MW00936738

A DROP OF ANGUISH

SHADOW HILLS ACADEMY: RELENTLESS
BOOK ONE

STACEY TROMBLEY

A Drop of Anguish

Shadow Hills Academy: Relentless / Book Two

Exterior cover design https://trifbookdesign.com

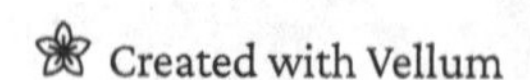

A DROP OF ANGUISH

SHADOW HILLS ACADEMY: RELENTLESS
2

STACEY TROMBLEY

I

My Only Source of Magic

Smoke streams up from the bubbling cauldron, and I watch as if hypnotized by the magic. I tap my finger on the cold stone table and wait. The instructions tell me to sprinkle crushed sage once the brew has been bubbling for fifteen seconds.

Someone else mutters the count under their breath. "Seven, eight, nine."

I ignore it. I've passed fifteen by several seconds, but still, my hands remain steady.

The air stirs, drawing in more and more power. Sparking like electricity.

This is the only magic I'll ever know. The only magic I'll feel and wield.

This is the only thing—in the magical world—that I'm good at.

My fingers absently roll the dried sage, crackling and crumbling into my awaiting palm, but my eyes never leave the liquid. My heart expands, and I breathe in deep.

Now.

Quickly, I tip the crumbled sage into the liquid then stir methodically.

Rumbling shakes me from my intense focus, and I lift my eyes to find a cauldron trembling two tables up. A short witch standing on a wooden chair to reach the table gasps as her potion bubbles over the rim, but it's not done there.

The teacher rushes forward and grabs the witch by the waist and carries her away just as the potion explodes, liquid splattering all the way to the ceiling and then over the table and pouring onto the floor.

Most of the students have fled the area, now standing against the walls, but I haven't moved an inch. Liquid sloshes up to my boots. I eye it then ignore it. If I'd been closer, I would have had to move—who knows what that half-baked potion would do if it touched uncovered skin. Luckily, I was just far enough away.

I continue my gentle stir.

The teacher drops the witch off on a chair near the edge of the room and then approaches me. Her expression is mild as she examines my potion and hands me a small black stone without comment.

I drop the onyx in immediately, and it clunks all the way to the bottom of the cauldron. Now, all I have to do is wait and hope I didn't mess it up somewhere along the line.

But the truth is, I know I didn't. This potion is perfect.

The witch's potion is still bubbling wildly. Smoke covers the ceiling, filling the room with an acrid odor. I retreat with the rest of the class to the edges of the room, but the teacher doesn't seem to think that's enough. She shoos us out the door and into the hall, where smoke leaks out and settles onto the ceiling.

A plump vampire with purple hair scooches next to me, wringing her hands together nervously.

"Did you really do it?" she whispers.

I shrug. "Needs another ten minutes to finish. I'll know then." It's impolite to be too confident when everyone else has likely failed. "Did anyone else finish?"

"Only three others even earned the stone," the vampire tells me. "And one of them was Patty. The moment her stone dropped, her potion went haywire."

"Candice was there with us," a lanky redheaded boy says with an eye roll. "Besides, I bet none of them are viable. That potion is way above our level. The point is for us to fail."

I *was* there, but I hadn't been paying attention to what everyone else was doing. Once I'm brewing, everything else fades away. My focus is intense, and I think that may be the real reason I'm obsessed now.

Yes, I'm good at it. Yes, it's literally the only form of magic I'm able to do. Yes, I have and will continue to use potions to defend myself against beings much stronger. But the real reason I've thrown myself into it so deeply is because potion-making has become my escape.

I'm tired of thinking. Tired of feeling. Tired of fear and pain and wondering.

It's our second day back at Shadow Hills Academy after an unorthodox break—our headmaster went super villain and tried to lure students into a to-the-death competition.

Good times.

Everyone knows I was involved, which has done wonders for my reputation. Add in the fact that the three most powerful students at the school—one of whom I was "dating" —haven't come back since those events, and well, I'm as popular as it gets. The whole school, including the administration, blames me for Jarron's, Trevor's, and Bea's absence.

And truthfully, they're not wrong.

But that's what I'm *not* supposed to be thinking about. I take in a deep breath.

When I'm brewing, my brain focuses on only the cauldron, books, and ingredients. They speak to me. Lull me into a quiet ease.

It's addicting.

The tension in the hall dies down as the streaming smoke settles, and the chattering builds. Eventually, the bell rings to signal the next class, and the hall is filled with even more bodies. I stay, waiting for my best friends to join. They'll want to see the chaos anyway.

Potions mishaps are exciting events, even in a magical school.

"Whose hair is on fire?" a tiny chirping voice singsongs. A purple pixie with black skin and two puffy pigtails drops onto my shoulder.

"No one," I say with a chuckle.

Lola pouts.

"What happened?" Janet asks when she arrives moments later. She stares up at the white steam still settled like liquid on the ceiling of the hallway.

"Teacher set us up for failure, supposedly." I shrug.

Janet's smile is wide. "But you passed it, didn't you?"

My lips twitch, but I manage to hold back the smile. "I don't know."

Lola nuzzles into my neck and whispers, "Yes, you do."

Still, I don't answer. We walk together toward our next set of classes. Lola has the farthest to travel, but she's also the fastest of us three, so she generally chooses to take the chance to socialize between classes as much as she can.

Janet and Lola chatter about Marcus, Janet's boyfriend. They were only talking before the break, but they became official during our time off.

He's a mage in Major Hall, a year younger than us, and they're sickeningly cute together.

"We went for a walk in the courtyard yesterday, and he picked me this daisy. It was the most amazing thing ever."

I force a smile, even as my stomach sinks. "Did you keep it?" I ask cheerily.

"It's sitting on my nightstand." Her cheeks flush.

I press my lips together and try my absolute best not to show her my real emotions. I wish I still had the dark purple flower Jarron picked me not long ago. "You should press it. In a book maybe? Do you keep a journal?"

She nods.

I bite the inside of my lip and ignore the pit in my stomach. Jarron had my journal delivered to my room in Minor Hall sometime during the break. I guess he knew I'd be back here, even if he didn't intend to return himself.

"You okay?" Janet says softly, eyes darting to the ground then up.

"Yep," I say, trying for a cheery tone. She curls her arm in mine and forces me closer, so our sides touch.

"You can be honest, you know?"

"Yeah, I know," I say quietly, face falling. "I just, uh, I'd rather be distracted than talk through my feelings."

She nods. "Yeah, I get that."

"It's just, too many things remind me of—things." Journals and headmasters remind me of my dead sister. Boyfriends and flowers and chai lattes remind me of Jarron.

"You've had a rough couple months," she says soothingly. "It's okay to not be okay."

I nod absently. A year ago, I was in some snooty human private school with my sister on a fast track into human politics. I'd have crushed that too.

But then, my sister was murdered by a supernatural being, and I threw that path away in the name of revenge. That was only eight months ago. My stomach aches now, the same way it did back then. Only now, the rage I used to cover up that pain is gone, and I'm left with... a whole lot of questions.

After Liz's death, I spent the next several months bound and determined to find her attacker and make him pay. To do that, I rejoined the supernatural community—something I'd sworn off years ago. I also started a fake relationship with the most powerful student in the school after he promised to help me.

Jarron was an old friend, but I also secretly suspected he was my sister's killer.

Obviously, I was making sound choices back then. Dating a demon prince who may have murdered my sister?

I'm lucky I survived the semester.

Good thing he turned out to simply be an incredible person that I'm not supposed to miss since I maybe possibly smashed his heart when I broke things off.

A bright-yellow pixie darts by us but gasps and doubles back. "Candice?" she asks in her tiny tinkly voice. Lola settles on Janet's shoulder, unusually still as the second pixie hovers in front of my face.

"I have a message for you," the yellow pixie says and then drops a letter into my hands. It's smaller than the average letter but still nearly the size of her entire body.

The pixie darts off, leaving her yellow glitter fading away in the air. I unfold the paper quickly. I honestly have zero clue what it could be.

But if I had to guess, it wasn't good.

Candice Montgomery,
Please see the headmaster immediately.

2

I WON'T LET ANYTHING TEAR THIS SCHOOL DOWN. INCLUDING YOU

"Candice Montgomery," a smooth voice drawls slowly as I open the mahogany door. I clench my jaw at the familiar view. A sleek, hand-carved wooden desk, curved computer monitor, and a wall of bookshelves. Mr. Vandozer's office.

Of course, it doesn't belong to Mr. Vandozer anymore, but I still remember sitting across from him—my sister's lover, statutory rapist, and the evil bastard that pushed her to enter the competition that ultimately led to her death.

If only I'd known then.

I cross my arms and take a seat across from the woman sitting with her hands clasped over his desk. Well, hers now.

Ms. Bhatt is the new headmaster at Shadow Hills Academy.

She's very pretty, with dark skin and sleek straight hair pulled back into a high ponytail. Her eyes are a normal honey-brown, but her winged eyeliner is meticulous. She's a powerful witch from an infamous family in India.

My parents spoke with this woman once already, and they seemed less than pleased by the experience. She's not exactly a fan of mine, apparently. Probably the kind of supernatural that thinks people without magic are worthless.

I puff out my chest and prepare to be looked down on.

"Hello, Candice. I'm glad to see you here and well."

"Thanks," I mutter.

"I must admit, I was almost surprised you decided to come back to this school after everything."

My eyebrows rise, but I give her no emotion—only the disdain I'm expecting to receive from her.

"Is there a problem?" I ask. Because my reasons have nothing to do with her.

"No problem." She forces a fake smile. "Of course, having a talented potionist in our school is a wonderful thing. However, your situation is rather *unusual*, given the events of the last several weeks."

"I suppose so." I squirm in my chair.

She hasn't flinched or shifted an inch since I sat. Is she even blinking? Honestly, someone could easily convince me she's a hologram at this point.

"I have several concerns I'd like to clear up with you."

"All right."

"Let's start with the simplest. I've taken a look at your records and your class schedule and," her eyes narrow just slightly, "I'm underwhelmed, to say the least."

My cheek ticks, but I otherwise manage to hide my emotions.

"You've spent the last three years in human school, so on paper, your level one classes make sense. However, I could list several reasons why I'm confident you are more talented than your class list implies. Including, but not limited to, the nullifying potion you used on two upper-level demons only weeks ago."

I somehow manage to hide the flinch. I used that potion on Jarron, my then sort-of-fake but kind-of-real boyfriend. And then, I used it on Mr. Vandozer, my headmaster-turned-mortal enemy.

"Did anyone else help you brew that potion?" she asks when I don't react.

I shake my head. "Jarron helped me get a few ingredients, but I did the work myself."

Ms. Bhatt nods sharply. "As I suspected. You were also the only student to complete a flying potion just this morning. Is that correct?"

Acid fills my belly. That happened minutes ago.

Releasing a quick breath, I decide we have more important things to discuss than how she's apparently keeping *close* tabs on me, so I simply nod.

"And yet, you're only in our second-level potions class. Why is that?"

I twist my lips. "If I was in high-level potion classes, I'd have to follow a specific curriculum and I wouldn't have had the opportunity to complete the nullifier."

Her eyebrows rise, her first reaction of any kind. "You made a successful nullifier on your first try."

My shoulders slump. I know where she's going with this, and she's probably got a point. "Yes."

"Then, I highly suspect you could follow a more advanced curriculum and still continue your independent studies."

I could launch into an explanation about how I have never had any intention of learning magic here. I came to find my sister's killer and nothing else. But I assume that's a pretty pointless conversation to have with a headmaster.

"What I want to know, Ms. Montgomery, is if you are actually dedicated to completing your education here."

My lips part, but then I shut them.

"I'm not sure I'm convinced you are here for the right reasons."

Well, she'd have been right a few months ago, but things have changed.

I take in a long breath, readying myself for the full explanation. "My relationship with the supernatural world has been complicated, I admit. I'm still figuring it out, if I'm totally honest. But I want to stay. I want to learn. I want to get better at potion-making. I'm here for the right reasons."

She nods and sits back, her shoulders relaxing ever so slightly. "In that case, I'm taking your instructor's suggestion and moving you into a level-six potions class. You can keep your slot in independent study rooms in the Under Hall. I'm also moving you into a level-four non-magic combat class."

"What?" My eyes bulge.

"You have been taking advanced self-defense and combat instructions since you were a child. Coach Tvanitti has also expressed concern that you're too advanced for a low-level class. You are well prepared for level four."

I bite the inside of my lip because I know there's no use in arguing. "Anything else?" I finally manage.

"Yes. I'm requiring you to choose two new electives and a foreign language. You can choose which classes you will drop to make space for them. I suspect you do not require History of Worlds, but that's up to you."

I huff out a breath. "Fine."

"I'll send you back with a catalog of elective options. I can put in your language choice now if you know which you'd prefer."

I consider it for only a few seconds. "High Orizian." The language of the royal line of demons. It might be useless, but if there is any language from another world that *could* come in handy, it's that one.

Besides the fact that it's Jarron's native tongue, it's also Mr. Vandozer's. It's a possible advantage to know my enemy's language.

"Interesting choice."

I shrug.

She jots down a note then continues. "Now, about the events that took place here two weeks ago."

I swallow.

"I'm very sorry that happened to you."

My chest expands with an emotion I can't name. Honestly, I didn't expect compassion from her. I may not fully trust or like this woman, but I do appreciate it.

"Mr. Vandozer is the worst kind of predator," she tells me. "And if I ever get the opportunity to rip out his throat, I promise you I will."

The back of my throat stings but I will not allow the emotion to well up any higher.

"And if you ever get the opportunity, please know that you will have my full support if you manage to kill him yourself."

"Thank you," I croak.

"Mr. Vandozer is currently at the top of the Supernatural Wanted List—mostly thanks to Jarron Blackthorn, who seems quite invested in catching him. It's rumored that Jarron has a *vested* interest in the situation." And now, back to beating around the truth she doesn't want to admit she's desperate for.

What is my relationship with Jarron?

I grimace.

Hell if I know, lady, I think, but I don't say it aloud, in part because I don't want to give her the satisfaction of acknowledging her unasked curiosity. Maybe in part because I'm a coward and it hurts to even think about it.

Jarron, the Crown Prince of the Under World, does indeed have a vested interest in Mr. Vandozer's crimes. But it's not what Ms. Bhatt thinks.

Mr. Vandozer seduced and manipulated my sister, Liz, into entering the Akrasia Games—a fight to the death. The winner is rumored to earn great power.

But no one has ever heard of an actual winner. Surprise, surprise. More lies.

Mr. Vandozer caused Liz's death, even if it wasn't by his own hand.

Jarron is passionate about getting Mr. Vandozer in the ground because Liz—

I swallow down a wave of pain. *Not now. Not here.*

I was beginning to fall for him, and damn if it doesn't suck to find out he and my sister were fated to be together. Jarron had *imprinted* on Liz several years ago. She would have been his lover. His betrothed. His queen.

If she'd lived long enough for him to woo her.

And believe me, it wouldn't have taken much to convince her.

Jarron wants revenge for his soulmate's death, that's his *vested interest.*

I want it too. She was my sister, and regardless of how her

potential relationship with Jarron affects me, I still want revenge for her death.

"Jarron desires justice," I answer simply. Which isn't untrue. Yes, he has a personal connection with the situation, but he's also *good*. Good in a way I used to think demons were incapable of.

He'd want this predator brought to justice regardless.

"Because of you," Mrs. Bhatt says. It's not a question.

"No," I answer. But I realize I probably shouldn't have. It's an easier answer than the alternative. No one is supposed to know of a demon's chosen. No one at all, not until the bond is accepted. Yet, several people have learned of Liz's role as Jarron's chosen, and that's exactly what put her at risk. Mr. Vandozer targeted her to get to Jarron.

One would think her death would have resolved that conflict, but demon culture demands every ruler bond to his chosen before they take the throne. It's an important show of worthiness. Though a demon can choose a replacement to be their lover and partner, they cannot replicate the original bond in the eyes of their people.

Liz died before she accepted Jarron, which means if the right people find out she was his chosen, he could lose his right to the throne.

"You were in a relationship with him before you entered the Akrasia Games yourself," she states.

I nod, ignoring the uncomfortable twist in my belly.

I hate that it's known that I entered the Akrasia Games. It's another source of tension in the school. People think Jarron dumped me and then I went seeking my own form of power, but the truth is that I only entered in order to hunt down the truth behind my sister's death.

Weeks before, I'd learned that the true cause of her death was the games, and I'd spent weeks searching for more information on them. When I got invited myself, how could I pass up the opportunity to face my sister's killer?

I never intended to actually enter the competition. I went along with their instructions to uncover information.

And it worked. Sort of. I figured out who was behind it. I learned the Akrasia Games are real. I now know who is worthy of my revenge fantasies—Mr. Vandozer.

But it sure as hell looks really bad to everyone else here. They all think I'm desperate for power.

Don't get me wrong, I want some form of power, but I wouldn't ever be desperate enough to rely on someone else for it. That's just asking to be manipulated. Magic isn't the only form of power, and anyone entering the games gives up their power willingly.

Plus, I would never kill innocent classmates for my personal gain.

"And you think his passion for justice has nothing to do with you?" Ms. Bhatt asks sweetly.

I just shrug.

"So, you don't think Jarron will return to this school?"

I squint. "Why would you think that?"

"Rumors. Just rumors."

I bite my lip. "I don't know what Jarron intends to do."

"And his brother, Trevor?"

My eyes widen. "I don't know, but I assume he's not coming back."

"Why?"

"Because his chosen, Bea, is in hiding."

Her eyebrows rise. "From whom?"

"Jarron."

She tsks. "You've certainly made a mess of things here, haven't you, Miss Montgomery?"

I want to clap back and deny any fault, but the truth is, I have made a mess of things. Not that any of it was really my fault, but it sure does revolve around me and my sister.

Bea is the one that paved the way for me to enter the Akrasia Games. I used her manipulation to my advantage in the name of my investigation, but Jarron was beyond pissed about it. Like "I'm gonna kill her" pissed. She won't be coming back here any time soon.

As for Jarron... I don't know.

I broke things off with him for good once I learned about his would-be relationship with Liz. He and Liz weren't ever actually together. They kissed once several years ago and Jarron insisted they hadn't seen each other since. I've chosen to believe him, but it doesn't make any difference.

I can't ever get over the idea that she was his *chosen*. I can't ever stop thinking about them together.

The what-ifs.

Knowing that if she were here, she'd win his heart in a second.

So, I care about Jarron. And I believe he cares about me. But there's no future for us.

Of course, I didn't expect that to mean I'd never see him again, but, well, I refuse to be bitter about that. Cutting off our almost-relationship was my choice, and I don't have a right to be mad about how he reacts to it.

"It's had a rather negative impact on our school's reputation," Ms. Bhatt continues.

I don't respond. This is the conversation I expected to begin with.

"The scandal with Mr. Vandozer was horrendous and terrible, and of course, I don't blame you for that. But when we add in that our three most powerful students left the school, mid-semester—well, it looks bad."

"You've stepped into a hard situation," I say sweetly. "I feel for you." I barely manage to hold back a grin. She didn't say it outright, but she's telling me she blames me for this. Maybe not Mr. Vandozer's betrayal, but the rest of it.

"Indeed."

"Well, is that all you wanted to talk to me about?"

She pulls in a long breath. Was that a sincere emotion? Yes, yes, I think it was.

Annoyance.

Well, it's a start.

"Yes, I suppose that will do for now."

"When will my new classes begin?"

She stands and wipes at her pristine black trousers. Then, she turns and strides to a large shelf and pulls a book from a pile. "You will find a list of available electives on pages 105-126. Choose wisely. Send word with your answer before dinnertime, and I will have your updated schedule to you by morning." She hands me the book. "You can take the rest of the school day off to look over your options."

After a pause, I take the book. I suppose that's a fair deal.

"But you should still have lunch in the main hall. And pass through the arches. Every day. That is more important than ever."

I swallow but nod.

"I believe in this school, Miss Montgomery. And I will not let anything tear it down."

I hesitate before walking the rest of the way out of the room. I heard the implied end to that sentence, exactly as she intended.

I will not let anything tear it down, including you.

3

A STELLAR REPUTATION

When I leave the meeting with Ms. Bhatt, I realize the lunch period is half finished by now.

I could just skip it and hide away in the courtyard. It's fairly nice out today for the season. Even in winter here, we get the occasional not-deathly-cold days. Okay, it'll freeze my butt in seconds. I sigh and recognize the truth—I'm just looking for an out. I should go chat with Janet and Lola anyway.

I'm tired of showing my fear in this school, where I'm the weakest being with the biggest target on my back. Certainly tired of letting fear dictate my actions.

I march toward the lunch hall, past the packed tables without looking anyone in the eye, and right up through the magical arches. Nothing happens, as usual.

The magical arches are meant to detect magical influence like potions and spells, for our protection of course. If someone slipped a student a love potion—for example—

they'd be found out the moment they get their lunch. I don't know what it looks like when magical influence is detected, and I hope I never find out.

I take my time looking over the food options. I usually just pick something obvious and simple so I don't have to remain in the spotlight for too long up here.

There are nearly ten major sections of food, three of which are entirely inedible for humans. I don't even want to know what that green gunk is. I've seen it on trolls' plates. Another tray has what looks like glowing tar. Then, there's a whole section of raw meat and a blood dispenser.

In the humanesque food areas, there is a Mediterranean section, authentic Asian food, a whole section of pasta with many kinds of sauce, a salad bar, fruit bar, and piles of at least a dozen different kinds of bread.

I opt for a pile of mac and cheese and breaded chicken strips. Again with the simple. I almost always choose some kind of chicken with either pasta or salad.

Oh well, I know what I like, and I stick to it.

When my plate is full, I finally cast my gaze out to the still very full lunchroom. Maybe my tactic of feigning confidence worked, or because I'd entered halfway through the lunch period maybe everyone was distracted, but no one seems to have noticed me up here alone.

It's kind of nice to be able to watch the different social groups converge without nasty glares in return.

Some are quiet and to the point. Others laugh and give exaggerated expressions. There are pixies who dart about the whole room in swarms.

I never paid much attention to the way pixies interact, but

based on what I'm seeing now, they keep in small packs, fluttering around here and there.

"Hey, ascension seeker," someone yells. I flinch and look up to find a set of three shifters who've noticed me lingering with my full tray in hand. "Your Minor Hall friends finally abandon you?" a redheaded boy says with a snide smile and piercing predator eyes.

"I'm surprised they let you back in their group to start with," a short fae girl says with a cruel smirk. "Knowing you were willing to kill them in a desperate attempt to get a little magic. How pathetic is that?"

I clench my tray tightly.

I begin marching toward my seat, but several eyes are darting my way now. So much for flying under the radar.

I'm fully willing to set them straight and tell them I had no intention of entering the games, but it wouldn't matter. Even if they'd pause long enough to actually listen to my words, they wouldn't believe me. They'd take my outburst as an opportunity to "set me in my place."

For those of us with little power, it's best to keep our heads down. Even when we're being verbally attacked.

"What's pathetic," a chipper voice drawls from behind me, "is that you feel the need to insult a lovely young woman to make yourself feel taller. Grow a few inches, would ya?"

I suck in a breath and spin to find Stassi pulling to a stop in front of me, arms crossed. His insult is a little ironic, considering he's not exactly tall himself.

The other wolf growls but turns his attention back to his heckling friends. Stassi smiles big and broad. "Is it possible you actually look hotter than usual today, Candice?" He's an

Elite wolf shifter himself, but apparently from a different pack than my hecklers.

I snort. "Shut up."

He shrugs and winks.

"Thanks. I appreciate the backup."

"Don't worry about it. I never turn down the chance to help a beautiful damsel."

As Stassi walks away, a little pixie with black skin and purple wings comes fluttering up and lands on my shoulder.

"Hey, Lola!" I say with my first sincere smile in hours.

She stays with me the rest of the way to the Minor Hall table.

Janet bounces in her seat as I sit across from her. "Oh my gosh, what happened? I was worried the new headmaster was gonna kick you out or something."

I laugh. "She probably would if she could come up with a valid reason."

"So, what was the meeting about?" Lola asks as she settles on her perch in the middle of the table.

"She's making me change my whole schedule." I sigh.

"Really? Why?"

"Too easy. If I want to stay here, she's gonna make me work for it." I shrug because as much as I'm annoyed at the forceful hand and I'm not sure how much I trust the woman, she does have some valid points.

"Oh, that sucks. What kind of classes are you moving into?" Janet asks.

"Level-six potions and level-four non-magic combat."

"*Ooh.*" Lola hops onto my shoulder. "That combat class gets kinda intense. Even Elite students have to take it before graduation."

My stomach sinks. "Well, that'll be fun."

"But you'll do great in potions, I bet," Janet adds.

"Yeah, maybe." It'll be challenging, but maybe that's a good thing. In my two weeks off of school after our *ordeal*, I spent hours and hours in my parents' studio, working on more potions than ever before.

My parents tried to get me to open up about my few months at this school, but I wouldn't give them much. Potions, though? That we talked about for hours. They even offered to make me an apprentice if I was that interested, but the truth is I'm not interested in a future career. I'm interested because 1) it gets my head out of the dark places and 2) it's a means to an end.

Potions are my only grasp on power. My only way to protect myself. I need it.

They didn't understand why I was determined to come back to Shadow Hills, and it's not something I could adequately explain. Mostly, I just refuse to run away.

The Akrasia Games are going to begin again, with or without me. Mr. Vandozer may not be here anymore, but there is one connection to the games left here.

Corrine.

My old witch roommate keeps to herself now, and I rarely see her, but she still attends this school, and she faced the jinn and contract moments before I did.

I told the authorities, whom I saw that night. There are at least three students with connections to the Akrasia Games now, but Corrine is my best bet. I intend to keep a close eye on her.

"You okay?" Lola flutters in front of my face, and I jerk back with a stiff laugh. She tilts her head.

"I'm fine!" I laugh, but my smile fades quickly. *Kind of* fine.

There's a lot on my mind and heart. I miss Liz. I'm angry that I missed the chance to give her justice. And I miss Jarron.

He and I were always more than—whatever you would call us.

We were childhood best friends before he manifested his demon side and hurt my sister. And though I was beyond pissed at him for that night, he made up for it and more during our weeks together at this school. He protected me, defended me, helped me, cared for me. And most importantly, listened. He actually cared.

If only he'd picked me from the beginning instead of my more beautiful sister.

I shake my head from those dangerous thoughts. "I have to pick two new electives too." I leave out the demon language class since that's a more complicated explanation than I'm willing to go into right now. "But the good news is, she gave me the rest of the day off while I look through the catalog and decide."

"Nice!" Lola chirps.

"Have you decided anything yet?" Janet asks.

I shake my head. "I haven't even opened it."

"Well, without magic, you'll have a few limitations," Janet says, tapping her finger against her chin.

"Right!" Lola says with a wiggle of her wings. "Like I'm in musical incantations where we learn to weave magic into music. It's *really* cool. But you'd need some magic to get in."

I tap my finger against my lips. "Right. Yeah, that does sound cool. What other classes are you in?"

"I'm in divination," Lola says, her chest puffed out.

"Really? You never told me about that. That's so cool!"

She shrugs, but her grin tells me she's proud of it.

"Have you seen anything? Made any prophecies?"

"Oh, plenty. It's just nearly impossible to interpret them correctly. That's the hardest part."

"That's so fascinating."

"I'm in spell crafting and art casting."

"Ahh. It sounds like all the best subjects will have a magical requirement." I purse my lips into a stupid pout.

"I also took human anthropology and runes my freshman year. They were okay." Janet shrugs.

"There's also cryptozoology, which is a really neat subject too!"

My eyebrows rise. "That's a thought. Do you get to ride unicorns or something?"

They both laugh. "More like take an acid slug home and keep it alive." Janet grimaces.

"Hey!" All three of us look up to find Marcus, Janet's boyfriend, approaching with a big grin on his face. He's a skinny, gamer-looking boy with pale skin, buzzed hair, and a spiked bracelet. He doesn't talk much, but his smile is kind. She blushes every time he's around, and it's absolutely adorable.

"Hi!" Janet squeaks.

I smile at her bashfulness.

"Hey, Marcus," I say. Lola soars in circles around his head, and by the time he takes a seat next to Janet, his eyes are unfocused.

"You're making him dizzy, Lola!" I laugh, and she darts to her perch in the middle of the table.

"Whoops. Sorry."

"No problem." He waves casually. "Hey, so did you guys hear about the new shifter?"

My eyebrows rise. "No."

Marcus leans in to spill. "We don't usually get new students mid-year so that's weird enough, but he's also a wolf shifter from a pack that's never been to this school before."

"He's alone?" Janet asks, eyes wide.

Marcus nods.

"Is that super out of the ordinary?" I ask, unsure why she sounds so shocked.

"Very," Janet says. "Shifters always come in groups of at least three. To leave a pack and join a school with no one else? It's *very* unusual. Do you think he's an outcast? Looking for a new pack? Or a spy or something?"

"Those are the only options?" I ask incredulously.

"It's very unusual to find a wolf shifter alone for more than a few days."

"Well, maybe he has pack members coming next week or something," I offer.

She shrugs. "I guess that's possible. But either way, it's big rumor news, which is good for you." She grins at me, like I'm supposed to know what she means.

"It is?"

"Yep. A new shiny thing for the masses to obsess over. It'll take some of the heat off of you."

"Oh, right." I twist my lips. That's true, I suppose. Being the ex of an MIA demon prince is super annoying. Having something new for people to obsess over is a good thing.

Case in point, heads of all shapes and sizes turn to stare at the entrance of the cafeteria, where a dark-skinned boy walks in. He's tall, with grey eyes and a sharp jaw.

"Is that him?" I ask.

Marcus nods.

The dark-skinned shifter doesn't seem fazed by the attention, though. His chin is high, lids hooded, like he is utterly at ease with all eyes on him. He pauses, scanning the room.

Then, his gaze lands squarely on me.

My heart rate picks up speed as he walks down the aisle without looking away. *What the hell?*

Why? What possible reason would a new Elite shifter have to approach me? Some of the other wolves seem to really enjoy taunting me, but he's brand new. It's his first day at a new school. How would he even know who I am?

No, I have to be imagining the attention. He's looking at someone behind me, right? I glance over my shoulder to find the wart-filled face of a goblin. I turn back quickly.

My internal questioning turns to utter panic when he stops next to our table. A powerful Elite shifter looks down at our reject group of Minor Hall kids.

"This seat open?" the shifter asks, amusement in his eyes.

Janet, Lola, and I are stun locked.

"Sure," Marcus responds for us.

The shifter smiles then scooches behind me to take the seat on my other side.

Marcus places two fingers under Janet's chin and lifts it shut. I chuckle at the image, and my shock dissipates.

I whip my attention to the shifter, all amusement gone in an instant. "Why in hell would you want to sit here?"

"Seemed like as good a spot as any." He shrugs.

"Bullshit. What's your game?" I cross my arms and meet his arrogant gaze. He's handsome, with that stupid cocky grin. But that only makes this worse. If he were an ugly shifter, I could at least justify his interest in our group a little.

"Game?" His smile remains, and boy if that doesn't get under my skin. I clench my fists. He's messing with us, and I want to burn him alive for it.

"What's my name?" I ask him.

His smile slips for the first time. "How would I know your name? We haven't met yet, and you're being very rude."

"Wonderful. If I'm so rude, then leave and go sit with the popular kids like everyone expects."

"You're not a popular kid?"

"This is the Minor Hall table. You're in Elite Hall. Go sit with the beautiful and powerful people and leave us alone."

His eyes scan the tables.

"Yeah, see, that's the problem. There's at least one shifter from a different pack at every one of those tables. So, unless you want me to have my throat torn out in my first five minutes here, I've got to find a different spot to hang out."

"So, you chose the weakest beings in the school?"

"No, I chose the smartest."

I roll my eyes. "Not how that works." Just because we're low in magic, doesn't make us top in brain power.

"As I hear it, you're a potions prodigy."

"See!" I say a bit too loudly, slamming my fist on the table. I flinch at my own outburst and then lean in to say quieter, "You *do* know who I am. And I don't believe for a second that you sought me out specifically for my potions work."

"No?" He tilts his head innocently. "What do you think I sought you out for?"

My lips part, but then I pause. What would be his reason?

To mess with me the way the other wolves have threatened to? To spy on me about the Akrasia Games? Whatever the reason, I can't just blurt out those theories.

His brows rise. "No?" He shrugs. "Well, my very own potion master bestie is a pretty good reason."

I cross my arms again and turn to face Janet and her boyfriend.

"I'm Janet," she says with a grin, ignoring my rage.

"Thompson. Nice to meet you." He turns his wide grin to Lola, who casually adjusts her pigtails.

"And you are?" Thompson asks.

Lola's wings flutter when he winks at her, but she remains on her perch. "Lola," she purrs, in what I assume is an attempt at sultry but nearly squeaks with her tiny voice.

"Nice to meet you all. Except you." He chuckles in my direction.

"I don't trust you," I say, crossing my arms. And I'm now super pissed that the whole "now everyone won't pay you as much attention" thing backfired big time.

"I don't trust you either." He shrugs. "I don't trust anyone outside of my direct family. That's just how these things go. I'm not looking for friends. I'm looking for leverage."

I purse my lips. Well, that's about as honest as it could get.

"So, no warm fuzzies?" I keep my voice steady, but my eyes are narrowed. I don't like this at all.

"Nope. Not my style. I mean, I don't mind the occasional benefits that come with alliances, but no pressure or anything."

I consider this. A brand-new shifter joins the school without any allies at all—which is exceptionally unusual for his breed—and heads straight for me. He admits he's only here for leverage.

So, he thinks he can get some kind of advantage from me.

That just leaves me wondering if that leverage will be to my benefit or at my expense.

4

DEAR CANDICE

When will you see?
When will you notice how much you do not belong?
You're like a child among giants.
One wrong move, that's all it takes.
One blink. One stutter. One moment of arrogance.
Who will be crying over your cold corpse? Who will be left to seek your justice?

The Jinn

5
FACING MY NIGHTMARES ALONE

I lay on my small, stiff twin-sized bed and stare up at the discolored ceiling.

Though Corrine did return to school, and she doesn't avoid me *entirely*, she did change rooms, leaving me all alone. She never explained why, and I never asked.

The biggest benefit of not being in my room is that she's separated herself from my *stellar* reputation. There have been whisperings of other students that were involved in the games, but those were forgotten fairly quickly.

Corrine has successfully flown under the radar since her return, despite the fact that she had a relationship with the school headmaster. That's also not something I'll ever bring up with her, since apparently, she shares that fact with my sister.

It makes me sick to my stomach, but my issue is not with Corrine or Liz.

Mr. Vandozer is a predator in several ways, and I will get

through each day by imagining the slow, agonizing torture I'll dole out when I finally get the chance.

I've spoken with Corrine exactly two times since school resumed—both very short conversations. Enough for me to make it clear I want to help her.

Though she never told me outright, I'm confident she did sign the magically binding contract to the Akrasia Games. She has no choice but to follow their call, and she's physically unable to speak about the games or what she witnessed.

It likely also means she can't outright tell me if she has contact with anyone involved, but I've made it clear I want to help her. I don't want anyone else to die for that sick form of entertainment.

The games are highly illegal, so I'm hoping the authorities are tracking Corrine after learning of her involvement, but of course, no one will tell me anything. Maybe Jarron knows, but I haven't talked to him in weeks either.

So far, Corrine has remained pretty scarce in the school halls. I only see her occasionally in the mornings just before classes start. She has made it clear she regrets her role with Mr. Vandozer and is terrified of the day she'll be forced to fight other students to the death.

I absently rub the inside of my forearm.

I am not bound to the games in the same way, but they left their mark regardless. Shimmering golden lines of a tattoo curl and twist over my veins in a half-completed symbol.

I did *sort of partially* sign the magical contract to enter the Akrasia Games. Jarron was injured, and if I didn't sign, Mr. Vandozer was going to kill him before help came. Pretending to sign the contract may have saved his life, but I did write part of my name on the parchment. I didn't feel the effects then, but when I woke up the next day, these golden lines, nearly translucent, shined up at me.

They're not very noticeable, unless light reflects off of them, and my uniform covers them anyway.

The authorities questioned me thoroughly about the games, and I was able to answer every question, so I know I'm not bound to the games the same way.

The fact that I bear a mark means something, though. I just haven't figured out what. Maybe the game runners can track me now. Maybe it's the reason I got that stupid taunting note the other night signed *the jinn.*

I'm certain some jerk student thought it was a hilarious prank to send me that note, but it still makes my gut clench to think about the actual jinn—the creature behind the power of the games—sending me messages.

My stomach squeezes, but I refuse to let it get under my skin any more than it already has. Instead, I roll onto my belly and stare down at my new schedule.

I spent hours this afternoon casually flipping through my book of elective options.

Janet and Lola were right; my options are extremely limited due to my lack of magic. More than two-thirds of the electives have a magical requirement.

I scrawled a list of the classes I could take without a drop of magic and ended up with less than a dozen, most of which don't interest me at all.

Several on my list sound boring as hell. The thought of anthropology and runes makes my eyelids droop immediately. I could do the cryptozoology class but truthfully, I'm not too into animals. I'm not patient enough, and I don't do good with icky things.

I bite my lip. The more I think about it, the more obvious the answer is.

There's something I've been thinking about since I started at this school. Potion-making isn't the only possible way for me to use magic; it's just the only one I have any experience in.

So, a class about magical objects is perfect. It's only a history class—background information and stuff—but it's necessary if I'm ever going to begin using objects that hold magic in them. Maybe I will, maybe I won't, but it's better to be prepared. It shouldn't be too challenging since it's a 101 class, and it could help me eventually. Win-win.

I sent off a message to Ms. Bhatt before dinner and then hid the rest of the night away in my room. That was probably a mistake, considering I feel so isolated now, but I still can't make myself venture out into the common rooms.

The sun is setting, and now dark shadows rise up in the already dingy bedroom.

Sometimes, it's nice to have the room to myself, but in the still darkness of my dorm, I occasionally feel utterly and suffocatingly *alone.*

I flick on the orange night light and glance at the copy of *Art of War* that Jarron gave me. I never had the chance to focus on it, and now I don't have the mental energy to give it a go. One day, I'll read it.

I miss him.

I want to talk to him. I want to hug him. I want to see if he's okay after everything. I want to tell him I'm sorry for how it all ended and thank him for saving me—more than once.

My journal stares at me from the side table by my bed. I haven't bothered to even open it since I got it back, not wanting to let my mind spiral down those tunnels of fear and doubt and shame and guilt. So much to wade through.

Biting the bullet, I grab it from the table and hold it tightly in both hands. Then, I flip it open. How much did Jarron read of it? I gave it to him, after all. He was welcome to read every page if he wanted. Even my stupid fears about how I thought he was a monster.

I might be human, but I'm more monster than he'll ever be.

I turn to the last page and find scrawled handwriting that wasn't there the last time I opened it—before that night.

I will never let you face your nightmares alone.
Jarron

I blink at the words. What does that mean? Did he write it before he chased me down and stopped me from entering the games? How could he have? He had minutes to get to me in time. There's no way he wrote that then.

It had to be after.

But then... why hasn't he come back to school? He's not here, and I'm facing my nightmares. I mean, maybe they're not the worst of my nightmares, but the pushback from students is only getting worse. Several powerful beings *hate* me here.

Maybe he's protecting me from Mr. Vandozer and the Akrasia Games, but they're not my only nightmares.

Winding dark thoughts slither in and leave poison in their wake.

My next several breaths are shaky. Reading those words have made a truth I'd been avoiding painfully clear.

My heart aches.

I'm tired and scared and so very *alone.*

I have Janet and Lola, and I love them, but it's not the same. There are things I haven't shared with them. Truths that weigh on me, carving deeper each day. Maybe I just need to open up to them. Maybe it's only me causing my loneliness by keeping them at arm's reach, but it hurts to even think those things, let alone say them out loud.

Maybe I shouldn't have come back to this school after all. What if I'm not ready for this?

Tears sting my eyes.

"I miss you," I whisper to the pages. "Both of you."

I miss my sister so much it's painful, but that anger I'd used to push down that pain is no longer as sharp. Instead, helplessness has made its way in. I'm nothing. No one.

Everyone at this school knows it.

And Jarron... I flop back on my bed. With him, I was beginning to feel powerful, and damn if that didn't taste sweet. Now, I'm left with the bitter reminder that I'll never feel that way again.

Not unless I achieve it myself.

6
A FIGHT WITH A FAE

I keep my hands tightly curled around the straps of my backpack as I march into the arena. A few of the panes of glass above are a slightly different color than the rest, but otherwise, you'd never know this place collapsed in on itself only a couple weeks ago.

Yep, just something else that was my fault, no biggie.

I try to get the note from the jinn out of my head before I start my first advanced combat class.

Even though this is a non-magical combat class, I'm no longer with the beginners. Shadow Hills Academy requires even their high-level magic students to complete this class, which means I'll literally be fighting Elite supernaturals in a ring.

I find a quiet spot and stretch, eyeing the groups of powerful people who watch me with confident grins, eager to get a piece of me. This is basically an academy-accepted way to kick my ass.

The only thing working in my favor is the fact that I have

taken self-defense classes since I was very young, and every person here will underestimate me significantly.

"Are you ready, Candice?" Coach Tvanitti asks quietly as she approaches the corner I've been huddled in for the last ten minutes.

Nope, not even a little bit.

The sharp-eyed Elite students are gathered together, glaring my way.

There are three high fae—one of them an icy blond with bright-blue eyes. Auren is beautiful and powerful, and we also happen to have something in common. We're both Jarron's ex.

She hates me.

Or at least, I think she still hates me. I did sort of save her life once, but I never got the feeling she was particularly thankful. She was more or less annoyed I had the power over Jarron to convince him to give her mercy. Most believe a human should never hold that over a fae. She was also the one to expose my journal and the fact that I was investigating Liv's murder—and that the students in this school were my suspects.

Now, Jarron is gone, and there's no one stopping her from showing me my place on the food chain.

There is another fae, two wolf shifters and an Elite-level witch. There are five other students from lower levels. Three from Superior Hall and two from Major Hall. I'm the only one from Minor Hall.

I drop my bag in the corner and approach the center of the arena. The ground is a massive field of AstroTurf with a large purple mat in the middle. A white circle painted on the mat acts as our ring. Not exactly intimidating, but it doesn't have to be.

The fae staring at me from the other side of the circle is intimidating enough.

"Everyone, welcome our new student, Candice. She'll be just warming up for the next few days, but we're going to get her a little experience in the ring today. A gentle warm-up spar is all we're going for. Got it?" Coach eyes the Elite students, who don't so much as acknowledge her.

I hate being looked down on. It's already making my skin itch.

Coach approaches me. "This will be your first practice fight against beings more powerful than you, but it's really not a big deal. We'll take it easy and slow. Would you like one of the Major Hall students to go first?"

My hands clench and unclench, adrenaline already pumping. I'm horrified and pissed that I have to be here, but I'm going to prove my worth.

I'd like to say no, but with so much attention zeroed in on me, I do think it would help to alleviate some of the tension. I nod.

"Melissa and Ryan. You two first."

One of the shifters leers in my direction. His arrogant grin tells me he thinks I'm scared.

He's right, but I'll never give him the satisfaction of seeing it confirmed.

"Remember, this is only practice. It will not be an all-out brawl, and tap-outs are not frowned upon. Skill is important, but fighting your fear is as much an opponent as the creature you will fight."

Melissa, a fae with pale skin, green eyes, and a long braid

down her back grabs a set of silver cuffs and claps them onto her forearms. The fae girl rolls her shoulders as her eyes dim. The bracelets stop her from using any of her magic—the only way I could even pretend to stand a chance in that ring against any one of these students.

A young mage from Major Hall steps forward. He's a good three inches shorter than the female fae he's facing. He does have more muscle, but not by a ton.

"Fight," Coach says firmly.

The mage boy pants excessively before they even begin then drops into a solid defensive stance. They slowly circle around the ring. The teacher instructs Ryan to enter the ring. He obeys.

Once within striking range, Ryan lunges, but the fae evades, simply stepping out of the way and then waiting again. Ryan grimaces and then tries again with a forceful punch.

I watch every move carefully. I've trained most of my life in self-defense, and I love winning a battle, so I'm not at all inexperienced in sparring like this. In my previous combat class here, though, we only did drills and exercises.

This will be my first time getting in a ring with beings even close to this strong.

The fae blocks and then goes in for her own strike. There's a thud as the fae's padded glove hits the mage's upper arm. The fae is fast, but her hits are light. Ryan strikes back quickly.

The fae is smiling as she retreats, blocking each successive blow, and then finally bends and kicks into Ryan's side, sending him flying out of the circle.

He twists and lands on all fours, sliding to a stop.

The teacher hops into the ring, hands up. "Fight over!" she

announces. She and the fae are smiling widely. "That was a wonderful job, Melissa and Ryan.

Ryan shakes off his rage and straightens. His cheeks are red, his chest heaving, but he manages to cool himself off and stands among the others, who pat him on the shoulder.

"Candice," she calls.

I stride into the ring, hands clenching. The dark-skinned fae remains in the ring, eyeing me quietly.

"Oh, I can do this one," a sweet voice calls.

My eyes widen.

"Sure, Auren," Coach says. "If you wish."

Fuck my life.

Auren gives me a wicked smile that tells me she's so going to enjoy this as Melissa clasps the silver cuffs to her wrists.

Adrenaline pumping, eyes focused on my enemy, I take my stance.

I'm not naïve enough to expect an easy fight, not with Auren as my opponent.

I can't know what's going on in her mind, but her sharp stare makes it fairly clear she wants to level the playing field and bolster her reputation. What better way than to *accidentally* go a bit too far during a school-sanctioned spar?

"Fight!"

Auren charges instantly.

Even without her magic, her movements are lightning-quick. I dive out of the way, only barely evading her attack. Okay, even expecting her to go too far, I didn't expect *that.*

I roll and land in a crouch just before she comes again. The small crowd sucks in a collective breath, pressing in tighter to get a better view.

"Auren," Coach chides.

She ignores her.

I leap away from Auren's second lunge in a similar way. She twists at the last second, and her fist clips my thigh. Pain ricochets up my back, but it's short-lived.

"Slow down, Auren," the teacher instructs.

She obviously has something to prove. I thought she'd take it slow in the beginning and then land a fierce blow once my guard was down. She's not even trying to hide her anger.

Truth is, I think this is exactly what I needed.

Anxiety is my worst enemy. Fearing the what-ifs kills me slowly. But put me in direct danger, and my mind turns sharp. There are no longer any questions. There is only the determination that I will not lose.

She attacks a third time, and now, I'm ready. I feint, like I'm going to dive away from her the way I have the two times prior, and she takes the bait.

Auren swings, which would have been a total takedown had I dove like she thought. Instead, I slide away and then slam my elbow into her exposed spine.

She drops to the ground, hard.

The room quiets, and I skitter across the mat, away from the very angry fae that slowly rises. Her eyes glow. Though I know she can't use her magic right now, it's meant to unnerve me. It works, but I won't give her the satisfaction of knowing it.

I only smile and wiggle my fingers in a taunting wave.

"I'm going to—"

"What?" I interrupt. "You're going to what?"

She flinches. Not only is she not supposed to be so aggressive during this spar, but the whole school is still uncertain how Jarron will react if I'm harmed. And since she's already on his bad side—

"I could have asked him to kill you," I say, knowing that's the moment she's playing in her head. "I still could."

She seethes, shoulders slumped. Anger pulses from her in waves. Some people think anger helps you fight better, and that can be true... to a point. But if you let it go too far, it clouds your mind. Auren is totally past that point.

"Candice, step out of the ring," Coach tells me, voice strained. She's watching closely, debating whether to interfere, but I also know perception matters.

"No," I say without taking my eyes off my opponent. I've got this.

"You think you're better than me? Did you know we bet on how long you'd keep his interest? I lost, of course. You lasted longer than three weeks. *Barely.*"

My cheeks heat. "Maybe we both lost Jarron, but you want to know the difference between us?" I ask, lips spreading into a vicious grin. I can't let her get the upper hand, even in the verbal fight. "You were so obviously desperate to get him back. You looked like an absolute fool. He didn't want you."

She charges, a growl ripping from her throat.

I evade her charge with an easy slip to the left. She spins and swings, but I knock her arm off its target and upper cut straight into her stomach. She bows forward with a grunt of pain, and I throw an elbow into her neck, knocking her down again.

This time, though, she sweeps my feet out from under me before I can get away. I land on my back, and the air swoops from my lungs. My vision spins for one instant, and then she's on top of me, hands around my throat.

For the first time, fear takes hold.

But her weight is surprisingly light, her muscles used to relying on magic, which it has no access to thanks to the magic-blocking cuffs. I grab her wrist and twist then rock my hips and throw her off of me.

She screams in rage as we both get to our feet. She's seething again.

Coach moves to step between us, to end the fight while we're apart, but Auren reacts first.

She flicks the magical cuff off her left arm, and then faster than I can blink, she throws a blast of icy-cold magic that barrels straight into my chest.

7
SORRY NOT SORRY

I groan and force my heavy eyes open.

There's cold pressure on my chest, and I try to roll away from it. "Stop," a harsh female voice chides. "I'm trying to help."

I groan again. "What are you doing?" I mumble, trying to focus. My vision is still blurry. The last thing I remember is frost magic slamming into me.

Auren.

I jerk up and swat her hand away from me.

"I said I'm trying to help you!" Auren says again. There's no warmth to her tone.

"Why would you do that when you're the one who hurt me?" We're still in the arena, on the stupid fake grass, with the rest of the class staring at us from a few feet away.

"Because I'd rather not die. Or be expelled." Finally, my vision clears enough to see the emotion on her face. It's not anger. Focus, yes. Maybe a sprinkle of fear.

"Why would you die?" I force out, collapsing back onto the

grass. But she never gets the chance to answer because Coach drops to her knees beside us.

"Candice, the healers are on their way," Coach says. "Are you all right?"

I nod again, already feeling the pain subside. I'm not sure what Auren is doing with her magic—Frost Court fae don't have healing abilities—but since I don't know what she did to start with, I don't bother asking. It's helping, whatever it is.

A minute later, Auren's arms relax, her magic finished. "I'm sorry," she says. "I—I don't always control my emotions well." She glances up at a wrinkled old woman in a white dress approaching. The woman I recognize as a healer kneels beside me on the AstroTurf and starts checking me. Her hands glow slightly as she moves them over my body.

"You seem well," she says in a gentle tone. "Best to have you up in the infirmary, though. I'll send a request for a potion to ensure the frost does no permanent damage. Better safe than sorry." She pats my shoulder twice then stands.

Coach whispers something in the healer's ear and she rushes off across the arena, presumably to someone else who needs aid. Injuries during combat class aren't particularly rare.

I sit up and face Coach and the rest of the class watching me carefully. No one is quite sure how fragile humans are. Their nervous expressions give me the feeling they expect me to implode at any moment.

"Will you be all right to walk up to the infirmary alone?" Coach asks. But then, without waiting for a response, she looks over her shoulder. "Anthony, would you—"

"I'll walk her."

Coach and I both blink up at Auren. Her face is solemn, her eyes dim.

"It's the least I can do."

"Auren..." Coach says slowly. "I don't suspect you of ill intentions, but you do realize helping her will not absolve you of any wrongdoing."

She nods.

"It was an accident," I say quickly. "There was no wrongdoing."

"Candice," Coach says then shakes her head. "That is really more of a decision for the headmaster. Do you feel comfortable walking with Auren? Or do you want me to select someone else?"

"Auren is fine."

I'm not afraid of Auren, though maybe I should be given what just happened. She has more than enough power to do terrible things to me, but her gloomy frown suggests not only does she feel guilt for her outburst, but she also has something she wants to say. I'd like to hear it.

"All right, Auren, ensure Candice makes it to the infirmary safely and then head directly to see Ms. Bhatt. Do you understand?"

Auren agrees, and they both help me to my feet. I don't feel particularly *great*—my limbs are stiff, and I have a dull headache—but I'm not in any intense pain.

I cross my arms and walk beside the fae princess who hates me into the main building of the school.

Only once we're relatively alone in the narrow halls of the south wing do I ask, "Why are you afraid of dying?"

She doesn't answer right away. The sound of our shoes

pattering on the marble tile is loud as hell in our awkward silence.

"Because if Jarron finds out what I did, even if you're not together anymore, he'll still murder me for it."

I let that thought settle in my mind. It doesn't exactly endear me to her, but it does distract me. Will Jarron come back soon? And if so, what will our relationship be like?

"You're right," she continues. "You could have had me killed back then. We all saw it. How obsessed he was with you. I swear he *never once* looked at me the way he looked at you."

My stomach squeezes. I don't want to remember how good that felt. "Is that why you hate me?"

"No," she whispers. "Maybe. But I'm smart enough to realize that's unfair."

She stops in the middle of the hall. I bite the inside of my lip and wait for her to say whatever it is that's been bothering her.

"I'm sorry. I haven't been the person I want to be lately. I guess, that's what I want to say. I don't know." She rubs the back of her neck.

"Yeah, I get that." I feel the same sometimes. I wish I were different. I wish I related to people better. I wish I communicated better. But I close up everything and let anger well until it strangles me. "Just seems so typical, you know? Girl hates girl out of jealousy."

Auren sighs. "Yeah. It's stupid, I know. But romance isn't the only reason I was jealous of you. *Am*, am jealous of you."

I ignore that last bit. She has no reason to be jealous of me now. I'm hated and alone and weak. I don't have anything she wants, except maybe wonderful friends like Lola and Janet.

"Yes, I've had a crush on Jarron for a while. He's hot and powerful, what's not to like? But there's more to it for me."

"Okay. What else?" I ask.

"Did you hear about the fae portals being closed for good? No one really knows how or why or if they'll ever open again."

My lips part. I had heard a little bit about that.

"Which means my brother and I may never return home. We may never see our family again. We're alone here on this magicless planet. A princess without a kingdom. Sounds fun, doesn't it?"

I pin my lips together. Better than not being a princess at all, I think. But I understand her point. She had something important torn from her grasp, and now she's left seeking something to fill the hole left behind.

"I wanted his *future*. I have been displaced from a wonderful world of wild magic, so much *bigger* than this dim place you call Earth. I miss it. And I'm scared of what my life will be like without it. So, if Jarron, the powerful prince of another world of wondrous magic were to claim me..."

"I see." Being with Jarron would give her a replacement future similar to the one she lost. It would give her purpose and a whole world that would cherish her.

"I don't think it excuses me being a jerk, but I guess I just wanted you to know. Or maybe—maybe I just needed to say it, so it stops rotting inside of me."

I sniff and rock back on my heels. "I appreciate you telling me. My friends in Minor Hall told me you were really kind to them, so I knew you weren't a *total* dick. Doesn't stop me from wanting to strangle you every time I think about you with Jarron, though."

She chuckles. "Fair enough."

We continue walking.

"Why did you two break up, then?" she asks.

I raise a brow. "This better not be an elaborate scheme to get information out of me for more rumors."

She holds her hands up in surrender. "It's not, I swear."

I don't answer her question, and she doesn't ask again. She parts with only an awkward wave when I reach the infirmary. I watch her smooth stroll toward the headmaster's office to face her consequences. I'm reminded of a phrase I heard at the Elite table a few months ago.

There's a thin line between friend and foe.

8

DEAR CANDICE

When will you see that it's all pointless?
A game.
A show.
You think yourself the vigilante
the rebel
But you don't realize that you are the puppet,
Controlled by the puppeteer
And this path does not lead where you think.
This is only act one.
The games have only just begun.

The Jinn

9
THE BIG BAD WOLF NEEDS MY HELP?

Something slimy flies through the air and lands on my shoe on my way to the lunch table. I look down at the spitball. Really? I go to a supernatural school, and they resort to spitballs? How pathetic is that?

I ignore it and keep walking to reach my friends. It's been a few weeks since school restarted, but it seems my reputation is only getting worse. Or rather, people are feeling more comfortable being open about their dislike of me.

Thompson, the Elite shifter, is already seated with Lola, Janet, and her boyfriend, Marcus.

"About time, potion master. I need you to help me with this," Thompson says dramatically.

I'm still not sure what to think about the shifter. He has to have some kind of agenda, but also, he makes me forget the bad. It's like he doesn't even see the hurricane of drama surrounding me, and the moment I sit at the table, all of it disappears.

His charming mix of goof and arrogance sucks my attention in. Almost like he knows it's what I need.

But I still don't trust him.

Thompson pushes an open book in front of me. "I've tried it three times and can't get the stupid foam to turn blue."

I glance over the potion instructions. Then, I shrug. "I've never done this one."

"Are you in level-three potions?" Janet asks, leaning across the table to stare at the book.

Thompson nods.

"That's impressive for a shifter," I comment, still examining the instructions. Shifters don't have a ton of usable magic. They rely on brute strength, which is built with inherited magic, but it's not exactly the same.

"What, you think because I'm a wolf I have to be a brute with no brains?"

"Pretty much," I mumble and grab a fry from his tray and pop it between my teeth.

His jaw drops, like it's the most offensive thing I could have done. I grin.

I chuckle. "After classes, you can come with me to Under Hall, and I'll see what I can figure out for you."

"Yes!" Thompson says, head falling back. "It'd be so embarrassing to fail this class."

"Really, though, wolves aren't usually into potion-making," Marcus says lightly. "What's your deal? Who you trying to impress?"

I roll my eyes.

"It's not like that," Thompson says more seriously, but there's a glint in his grey eyes. "My pack isn't very big, but we've got pretty strong witch blood. That's what sets us apart, and as future alpha, I'm expected to be proficient in multiple strains of magic. Having pretty girls who help that endeavor is just the cherry on top." He shoves three fries into his mouth and chews quickly. "Besides, I know better than to think I could compete against Orizian royalty."

I freeze. Thompson hasn't mentioned Jarron since the day he joined our group. I got the feeling he was trying to ease into it, butter us up so we're less suspicious of him. Him dropping that comment now only makes my Spidey senses tingle even more.

"Jarron isn't here," Janet says with a wiggling brow.

"He will be, eventually."

"What the hell do you know about it?" My fists clench. I shouldn't be so fast to react harshly; I know that. I'd get so much more information from the suspicious wolf shifter if I'd act casually, but apparently, I'm worse at that than I am at magic.

Thompson raises a brow.

"You weren't even here when we were together. You're just talking crap to bother me."

Thompson's expression falls, giving me a more serious look than I've ever seen on his face. "I'm certainly not trying to bother you."

"Then, why would you make comments about an ex—that you've never met—coming back?"

He rolls his shoulders. "I just... think that. Based on what I've heard."

"And what's that?"

"That he was incredibly into you. That he's the sexiest guy alive, according to the Major witches in my potions class. And that he and his brother almost died trying to save you from entering the Akrasia Games *after* you broke up. Exes who don't care don't put themselves at risk like that."

"Is that what people are saying?"

"What?" Janet asks, tilting her head.

She didn't hear the subtle difference?

I sigh. "I never intended to enter the Akrasia Games. Saying they saved me 'from entering the games' sounds like I wanted to enter and they stopped me. Really, I was saved from my sister's killer when he tried to force me to enter. They're making me not only the villain but a weakling at the same time." I guess it's not far from what I expected people to think, but it still gets under my skin to hear it.

I know the whole school thinks I entered the Akrasia Games, but I thought the rumor was that I'd changed my mind. Or maybe that was just wishful thinking. Now, they think the handsome, powerful princes stopped me from getting myself killed while desperately seeking power.

No one speaks for several long moments.

"Whatever, it doesn't matter." I push away from the table.

"Where are you going?" Lola squeaks.

"To get food. I've got to walk through the arches anyway."

No one follows me as I march past the rows of tables to the front of the lunchroom.

My "fight" with Auren caused another dozen stories to surface about me. Auren was suspended for a week, and even though it was clearly her fault, everyone blames me. Another powerful student absent from the school because of one meaningless human.

Then again, some of those whispers have been about how Auren couldn't beat me in a fight without magic, so she cheated. At least that one makes me sound strong.

Even though in real life, they all have magic, it's nice to know word is getting out that I'm not completely useless.

I grab an apple and a chicken salad wrap and head back to the table. My friends are still quiet when I sit back down, and I pick at my food without actually taking a bite.

"So," Thompson says after another moment of awkward silence, "what kind of potions are you working on in your independent study?"

I sniff and force a bite of my wrap. Again, he brings up the exact subject I need to refocus my mind from bad to good. "A couple things," I say with a shrug.

"Will you really let me see it?"

I nod. I don't know what's up with Thompson, but I don't mind helping him with a potion. Maybe I should avoid being alone with him, but my gut isn't telling me that's something to be concerned about. There is something about him that concerns me, but outright violence isn't one of them.

Unlike many of the other wolves eyeing me now.

10

WOLVES CAN BREW POTIONS TOO

Thompson whistles a joyful tune as we walk through Under Hall. It's chilly down here, even more so now that it's winter. Though there's a fireplace at the end of the hall and a few scattered torches, it's not enough to truly warm the brick tunnel leading through the basements, where my independent brewing station is located.

A set of wolf shifters stare openly from the end of the hall.

I try not to make it obvious how closely I'm watching their every move, as if they might pounce at any moment. I barely notice a vampire exiting a room until she leans close as she passes.

"Got yourself a bodyguard, have you?" she whispers. Her bright-red lips curl into a cruel grin as she saunters past.

Thompson doesn't comment or even react, and so I follow his lead and push through the heavy wooden door to my personal haven without a word. Steam pours from the room, billowing up to the hall ceiling.

"Whoa."

I smile the moment the acrid smoke dissipates as I enter my potion chamber. Thompson blinks several times as the air clears, then he follows me in. I release my final bit of tension as the door clicks shut.

"How many are you making? You said a few. This is more than a few!"

Pride wells in my chest. "I haven't really been keeping track. Half a dozen?" I purse my lips and count my active cauldrons. "Seven," I answer definitely.

He just stands there, staring for a very long moment. I wait for his brain to kick-start back up. Finally, he shakes his head. "What the hell, Candice?"

"It's not that many. I've got a list of a dozen more I want to do."

He throws his hands up. "Well, why not? Make 'em all, why don't you?"

I grin. "I would if I could. But the timing would be impossible for just me, while also taking classes. Plus, some potions have different temperature requirements. I can't make the cold potions and hot potions at the same time."

"You're saying that even *you* have a limit? Shocking."

I shrug again.

"So, what are you working on?" He leans over a copper cauldron that's not steaming as much as it should be.

I point to one after the other. "Stunning, confusion, poison —don't tell anyone about that one." I leave out the fact that it's a lot more than just poison and is very, very illegal. I continue pointing. "Truth-telling, sleeping draft, and another nullifier."

"*Another* nullifier?" he asks.

"Yep. The nullifier is what saved my life when—well, you know."

"So, that stuff is true?" For the first time, Thompson seems out of his element, an innocent sense of wonder enters his eyes.

My chest tightens, but I decide it's worth it to give him the cliff notes version. I speak casually as I stir the neglected potion, trying to figure out what small element is off. "My sister died in the Akrasia Games this past summer. When I had the chance to enter, I took it to learn what really happened to her. I refused to sign the contract, though."

"And you used the nullifier on—"

"Well, Jarron first. He wasn't going to let me enter Minor Hall, where the contestants were supposed to start so I used it on him, to stop him from stopping me. He followed me anyway—long story. I then used the same potion on Mr. Vandozer after he injured Jarron. It was really just to stall until help came. It didn't actually do much. But it still pisses me off that people think so little of me."

"Thanks for telling me," he says. "Do you really think Jarron won't be coming back?"

My brows pinch together. "I don't know. To be honest, I was surprised he didn't come back to start with. He could show up anytime. Or never, for all I know."

"Why do you think he's stayed away?"

"What's with the Jarron inquisition?"

Thompson grins, leaning onto his forearms on the concrete table. "My toxic trait is that I'm fatally curious."

"Mhmm." I cross my arms. "Show me this potion of yours."

"Right!" Thompson grabs a book from his bag and flips to

a page about midway through. "This one. I've got to complete it for midterms, and considering I missed most of the semester—well technically all of it, but the break was extra-long for, ya know, reasons, and they're making everyone, including me, finish the final projects that were due in the fall, now to make up for it. Anyway, I lost out on all the teaching and practice time."

I look over the instructions a little more closely than during lunch. I try to play the steps out in my head and figure out what could be tripping him up, but it's hard without going through the motions myself.

"Right. Get to work," I say, holding the book out to him.

"What?" He takes the book from my hand, but his expression is humorously panicked.

"It only takes a half hour to complete," I say while I grab an extra cauldron and place it on one of the few extra burners. "Do it here and I'll watch, see if I can figure out what your problem is. I can't tell just by looking at the instructions."

He frowns then after a beat sighs. "Fine."

He stands and wipes off his pants and heads to the ingredients. I help him gather the right ones because there's a ton in here and that could add a half hour on its own. Once he has all of his ingredients in order, he rubs his hands together and sets to work.

While he's prepping and getting started, I work on my own. I add a dash of hemp to my truth potion, which is now billowing nicely.

Then, I hop around to each of the others, giving them a stir and checking the consistency. The stunning spell is a bit thin for where I think it should be, so I add a dash of rock salt and pixie dust. The death potion is hard to read, but I think it's all right.

"You're not even watching," Thompson complains.

"You're doing good so far," I say.

"How can you even tell?"

"Just can. Keep going."

I head to the nullifier and tap the side a few times to loosen the tar that's settled at the bottom. The air stiffens as Thompson moves to complete the next step of his potion.

"Wait."

Thompson pauses, crushed hemlock in his open palm. His eyebrows rise.

"Give it a minute."

His forehead crinkles, looking down at the potion. "Why? Also, how do you know?"

"Just do."

His frown deepens, this time examining me, like he's really seeing me. "You sure you're not a witch?"

I chuckle. "Define what a witch is."

His head bobs side to side. "A human with magic, I guess."

"I have no magic. But I do have some very-far-removed fae blood."

"And demon," he says.

"Yes. I've tried multiple forms of magic, though, and nothing works. But I do seem to have a sense for potions. Kind of an intuition? No witch would accept me as one of them with only that, but I suppose I'm not *entirely* human either."

"Technically, I'm a witch," Thompson says. "And I'd consider you a witch."

"Thanks." I nod to the hemlock in his open palm. "Now."

"How do you know?" he screeches, but he obeys and drops

the hemlock into the liquid. "Using *your* intuition isn't going to help *me* pass the midterm."

"You need to be more patient and listen to the potion. The steam changes. Watch how it swirls, its speed, its thickness, its smell. It takes some time to learn it, but if you pay attention, you'll figure it out."

He sighs. "How do you just know what a potion is supposed to look or act like if you've never made it before?"

"Most people can't. I kinda feel like—" I twist my lips, considering. "It's like getting to know someone. You're awkward and unsure at first. But the more you're around them, the more you understand. I've been around potions my whole life. I've seen my parents make massive messes. I remember the smells they made before it happened. I learned that when my mother hummed it meant her potion was going well. After many years, I've learned all the signs and can watch for them. I don't usually think about it but they're there. Like—like they're talking to me. Which obviously, they're not but—"

"I get it. Kinda. I have to learn how potions work the way I learn how people work."

"Each one is different, but there are patterns you can follow. Occasionally, you'll find one that totally stumps you, but as you spend more time with it, eventually it will click."

He stares at me like I'm the thing he can't quite figure out.

"Salamander now," I instruct.

Thompson shakes his head, as if breaking from a daze. He quickly grabs three scales and drops them in.

"Stir very, very slowly. Don't disturb the magic but facilitate the transitions."

"You know that sounded like straight mumbo jumbo, right?"

I smile. He follows my instruction and swirls the bubbling blue liquid smoothly, like he knew exactly what I meant. Thompson isn't entirely inept with potions, or else he'd never have made it into a level-three class.

"Now, leave it alone for around ten minutes."

He slumps onto the stone bench, shoulders hunched.

"Tired already?" I ask.

"Stressed. Starting here mid-year was a terrible idea."

"So, why did you?"

"I wanted to. And it seemed like a good time to come while things were in the middle of a transition. Not so sure that turned out to be wise."

"Or maybe you just like to be dramatic."

He chuckles. "That too."

"I guess it's hard, but also, everyone is struggling to figure stuff out, so at least you're not alone." I almost consider asking him if that's why he chose me to cling to. I'm also in the middle of an upheaval. But I don't want to give him an easy excuse. I want to know the real reason, even if it takes a while to uncover it. "I just had to change my entire schedule."

"Mid-year?"

"The new headmaster isn't my biggest fan and decided I needed more *challenging* coursework."

"Ms. Bhatt? She loves me."

I put my hand on my hips and huff. "Why am I not surprised? She hates me because she blames me for Jarron's absence."

"Ahh. I see."

We're quiet for a few minutes, watching the cauldrons

bubble. The acrid steam fills the air, warming the room to the point of near discomfort causing Thompson to wipe sweat from his brow.

I ignore the heat and begin a slow stir of my truth potion.

"I know you don't really trust me," he says, breaking the easy silence. "And I don't blame you. But I want you to know I don't mean you any harm."

I pause my stirring to look at him. "I wouldn't have come here alone with you if I thought you did."

He looks around as if just realizing we're alone in a room together. "Oh. Right."

My attention returns to my potion. "I do think you have an agenda, though. I just haven't figured out what it is."

He sniffs and then smiles that arrogant crooked grin. "Got any guesses?"

I narrow my eyes, focused on the swirling liquid as I consider my response. "At first, I thought you were trying to get to me the way the other wolves are. Messing with me. Taunting. I don't think that anymore."

"Oh?"

"No, you go out of your way to make lunch easier. You purposefully distract me from the stares. That's not something a bully would do, even if you were trying to get me to let my guard down."

"Interesting."

"Maybe you want to get in good with my parents since you are a potions student yourself. That seems far-fetched, particularly since you say you're the future alpha of your pack."

"Hmm." He leans back on the bench, oozing ease. He's enjoying having all of my attention on him.

"You could be trying to get to Jarron," I say, but then I stop.

I don't really want to explain that one too thoroughly because it's the most likely option and I don't want him to close up if I'm right. "But in that case, you could be waiting a very long time."

He doesn't respond, and I don't even glance his way.

"Or something I haven't thought of yet. Something to do with the Akrasia Games? Who knows."

His voice is quiet as he asks, "you think I want to be involved in the Akrasia Games?"

I meet his tense gaze. "There are only a few connections I have that a powerful supernatural could want, and that's one of them. I don't know why you'd want that connection, but it's possible there's something. Maybe you had a loved one killed by it too and want revenge. Maybe someone you know signed the contract, and you want to stop the next set of games too. I don't know."

His expression relaxes.

"No clues?" I ask playfully now that his tension has eased a bit.

"I'm not even admitting I have an agenda."

"But you're not denying it either."

He smiles as he stands and approaches his potion. He studies it for a moment, breathes in deeply.

"Feel anything?"

"It feels... like it doesn't like me."

I laugh.

Without my bidding, he grabs his last remaining ingredient: a vial of liquid ash. He pulls in another deep breath, as if unsure and trying his best to figure out the right move. I wait, wondering if he'll do it all on his own or if he'll wait for me.

Carefully, he tilts the vile to let one small drop fall into the liquid with a tiny splash.

I purse my lips. "Maybe too small?"

He rubs the back of his neck. "Should I put another?"

"No, that'll be too much. Next time, try for a larger drop."

He nods.

Even so, the potion begins bubbling, oozing up with a light-blue foam. He leans in eagerly.

"Still a bit light," he says. "Rebecca's was like a royal blue."

The foam rises, nearing the edge of the cauldron, then settles back to a simmer.

"Did I do anything else wrong?"

"No. It's close. That's probably a passing grade as it is."

"Barely. And it was with your help."

I nod. "Try again. I bet you can repeat that success on your own. Then, try again. Listen to the potion. Feel the air and how it changes. It may take a few more tries to really get it right."

"Should I do it again now?"

"I'll be here for at least another hour, so you're welcome to try again if you want."

His chest puffs out with determination. "All right. Let's do it."

II

THE DEVIL'S RETURN

The lunchroom is buzzing, and when I walk in, all heads turn to me. That's become my norm, though, so I don't notice that something is very off until I'm halfway down the aisle toward my table.

The room hushes, and the weight of overwhelming power settles over me, tensing every muscle. My next breath comes out in a puffy white cloud.

Like drawn to a magnet, my eyes drift straight to his. The most handsome face I've ever seen. Golden bronze skin over sharp cheekbones and eyes so black they're like staring into a void.

His hair is longer than even just a few weeks ago, dipping into his lashes.

My blood runs cold, but I keep walking slowly toward the demon prince I was starting to think would never return to this school.

He watches me intently, with an expression I couldn't begin to describe. It's nearly empty. I'm not sure I could tell there was a massive amount of emotion behind the blank stare if I didn't know him so well. Or if I couldn't feel the pressure of his magic like a blanket over my shoulders.

Prince Jarron has returned to Shadow Hills Academy, and everyone is watching to see what I will do.

Jarron sits in his usual spot, with the chair next to him empty.

That used to be mine.

My heart continues to race as I stop next to the Elite table. Part of me wants to keep walking and pretend like none of this is happening. Jarron didn't come specifically to see me. If he had, I'd have spoken to him already. At the very least, he'd have sent a note or something, giving me a heads-up about his return.

Nope. I'm more shocked than anyone else.

So, I fully consider turning my heel on the issue and pretending not to care. But Jarron is more than an ex, and what's between us is more than school drama. I don't want this awkwardness to linger any more than it must.

"Candice," a low voice says. My attention twists away from Jarron to another familiar face on the other side of the table.

"Laithe," I say, surprised. He's sitting in Trevor's usual seat across the table from Jarron. The seat next to him is also empty. That's where Bea would usually sit—when not right in Trevor's lap.

That's another reminder of how much has changed.

Auren is back too, I note, her icy gaze a tad less cold than usual, but I can't spare the attention. I'm too distracted by the demon prince's emotionless stare.

"You're back," I say as casually as I can manage. "Both of

you." His expression doesn't change. No smile or nod or acknowledgment of any form. Though his body is positioned in a casual posture, it almost seems rehearsed. His body is rigid. I can feel the pressure building inside of him, like he might explode out of his skin if he moves.

My fingers begin tapping on my thigh nervously. I'm not sure what to do, especially with Jarron's tension.

"It's good to see you." Laithe bows his head slightly.

"Same to you. Is everything all right?"

"As well as can be expected. No news on the Mr. Vandozer situation, I'm afraid."

"I see," I murmur. When I glance back at Jarron, he's examining me. "I'm... gonna go sit. I'll see you guys around?" I ask, aiming for a hopeful tone. *No big deal. No drama to be found.* I force a smile.

Jarron's hands are in tight fists. He still doesn't respond, and it leaves me wondering what is going on in his head.

"I'm sure you will," Laithe answers for him.

Finally, I tear myself away from the most awkward conversation of my life. The moment I face Janet and Lola, I give them a shocked expression but quickly smooth out my features and hide it all. I flop into my seat, staring at the table, mind entirely blank.

Lola flutters onto my shoulder and leans in close. "Are you okay?" she whispers.

Nope. So much nope that I can't even speak the word. I can feel the blood pulsing in my head, which I assume is a bad sign.

I don't know what I feel, but absolute shock is the biggest. There's a whole hurricane of other emotions in there too. Longing, sadness, hope, terror, pain, adoration. I'm not sure what to make of Jarron's reaction, which I think is part of my internal panic. And it sure didn't help that all of this happened right in the middle of the damn lunchroom, where I have the most witnesses.

I finally pull in a long breath and release a little bit of my tension. *Holy crap.* All right, well, at least that bit is over with. I don't know what will happen now, but Jarron is back. That's probably a good thing in the long run. I'll be less of a target with him around.

Plus, maybe he and I can figure out how to be friends again. Because even though I've learned that my sister was his soulmate—my stomach twists, and my mind shuts down. *Shit,* all right, I'm not ready to face that one yet.

Every time the thought even crosses my mind, blinding pain shoots through me.

I rub my chest absently. The pain is intangible, but my chest is still super tight.

Okay, so even though we can't be together, we still care. That's still true. It has to be. Even though he's aloof, he's still Jarron.

A high-pitched whoop rings out through the room, and my attention darts up just in time to find Thompson rushing toward me, paper in hand. His expression is open and eager.

He has absolutely no clue what just happened.

"I did it!" he hollers. "I passed, baby!" He slams a piece of paper onto the table and then wraps his arms around me.

I'm too shocked to move or react or say anything. Lola, Janet, and Marcus let out panicked gasps, but it isn't until the walls begin freezing that Thompson notices something amiss.

His arms tense around me, his body frozen in place. We

watch the frost cover the walls and crackling over the windows just a few feet over.

"Oh, shit," he murmurs. Slowly, he removes his arms from around me and gives me a look full of panic. "Is he going to kill me?"

"Sit," I demand.

He obeys immediately, slipping past and sliding into the chair on my other side.

"No, he's not going to hurt you," I say loudly, forcing my gaze up to meet Jarron's. I nearly wince at the pain I see there, but this is important. "He wouldn't do that."

Jarron turns his back to us, and the ice begins to retreat. Excited voices fill the room as everyone begins chattering about what just happened.

"I saw my life flash before my eyes," Thompson says, head bowed low.

"Yeah, dude, I thought for sure you were a goner," Marcus whispers.

I shoot him a glare. "Not helping."

Janet chuckles. "Jarron doesn't seem the type to kill his competition."

Thompson's eyes are still wide as he shakes his head. "That ice is bad news bears. That means his demon is close to the surface. Who the hell knows what could have happened?"

I squint. That's an interesting demon fact. How does he know that? I didn't even know that. I mean, yeah, I knew it meant Jarron's emotions were heightened and his power was on edge, but it connects to his demon?

Creatures from Jarron's world are casually called demons for no other reason than their true forms look a bit like our human legends of demons. Most of the time, he looks entirely human, but I've seen the beast beneath the surface. I've seen everything that makes the boy I care about disappear and leave only the monster within.

It still chills me to the bone. That night still haunts me, even if I've seen his demon in a more positive light since then —like when he saved me from being crushed by the crumbling arena and carried me back to safety.

Bea explained their "demon" as *the spirit of the beast inside.*

It's that spirit that chose my sister as his mate and ruined everything.

"I might need a place to crash tonight," Thompson muses.

I snort.

"I'm serious. Can you imagine going back to Elite Hall after that? I have no allies there as it is. If he decides I'm a threat—"

"Jarron isn't going to harm you for hugging me. I'll talk to him if that'll make you feel better."

Thompson flinches. "I don't think you understand." He rings his fingers together, staring absently at them.

"I understand just fine. You don't know Jarron. He might get worked up, and I don't suggest you taunt him or anything, but there's literally nothing happening between us. And even if there was, he's not going to hurt you unless he thinks you will hurt me. So, don't be a threat to *me,* and you're fine."

"You're welcome to sleep in my room," Marcus says. "Just in case."

Thompson releases a breath and nods. He runs his hands over his short-trimmed hair. "Damn, that was terrifying."

I roll my eyes. "It's kinda funny how scared you are, Mr. Alpha Wolf."

"Did you see that guy?" Thompson's eyebrows rise comically high.

I pause, waiting for him to think that through. "I've seen that guy plenty," I say slowly.

His expression doesn't change. His eyes are massive, his nose flared. Does he know how ridiculous he looks?

Don't get me wrong, Jarron is scary, I get it, but the big bad rebel wolf is shaking in his boots at the thought of Jarron looking in his direction. I don't know why, but a hysterical laugh builds up in my chest, and I can't stop it. I bark out a laugh at how ridiculous this entire situation is.

The others at the table are staring at me like I'm insane. My amusement settles when I look up to find a set of pitch-black eyes staring at me.

Well, that's one way to sober me. Jarron jerks to his feet and then marches from the lunchroom. I find Laithe's concerned gaze. He gives me a sympathetic smile.

"Don't worry," I tell Thompson, "I won't let the big bad demon get you." I pinch his cheek, then I rise and follow Jarron from the lunchroom.

12

WE'LL BE NOTHING

The lunchroom hushes as I march out and stop in the empty lobby. All the attention is really grating on my nerves, but with Jarron back, I'm hopeful things will settle soon. So long as my new wolf friend and my ex don't decide to get into a pissing match.

This whole dynamic should expose a bit more of Thompson's motives though.

A chill breeze floats through the air, rustling a few pieces of paper pinned to a corkboard in the corner. No sign of Jarron.

My fingers tap against my thigh. Anxiety curls in my belly, and I really just want to get this over with. I know it's too much to hope for, but I want things to go back to normal.

Although, I guess I don't even know what normal is now.

Normal would be Liz with me. Jarron and I not speaking. Me avoiding all things supernatural. I don't want that form of normal anymore.

Yes, I want Liz back. But I wouldn't want to lose Jarron.

I need a new normal. Liz is gone; I can't change that. And

my relationship with Jarron is over, but our friendship doesn't have to be. That's my goal now.

- **Kill Mr. Vandozer.**

- **Ease back into a friendship with Jarron.**

- **Maybe kick some supernatural ass with my potion-making skills.**

I peer out the doors to the courtyard but see no sign of the demon prince. There isn't anyone to ask either. But I really, really want to find him. We need to speak to get over some of this tension.

I want to tell him that Thompson isn't a threat and we're only friends. I want to tell him I still care about him, even if I don't want to date him.

Somewhere between the anxiety and sadness, there's a tiny tug in my gut.

I turn back to the courtyard doors and push them open. The icy air bites at my exposed skin and tosses my hair back.

My fingers wring together as I walk through the chill air over the cobblestone walkway and toward the small courtyard garden ahead. The path winds around several sets of trees and flower bushes.

When I finally find him, Jarron is leaning against a shadow maple, hands in his pocket and head drooping.

He must hear me approach, but he doesn't move. Doesn't react.

My heart pounds as I examine him. The curve of his body is like artwork, and it makes me think about all of the things I never got the chance to do while we were still together.

My eyes snag on the buckle of his belt, but I force them higher. I can't think about him like that. Not if I want this to work out. If we weren't friends, I could live in my fantasies about the sexy, powerful demon prince all I wanted. But those feelings must be smothered if I'm to make a friendship work. And I desperately want that, even more than I want in his pants.

"Hey," I whisper.

Jarron pulls in a long breath then finally looks up. His eyes are back to his regular honey brown, but there's a deep sadness, along with a flicker of interest.

"Are you okay?" I ask.

He straightens, leaning his head back against the bark. "I'll be all right."

I tilt my head, watching him. As I consider what to say next, I realize part of me is angry with him. I'm not sure that's fair or rational, but he left me alone here. "I didn't think you were ever coming back." My voice dips lower, grows sharper.

His brow pinches. "That bothered you?"

"Of course it did."

His lips part, but his expression remains the same. "Why?"

"I... care about you. You're my friend, if nothing else. Right?" Does he not want to be my friend anymore? My cheeks warm. Maybe I couldn't blame him for that. My heart aches, both hopeful and scared.

The lines on his face deepen, as if completing some inner war. Then, he rolls his shoulders and pushes from the tree. His steps toward me are slow, and my heart races.

Anticipation chases my anxiety away, but the relief is short-lived.

He stops only inches from me, his expression somber but curious. "Friends like that wolf shifter of yours?" There's no accusation in this tone, just a gentle question. Deceivingly casual.

"Thompson is only a friend. I helped him pass his potions midterm. That's what he was excited about."

"He's new here. He has no other pack members at the school. And he gravitated to you immediately."

I purse my lips. "You sure seem to know a lot about him already."

"He's all Elite Hall is talking about. And you, of course."

Several emotions swirl through me. Bitterness, anxiety, annoyance, bone-deep exhaustion.

"You've been back long enough to catch up on all the rumors and school drama, but not long enough to even send me a message?"

He tilts his head slightly to examine me. "I didn't think you'd want to hear from me."

"Why would you think that?" My voice rises too high. "I thought—" I shake my head.

"You thought what?"

"I thought we were friends." Because honestly, I don't know what else to say. We're more than friends but there's no label I could find to explain it. No box we fit.

He winces. "Last I heard, you wanted nothing to do with me."

"No." My voice wobbles. My mind is drawn back to the last time we'd been apart. When I was thirteen, I told him I wanted nothing to do with him after he'd scared me with his true form—a scaled monster with fangs, talons, and alien eyes that did not see me as a friend. It saw me and my sister as prey.

When he spilled her blood and ignored my pleas.

When he showed me what it felt like to be weak and meaningless.

He was the reason I hid away from the supernatural world.

Though that night was terrible and still bothers me, I know now that Jarron is so much more than a monster. To run from him was an unfair reaction out of fear.

Maybe I can't blame him for assuming this is the same. I did push him away again, but not for the same reasons.

"You think I'm a monster," he says it like it's a fact. As simple as discussing the weather.

"No," I say between clenched teeth. "I swear I don't think that."

"Do you fear me?" he asks, his tone filled with that alien power. He doesn't usually use his magic to intimidate, especially with me, but I feel that darkness now. The threat of what he's capable of scrapes against my mind.

"Yes," I whisper. "But it's not—"

He huffs loudly and spins away from me.

"Jarron."

He turns back, that mask of indifference over his face once more, but I can see the pain and confusion in every tight muscle, and it's killing me. How do I bridge this? How do I assure him I care and trust him but can't be in a relationship with him? Our feelings are so jumbled up together.

How do I control the ridiculous urge to nestle into his arms? To leap up and kiss him. Those stupid feelings make this so much more difficult.

I rub the back of my neck.

"What do you want, Candice?"

You.

I pause for maybe too long.

He takes a step back. The distance is slight, but I'm suddenly cold, like he's taken his warmth with him.

I want things to go back to normal, but what does that even mean? I want the comfort and safety of Jarron's friendship, but what if he no longer wants to give me that? Maybe I'm asking too much. "I want to feel safe in this stupid school. I want people to stop treating me like a power-hungry bitch that would kill my friends for magic. I want Mr. Vandozer to pay for what he did."

His back straightens, and his face hardens. "You don't want me or my friendship. You want what I can do for you."

My stomach drops. "No. That's not what I'm saying." I don't need his help, but I do want it. There's a difference. And I'm a little annoyed that he left me vulnerable. Doesn't he care?

"You see me as a means to an end."

I fight back frustrated tears. He meant so much to me when we were friends all those years ago. I was an idiot and ruined it by pushing him away, and somehow, it turns out I've done that again. I ruin everything. "That's not true."

"Isn't it? You want me back here to make everything better. Make the Elite like you again. Track down your villain for you. I'm a tool to be used to you. Same as everyone else."

"I thought we'd work together," I say through gritted teeth. *I thought I mattered to you.* "But clearly, you don't think I'm capable of being an equal partner since I *need* your help so badly. So, go ahead and treat me like a weak human, and I'll prove you wrong along with everyone else."

He pauses, eyes softening. "I don't think you're weak. And I am willing to help you. I'm still working to find Mr. Vandozer. That hasn't changed."

"Right," I say bitterly. "You obviously need to get revenge on the person who hurt Liz."

"The person who hurt *you,*" he says quickly.

I don't respond to that, in part because I'm fairly certain whatever would come out of my mouth next would only make this worse.

"Fine," I whisper. "We'll be allies but not friends. We'll only ever talk if something comes up about the Akrasia Games or Mr. Vandozer. Other than that, we're nothing to each other." And I'll deal with the rest of it on my own. I won't ask him for any help if he doesn't want to give it.

Jarron sucks in a breath, but I don't wait for another reaction. I turn on my heel and speed away from the demon prince that still holds my heart without even knowing it.

13

Not the Flowers My Heart Wanted but Maybe the Ones I Deserve

I wake up with a pounding headache, eyes burning from crying myself to sleep, my journal clutched to my chest.

Jarron left me a note at the end when he returned it. It's the only words we'd shared since that night until yesterday.

I will never leave you alone to face your nightmares.

Lies. Those words were lies because I'm facing my worst nightmare now.

Losing him.

Worst of all, it was my own doing.

I shake my head. It's a new day, and I'm supposed to put all of this behind me. If I don't get some makeup on, food and water in my belly, everyone will see my puffy eyes and know how pathetic I am.

But when I sit up, something rustles in the corner of my vision. I twist to find a massive, beautiful bouquet of flowers. Calla lilies so dark they almost look black but are actually in varying shades of blues, reds, and purples.

My heart leaps, and I reach for the note.

He's not yours.
He was never yours.

The note slips through my fingers and flutters to the floor.

What. The. Hell.

Someone sent me flowers to mess with me? That's—God, that's so messed up. I run my fingers through my hair. The ache in my chest is heavy, but instead of letting it consume me, I suck in a long breath and pick up one of the lilies. I sniff it, and for another few minutes, I let myself remember the good.

These flowers are not from Jarron, but he did once send me some just like it. It's those flowers I will remember. I didn't appreciate him at the time, but I do now. Even though I'm mad at him. Even though he's hurt me, and I've hurt him. Even though I can't be in a relationship with him, in my heart, I can remember and cherish the beautiful moments.

Because at my very core, I am a stubborn bitch, and I refuse to allow a bully to ruin a wonderful memory.

Then, I force myself to my feet and head to take care of myself to a lavish extent.

My self-care includes a long hot shower, detailed makeup, and a massive plate of bacon and eggs. And finally, my potions lab, where I imagine the face of whoever sent me the flowers while I stir my instant death potion.

14
LEFTOVERS

The relief at the constant stares and whispers settling to a simmer is the only positive feeling I could pinpoint in the following days after Jarron's return.

Even with less attention on me, there's still this sense of a collective breath being held as I walk into the lunchroom each day, like everyone anticipates something could change at any moment.

But every day, I walk past the Elite table, and every day, Jarron barely looks my way. The moment I'm past his table without incident, the unwanted attention shifts away, and I can breathe again.

Along with that change, though, has come a different sort of unwanted attention. It's subtler and more unnerving.

The average students are paying me less and less mind. Which is good. But there are still three sets of silvery predator stares that won't leave me—and I mean *constant* contact. I don't think those three have blinked or looked away from my table in the last thirty minutes, and it's been like that every day this week.

"What's their deal?" I ask Thompson. I nod subtly to the table full of shifters eyeing me. "It's creepy."

He follows my gaze to the shifters. They either don't notice or don't care that Thompson has focused on them.

"Well," he says slowly, rubbing the back of his neck, "there's some talk about you being 'free for the taking'."

"What the hell does that mean?" Janet asks on my behalf.

Thompson winces. "Wolves have this weird thing where they covet a powerful supernatural's leftovers."

I cough. "*Leftovers*?"

"For lack of a better word." He shrugs. "I kind of think of it like a sickening form of curiosity. They want to experience what that being experienced. They want to know what they desired and what turned them away. Almost like how wild wolves roll around in dead animal carcusses."

I cough. Would it be overkill for me to exclaim "*what*?" again? Probably. But I sure as hell yell it in my mind.

"That sounds... pleasant." Marcus looks as though he may gag.

"It's not," Thompson continues. "It tends to be a *violent* sense of desire."

Janet's eyes widen. "What does that mean?"

"They equal parts want to kill and screw her?" Marcus asks.

"Pretty much," Thompson admits. "I mean, the good news is that wolves are not into rape. That's a big no-no. But the bad news is that if you deny their advances—"

"They'll revert back to wanting to harm me," I say dimly. *Wonderful. This is great.*

"They've been keeping their distance for a while because it wasn't entirely clear where you stood with Jarron after everything. Everyone was afraid he'd show back up, claim you, and anyone who'd shown interest would be on his bad side. The more he ignores you, the more their interest grows."

"That's so sick."

Thompson shrugs. "We're not human. Sometimes, our instincts push us to desires that make little sense to other species."

"So, uhh..." I pause, watching the shifters again. My stomach churns. I don't like this new information at all. And it sounds like it's only going to get worse. "What do I do? How do I protect myself?"

"You could talk to Jarron. One word from him and they'll drop the pursuit."

I twist my lips. "Not an option. He made it clear he doesn't want me asking for his help." Sort of. He implied I was weak, that's enough for my stubborn butt to avoid asking for his help. Even though I'm pretty certain if I mentioned this, he'd be enraged, I'm not going to go begging him for help. Maybe if I get the chance, I'll drop the hint that the wolves are being weird and he'll figure it out, but that's only if we ever actually speak again.

"Well, option number two is to screw one of them and get it over with."

I throw my hand over my mouth and whisper-shout, "I'm not screwing some random violent shifter just to stop them from hurting me. I'd rather poison them in their sleep."

Thompson scoffs. "Unless you plan to poison all of the shifters in the school, that won't help. There's only a few considering pursuing you right now, but any of the others could change their minds the moment the other competition is out of the way. Besides, you don't have to sleep with one of *them.* Any wolf would do. Or a vampire for that matter."

"What about you?" Lola asks with a deep scowl and crossed arms. She's not pleased with this turn of conversation any more than the rest of us. "Does she have to poison you too?"

My lips twitch into an almost smile. I kind of love that she feels protective of me.

He waves her anger away. "No. You don't have to worry about me. One, I don't bow to my baser instincts as freely as some of these fools. And two, I'm not stupid enough to think Jarron is actually through with her."

"You're still scared of him." I narrow my eyes.

"I'm not scared; I'm wary. There's a difference."

"Right."

He shrugs. "Think what you want. Wolves recognize those more powerful, and only the foolish children aren't willing to bow when necessary."

I sigh. "So, you wouldn't sleep with me to save my life?"

Thompson freezes. "Is that you asking?"

I snort. "No, I'm just curious."

"I'm not sure what I would do. I'm just saying that's not what I'm after. I didn't befriend you to get in your pants—or harm you."

I want to ask him again why he did befriend me, but I leave it be. I've barked up that tree enough for the month. "So, my choices are to ask Jarron to verbally claim me again or sleep with a shifter or vampire to get them off my scent."

"Those are the best solutions, yes. You could also run. Leave the school. It's unlikely any of them would follow you."

Unlikely.

"Or you can lay low, never put yourself in a situation to be cornered, and hope it resolves itself."

"Resolves itself," I repeat.

"The desire will fade eventually. Or maybe your romantic life will alter in some way to alleviate the issue in a more organic way."

I frown. "I don't like this."

"It's not a particularly good situation to be in, but being in Minor Hall gives you some protection. Be careful not to walk around the school while the halls are empty, especially at night. I'll go with you to Under Hall the next time if you want. It's best not to be alone as much as possible."

I pull in a long breath. "Yeah. Are you free this afternoon? And tomorrow morning? And the next morning?"

Thompson groans. "You really go that often?"

I nod. "When you're brewing seven potions at once, they require a lot of babysitting."

"I guess I just volunteered to be your personal bodyguard for a while."

15

A STUN-GUN COULD NEVER

The set of wolves watching from the end of the hall has grown to four. The same four silver-eyed fools that watch me during lunch. I pretend their presence doesn't unnerve me, but more and more, it's making me physically ill.

It's only a matter of time before they act on this sick obsession of theirs.

The redhead licks his lips and winks at me before I slip into my potion's chamber.

"So," Thompson says the moment the door shuts behind him. He rocks back on his heels casually. "Do you keep any of these potions on you regularly?"

I sigh, dropping my bag on the back counter. "Yeah, but I don't have much yet. I only have one finished nullifier left over from my last batch. I have a couple smoke bombs. After that, I have a couple I brewed in class and kept. A blood clotter, a noise amplifier, and a weak floating potion." None of those things will be very good for defending myself against wolves. "I should have a few more ready by the weekend."

Thompson nods. "You should keep as much on you as possible. Wolves aren't fans of potions usually. Messes with our noses."

"And yet, you're a wolf studying potions." I tilt my head. The mystery of Thompson continues.

He smirks and leans back on the table behind him. "My pack is certainly unusual. We're small in population and low on standard strength, but our lands are highly sought after. We've only survived because of our witch blood. We use what we must to keep our advantages."

"You don't seem like a weak wolf."

He's not particularly large, but he's fit and confident, with bright silver eyes. And considering he's in Elite Hall, I know he's powerful.

His brow quirks. "Are you admiring my bulky biceps on the sly, princess?"

I roll my eyes.

"Yes, I'm one of the strongest born to my pack in a few generations. I'll be alpha as soon as I come of age. Assuming our pack survives."

"Are you at risk of not surviving?"

"There are three other packs sniffing around our territory as we speak." He sighs. "Although, it feels like we're always on the verge of a territory war."

I twist my lips. Does that have something to do with why he's come here?

"Anyway, you, my friend, need to keep as many weapons on you as you can right now. A single wolf guardian won't keep them at bay long."

"Oh, so you *aren't* that strong?" I poke his biceps.

He flexes. "Not strong enough to go up against four wolves alone."

I look down at my stunning potion. It's done, but the constitution is still pretty high. I'd prefer to let it boil down for a few more days. "By your expert estimation, when do you think I'll be needing to use these potions?"

"At any time." He hops up on the stone table behind me. "Honestly, I've been considering suggesting you give up your potions work for a little while. If you went straight to and from Minor Hall for classes for the next couple weeks, you could get through this without a confrontation, but as it is..." He looks at the door. "I think they're plotting something with the way they've been sniffing around here."

I let his words sink in for a few moments before heading to the shelf to grab three large vials. It's not ideal, but I suppose a weak stunning potion is better than no stunning potion. "I am most definitely not going to stop potion-making."

"Or you could suck up your pride and talk to Jarron. I'd bet my tail he'd help you if he knew what was going on."

"If he doesn't know what's going on, then he's blind."

Thompson sighs. "Yeah, but men tend to be blind when it comes to women. He pays attention to you but no one else. He doesn't talk to anyone at his table at lunch; have you noticed that? He's like off in his own little world. And in Elite Hall, he's never seen in the common areas."

I shrug, feigning like I don't care. But I do. This Jarron is very different from the Jarron I know. The one who is open and sweet. Who showed me around every inch of Elite Hall and spent time in the library and in the sunroom chatting with his group of friends. He was never overly social, but he wasn't a recluse like he seems to be now.

"I've heard Trevor used to throw parties in his room weekly, but Jarron has not picked up that mantel, so far as I can tell. But anyway, my point is, I don't think Jarron's giving himself much opportunity to see what's actually happening at the school."

I shrug.

"Let me ask you this. If you told him, what do you think he'd do?"

I slip on a set of gloves and begin the process of scooping the steaming red liquid into the large vials. "I think he'd put the wolves in their place before I could even blink." I recall the time he strung up a wolf for making an offhanded comment about taking a bite.

"Exactly." He nods sharply. "So, the only reason you're not saying something is your pride. Is your safety and well-being really more important than your pride?"

I bite the inside of my lip. The large vial holds nearly four ounces of liquid. Too much. Other than the fact that the potion will require most of this liquid to hit skin to have much of an effect, the larger vials also tend to be harder to break. It won't be ideal in a fight.

"I think I should invent a potion water gun," I mutter.

Thompson smirks. "I think witches have tried that."

"I'm sure they have. But most witches are not the battling type, so it's never been a large priority for them." Most fighting supernaturals have different sorts of magic to rely on. Potions are generally for less immediate needs.

"It's nearly impossible to create a gun that won't leak in

some form or another, or with a material that won't affect the potion."

Hmmm, true.

"Paintballs have been theorized, but so far as I know, nothing has worked well yet. Besides, the potions would have to be incredibly small doses."

Thompson stands and approaches my potion.

"This is a stunning potion, right?"

I nod.

"Using thread of torrent?"

I nod again.

He chuckles. "Couldn't you just buy a stun gun and call it a day?"

I roll my eyes, although he does have a small, very short-sighted point. This potion may be subpar to a stun gun, but I'm still learning. As of now, it will cause pain and shock, hopefully enough to put someone down, just like a stun gun —assuming I can get all of the liquid onto the target. Once I get it right, though, a solid stunning potion could put a supernatural down way longer than a stun gun.

A stun gun also won't work on all supernaturals. I didn't begin brewing these potions with wolves in mind. I was more concerned about High Orizians—AKA demons from the royal line.

The nullifier worked well at sucking magic from Mr. Vandozer, but he was still physically stronger than me.

Once I perfect the recipe and give it the time it needs to condense properly, I'll have something I can use to put down Mr. Vandozer in one hit. At least, long enough to put a dagger through his heart.

A stun gun could never.

"Do you have access to a double vial?" Thompson asks.

My brow furrows. "I'm not sure. But I could get one from my parents if needed. Why?"

"Try to find a recipe for a stunning spell or something similar that uses amiximide instead. You'll also need an expelling potion. Put those two on opposite sides of a double vial. Shake, and toss."

If he's saying what I think he's saying, it would create a tiny stunning spell bomb. "That will really work?"

He nods. "It's a signature of my pack. We don't use them to throw, but we create land mines all around our territory. Enemy wolves find quite the shock if they overstep. They hate it, and us by extension. But it's better than the alternative. Don't tell anyone else about it, though. If our enemies figured out what we use, they'd be able to find a way to neutralize our mines."

I blink. "Why use not actual mines, then?" A real explosion would work better than a stunning potion.

"Dead wolves equal war. Stunned and confused wolves equal them backing off."

I grunt in approval. That's an interesting thought.

I finish my process of packing up my subpar stunning potions and double check my others. The knife Jarron gave me is strapped to my thigh. I haven't needed it yet, but based on Thompson's concerns, I'm worried I will soon.

"Well, this has been an interesting conversation," I tell him and pull my bag over my shoulder. "I'm not going to stop making potions, but I'll consider talking to Jarron."

He nods and hops up.

We head out the door into the chilly stone tunnels of Under Hall. It's not until we're nearly a hundred feet away from the door to my private potions room that we see the pack of wolves waiting for us.

16

TAKE A BITE

My vision tunnels, and suddenly all I can see are the sharp canines on the cruel boy's face. There are four wolf shifters in total blocking our exit.

Thompson and I are frozen in place, facing the shifters in the middle of a suspiciously quiet Under Hall. Usually, there would be at least a few other potion students wandering around, but everyone has made themselves scarce.

The shifters are still in human form, but they aren't hiding their nature. They are crouched, backs hunched, too-sharp teeth gleaming.

"Hello, Candice," the one in front practically purrs. "We've been waiting for you."

I swallow. They're blocking the only way out.

Thompson huffs and takes a casual step forward, putting himself between me and them. He speaks quietly to me. "If you run, they will chase you. That's what they want." Then, he sends a fleeting glance to my bag, and I receive the message.

Don't run. Fight.

Slowly, I unzip the front section and reveal several vials. So many thoughts fly through my head—I need a better way to store these, for example—but those things won't help me right now.

I don't have much that will help me right now.

Flying potion—which would make me stick to the ceiling for thirty minutes or so, but unless I had help on the way, what use would that be?

Several smoke bombs—I suppose those aren't a bad idea, but they'll do little to actually help.

A noise amplifier.

Three stunning potions in those stupid massive vials—still better than nothing.

One nullifier—which will do little against shifters. Magic isn't their most dangerous weapon, and it won't drain much of their natural strength or speed.

If I use my stunning potions perfectly and Thompson takes one of the shifters...

Those margins are too thin for my liking.

The knife Jarron gave me weighs heavily on my thigh. That could be what saves me today, but what kind of consequences will I face if I gut a shifter in the school halls?

I guess I may find out soon enough.

"Jimmy, right?" Thompson says casually.

The shifter in front pulls his gaze from me for the first time and glares at Thompson.

"Get out of here, foreigner. Your blood doesn't need to spill along with hers."

"Not happening."

Jimmy smiles cruelly. "Her screams will soon echo

through these tunnels. Every wolf in the school will know that she is mine now."

"The way I see it," Thompson rocks back on his heels, oozing arrogance, "it will be your blood decorating the stones. Your screams of rage making the entire school *laugh*."

All four wolves jerk forward in reaction to his words. My heart leaps, blood running cold, but they don't attack—yet. Adrenaline pumps through my veins.

Keep your cool, I tell myself. My mind is my best weapon now.

I hold my first chosen potion. A tiny blue vial. Then, I wait for the wolves to make their first move.

It doesn't take long. Thompson shifts into a defensive stance and holds out both hands, fingers splayed at his sides. His nails grow into sharp points.

One of the shifters growls.

The next several things happen so fast and are so surreal that I can barely register them. In a series of jerks, flashes, and cracks, all five boys shift into massive wolves of varying colors.

Two of the wolves lunge at the pitch-black wolf I know to be Thompson. The other two head for me.

Snarls and snaps and flying fur *almost* distract me from my first planned move. But before any of the wolves can reach me, I throw my tiny blue vial against the stone wall. It shatters, and the whole hall is filled with *shrieking*.

The blasting sounds bouncing and echoing over the stone is painful even to my ears. All five wolves—one of which was less than a foot from reaching me—drop to their bellies and howl in pain.

I thought the noise amplifier was a pointless potion, but then I realized wolves have impressively sensitive hearing.

This is going to hurt like hell for the next ten minutes. It worked even better than I expected.

Sorry, Thompson.

There's a path past the wolves, wide open, with them cowering in pain. Next potion in hand, I sprint toward my freedom.

A paw clips my ankle, and I slam to the ground. The breath rushes out of my lungs, black peppers my vision, but I scramble up to my knees. I cry out when claws dig into my thigh, pulling me back. A grey wolf stands over me. His ears are back, but he's no longer immobilized by the sound amplifier.

His rancid hot breath blows into my face as he snarls. Drool drips onto my neck. *Ew.*

Growls and whimpers alert me that the other wolves have restarted their fight.

Now, it's my turn.

As I reel back, I realize what's going to happen, and yet I don't hesitate because it must be done. I aim for the side of the wolf's chest because when the potion inevitably drops to me, at least it won't hit my face.

With all of my strength, I slam the stupidly thick vial into the wolf's chest and do my best to twist out of the way—I hope.

The vial shatters. The red liquid sloshes all over my hand sending raging pain all the way up my arm. An instant later, that same pain hits my hip.

The wolf and I cry out in unison.

My whole body shudders, muscles tensing and pulsing like one terrible charley horse. For moments, I can't think beyond the agonizing pain.

The weight of my attacker is gone, though, and I roll to the side. The waves of pain begin to recede. The wolf remains crumpled in a ball, only a soft whining to suggest he's at least somewhat conscious.

Well, my potion worked.

The bulk hit the wolf, but my body is still aching, and my head is still pounding.

Thompson is fighting a brown wolf. Another lies on its side against the wall, breathing fast and making no attempt at getting up. Thompson downed one. I've downed one.

Where's the last one?

A quiet growl behind me answers my question. I grab another stunning potion and spin to face the red wolf.

He crouches low, baring his teeth.

I stand slowly and take careful steps backward. His attention darts to the vial in my hand then to my face and back. My fingers are shaking. My right hand aches from the potion ricochet.

The look in the wolf's eyes promises pain. And he knows what my potion does. He's going to go for it quickly. I just don't know what I can do to stop him from getting it.

An idea pops into my mind, and I act on it immediately. I quickly grab another potion, and I throw it into the empty hall beyond. The red wolf ducks, ears back, expecting some unknown effect. Nothing happens, but I hadn't expected it to.

I leap at the wolf, stunning potion in hand, but he twists so fast I couldn't even pretend to see it coming. His jaws latch onto my forearm.

I scream, back arched. The potion hits the ground. The vial cracks and leaks out in spurts. The wolf's teeth carve through my skin, and soon the potion isn't the only liquid pooling on the stone floor.

The wolf whips me down. My back slams onto the stone floor, and I can't help the pathetic whimper. I can't manage to pull enough air into my stressed lungs. My head throbs. Sharp pain shoots through my arm.

I can't think. Can't move.

I don't know how he changed so quickly, but the next thing I know, Jimmy's cruel face is over mine, back in his human form. His hands are on either side of my head, and he smiles down at me, revealing those sharp teeth, dripping blood.

I reach for my last possible weapon. My hand is barely strong enough to even pull the dagger free from the sheath on my thigh.

"I'm going to enjoy this," he growls.

I scream as his teeth carve into the flesh at the base of my neck.

17

I BITE BACK

I scream.

Pressure and pain and warmth running down my arm, are my only sensations.

All thought escapes my mind, and there is only the force of the shifter's teeth digging deep into my muscles and veins and ligaments.

The world spins.

There is snarling and whining and a howl so full of sorrow it actually makes me sad. There is something warm and slick beneath me.

Blood.

Mine? I wonder.

My vision flickers in and out of focus. Above me grey stone lines the curved ceiling in a corkscrew pattern. When my vision blurs and whirls, it's almost like they're dancing.

Weight leaves my chest, but I can't move.

Someone is talking. He's frantic. Panicked.

"Candice!" I finally hear.

I try to respond, but it only comes out in a mumble. Why won't my lips work? Maybe because my lungs aren't working.

"We have to go," Thompson says, voice raw. Pained. Is he hurt too? "More wolves will come."

Go. That I can agree with. I want to get away from the sticky slick blood under me.

I'm lifted and somehow find my feet. I shuffle forward. As we walk, more and more of my mind clears. Thompson has his arm under me, supporting me as we walk up the spiraling steps out of Under Hall.

"What happened?" I finally manage. I remember the wolves. The attack.

Then—

"You stabbed him," he says, voice hoarse. "You stabbed the heir of the Lonecrest pack in the heart."

18
TROUBLE

"I think she may have killed him," a hoarse voice whispers nearby.

I groan, head throbbing. Dammit, I have to stop waking like this. So much of my body hurts. My right arm burns, and my left arm and neck are paralyzed by sharp, shooting pain.

"Killed?" I whisper.

"You're awake?"

My breaths start coming faster as I focus on my surroundings. I'm lying on a small white cot, stone walls surrounding me—the infirmary. Janet and Thompson are standing over me. Lola lands on Janet's shoulder.

"I suppose so," I answer.

There's dried blood on Thompson's head and scrapes up and down his arms, but otherwise, he seems generally unscathed.

I cough and then wince. How does breathing hurt? "What

the hell happened? You're not hurt?" I ask Thompson. If he were, he'd be in a bed too.

"It's you we're worried about!" Lola chirps.

"I only have minor injuries," Thompson answers. "Probably had a concussion and was carved up pretty good, but between my shifter healing and the healer's potion, I'm already doing much better. You, on the other hand—"

"I'm not going to die," I say. Even though I feel like I was hit by a bus, I'm fairly certain death isn't a risk at present. Janet squats next to me and grips my hands.

I wince, but she doesn't let go.

"No, but that doesn't mean you're okay," Thompson says, his voice somber. Well, that's encouraging.

"Did you say someone died?" I ask, trying to remember the details of what happened. We were cornered by wolves and fought our way out. I used my stunning potion on one, but the other pinned me and... bit me.

I don't remember much beyond that.

"I didn't realize you had an obsidian blade," Thompson says. "You—you stabbed Jimmy in the heart."

My eyes bulge. "I killed him?"

"We don't know yet. It sounded like they were getting him emergency care, but from what I overheard, it didn't sound good. For him or for you."

"Me?"

"The pack is going to want your head. He was the heir to their pack."

I curl a lip. "He attacked *me*."

"And you used an illegal weapon to harm him."

"After he attacked me."

Thompson shrugs. "You know how politics affect everything here. If the pack is that pissed—"

"She doesn't need to feel any more stress than she already does," Janet barks, then her eyes soften as she takes me in. "You just focus on getting better. Are you feeling okay?"

"I feel like I got hit by a truck," I admit.

Lola chuckles. "You kinda look like you got hit by a truck."

"Hey!" I say with a laugh that turns into a groan.

"The healer said you'll be okay," Janet says gently. "You got hit with the stunning potion and have some bites. But those will heal with time."

"Jarron is going to flip his lid when he sees you," Lola says in a hushed tone.

My stomach sinks. That was true a few weeks ago, but now? Now... what if he doesn't care?

I know whatever is happening between us won't stop him from caring about my well-being, but, well, I recall his reaction in the autumn when someone tripped me in the hall and the fall made me bleed. With his new emotionless persona, I don't think I'll get quite that same level of passion this time around.

"Does he know already?" I ask slowly. If Janet and Lola are here, I'm guessing word has spread at least a little bit.

Lola nods. "Ms. Bhatt apparently won't let him in. She kinda implied you were fine and already went back to Minor Hall."

My eyes narrow. "Why do you think that is?"

"Because you need to heal, and him flipping out isn't going to help that," Janet says.

"Or maybe because she wants to get ahead of what

happened," Thompson adds. "The how and why before she lets more politics get involved."

I groan. "This is terrible."

"In positive news..." Lola says, her wings wiggling. She pauses a bit too long. Is she trying to come up with something positive? "Thompson said you were awesome in the fight?"

I scoff. This time, the pain is slightly less. "Yeah, sure."

"I mean, you downed two wolf shifters. Honestly, there are few students here outside of Elite Hall that could manage that."

It doesn't feel all that impressive with the way my whole body is throbbing.

"If we can survive the implications of killing an heir to a powerful pack, you'll be a legend." Thompson crosses his arms and raises a brow.

"Thank you for your help, Thompson," I say seriously. "If it weren't for you—"

He shrugs. "What are friends for?"

"I'll repay the favor if I'm ever able." I spent a lot of time questioning his motives for befriending me, but now, I'm not so concerned. Anyone willing to put their neck on the line to help me is worth the trouble.

I don't mention how much trouble he'll likely be in too if Jimmy dies and the pack comes after me.

Someone clears their throat, and Janet leaps to her feet. "Ms. Bhatt!" she squeaks.

"Hello," Ms. Bhatt says smoothly. Her dark eyes drift around the room, meeting each of our gazes one at a time. Her hair is in the same sleek ponytail, her makeup perfect, and not a wrinkle to be found on her pantsuit. "I'd like to speak with Candice."

"Of course!" Janet says. She grabs Lola by the waist and turns to me. She smiles, but there is clear panic on her expression. "Feel better, Candice! We'll see you in the morning." Then, she rushes from the room, taking Lola with her.

"You," Ms. Bhatt says to Thompson the moment they're gone, "I want to see you once I'm done here. Don't rush off."

Thompson nods, sends one fleeting glance to me, and then exits the room, leaving me with the stiff new headmaster.

Ms. Bhatt sighs. "Just when I thought things may be settling into a new normal."

"I have to go and mess everything up again," I complete her thought for her.

"I don't like to make a habit of blaming victims," she says.

"You may not like it, but it seems like that's what you're doing."

She ignores me. "What were you doing with an obsidian blade, Candice?" She sounds tired.

I shift my attention to the fascinating pattern of stones on the ceiling.

"Candice, do you know what could happen from here?"

I don't respond, knowing she'll tell me regardless.

"Jimmy is in critical condition. There is no telling if he will survive. As I understand it, he attacked you, and the use of potions I can easily excuse. But that blade complicates things. If Jimmy dies, the pack may demand your head, and there is very little I could do to stop that."

"Would you even want to?" I spit.

She pauses. Silence stretches for a long moment. "Is that what you think? That I want to see you fall? I am not so vindictive. But you put yourself in the situation—"

"So, I should have let myself die?" I bark, meeting her gaze with a sharp one of my own. I'm done taking the blame for everything. "They cornered *me.* You didn't do your job of protecting *me.* Again. And I am only alive right now because I had a backup plan. I haven't touched the blade since I got it until today because I needed to."

"You're right," she says. "I'm sorry I didn't protect you. But I want to protect you now. That's what I'm trying to do. I know it sounds harsh, but the reality is that the consequences of this situation come down to more than morality.

"I can't stop every altercation from occurring in a school like this. Next time, perhaps you should ask for help instead of taking on what is clearly over your head."

My nostrils flare, but I hold my tongue. Anger simmers in my chest.

"How did you get it, Candice?"

I consider telling her that it was a gift from Jarron. Once we go down that road, it lessens the likelihood that I'll get in trouble, but I'm still feeling rather stubborn. That bit of truth can wait.

She sighs. "Very well, Candice. I'd like for us to be allies, but it seems you're against that idea." She clasps her hands in front of her and rocks back on her heels. "Let me explain what will happen from here. No one, other than a few members of authority are aware of the situation with the blade, and we intend to keep it that way. If Jimmy survives, this will blow over, and assuming no other such events occur, all will be well. There will be rumors, of course, and I cannot control what the students say about you. If you feel threatened, please come to me. I *will* protect you." Her jaw clenches, her expression clearly determined. She means it.

"And if Jimmy doesn't survive?"

She sighs again. "We will cross that bridge when we come to it."

"What does the rest of the student body think happened?"

"They are aware that wolves of the Lonecrest pack ambushed you and Thompson. They know that you both escaped relatively unharmed, but Jimmy was seriously injured. Other than that, I do not know what they will say."

Relatively unharmed. Is that what they told Jarron too?

"And I'm to return to classes in the morning?"

She squints. "I will heed the advice of the healers. They want to make sure you sleep well tonight, and as long as there are no other complications, you will be free to go to class. If you don't feel up to it, you can send me a message. However, I think it is in your best interest to resume your normal activities if possible. If you miss classes, that will exacerbate the rumors and potentially cause more issues. That decision is up to you, however."

Pretend everything is fine and maybe it'll blow over. I want to be annoyed with the advice, but she's probably right.

"Okay. I'll see how I feel, but I'll intend to go to class."

Ms. Bhatt nods, her expression blank. "Anything else?"

I pull in a long breath and suck up a little bit of my pride along with it. "Thank you. We don't particularly see eye to eye, but..." I pause, considering the right wording. Mostly, I'm just grateful she's keeping the information about the knife to herself. "I do believe you have my best interest in mind." Kind of.

She raises one brow.

"So, thank you."

"You're welcome. I'll send the healer in after me, then see about that rest."

I nod and nestle into the stiff cot. Pain carves through my shoulder, but I finally find a vaguely comfortable position. Tonight won't be fun, but it's tomorrow I'm dreading most.

19
DEVASTATION

I stand in front of the mirror in my bedroom in Minor Hall, trying to figure out how to hide the bite marks.

I slept in too late to make it to my first class unless I skipped a bath, which considering the dried blood all over my skin, seemed like an unwise choice. The healers bathed me in the infirmary, which was awkward but probably necessary. The bite on my neck is still a gaping open wound they'd covered in white gauze. The bite on my forearm isn't much better but stings considerably less.

Now, I have about fifteen minutes to get dressed and make it to my second class.

The ache and burning from the stunning potion are completely gone now, though, so that's a bonus. I'm still a little sluggish, but otherwise, it's only the bites that bother me.

My left arm is basically useless since the worst of the two bites is right at the intersection of my shoulder and neck. I can't move my arm without shooting pain. I shift my collar, trying to hide the gauze on my neck. I pop the collar up a little. I look like an idiot, but maybe it's better than showcasing the bandage.

I'm supposed to pretend like this wasn't a big deal. Supposed to let the rumors run their course and then fade away. But I'm not a shifter, and my wounds will take weeks to heal completely. And even then, I'm terrified the bite mark will remain for months or even years. *If he was trying to claim me...*

I swallow. If he was trying to claim me, then it was more than puncture wounds. There was magic in the bite, and it won't fade for a very long time.

My stomach aches terribly. I suck in a deep breath and release it slowly, eyes closed. Maybe I should invest in some turtlenecks.

I run my fingers through my still-wet hair. I probably should have asked the healers to put it in a ponytail before I left the infirmary, but it's too late for that now. Luckily my shoulder-length hair is generally easy-going. It'll dry okay within an hour or so. Until then, it'll just be stringy.

It is what it is.

I grab my backpack and sling it over my right shoulder. My left arm hangs limp, but with no pockets in the stupid uniform skirt, there isn't much else for me to do with it. I can't hold books or anything.

This is going to be awkward as hell, but here it goes.

#

I'd enjoyed the lack of attention on me for the last week,

but of course, it's now come back in full force. I do my best to ignore it today.

People eye me in each class, and the teachers do their best to pretend like every whisper isn't about me.

By lunch, I'm already exhausted. Doing everything one-handed, and hiding the pain in every movement, takes a considerable amount of effort.

I'm in a bit of a daze when Janet stops me in the lobby outside of the lunchroom. I frown at her concerned expression. I saw her in the hall an hour ago and she seemed fine then, so what changed?

"Jarron is waiting for you."

My breath hitches. "What do you mean?"

"I mean..." She looks over her shoulder. From here, we can only see the first couple tables through the open entrance and people are staring at us. "He's apparently been looking for you between classes, and now he seems... agitated."

My stomach sinks. Is Jarron concerned? Or angry with me?

"The whole school is on edge."

That's when I notice the girls watching us from the back table are shivering. That can't be good.

I swallow and squeeze Janet's arm. "You don't have to walk in with me."

"You sure?"

I nod. "If I make it to my seat without incident, come sit with me. It's better if I talk to him alone anyway." I don't know what to expect, and she's clearly nervous, so this makes the most sense.

"Good luck," she whispers.

I adjust my collar, trying my best to cover the bandage, and then I stride into the lunchroom.

The whispering stops when I enter. All eyes turn to me, but I see only Jarron.

He's leaning against the side of his usual table, hands in his pockets, head drooped down. He looks up at me through long lashes.

His expression doesn't change as he takes me in, which only makes me more nervous.

When I approach, his attention narrows on mine. "Where have you been?" he asks casually, as if this were just a simple conversation between friends.

I stop a few feet from him and cross my arms. "Class?"

"Did you change all of your classes since last semester?" He bites out.

"Yes." I shift my weight from foot to foot.

His brow furrows like that's the most peculiar thing in the world.

He does another once over, only this time, his eyes pin to my collar.

The whole room chills. My breath comes out in a white cloud. That means his demon is close to the surface—that's what Thompson said. The demon that chose my sister as his mate.

He quickly steps forward and reaches for the bandage. I jerk back.

He snarls when I wince. The image of sharp canines are much too recent and that sound... My eyes remain pressed tight but when nothing happens, I peek up at him.

He's utterly still, watching my face closely. In his eyes, I see what he tries to hide—fear and maybe a little sadness.

His chest rises and falls with heavy breaths before he reaches again, this time slowly. I begin to pull away again, but he grips my wrist instead of going for the bandage. "Candice," he says firmly but gently.

I close my eyes and nod. He's not going to let it go until he sees the wound.

Very carefully, he peels back the gauze, and then the room ices over. The last time, it was a slow rise of frost crossing the floor and walls. This time, it's a flash and every flat surface I can see is covered in a thick layer of ice.

The students around us gasp and scramble away from the tables, and especially away from us.

Jarron's face is pure horror.

He looks like someone just stabbed his best friend in front of him. Like his every hope and dream was crushed right here and now.

I take a stumbling step back.

He doesn't move, not even his eyes. They stay pinned to the place my neck was moments ago.

And that's when I realize this isn't Jarron anymore. His eyes are pitch-black. His skin has lost all pigment. Horns slowly grow from his shaggy black hair.

"Jarron?" I whimper pathetically, taking another step back. Even when I had feelings for him, his demon always terrified me.

"He *bit* you," he says, but his voice is all wrong. Echoey and gravelly.

"Candice, move back." Laithe slips past Jarron and wedges himself between us. Thick grey wings spread behind Jarron's back. Black scales form over his grey skin until he is utterly unrecognizable.

The monster bares his teeth at Laithe. I take his advice and flee to the edge of the room with the other terrified students. Wisps of black magic stream from Jarron's back. The ground begins to tremble, along with Jarron's arms.

Laithe crouches, and a shadow spreads over his face. "So, you're sharing now, are you?" Laithe says with a smirk.

My stomach sinks. Why the hell is he taunting him?

Jarron's response is a roar that shakes the foundation of the school. I whimper and cover my head. Frost falls from the ceiling, crumbling down on the students below.

Laithe takes a quick step back. "I'm sure she's delicious. Mind if I take a turn next?"

Jarron's massive talons swipe at Laithe, but he spins out of the way with fluid grace. Jarron exposes his massive fangs and lunges.

Laithe sprints out of the lunchroom with the winged demon in pursuit. Jarron crashes through the door, smashing stone as he goes.

I suck in a breath as the two demons storm outside, shaking the walls of the school as they go. I blink rapidly, trying to wrap my mind around what just happened.

The lunchroom is utterly still, with only the distant sound of rumbling and the desperate breaths of those surrounding me.

No one dares to move or even speak. There are no whispers, just panicked stares.

Then, Ms. Bhatt enters the room, hands clasped behind her back.

Once all attention is on her, she holds up her hands, as if surrendering. "All is well. Please return to your meals."

I huff. Is she kidding? The tables are frozen solid, and everyone is petrified.

Her lips twist into an annoyed frown when no one moves.

"As you all know, this is one of the risks of housing such powerful supernaturals. Prince Jarron's passion got the best of him, but he is working out his emotions in the arena with his companion, as is part of our protocol for such situations."

A blast in the distance makes me flinch. *That's what they're doing?*

Many students lean to peer out the window in the corner. The arena can just barely be seen. Black magic flashes then recedes. Oh my God.

That was not the reaction I'd expected. I don't know what I expected. The last time I was injured, we were in a public relationship and he had to react—it was expected. Not that I thought it was false, I just... was prepared for it.

But this time, it wasn't really like he was angry. It was like he was devastated.

My cheeks warm. I don't even know what to make of that.

The other students seem to finally take Ms. Bhatt's words to heart and begin shuffling back to their seats. I don't move until Janet comes up next to me. She twists her arm in mine. Lola flutters over too and sits on my good shoulder, nestling into my hair.

Janet guides me to our usual table and sits next to me without a word. I'm certain the rest of the lunchroom is talking about me, watching me. But today, I don't hear it. I don't see any of it.

"Are you okay?" Janet finally asks.

"What the hell just happened?" I whisper. It's not an

answer to her question, but I don't have one, so it'll have to do.

"Jarron lost control," she says gently, like a mother explaining a hard truth to a toddler.

"Has he ever done that before?"

She shakes her head. "He's shown his magic before, like the frost, but I never got the impression that he had no control over it or that he was on the verge of exploding like he was just now."

"Yeah, that was really scary." Lola shivers against me.

"We basically had an atomic bomb land in the middle of the cafeteria," Janet says.

Lola clears her throat. "But, uh, the good news is, I don't think anyone else is going to mess with you. Like, ever again."

I huff out a bitter laugh. Then, I force a deep breath. "Where are Marcus and Thompson?"

"Marcus is over there." She nods to a table across the aisle. "He decided it would be safer to stay with his Major Hall friends for now. And Thompson never came to lunch. I think he suspected something might happen, and he wanted to steer clear in case Jarron's rage turned on him."

"He—he expected this to happen?"

Janet shrugs.

"We expected him to react," Lola answers. "We just didn't know how."

Another distant explosion rattles the room. "Is Laithe going to be okay?"

"Yeah. They're bonded, so he can't technically harm him."

"Really?" I was unaware of that part of their relationship. I mean, I knew they were platonically bonded, but I didn't realize that meant they couldn't hurt each other.

"Yeah. Their magic is linked. They can fight, and it can cause pain, but it's never serious. Honestly, when Laithe said those things, it's likely Jarron knew he was trying to bait him into leaving the area."

"But he still went," I say.

Janet nods.

Interesting. "I'm still having a hard time wrapping my mind around all of this. I don't understand his reaction."

Janet shrugs, but her expression is soft, almost pitying. "He has feelings for you, babe."

My gut twists.

"You never did tell us the full reason you guys broke up."

I bite the inside of my lip. "It's complicated."

"Yeah, you said that before. But clearly, he adores you."

"And he's crazy hot and powerful," Lola says. "So, unless he did something really bad—"

"Please stop." I hold up a hand. "I don't have to explain it. But he and I are not getting back together."

Even if that thought physically pains me.

Lola sighs.

"I think you're crazy. But you're right; it's your choice." Janet shrugs.

"Your choice, even if it's the wrong one."

20

DEAR CANDICE

The games are beginning again, and I can't wait to see your face when you uncover what's in store for you next.

Good luck
The Jinn

21

DO YOU LIKE IT? OR DOES IT SCARE YOU?

The still-healing bite on my neck itches, but I try my best not to scratch it as I stir my potions. Today, I need to bottle my new set of nullifiers.

"Your brew house almost looks like a normal student's lab," Thompson comments, flipping through a textbook in the corner. Even though you'd think I have the plague with how much space literally everyone in school is giving me today, he still insisted he come to my potions lab this afternoon.

"Yeah. I'm almost through with this set."

"You're not starting up any new ones?"

"Yes, on Monday, but they're going to be a cold set, so I have to finish this one before the potions department complete the temperature shift. It's scheduled for Sunday."

Many potions have a very delicate temperature requirement—just a few degrees off can alter the outcome dramatically. The nullifier requires a warm environment, and that has always been my priority. I couldn't fight a powerful magic user without it. So, I've had the room spelled to eighty degrees since I started. Now, with my new double batch of nullifiers, I'm content to try some new things.

One of the witch instructors is going to alter the spell to cold for next week.

"Bring a jacket next week, got it. Thanks for the warning." He holds up a thumb and flashes a goofy grin.

I roll my eyes. "You're a wolf. I'm pretty sure you'll be fine."

"I'm a wolf born in a warm climate."

"You're from Tennessee, not the equator."

He shrugs.

"As I was about to say, my new set will include an expeller and a stunning potion using amiximide. My parents have put in an order of double vials for me."

He looks impressed. "You have a lot of connections, you know that?"

I nod as I cork the final nullifier vial. My invisibility potion is the last brewing. "Yeah. I was a spoiled rich kid growing up, and honestly it was a shock when I realized my real place in the supernatural world. Maybe that's why I'm so bitter about it."

In some ways, my lack of power may be a good thing. If I had strong magic, I might have been a complete bitch. As it is, I know what it's like to be considered less than, so I've got some perspective. Even so, Thompson is right. I've been super lucky.

"And why I thrived in those snooty human boarding schools."

He chuckles. I won't pretend like I've always done the right thing when it comes to treating those with less, but like most of us, I'm a work in progress. I don't want to make anyone else's life harder, and I do my best to limit the pain I cause.

A loud banging noise makes me jump. Someone pounds on the lab door.

"Candice? It's me."

My jaw drops. The low voice is strained but familiar.

My gaze turns to Thompson, whose eyes are wide and full of panic. "He won't hurt you," I tell him. "I won't let him."

Thompson doesn't look convinced.

I march over to the door and open it only a few inches.

Jarron's face is gaunt. His hair and clothes are wrinkled and twisted wrong. "Can we talk?"

I bite my lip. "I'd like to talk to you, but—" I glance over my shoulder then back. "Can you control yourself?"

Jarron winces, and I wonder if it was the wrong choice of words. But then, he nods. I hold open the door.

Jarron takes one step in, notices Thompson, and freezes. The hair on my arms rises.

"Hey," I warn, finger pointed at the demon prince. "No demon-y frost. You'll mess up my potions if you change the temperature."

Jarron's lips flatten ever so slightly. "Sorry," he mutters.

Thompson is shocked still. He hasn't even blinked.

"I'm glad you're here," Jarron says without inflection. "I wanted to thank you."

I blink. He's talking to Thompson.

Jarron's chest rises and falls with heavy breath. Nothing about him is relaxed, and it has me on edge. His words are kind, but I'm not convinced that Jarron is okay.

Thompson's lips remain parted. He doesn't respond.

"You protected her when I didn't. I'll never be able to repay that debt."

Thompson leans back, his jaw tight. "I'm not sure I did a good enough job."

Jarron shakes his head. "You did more than was expected. More than you should have had to."

Thompson blinks rapidly. "All right," he says. "You're welcome?"

I smirk, though it fades quickly. "Something you wanted to talk about?" I ask Jarron casually.

"Yes."

I pause. He doesn't continue. My gaze darts between the two males. Jarron doesn't seem intent on continuing the conversation right now, but this awkwardness is too much for me to continue my work.

"I'll be done in about five minutes," I say, looking down at my vials lying in a pile on the counter. These are my most precious cargo. I can't just toss them in my bag. I have to organize the compartments to make sure everything is snug and in its place. Mixing up potions could be disastrous. I look back at the very tense supernaturals. "Maybe you should wait outside?" I say to Jarron. I can't very well ask Thompson to leave when he's been with me for days now.

Jarron lifts a brow.

"No," Thompson says, hopping to his feet. "I can leave. You'll walk her back to Minor Hall?"

Jarron nods solemnly. "Please consider me an ally. If you need anything..."

Thompson's eyes light up.

I narrow my eyes at his reaction, but I shake those thoughts away for now. Everything everyone does in the supernatural world has deeper motives, it's not unusual, but there's no point in speculating just yet.

Thompson nods. "Thank you." Then, he slips out through the door, leaving me alone with a very volatile demon.

I twist my lips and look down at my now empty cauldron. Then, I sigh and move to my next task of storing my vials. If Jarron is walking me back, then we'll have plenty of time to talk.

Seeing me get to work, Jarron settles in on the bench Thompson abandoned and waits. I grab my new bag, which was delivered yesterday, and I'm super excited to try it out with all the new potions.

I carefully strap in three of my nullifiers into the tiny holsters. This backpack was sold as a makeup bag, but its real purpose is for witches. Or you know, humans who brew potions. There are only a few slots, though, and I have way more potions than it will hold. I put three vials of the nullifier in the smallest slots—this nullifier is only one hundred milligrams, like a tiny perfume size. My last stunning potion goes in the largest slot.

I consider my options for my last two. I still have several smoke, truth-telling, and invisibility potions. I select the invisibility and the smoke. Truth-telling, I put into a smaller makeup container. It's important but unlikely I'll need to use it quickly. This pouch is my best bet for emergency use. If I decide to use my truth potion, I should have time to unzip a few extra pouches.

Content with my work, I put the cauldron on the muting tray and decide to clean it out tomorrow. Right now, I've got a demon waiting for me.

I take another long breath and then turn to face him. His

gaze flits up to mine the moment my attention is on him.

"I'm sorry," he says immediately, and is it just me or is his voice wobbly? "I'm so fucking sorry." This time, his voice clearly breaks.

I swallow and look down at my feet. I don't know how to deal with this Jarron. He's always been so sure, so confident. He was *my* comfort. Am I even capable of giving it back?

He stands and approaches me slowly. His eyes are bloodshot. I don't know if that's new or if they were like that when he walked in. "I don't think you'll ever fully understand..." He pauses, eyes unfocused. "I don't think you'll ever know how much I hate myself for this. How much of a failure this makes me."

I pinch my bottom lip. "Jarron, I don't blame you."

"It doesn't matter if you blame me," he barks. "I blame me."

I wince. I don't know what to say to this. What to do. I was a little mad that he dismissed me the way he did last week, but I didn't want his help. Do I tell him that? Or will that only make this worse?

"Part of me wanted to prove myself," I tell him softly. "Wanted to prove that I was strong enough to do it on my own. That I didn't need a big strong protector. But I failed too."

He shakes his head. "You didn't fail."

"Of course I did. I needed Thompson's help, and I—" For some reason, I really don't want to say I was bitten or hurt. Without even saying the words, Jarron's gaze turns darker.

"You killed him."

"No, I—"

"He died yesterday afternoon, and that was a mercy for

him." He clenches his jaw.

My stomach sinks. "He... died?"

Jarron nods. "He bit you. And you killed him. You did not fail; I did."

My heart is suddenly racing. He died. I killed him.

I killed him.

"Candice?" Jarron asks. He takes another step toward me.

My breaths are coming too fast. I'm not even certain what I'm freaking out over. The fact that I *killed* someone. Or the very real fear that his pack is going to retaliate.

Jarron grips my forearm, it's not hard, but it still sends a wave of pain up my arm. I whimper and pull it back.

"What's wrong?" he asks, confusion on his face. "Is your arm hurt too?"

I bite the inside of my lip and nod. "Just a small cut," I lie.

His shoulders tense, but he holds back any other reaction. "I swear to you, Candice, I will never let anyone touch you again."

"His pack," I whisper. "They're—"

"They're going to be *thankful* I don't hunt each and every one of them down for what *he* did."

I blink. *What?*

"The message has already been sent. You will never see a member of that pack so long as you live. They will cower before you. One word from you and they're all dead."

"Jarron—"

His jaw ticks. "It takes honest effort not to hunt them down and tear them all apart now. I'm almost disappointed he died by your hand. I would have enjoyed ripping him apart. If it weren't for the extra level of protection it's now giving you, I would be."

I tilt my head. "Protection?"

"You haven't heard the rumors yet? You will soon. People are scared of you. And not because of me this time, but because they think you're an even better potion master than your parents."

I suck in a breath, and then I realize. "They think I killed him by potion." Ms. Bhatt said she'd keep it quiet about the obsidian blade. So, with that missing part of the equation, the school knows I killed him, but they're assuming it was a potion that did him in.

He nods.

"So, his pack really won't do anything?"

"If they know what's best for them, they'll already be in hiding. If a wolf, or any creature, for that matter, starts sniffing around you, tell me. Don't ever hide that from me again. Ever."

I press my lips together tightly, then I nod. Things between us are so complicated. I don't understand it at all, but for now, while we're here in school together, I'll take it for what it is. He cares enough to keep me safe. That's all I know.

"I'm sorry I made you feel like you couldn't come to me."

"I told you I don't blame you. I knew if I told you that you'd stop it. But I chose not to."

"Because of what I said."

I shrug. That may have played a role, but he doesn't need to hear that. "I was planning to talk to you. Just minutes before..." I swallow. "Thompson convinced me to talk to you. It was just a little too late."

He absently picks at a loose thread on his cuff. "You and Thompson—"

"Are friends. Nothing more." I like him, sure, and I guess

under the right circumstances, I could be interested, but not now. Not like this.

Those are also things Jarron does not need to hear.

"It's not really my business, I know."

"It's all right. I'd want to know too if it were the other way around."

He pauses, staring down at his sleeve. "Would it bother you? If I—"

"Yes." Maybe that was too honest, but it's true. I'd be flipping out. That's part of what makes all of this so unfair. I recognize that. I have legitimate feelings for him. I wish really, really hard that things were different. And it sucks that it's hurting him too.

But I can't live the rest of my life knowing that if my sister were here, if Mr. Vandozer hadn't manipulated her into the Akrasia Games, she'd be with Jarron. He'd be devoted to her. Kissing her. Touching her. Protecting her.

It makes me sick to my stomach to even consider the possibility.

I don't know why it matters so much, but it does. Maybe if it weren't my sister. Maybe if I didn't know her. There's just something so icky about it being *Liz*. Maybe I've got some kind of complex about my sister I haven't worked out yet. Or maybe it's just the fact that if I were to give in to Jarron, to be happy with him, then I'd begin to feel grateful my sister is dead.

That's not something I ever want to feel, and I don't trust myself enough not to.

"I wouldn't stop you or anything," I say. "If you wanted to date someone else, but yeah, it would hurt."

His brow crinkles, and his jaw clenches. He remains that

way for the next several moments, like he's thinking over several things. I watch him. And soon my eyes are wandering places they shouldn't, like the slope of his shoulder, the skin of his chest exposed by his loose top two buttons. His folded-up sleeves, exposing muscled forearms. The silver rings on his long fingers, and the veins on his hands.

I blink and look back up to find Jarron's focused stare on me.

"Did I scare you?"

The breath freezes in my lungs. "What?"

"Yesterday. I changed in front of you. Did I—"

"No," I whisper, back straightening quickly. I mean, yes, sort of, but not in the way he's implying. I wet my lips absently. He watches my every move closely. "I don't fear you."

"Then, what do you feel?" The muscles of his forearms flex.

I turn away to cover my reddening cheeks. "I'm ready to go whenev—"

He grabs my upper arm and pulls me to face him. I suck in a breath, shocked at the sudden change. His movements are almost feline, slow and smooth, as he shifts his body closer to mine.

My heart picks up speed, and my stomach flutters.

His body is still human, except for his sharp gaze and his mannerisms. I swallow. Is his demon in control while he's human?

"You're hiding something, bright one," his voice echoes slightly.

I rip my arm from his grip and retreat a step. That is most certainly *not* Jarron.

I watch in absolute fascination and only a drop of fear as he tilts his head, like a curious animal. I've spoken with his demon before, but not like this. Not mid-conversation.

"Do you truly fear me?" he drawls. "Or is that a falsehood used to hide something else?"

When I say nothing, he takes a slow step closer.

"You do scare me, but not in the same way as before," I finally say.

He stops, examining me with those eternal eyes. "In what way?"

I blink. How do I explain without admitting that the things I feel are good, not bad? Because if I admit that I'm kind of, sort of into it, how do I keep him from convincing me to take him back?

"If it were up to me, bright one, I'd track down every wolf within a hundred miles and slaughter them. If it were up to me, I'd wipe out that gh'atan pack for good." His voice rumbles with power. "I want to kill something, anything, because of what they did to you."

My next breath trembles.

"Do you like that?" he purrs. "Or does it scare you?"

I shouldn't like it, and yet...

Jarron suddenly stands up straight and blinks rapidly, his expression full of tension. "Candice?" he whispers, staring into my eyes, like he's just now realizing where he is. He finally breaks the connection with a curse under his breath.

"What the hell just happened?" I ask. The regular Jarron is back, and I don't understand how or why they transitioned liked that. It sure looks like this Jarron did not have control over it.

As much as I don't fear his demon the way I used to, that

still seems like a very bad thing.

"I'm sorry," he says.

"Did you just lose control of your demon in the middle of a conversation with me?"

His face falls. Shame. He feels shame for this fact.

"I'm not mad," I tell him. "I'm not afraid—I mean, worried maybe, but not like traumatized." I take in a long breath and hold it. "Talk to me? Please?"

Anger flashes over his features for an instant, but it fades quickly. "I'm—It's hard to explain, but my demon and I are," he runs his fingers through his hair, "not on the same page about some things."

I huff out a laugh. "That's not the explanation I was expecting."

His eyes soften, shoulders relaxing ever so slightly. "What were you expecting?"

I shrug. "You make it sound like you're having a tiff with a friend, not having some deep inner struggle."

His lips twitch.

"Is it something bad?"

"No," he says quickly. "My demon will not harm you, even if," he points between us, "this happens again."

"Oh." My cheeks redden. "I was more concerned about you, actually. Are you okay?"

He looks surprised. "I'm—Yeah, I'll be all right."

Something is clearly off with him, and I can't imagine losing control to his demon at random is a good sign, but he also doesn't want to share details. I can't exactly blame him for that.

"We can go now, if you're ready."

When I nod, he silently glides toward the door while I

grab my bag. He waits, holding the door open for me.

We walk in silence through the halls. People stop to watch us, but I find I'm starting to get used to the attention. It's annoying, but I've run out of the capacity to actually care. *Stare, don't stare. Whatever. Just leave me alone.*

And right now, everyone is definitely leaving me alone. I'm not sure I'm convinced they are afraid of me and not the demon who's threatened to destroy anyone who harms me, but for now, the result is the same.

The silence between Jarron and me is thick but not necessarily uncomfortable. It's tense because there's so much I'd like to say, but at the same time, I feel good just being around him again.

I want to tell him I missed him.

But that seems unfair.

We finally reach the entrance to Minor Hall and stop, both just staring at the shimmering magic that blocks any powerful being from entering. It doesn't feel as formidable now that we both know how to override the magic. Only a few weeks ago, Jarron, the most powerful being in the school, entered through it after I used the nullifier on him.

Is he thinking about that too?

"Candice," he finally says. I twist to meet his stare. "I want you to know that, no matter what I do or say in the coming days, I'm doing it to keep you safe." He looks up to the ceiling, his muscles tense. "But my threats do not include anything you consent to. I'm not going to stop you—"

I hold up a hand. "I know. And I don't want anything else anyway." I don't want any*one* else.

I only want him. But he can't know that because this is already too complicated as it is.

22
THE DEVIL LOSING CONTROL

The next days are *weird.*

Jarron is weird. No more is the sweet and attentive prince I dated last semester. Now, he is a domineering immortal raging through the halls. I can feel his magical presence everywhere like a thick sheet. Walking through the school is like wading through cold, ever-shifting waters.

This is not like last semester, where I'd been told that Jarron worked hard to make it clear I was *his* without needing to mark me.

I didn't see evidence of that effort. Now, it's clear as day. Or more specifically, as dark as night.

Literal darkness permeates the halls. Black fog clings to my ankles and swirls over the walls.

Jarron's warning lingers over everything and everyone.

On top of Jarron's magical warnings, I'm now receiving apology gifts from wolf packs I've never heard of. Nearly a dozen flower arrangements, two boxes of silver jewelry, and a bunt cake.

The supernatural world is weird.

Why are they sorry someone from their species hurt me? No idea.

There are rumors that the entire Lonecrest pack is utterly terrified. They've lost several alliances and are now withdrawing into the rural parts of their territory. Not that I care. Don't raise super creeps and maybe they wouldn't be in this situation.

Now, it's like I've got the plague again. The whispering is louder and more obtrusive than even a few weeks ago, but I may as well be in a literal bubble. No one will walk within four feet of me.

Except, of course, my small group of friends.

My potions class goes by quickly; I can block it all out and focus on my work. I think the most annoying class is combat, in which everyone just forfeits every time they step into the ring with me.

Janet curls her arm in mine and leans in close.

Various students pass me and dart to the side of the hall, as if I held a venomous snake on my shoulders.

"Everyone says you're a mad potions master that's going to take over the school and poison anyone who threatens you," Lola whispers in my ear.

I chuckle at that. "Better than some of the other rumors I've heard."

A set of wolves pass by with their heads bowed dramatically.

We enter the lunchroom, and I decide to bite the bullet

and pass through the archway right away. I grab a wrap and chips, but I don't touch them when I sit.

"It's lasagna night in Minor Hall." Janet winks, and I give her a sincere smile. They know me so well.

Thompson is sitting at our table, waiting. His expression is casual, but his shoulders are tense.

"Everything okay?"

His eyebrows rise. "It's been an interesting day."

"Oh?"

"I'm sure you'll see soon enough."

Heads turn to watch Jarron, the demon prince, march into the hall, shadows billowing behind him like a cloak. His magic is a heavy weight over the whole room.

It's a bit dramatic, bordering on cheesy, but still hot.

The things I imagine doing with this new darker version of Jarron are... degrading. And delicious.

Jarron stands beside the Elite table and points to a fae boy. "Move." The boy scrambles away like a live bomb dropped in his lap.

Jarron drops into the newly vacant chair and stares in my direction. He scans the area around me methodically and stops to glare at every person who walks past my table.

He moved his usual seat so that he's facing me. So he can watch my every move. Or rather, anyone else's move against me.

Is it just me or are there shadows lingering on the ceiling making everything just a tad darker?

Jarron does nothing else, just sits in his chair like a king on his throne, arms crossed, gaze diligent. He doesn't stare directly at me again, but he tenses and the temperature noticeably drops every time someone even walks near my table. Before long, everyone is using the other side of the lunchroom to pass by, even if it means going the very long way around to their seat.

"He seems—" Janet begins.

"Different," Marcus completes the sentence.

"He's—"

"Not okay," Lola whispers, her wings fluttering slightly.

My stomach sinks. I never told them about my surprise conversation with the demon soul inside Jarron. The conclusion that he's *not okay* bothers me significantly, given what I know.

"He's making sure everyone fears him adequately, so they never even consider touching what's his."

I glare at Marcus. "I wasn't *his* before, and I'm certainly not now."

Marcus shrugs. "Just repeating what he said."

The tension remains for the entirety lunch period, even though nothing of note happens. Is it bad I think he looks really good? Like mouthwatering.

I shake my head from those thoughts. I've been planning to find a time to talk to him and tell him about the letters.

"There have been some rumors about Jarron lately," Thompson says, looking over at the Elite table.

"What kind of rumors?" I ask hesitantly.

"That he's losing it."

My expression drops to horror. "What the hell does that mean?"

"He's... well, he's losing control of his magic, which is a bad sign in our world. Ms. Bhatt tried to make his outburst seem normal for beings like him, but truthfully, for High Orizians, it's extremely unusual. A reaction this intense only has a few reasonable explanations. And last night, in Elite Hall, he did something similar at just a comment from a wolf. It's strange, so it has people talking." He shrugs like it's not a big deal, but I can tell even he thinks it is.

"He is very different," I say.

"He's sad," Lola says softly.

"It's more than that." Thompson runs his hand over his short hair. "Everywhere he goes, the light dims and it turns colder. Some beings do that sort of thing on purpose because they like to see the fear they evoke, but Jarron has always been so even tempered that it's off. Something is off."

"So, what are the rumors, then, exactly?"

"There's a rumor that he's fighting his own demon, and if he loses that battle, he'll murder the whole school in a fit."

"Jesus," I hiss. "What the hell is wrong with people?"

Thompson shrugs. "It's never happened in a school like this, but there have been events like that, historically speaking."

My palms begin to sweat.

"But we know that's not what's happening, right?" Lola says in a hushed tone. "He's acting like this because he's in love with Candice." She sounds hopeful but uncertain.

My blood runs cold. *In love?*

"Maybe," Thompson says. "It's all just very extreme."

"What do you think, then?" I ask, heart throbbing. Is there something more going on with Jarron than I realized? It's strange, but he did say he was okay.

"I think it might be a mix of both."

Anxiety curls in my gut. "What would cause it? The conflict with his demon or whatever." That's probably not a question I should expect a wolf shifter to know the answer to, but Thompson has always known a bit more than usual about Jarron and demons. It's one of the things I've been keeping tabs on, but at the moment I'd like to exploit that knowledge if I'm able.

He purses his lips and pauses for long enough that I begin to question his motives. He doesn't seem to be searching for an answer, he looks more like he's measuring his words, like he doesn't want to say what just came to his mind. "An illness, maybe?"

My stomach sinks.

That's a simple answer. Is it truthful? And if so— is Jarron really okay?

Over the next several minutes, I absently pick at my nails so much they start bleeding. Dammit, bad idea with vampires around.

Janet watches my nervous fidgeting. She reaches out and grips my non-bleeding hand. Lola flutters over to my shoulder and nuzzles into my neck. "Give it a few days. Maybe it will settle. He just needs some time to cope with everything."

23
V'RTA

My blood is pumping hard and fast the rest of the day and the next. The thought that there might be something legitimately wrong with Jarron does not leave my mind for one single second.

And there's this irrational fear that it's my fault.

I barely focus during classes, which probably should be bad because I am not coping well in my High Orizian class. Language is not my best subject, and I'm already significantly behind. But I've learned that most of the teachers aren't particularly concerned about grades, especially this one. Maybe it's because it's taught by a demon, who doesn't understand the American culture of grades and accolades over actual knowledge. He wants me to learn, and so long as I'm trying, he doesn't intend to punish me for not meeting his expectations.

I'm not sure if Ms. Bhatt will feel the same, but it does take some of the pressure off of me when I stare down at a page of very simple Orizian words that I'm supposed to be able to read but can't.

"We'll try again tomorrow," Professor Zyair tells me before heading up to begin a lecture.

I half-listen to his lecture in High Orizian. Though I enjoy the cadence of the professor's voice as he speaks in the guttural language, I'm barely able to make out even a few words.

His general philosophy is that the more we hear and become comfortable with the language, the easier it will be to learn. So, even if we don't understand what he's saying, it's helpful for us just to be around someone speaking it. He's given us recordings of stories told in Orizian for us to listen to while we sleep.

It's a much better tactic than just memorizing a bunch of words I'll forget in a week, but I'm not sure how much it's helping just yet. Right now, he's apparently telling us about the Orizian culture. Things I'd very much like to understand, but the words are too foreign and I give up trying after a while.

He begins writing on the dry-erase board. He lists five different words. I don't know what they mean, but again, that's not the point of the lecture. If I retain nothing, I won't fail.

Still, one of the words catches my attention.

"V'Rta"

I straighten. He says the word several times in his casual tone, pointing to a word in symbols I haven't quite mastered.

I've heard that word before but can't place when or what it might mean.

Recognition sparks somewhere in my mind, just out of

reach. I stare at the strange letters, trying to remember where I've heard it. Did Mr. Vandozer say it while trying to convince me to enter the games? Jarron's parents at the banquet? I don't know where anyone would have spoken Orizian to me except here.

The bell rings to signal the end of the class, but I wait for everyone else to leave, and then I walk up to the front of the class toward the young male teacher with toffee skin and two red horns sticking straight up. His appearance is very similar to Laithe's, and I wonder if he's of the same species.

"Candice Montgomery. What can I help you with?" the young male demon says with a perfect American accent.

"There was a word you said that I'd like to know more about."

"Picking out individual words in a fast-paced speech is impressive. Which word did you recognize?"

"V'Rta."

One of his brows quirks. "Interesting choice." He smiles big and wide. He's handsome and charming, if I'm entirely honest.

"I've heard it before but don't know when or how. I don't think I even knew it was Orizian."

"Well, it simply means choice, or chosen, depending on context."

My brow pinch. "That's it? No deeper meaning?"

"That is indeed it, but that does not mean there isn't a deeper meaning."

"Are you being purposefully vague?" I accuse, half-annoyed, half-amused.

He smiles. "To be honest, that one word could be an entire study. It is indeed just a word with a simple definition, but it also signifies a very important rite of passage to royal demons in Oriziah. Culturally, it is quite significant. In fact, that's what my lecture was about—rites of passage for young Orizians of the royal race."

My stomach twists with emotions I can't define. "Any chance I could get that lecture in English?" I ask hopefully.

"Generally, I'd say it would be a pointless endeavor. A human needn't learn about demon rites of passage, unless they intend to spend time in Oriziah. Young royal demons are kept quite secluded from the outside world. You are one of the few on Earth who can say they've spent more than moments around young demons."

"I spent two entire summers with the princes," I say.

"An extremely rare honor." He bows his head.

"I didn't realize," I say again, vaguely annoyed. "Is that because it's not safe?"

"Not at all. Orizian royals have impeccable control over their baser instincts, except in a few rare circumstances. As adolescents, they have little magic, so the risk is low. Once their shifting abilities manifest, it can get more interesting, but so long as they're closely monitored, they are generally considered safe."

Generally. He uses that word a lot. Like I'm some kind of exception. Is he trying to say what happened with Jarron and Liz was an anomaly?

"So, the word means chosen. Does it have to do with their chosen mates?"

His eyes flare slightly. "Indeed it does. And I'm afraid I should say no more on the matter."

"Why?"

"Because it is a sacred and sensitive topic. Perhaps you can ask Prince Jarron more about it."

I recognize the words as the dismissal they are. He begins erasing the words from the board quickly. I almost wish I'd taken a picture so I could study the whole thing, but it's too late for that now.

"Wait, I have one more question if you wouldn't mind?"

He sighs and stops his erasing to face me once more.

"There are rumors about Jarron's demon soul splitting or something? I was wondering if there is an actual precedence for that?"

Professor Zyair takes in a long breath. "You stretch the boundaries of propriety, Candice. But I also appreciate your situation and your concern. I have also heard the rumors. From everything I have seen and can tell, Jarron is simply going through a transition period. People from all different walks of life and worlds have internal conflicts all the time. He is a powerful being that is dealing with and balancing a lot of emotions, and in that way, he is acting in a very understandable manner. He is not at risk of blowing up the school anytime soon."

I huff out a bitter laugh. That's not my actual concern. "But is he okay?"

Professor Zyair's gaze softens. "That, I cannot tell you. He... This is his personal journey that he must work through on his own."

Disappointment drops into my belly. No answers at all, just more vague puzzle pieces. I mumble a thank-you and then head out to my next class.

24
A MISSING CHAPTER

My anxiety doesn't decrease at the end of classes when I look out the window and notice black clouds hovering over the school. I want to talk to Jarron, now for several reasons. I'm just not exactly sure how.

It's the end of the day, but I couldn't tell a single thing that happened in any class aside from Orizian. I've been in a complete daze, even now as I shuffle through the halls.

Thompson usually meets me to walk with me to Minor Hall or the potions room, but he's not here today, and I don't have the energy to be bothered by that. Not to mention the fact that I don't feel at all at risk anymore.

Everyone knows the shadow magic and chilly halls are a threat to anyone who would even consider touching me.

"Candice," someone whispers softly. I spin around but find no one within feet of me except a friend. A male friend who was definitely not the one who whispered.

Stassi looks down at me, concerned, which is a strange look for the usually smiley shifter. “Everything all right?”

I shrug. “I guess so.”

“Well, you’re looking very… adequate today,” Stassi says then frowns like he’s unsure where those words came from.

I stop in the middle of the hall, stuck between annoyance and amusement. “What?”

“I… well. You know.”

“I’m not looking ‘lovelier than the flowers’?” I say with an eye roll. “Do I really look that bad?” If Stassi of all people can’t compliment me, maybe I’m doing a worse job at hiding my bad mood than I realized.

“Well, you do look a little down, but…” He glances over his shoulder. “Jarron doesn’t seem to like it when you’re complimented lately. He, uh, scares me.”

My lips twitch. I’d like to smile, but there’s so much weighing on me that it’s hard to let one emotion take the reins.

“Well, thank you, then, I guess.”

He beams, his steps suddenly lighter.

After another moment, Stassi remains by my side, and I assume he’s my alternate bodyguard for the moment, so I bite the bullet and blurt out the question still thundering inside my mind. “Is he okay?” I ask. Jarron doesn’t have many close friends, but Stassi was in his inner circle, so they have to have some level of friendship.

“Who?”

“Jarron.”

He blinks, and I can almost see the gears turning in his head as he catches up to the conversation. What was he thinking about before?

"Oh, right. Uh, no. He's not—well, I don't know for sure what it all means, but he's clearly unwell. Hasn't been okay since he came back, actually. He doesn't talk to me, though, so I couldn't say exactly what's going on."

"Did he used to?"

"What?"

"Talk to you?"

"Sometimes, but he's always been reserved. I think he liked me because I never bothered him about the deep things. That, and I always point out the loveliest ladies." He grins.

"You think every lady is lovely."

"Exactly!"

I shake my head and finally a smile snags on my lips.

"Laithe and you are the only people he ever really confided in. I don't know how he does that, just not talk to people. I'm just blurting out my every thought all the time."

I snort.

We make it to the main corridor, where I turn toward Minor Hall and Stassi rushes off chasing some beautiful vampire girl before I even get the chance to say goodbye, leaving me with even more thoughts to sort through.

I head straight into my room today, ready to crash early, or at least hide from the world for a while, but I stop dead in my tracks when I find a piece of ripped notebook paper nailed to the door of my dorm room. It's covered in shockingly familiar handwriting in pink ink.

Dear Diary.

My blood runs cold. I look around, only to find myself alone in the hall, so I quickly work to get the nail dislodged so I can pull the page down without ripping it.

My throat burns. This takes the harassment to a new

level—if someone were to fake a note from my sister's journal. The handwriting looks so similar, though. It would have to be someone who had either seen the journal or knew my sister.

I'm afraid to read the words.

I open the door to my room while staring at the pink swirly letters and examining the ripped edge. It certainly looks like it could have been ripped from the journal. And I suppose there were a couple places there was evidence of pages being torn out, but there's no way it's real, right?

I set the paper down on my bed, jaw clenching so hard it's beginning to hurt, and carefully pull out my sister's journal from the bedside table. I flip through it, setting aside my other harassment notes, and search out a spot where it looks like a page could have been ripped out. I know it's a long shot, but I want to know what I'm dealing with before I torture myself with the message on the mysterious page.

I find a spot with remnants of torn paper in the crease and try matching up the page, but it's not even close. I try again with another spot. Not that one either.

The pressure on my chest eases slightly. At least if I can convince myself there is no way the journal entry is real, I can dismiss whatever terrible things are in the note.

Still, I keep trying. I notice a spot where a large corner is torn away from a page. But I skip past it, wanting to focus on one theory at a time. I find one last spot with tiny shreds of paper in the crease, right before the final entry.

My heart pounds as I line up the page to the remnants. They match up perfectly.

My lips tremble, but I refuse to cry, for now at least.

It's hard to think straight, but I can't come up with a

reasonable explanation. I read this journal a dozen times or more, trying to figure out what happened to my sister.

There wasn't an entry between these two before. I didn't necessarily notice the ripped pieces left behind, but they're small enough I may have just missed them.

Before I torture myself with reading the possibly authentic missing journal entry, I flip back to the entry with a missing corner and I pull out the folded note I found a few days ago—the corner remnant of a page.

You haven't escaped. Beware the games.

The jinn.

They fit perfectly together.

I curse and slam my fist against the bed. Whoever has been sending me notes, had access to my sister's journal—before the investigation was complete. That's the only explanation I have.

My stomach clenches tight.

Finally, I take in a deep breath and force myself to read the journal entry from my sister before she died.

25

DEAR DIARY

There is a way.

I keep thinking about all of the things Candice told me over the years about demons. How they're heartless, soulless. How they think of humans like lesser creatures. I don't think I ever fully believed her, but I did go along with her wishes because I trusted her to take care of me. We're barely a year apart in age, but she's my big sister. She's smart and driven and honestly, never wrong.

Except in this.

I think even she knows how close-minded she's being about the magical world, but she's too stubborn to admit it.

Even knowing all of that, it's still been mind-blowing to meet a demon who cares. Who listens and takes care of me. Even in his demon form, his leathery wings and terrifying fangs and horns—he's compassionate.

Yesterday, I talked with Candice on the phone, and it took everything in me not to share my news. I wish I could tell her how everything has changed. I wanted to tell her to read the book Behind Alien Eyes, *which opened my mind about these "monsters." I want her to understand too. But I know how she feels, and her mind will not be changed easily.*

I felt it too, that terror and helplessness.

I remember that night when the boy I had a crush on turned into one of these creatures. His growl was full of absolute rage, and it left me barely able to think beyond that fear. My sister tried to save me from his wrath. I don't know what I'd done to make him so angry.

He was my friend!

So, I understand Candice's fear and her anger at him. Someone we trusted hurt us. He hurt me. My sister told me she knew the solution to all of our problems.

We were weak and meaningless to the supernatural world, but that wasn't who we were on the inside. We could be powerful if we hid from the things that scared us.

Well, of course, she didn't say it like that. She said it was to put ourselves in situations to showcase our strength. But what she meant was to hide from those who would make us feel powerless.

She told me to hide. So, I did.

But I never felt weaker.

I couldn't undo the knowledge that beings like Jarron existed. It doesn't matter how hard you pretend; monsters are real. I couldn't stop looking over my shoulder. I couldn't stop fearing, all the time.

Until I met him. Another monster.

A monster who made me feel safe for the first time in years. He told me that the answer to conquering my fears wasn't removing myself from them but facing them just the way I've faced him. Vincent, my *monster.*

But that is only step one.

I can't wait to see the look on my sister's face when she realizes what I've done. When she sees that she was wrong the entire time and power was accessible to us.

I will be more than powerful.

I will be invincible.

26

TO HER, I AM THE BULLY

I toss and turn the entire night, unable to rest more than minutes at a time. Mostly, I wonder who would have done this. Who would nail a missing entry from my sister's journal to my door?

Mr. Vandozer must have had contact with Liz's journal before the investigators got to it. That makes sense because this entry would have pointed straight to him.

But then again, why rip out a single page? Or were there more? Will other entries show up on my door in a week?

Why not just destroy the journal altogether?

I also consider who would have delivered the message.

There is only one name that comes to mind that would have access to both my villain and Minor Hall.

So, I wake early, spend time doing my makeup and carefully covering my bite marks—they still make me physically ill to look at, and this nonsense with the notes and the journal is not helping.

I drink a coffee and munch on a pastry in the corner of the Minor mess hall, waiting for a certain someone to arrive.

Corrine finally walks in a few minutes before classes start, her hair a mess and dark circles under her eyes. I almost feel guilty when I walk over and slam the journal page onto the table in front of her.

She jumps and curls into herself in fear.

"Did you do this?" I demand.

Her expression is full of utter terror. Tears instantly well in her eyes, but she doesn't respond. I'm honestly not sure she's even capable.

"Are you still in contact with him?"

Her eyes widen, and she shakes her head rapidly. "I didn't do it," she whispers. "I haven't seen him."

My stomach twists uncomfortably. "You're sure?"

She nods. "I don't want to see him. I want to be free of this." Her lips tremble.

It would be so much simpler if she were my messenger, but I believe her—or at the very least, I pity her enough not to push it. "You've heard nothing new about the games?"

She shakes her head again. I sigh and slump into the seat across from her. "Someone has been leaving me notes. You haven't gotten any?"

She shakes her head again. *Dammit.* What does that mean? It's all a hoax? Someone's messing with me? I don't know what to think.

"Okay," I say finally. "Sorry for bothering you." I try for a compassionate tone, but I'm too frustrated to succeed. Corrine skitters off out of Minor Hall, leaving me alone with the last few students staring at me in horror.

They all think I'm the bully. Wonderful.

27
YOU SHOULD HAVE TOLD ME SOONER

I'm later than usual this morning, but Lola, Janet, and Thompson are chatting outside the Minor Hall gates, waiting for me, so I try to hide my internal panic and grin.

Even though Jarron's threat is clear as a full moon, and I don't suspect there is even the slightest chance someone would dare harm me now, Thompson still walks me to and from Minor Hall every morning and most evenings.

I sometimes get the feeling that he stays with me for his protection more than mine. Jarron is rather scary these days. But I've never brought that up. He goes out of his way to walk with me, Janet, and Lola every morning, and I've come to enjoy the tradition.

Today, I even brought him out a blueberry muffin from Minor Hall because I feel bad for the last two mornings the three of us came out holding our remaining snacks and he had nothing. His face lights up when I hold it out, making it very easy for me to drop the act and smile sincerely.

The muffin is nothing but crumbs within seconds, so obviously it's a hit. Maybe I'll bring a few tomorrow. Wolfy appetites are massive.

"So, how's this professional-level potions class going?" Thompson asks casually as we walk toward our classes. We only have a few minutes before we're officially late, but no one comments. I suspect they know I was dealing with something stressful and don't want to put any more pressure or shame on me than I already feel.

I have the best friends ever.

I sigh. "Kinda annoying. I'm forced to study potions I'm not particularly interested in, which sucks. But the professor keeps droning on about foundations. Learning these processes can help with others further down the line, yada yada." There are also only five other students, four of whom look at me like I'm the Wicked Witch of the West. "But it's cool to be in class with some Elite. Ya know, the ones that don't hate me and aren't forced to literally fight me."

"How is that combat class going? Any changes?"

"Nope. Every time Coach tries to put me in the ring with someone, they forfeit automatically, even if she threatens them with low marks. She's given up for a while, and now I spar with her every day. Stupid."

Lola flutters a few feet ahead. "I don't blame them, though. Jarron has been *scary*."

"Well, it wouldn't be like this if they weren't jerks to begin with."

Lola shrugs and does a lap around the three of us.

"What about your classes? Any new big projects?"

"I'm writing a sleep song," Lola shares. "Which is cool, but also kinda pointless since I can just use my pixie dust."

I laugh. "I guess that's the downside to so many different species taking classes together."

She wiggles in agreement.

"I'm just starting up our final project in art casting," Janet chimes in. "It takes so much focus to keep the magic lingering over every stroke. I've got this massive canvas to complete, though. Like the entire rest of the year will be dedicated to that, which is awesome."

"Nice. What are you painting?"

"I haven't decided yet. I'm still structuring it. The spell should be a version of hypnosis that makes the person literally think they've fallen into the painting and keeps them there for hours. I haven't decided what the actual image should be yet, though."

That sounds insane, and it's a *class project.* "How do they grade that? Do you test out the spell on someone?"

"We each have to volunteer as a guinea pig for someone else's project, so we'll get a full pass one day at the end of the year. It's... interesting."

"Are they all hypnotizing? So, you're going to think you're stuck in a painting for hours as part of your class?"

"Yep. And we have to write a detailed description of everything we see and experience while inside it."

"That's so insane."

She nods. "It's a little scary but not dangerous. They won't allow us to do anything violent in the spells or the paintings."

"What about you, Thompson? How are your classes going?"

"All right. I'm caught up on most of them, thanks to our friendly neighborhood potions master." He nudges me. "Only one I'm having trouble with now is numerology. I've never been much for numbers, and this class is savage."

"I've heard those advanced classes can be brutal," Lola says. "My cousin is in that track, and she's had three mental breakdowns since last year."

My eyes widen. "That sounds unhealthy."

"Her parents are crazy strict. The pressure is really high."

My lips part, but I shut them. Is that all pixies? Is that why her family treats her so badly for being in Minor Hall? I'm not brave enough to voice the questions now, especially considering I don't know if she'd want to discuss her less-than-pleasant family dynamics in front of Thompson.

The moment we pass into the main hall, we all stop and shiver as one. Yep, that heavy magic is even worse here.

"Is he ever going to chill out?" I mutter.

"Nope," Thompson says definitively.

I groan. "Ever? You really think he's gonna try to suffocate the entire school with his magic for the rest of the year?"

"And beyond, I'm afraid. Of course, you could alleviate some of the pressure..."

I cross my arms. "What does that mean?"

Thompson stops and gives me an uncharacteristically serious look. "The Crown Prince of the Under World is desperately in love with you, and you won't give him the time of day." His gaze softens when I tense. "I'd be willing to bet things calm down a little if that were to change." He nudges me with his elbow, and we resume walking.

Is Thompson really pushing me to get back together with Jarron? Just three days ago, he was convinced it was at least partially due to an illness. Now, he thinks I can solve everything by dropping into the demon prince's lap?

I cross my arms, but it sends a shooting pain up to my shoulder, a reminder that my wolf bite is not even close to gone. It's getting better, but it still hurts, and it's not fading. I don't want to think about what that means.

"Word on the street is that, even when you were dating, you wouldn't let him mark you. What's up with that?"

"None of your business, that's what."

"Mmhmm."

"She's just afraid," Janet says sweetly as we wade down the hall through the overwhelming darkness.

"Hey," I complain.

She shrugs. "The supernatural world is still kinda new to her, at least like this. She wouldn't let him bite her or anything."

"Janet!"

She smirks. "What? It's true."

"Interesting," Thompson purrs. "I wonder if we'll need to give her an intervention."

"Oh my God! Stop."

The rush of an icy wind swoops over us, and we all freeze.

"Something wrong?" a gravelly voice asks.

My eyes widen at a certain demon prince leaning against a doorframe only a few feet ahead. Where the hell did he come from? His posture is casual, one hand in his pocket as usual, but his eyes are sallow with dark shadows beneath them.

"No, nothing is wrong," I say, maybe more harshly than I should.

Jarron's gaze lingers on the bandage on my neck, then they flash up to meet my stare. He exposes no obvious emotions, other than general unease.

"You guys can go ahead," I tell my friends.

"Oh, would ya look at that, we're late for class!" Thompson says as he skitters off. Lola and Janet rush after him.

I've needed the chance to talk to Jarron about the letters. I've put it off long enough, so this is a good opportunity to slip it in.

Jarron flicks a brow.

"Lovely morning," I chirp sarcastically. "So bright and warm."

Jarron's lips twitch. "Are you all right?"

I nod. "Are you?"

He shrugs. And that, I believe. No one could look at him and think he's anywhere near good. "I think you're stuck walking me to class now."

"Did you think I'd mind?"

I shrug. Not really, I suppose. "You don't have to suffocate the whole school, you know."

He doesn't react. "Maybe I want to."

"This?" I hold out my hand, pushing at some of the wisping black magic. "This is what you want?"

"Feels like home," he jokes then lets out a rumble of a laugh. "Actually, it just feels good to make everyone else feel as miserable as I do."

He's smiling, but it's more of a grimace.

"Are... you serious?"

He chuckles lightly. His expression is softer than before but still missing the lightness and joy he held months ago.

"Jarron, are you okay, really? If something is *actually* wrong, will you tell me? Please?"

He shuffles his feet and looks up to the ceiling. "I've had a hard couple of weeks. Sometimes, when you feel dark, it's better to expel it than hold it in."

"I'm not so sure making others miserable is a healthy form of expression," I chide lightly. "And that wasn't really an answer."

He rubs the back of his neck. "I've had a hard time, but it's not easy to explain. It's internal. Something I have to work out on my own. Manuela keeps calling it anxiety."

"Oh," I say stupidly. I'm not sure why, but it seems odd to think of powerful demon princes dealing with things like depression and anxiety. I suppose they could, though. "I mean, anxiety can be a really serious issue. You don't have to work it out on your own."

He sighs. "Therapy might help," he admits. "But it's not an option at the moment."

"Why not?"

"Only another High Orizian could realistically understand enough to help."

"Even Laithe can't?" Other than the fact that he's not a trained professional, at least he's someone who would understand, right?

"He does help, but we're still different species with different needs. My parents wanted me to stay in Oriziah for a while, actually, but I knew I needed to get back."

I itch my ear awkwardly. I stop in the hall and face him. "You—you don't have to be here, at school, for me. I mean, if that's why you returned."

Jarron's face pales, and my stomach sinks.

"I mean, I want you here. I do. But I feel like you're telling me you're unwell and should be home. And then, I think you came back here against your own well-being to protect me."

Which makes me feel terrible because I guilted him from the beginning.

I never really considered that he had his own personal demons to deal with.

"It's not just that," he says. "Besides, I want to be here. Need to be, if I'm honest."

My brow furrows. "Is there anything I can do? To help?"

"No." He shrugs. "Be my friend. That would help."

I give him a small smile. "I've been trying to do that. You make it kinda hard."

"I know," he whispers.

"Was there something you wanted to talk to me about?"

"Do I need a reason to talk to you?"

I twist my lips. "Of course not. I just..."

His eyebrows rise.

"Nothing. Never mind. I just thought maybe you had something to say."

Something crosses his expression then, but it fades too quickly to analyze. "There are many things I'd like to say."

I wait. He rocks back on his heels, staring down the hall, lines of stress on his mouth.

"But you're not going to say them now?" I guess.

He shakes his head. "So, where is your first class, now that Ms. Bhatt changed your entire schedule?"

I open my mouth to answer, but then I shut it. I don't want to give that answer.

"Something wrong?" His face brightens with curiosity, the first non-intense emotion I've seen cross his features.

"Language," I answer and then turn on my heel and begin down the hall, assuming he'll follow.

"What language?" he answers as he rushes to keep up.

I withhold a sigh. "High Orizian."

His next step falters, but then he matches my casual stride. "That's interesting."

"Is it?" I ask, voice too high. "I did have something to talk to *you* about."

"Oh?"

"I've been getting notes lately. And a few nights ago, I received something else of... interest."

His jaw clenches. "Interest?"

I nod, chewing the inside of my lip.

He grips my elbow and pulls me to a stop. "Explain," he demands, "because I have no idea what you're talking about, but it sounds like it's serious to you."

People buzz about around us, all breaking their necks to see what's going on and hear what we're saying. I grab his upper arm —which is thick and firm, and I should not be thinking about that at all—and pull him to a corner, where we can talk more privately.

"I've gotten three notes since we came back. Ominous and... weird. All signed, 'the jinn'."

Jarron's eyes darken. The magic filling the hall pulses and zings, making it harder to breathe.

"And then, I got a journal entry that had been ripped from Liz's diary. It would have been pretty incriminating to Mr. Vandozer if it had been there before."

The air around me turns icy.

"Jarron?" I whisper, but his eyes are not his any longer. "I don't think it's that big of a deal," I say, hoping to absolve the stress building in him as we speak.

"Not a big deal?" he repeats, his voice more echoey than usual. "Worst case, it means someone connected to the games is stalking you. Best case, someone in this school is taunting you. Neither option is okay with me. And if the journal entry is real..." He runs his fingers through his messy hair. "I can't believe you didn't tell me this sooner."

I release my breath and mutter, "sorry."

"Okay. I need you to bring me those letters. I need to see them."

I shift my weight from foot to foot. "Bring them—"

"To Elite Hall."

It takes me a tad too long to respond. "You want me to come to Elite Hall?" I finally force out.

"There isn't much choice," he says slowly. "I need to examine them. Test them. We shouldn't do that in public, and I can't go into Minor Hall."

I suddenly feel lightheaded. He's all but confirmed my assumption that he means his room. We'd need to be somewhere private.

Emotions I've fought very hard to shove into little boxes begin to emerge.

He must read that fear on my face because then he says, "I suppose, if you don't want to be alone with me, you could just give them to me and I'll do it all myself and bring them back when I'm finished."

"I—no, I can. I can come." I blink rapidly. This is going to be awkward, and overwhelming and so many other things. But it's Jarron. I want us to be friends.

So, this shouldn't be that big of a deal.

Right? Right. Not a big deal.

I'll just conveniently forget the fact that he is losing control of his demon side. The demon that seems very interested in me for reasons I can't fully understand because it didn't choose me three years ago. It chose my sister.

I'll also have to pretend that I don't want to relive those intimate moments I shared with him in that room while we were still "together." My cheeks heat even now. This is going to be tough.

"You're sure? I understand that you're afraid of me—"

"No. It's not that," I say quickly. "I'm not afraid of you."

I'm wary. I'm confused. I'm hurt.

I'm terrified, but not of him, of my own lack of self-control.

He doesn't seem to be convinced, but he doesn't comment again. "So, this afternoon?"

And yet, somehow, it feels like the whole Earth has shifted beneath me as I answer, "Yes."

28
I DON'T WANT TO LOSE YOU

To my surprise, when I meet Jarron in Elite Hall, he turns the opposite direction than his bedroom. My heart sinks and swells at the same time.

I follow Jarron down a familiar narrow hall. My shoulders relax when I realize where he's taking me. I almost grin when we turn into the dimly lit room I'd dubbed the speakeasy.

The back wall is covered in old red brick, where there are wooden shelves lined with hundreds of jars of liquids and herbs. There are three small cauldrons and two machines on the countertop.

The only light comes from two hanging industrial lamps and a massive fireplace at the far end.

It feels good to be back here. This was the first location in Elite Hall that I felt any sense of ease. Maybe the only place, other than Jarron's room for a time.

And now, Jarron's room would bring up a lot of really negative feelings, but this place still feels right.

An escape among the chaos of Elite Hall.

I'm a potionist, but I've never actually made my own beverage here. Jarron has always done it for me. And once again, without a word, he begins combining several of the jars into the steamer and pours the creamy, spicy liquid into a copper mug.

In only moments, he's made a masterful chai latte—my favorite.

"Thanks." I grip the hot mug between my hands and bring it up to my nose to breathe in the delicious spice-filled aroma.

He pours a second for himself.

"You're drinking chai now?"

He shrugs. "I don't have any particular preference."

Jarron takes a seat at one of the six bar top tables clustered around the room, with dark metal chairs and red velvet cushioned seats. We didn't use to sit here.

I look over my shoulder at the velvet bench in front of the fireplace, and I picture past-us, sitting there together, filled with uncertainty, but at the same time, I found such comfort being here with him.

I hate how different things are. Guilt swirls in my chest because I ruined it. I ruined a really good thing, all because I can't seem to get over the jealousy.

The wondering. The what-ifs. They keep me up at night even now.

"I'm surprised there aren't more people here," I comment as I take a seat opposite him.

"There usually are. I asked Laithe to clear it out for us today."

"Really?" Why? I don't voice the second question.

He nods. "We needed privacy for this, and I figured—well, I figured this was best."

My stomach squeezes uncomfortably. He doesn't want me in his room?

Or did he do this for my comfort, assuming I wouldn't want to be in his room?

Slowly, I lift the cup and tilt it back, allowing the warm frothy liquid to distract me from these conflicting feelings and doubts. The spices zing over my tongue. Pure joy fills me with just a taste.

I've always thought chai tastes like magic. The way it settles my nerves is incredible.

I open my eyes to find Jarron staring at me with a look of awe. "What?" I whisper.

"This feels good," he says, the tiniest hint of a smile on his lips.

I haven't seen him truly smile in, well, weeks. Not since the morning I woke up in his bed. "Things between us are complicated, but it feels good to be here with you."

He stares down at the liquid in his cup, the smile already fading. "I was wrong to push you away. Just because we want different things from this doesn't mean I don't want you in my life. Literally the last thing in the world I want is to lose you entirely."

My eyes widen as I let his words settle. I could let myself freak out over the implications, but—*friends*. We're friends now. That's what I want.

Right?

I force a smile and allow a little spark of hope to well in my chest. "I don't want to lose you either."

He watches me, all while his drink remains firmly on the table.

"So," I say, looking for something more to thin the tension

between us. I pull out the three notes and set them on the table between us. "Here's what I have."

I swear Jarron is not breathing as he carefully picks up the notes and reads each one. He sets them back down carefully, every muscle tense.

He flexes his hands, fists them, and then sets them in his lap beneath the table. "What do you think?" he asks, feigning calm. "Do you think it's the jinn? Or someone messing with you?"

I swallow. "Honestly? It could be either. I guess it's bizarre to think the jinn would really care that much about me. Like is it really likely an immensely powerful being would care about a little meaningless human?"

Jarron's eyebrows rise. My mouth dries. Right, uh, besides him. That's different, though, right? We were friends. We grew an emotional attachment. To the jinn, I'm no one. "I mean, the only real connection I have to her or the games is that my sister died in them. Is there any precedence for this? The games specifically seeking the sibling of someone previously in the games?"

Jarron shakes his head. "I find it unlikely. It would decrease the security of their secret."

"So, it seems more likely it's someone in the school messing with me. I mean, everyone here knows I was involved in the games. Most think I tried to join them and you stopped me."

Jarron frowns.

"It's not a far stretch to think they'd try to bully me this way, is it?"

Jarron closes his eyes, his jaw tight.

"Are you okay?" I whisper.

"No," he whispers. "I'm not going to be okay for a very, very long time." Did his eyes flash to the bite mark on my neck, or was that my imagination? Either way, sympathy fills my chest. I hate seeing him like this. It's incredible the difference between this Jarron and the one he shows to the school, now most of all.

To them, he looks like a dominating world leader, or even a villain. Powerful, determined, and sure of himself.

This Jarron is lost and afraid.

Part of me absolutely hates seeing him this way. Part of me feels honored to be someone he trusts enough to reveal this vulnerability. Mostly, though, I want so badly to comfort him. I just don't know how. Now that we're "friends", where is that line?

I place my hand over his closed fist. A small, gentle gesture. His eyes snag on the place our skin connects and remain there. His shoulders relax, but I don't get the feeling it's out of relief, more like resignation. Like he's giving up. Letting go.

I hate that too.

"I feel like so much is out of my control," he mutters. "I want to burn down this entire school. Or hide you away for years until this blows over."

I pull my hand away, and his eyes flash up to mine.

"No," I state simply.

"I know," he whispers. "I won't do that. I know you need to do this. But every instinct is screaming at me to take you somewhere the jinn or Mr. Vandozer or those wolves or any one else here can't even lay eyes on you."

I want to ask him why he cares so much. Because it seems

like such a foreign thing to me. But one, it's not a fair question. And two, I suspect it's just who he is.

He is loyal and caring. He chooses his people, and he will tear the world apart for them. The same way his brother tore down the entire arena to help him, even though Jarron is the only thing keeping him from taking the Orizian throne.

Maybe it's a demon prince thing, this loyalty to a fault.

"Thank you," I whisper.

He tilts his head.

"Thank you for caring as much as you do."

His lips twitch ever so slightly. "What the hell kind of fool was I to ever think that pushing you away was a good idea?"

Jarron's nostrils flare and his jaw tenses as he reverts his attention back to the notes I found in my room over the last few weeks. He examines each closely, looking for a clue I missed. Someone has been stalking me, and he's even less happy about it than I am.

He's not yours.

He was never yours.

I don't want to know what his expression shows over that one. The jinn obviously knows what's been digging at me most. Very few people know that secret.

Jarron belonged to my sister, not me.

Never me.

That's fine. I don't need a handsome, powerful, considerate prince as a boyfriend.

As incredible as Jarron is, and as much as my stomach squeezes uncomfortably whenever I think about how we can't be together, that isn't the future I ever considered before this year.

It was, however, something my sister would have wanted.

So, really, it's another thing that the jinn and the game runners stole from my sister. And Jarron.

If I hadn't caught feelings like a dummy last semester, things would have been just fine. I wouldn't have known what I was missing when Liz and Jarron eventually found each other and fell deeply in love.

I would have been happy for them both while I went along my ambitious path toward human power, where I could make an actual difference.

Now, I don't know if I can ever go back to that life. I'm too far into this world. Magic has dug its claws into my soul, and now I'm hooked.

"What are you thinking about?" Jarron asks.

I jerk my attention back to him. "Oh... what-ifs, I guess? What my life would have been like if none of this had ever happened."

He examines me long enough that discomfort squirms through me. Why do I feel like he can see into my soul? Why do I want him to?

I shake that thought from my mind. Nope, Jarron isn't getting any deeper into my heart. I can't let him.

"You're very confusing, sunshine."

My lips curl into a bitter smile. "I know." I clear my throat and sit up straighter. "So, what now?"

"Well, I don't know if you realized, but this room is good for more than just chai lattes." He nods to the counter with shelves and shelves of vials.

"I assumed." There are certainly more substances in those jars than just edible ingredients. Most of them are consumable, but some, not so much. "What do you plan to do?"

"Well, I'm going to have Laithe track one of the notes, so we can possibly see where the writer or messenger came from. Which one is the most recent?" I point to the one with the journal entry.

He squints at the ripped page. "I wonder if the fact that it originated in your sister's journal will make it harder to track. It'll have passed several hands, including hers."

"This is from the journal too," I state, pointing at the ripped corner. "These two are on different parchment."

One is the longest letter of the bunch, and the other is the ripped parchment that came along with the flowers. ***He was never yours.***

"The writing looks similar," he comments, staring at the two in question.

"Yeah. Why?"

"The messaging seems different, though. This one," he holds up the longest of the three notes, "I could believe came from the jinn. Threats and taunts about your perceived inadequacies. They want you to feel weak so they can manipulate you into the games. But this one reads more like a jealous ex."

My brows shoot up. "Do you think Auren wrote it?"

He shakes his head. "I doubt it. She's not the note type. Too personal. She's more about whispers and rumors."

"Well, there's been plenty of those too."

Jarron stands and takes the jealous-ex note and the longer poem over to the counter.

"Anything in particular?" he asks casually as he reaches for a jar of red liquid.

I shrug. "I feel like I don't hear as many of them as others. I can see that people are talking about me, but what they're saying is usually outside of my reach. Maybe because my hearing isn't as sensitive as the supernatural's here."

Jarron crunches up a few different leaves and then combines them. "Well, right now, there are certainly rumors about your potions work," he says, all the while completing his own. "Your relationship with Thompson is being scrutinized constantly. I still haven't decided how I feel about him."

"You don't have to feel anything about him."

He pauses his spell work. "If someone is untrustworthy and placing themselves close to you, that's not something I'll ever ignore. However, he did put himself in danger to help you."

I nod.

"What do you think about him? You trust him?"

"I—not completely, but mostly. He's hiding something, for sure. And I reserve the right to change my mind once his secret is revealed, but my gut says he's sincere and generally good."

He nods, accepting my answer.

"What's this going to do?" I couldn't follow all the ingredients. Some of them appear to be pre-brewed concoctions. Likely to make new potions easier to create. It could be some kind of tracer, but he said Laithe would do a spell for that. This is something different, I assume.

"It will reveal the essence of the author."

"Essence?"

"Should reveal their species or world origin."

"Oh, interesting." I watch him use a dropper to withdraw a small amount of his potion. "Could we have done something like this on the Akrasia Games calling card?"

He raises a brow. "If you hadn't gone running into danger first."

Right. I ran right into that one, didn't I?

"The investigators did even more than that during your sister's investigation. They came back inconclusive. I assume those behind the games used a spell to conceal their essence."

I bite the inside of my cheek while Jarron lets one single drop fall onto the short note page, followed by a single drop on the longer note.

There's a spark then white steam. My head tilts. "What does that mean?"

He grimaces. "There should be a color, or at least a smell."

"So..."

"They're both inconclusive."

I match his grimace. "How easy is it to conceal your essence?"

"Not easy."

"You sure you did the potion right?"

He glares at me, and I shrug. "I did it correctly."

Wonderful. That means it's unlikely the note came from a taunting peer. If Auren, or even Corrine, had been involved in the messages, that would have shown.

That very likely means the actual jinn has been sending me letters.

29

THE JINN WAS HERE

I ignore the glances in our direction as Laithe leans over the notes.

Those ugly words stare up at me.

He's not yours. He was never yours.

I should have just left that one behind. He had enough information to look into with the others. Then, I wouldn't have had to share that message with anyone else, and I wouldn't have to let it stare at me for what feels like hours.

Not that Laithe reacted to the words. He may not have even read them.

We headed back into the main entryway of Elite Hall to meet with Laithe.

The few wolves that were in the area scattered the moment we arrived, leaving the area more bare than usual. Only Manuela and Lucille, her girlfriend, sit in the leather armchairs by the window, watching closely.

I half expect Laithe's spell to do nothing.

If it is from the jinn, what are the chances he'll be able to track her?

But only a moment after, a thread of silvery blue magic drifts up from the notebook page and hovers in the air in front of Laithe's nose. It dances midair, like a tiny shimmering snake, and then in a blink, it darts down the hall.

I suck in a breath.

The silvery thread heads straight out of Elite Hall, like someone threw a ball of glowing blue yarn and held the end taut. Moments later, it doubles back, crisscrossing this room, creating a web of glowing string through the halls.

It darts down the hall to the right—toward Jarron's room.

Jarron lifts his chin. "Manuela," Jarron says firmly. "Can you please double-check where it ends?"

Manuela and Lucille both hop up and head down the hall toward Jarron's room, following the glowing line of the tracing spell, while Jarron and Laithe follow the other thread.

I jog to keep up with their rapid pace. "What exactly does it show? Everywhere the being has been?"

"Everywhere the note has been," he answers. "So, the path from Elite Hall to Minor Hall makes sense. That's where you carried it. We want to check where it was before that."

"So... that note was carried to your room?"

"Or possibly Trevor's. Or Bea's. There's very little else down there."

Right, so that's what Manuela is checking. If it went to Bea's, we'll have a whole different suspect on our list. Trevor's girlfriend had been involved in the games before. I don't think I could negotiate her out of Jarron's wrath a second time if she were involved now.

We march out of Elite Hall toward the south wing. Several

students stand with their backs to the walls, watching us chase the path of the silver magic.

We follow the thread to Minor Hall and then where it diverges. The silver thread winds down and around several corridors. Whoever wrote the note did a bit of trekking around the school, then.

Finally, we follow the thread into the portal room, where the silver thread leads straight into an empty archway. A portal. There's a symbol on the top of it I only vaguely recognize. "That's not—"

Jarron nods gravely. "Oriziah."

30
DUTY VS DESIRE

"I'll call Ms. Bhatt to open the portal. I need you to follow it," Jarron says to Laithe.

"I'll take care of it. Go back and rest."

Jarron clasps Laithe on the shoulder and then beckons me to follow him away from the portals back down the hall. "I can walk you back to Minor Hall if you want. I, of course, wouldn't mind more company in Elite Hall if you're willing. But I understand if you don't want to."

I start walking, and Jarron skips to catch up. "Why did Laithe tell you to get rest?" Does this have to do with his mysterious illness slash anxiety?

"He's a worrywart. I've been expelling a lot of energy lately. All that darkness doesn't come from nothing."

I elbow him. "Then, stop it."

"I don't have control over all of it, if I'm honest. My demon is... unhappy."

Unhappy. A new thought crosses my mind. "Are you in pain?" I blurt out. "Like, real physical pain?"

Silence settles between us for far too long. It's then that Jarron seems to realize we've passed the route to Minor Hall and are headed up the stairs toward Elite Hall. His eyes light up, and his lips curve into a small smile. Almost there.

"You didn't answer my question," I say.

"Yes, there is some physical pain. I have to actively fight it back sometimes, and it... carves through me. Much like my bond with Laithe, my demon cannot do true damage to me, but there is pain."

I bite the inside of my cheek. I wait for any additional questions until we're inside Elite Hall. "To the speakeasy?" he asks.

I grin, knowing that nickname came from me. "Will we be alone?"

"If you want us to be."

My stomach squeezes, not altogether an unpleasant feeling, but the implications do make me nervous. "Yes," I say, hoping he doesn't read too far into that.

He doesn't say a word as we walk down the spiral stairs to the speakeasy. It's still empty, and our mugs are sitting where we left them on the high-top table. I grab mine, only to realize it's cold already.

Jarron pulls it from my fingers.

"Hey, I could still drink it."

"No, you can't. You'll get a new one and like it." He dumps my leftover chai into the sink and begins brewing a new one.

I ignore the flutter in my belly. "So, demanding. Why couldn't I finish it?"

"Because we left them unattended and that's not a risk I'm willing to take."

I purse my lips. He does make a good point. When Jarron

finishes my fresh, piping-hot chai latte, I lead us to the velvet bench.

I'm not sure why I'm feeling so much more comfortable now than even just thirty minutes ago, but I've stopped thinking about all the things that bother me, and instead I'm focused on him.

My friend, who is in pain.

My very sexy friend, whom I'm not supposed to think about that way at all.

Jarron wordlessly sits beside me and takes in a relaxed breath, seeming more at ease than I've seen him since... before.

"I've missed you," I tell him honestly.

His fingers still on his copper mug, his eyes remain steady on the steaming liquid. "I've missed you, sunshine."

My stomach flips. Dammit, this is hard.

I turn partially to face him on the bench. "Tell me how it can get better. The anxiety."

He huffs, like he's surprised at the question. Maybe it's a stupid one, but I get the feeling there's more going on here than he's willing to admit. When he meets my determined stare, the sadness I swore I'd seen moments ago slips away leaving only ease. "I am quite relaxed currently."

I roll my eyes. "I don't mean right now."

The silence feels like it's pulsing, growing, pressing down on us. I jump when the fire sparks to life. "Did you do that?"

"Yes. I'm sorry if it scared you."

"Not all fear is bad," I answer quickly. I turn to watch the now flickering flames, my cheek hot.

He watches me carefully, measuring my every move.

We remain like that for a few minutes, just soaking in the warmth and comfort of being near one another.

"Can you tell me what's going on inside of you? Why is your demon carving you up from the inside?" I don't know if I'm being pushy but I can't relax until I at least have an idea of how to help him. Even if he makes one up. Give me something to do.

I hate feeling helpless while someone I care about suffers.

"My thoughts are constantly warring, that's what makes me anxious. Like I'm never doing enough, but there's nothing more to do. I'm a constant failure, but I haven't failed yet."

That's not confusing at all. "What—what are your thoughts warring about?"

"You."

My heart skips a beat. "Me? What—what's warring about me?"

He sniffs but keeps his shoulders back, his eyes trained on something in the distance. "I'm warring between duty and desire, I guess."

My eyebrows rise. I'm not following his meaning.

"What's your duty?" I ask. He's never mentioned anything about his role as a prince, so I have no idea what he could mean.

He turns to me, face still lacking any emotion at all. He examines me, with those dead eyes. "I should woo you. Convince you to be mine at any cost."

My stomach sinks, and for a moment, I feel like I might be ill. How is wooing me his duty?

"What's your desire, then?" He doesn't want me, but somehow thinks he should? Does that have something to do with Liz? Is there some kind of magic in the blood of his chosen that I share with my sister? He can't have her, but he can replace her with me and regain some of what was lost?

"My whole life, people have desired me because of what I am. Not who. I desperately want someone to choose me back."

My mind spins through his words. *Choose me back.*

This is so messed up, and I'm so lost. In my own thoughts and feelings, and his. I don't understand any of it.

"I don't want to hurt you, Candice, and I don't want to push you away, but if you are going to push me to open up—"

"Tell me, even if it hurts." I clench my jaw, ready for whatever criticism he'll share. Ready for him to tell me I'm his second choice, but he needs me. I know it'll hurt, it'll slice through me the way his demon is slicing through him, but I'll take that pain if it will help him. I'll take that pain because I've been bearing it anyway.

Even my sister knew my true weakness—I hide from what scares me. Well, if Jarron wants to be open about his, I'll face it. For him.

"I thought you were different," he says, voice low and emotionless. "I thought I mattered to you, but it turns out you were using me just like everyone else."

My stomach clenches. It wasn't the hard truth I was ready to hear, but he's right. I did use him. I know it hurt him, to learn that I truly thought he was a monster who killed my sister. That I spent time alone with him, wondering if he'd kill me too. All while he did everything in his power to make me feel comfortable and safe and loved.

"Maybe it shouldn't matter, but it does. And I... don't want to play games. I don't want someone who doesn't want me back, even if it kills me."

My heart aches.

"Of course it matters," I whisper. "I'd hate me too. I do, sometimes."

Concern flashes across his features. "You hate yourself?" he asks in a near whisper.

I nod. "I hate that I'm weak. I hate that I'm meaningless. I hate that I wasn't there to stop Mr. Vandozer from hurting my sister. I hate that I'm stupid enough to be jealous of a dead girl. I hate that—I hate that you'd rather have her here than me."

Jarron's eyes turn completely black in an instant. Horns sprout from his head.

I stand and stumble a few steps back until I can feel the heat of the fireplace licking at my legs.

The hair on my arms rises as he stalks forward. I reroute my retreat with careful steps backward. His movements are smooth and strange.

My back hits brick. He presses his hands to either side of my head. "Say that last one again?" he growls.

"I-I..." My voice trembles, his powerful presence looms over me. "I hate that you'd rather have her here than me?" I whisper uncertainly.

His canines elongate as he closes his eyes against some wave of emotion I can't identify. He winces, his muscles tense, but when he opens his eyes, it's very clearly Jarron staring at me, and he is not pleased.

"Why in fucking hell would you think that?" He forces the words out, jaw clenched.

My lips part, but no words come, only quick breaths. My thoughts are confused and scattered. His body is so close I can feel his warmth. I want to press into him, but I won't let myself. I'm not even sure where he's at now. Is this Jarron or his demon? Maybe it doesn't matter. His demon once told me they were the same, he is simply part of him. But his demon is battling him. How does that work? Is that what's happening now?

His jaw clenches so tightly I'm concerned he'll break a tooth. Is he in pain now?

"What's wrong?" I whisper.

"Everything is wrong," he says, leaning forward until his forehead is against the wall next to my ear.

Without permission, my hands find their way up to his chest. His chest stops moving. The whole world stops, I think, at that first touch. Finally, he releases a breath, tension slipping from his body like a cloak that drops to the floor.

"I don't know what's going on in your head, Candice, but let me be perfectly clear about this." He pulls back, fingers gripping my chin forcefully.

I stare into his black eyes, trying not to tremble.

Is the shaking from terror or desperate desire? Because I'm feeling a whole lot of both right now.

He speaks slowly, gaze so intensely pinned to me I couldn't move if I wanted to. "I want you. Not her."

Could he really mean that? I don't know if I believe him. Maybe when Liz died his connection to her died too? Or maybe Jarron truly, desperately desires me the way I desire him, and it's only his demon that feels differently? That instinctual, beastly part of him.

Maybe... Is that why he's battling his demon so hard? Is that what's causing him such pain?

That's what Trevor was implying, right? Their demon souls don't always agree with their conscious minds. Who wins the battle? The human part of Jarron desires me. Maybe he always did.

"Do you?" I ask uncertainly.

A soft growl reverberates from his chest.

"Because you said I was your duty, not your desire."

His nostrils flare. "That didn't come out how I'd intended it," he says breathlessly. "You are everything I want."

That's not new information but somehow seems so significant.

It still hurts that I don't know who would win that battle if Liz were around. But Liz is gone. There is no more battle.

"The difference is the how," he continues, searching for the right words to explain. "My demon has different intentions than I do, and sometimes, it's—sometimes, we are warring. It takes a lot of effort to stop him from taking over, but I don't want to hurt anyone."

"Would he? Hurt people?"

I recall his violent speech about killing wolves in my honor, and I realize I already know that answer.

"Yes. But not you. No part of me would ever hurt you. But I cannot promise the safety of your friends—especially Thompson—if he were to take control in the wrong circumstance."

"I still don't understand."

He's battling with his demon about me, that's the truth I've uncovered, but I still don't fully grasp what that means. How? Why?

"I don't understand you either," he admits.

I allow a small, bitter smile to spread on my face.

He's still standing so close I can feel this warmth. For a moment, I think he might kiss me. I desperately hope he does.

There's a flood of emotions overwhelming me.

Jarron must read something in my expression because there's a flicker of disappointment on his face. He pulls away, wiping all emotion from his expression.

He's become an expert at masking his feelings.

I know I hurt him in several ways. I wish I was brave enough to blurt out all my fears. But again, I hide. I don't ask him if he's battling his demon because it doesn't want me. I don't ask him why his demon seems protective of me.

I don't ask why he chose my sister all those years ago. What did she have that I didn't? I know those kinds of questions are pointless. Love and devotion don't work so logically, and even if they did, I could name a thousand reasons why Liz was better than me. I would've chosen her too if I were him.

I just want someone to choose me back.

Maybe that's what he needs. He needs me to be selfless enough to choose his love, despite the rejection. Maybe a chosen love could be more powerful than a fated one.

I just don't know if I'm strong enough to do that.

I grab my bag from the bartop, and Jarron escorts me out of the speakeasy, and out of Elite Hall.

"We can start over, right?" Jarron says softly. "At the whole friend thing."

I bite the inside of my lip and shift from foot to foot. "Yeah."

"Come to Elite Hall this weekend."

My stomach twists pleasantly. More memories flash through my mind. Times when we were so uncertain and yet comfortable. There was structure in our relationship then, though. Even when I was confused, there was purpose behind our time together.

Now—now we'd be spending time together just because we want to. And somehow, that's so very, very different.

And yet, I want to be his friend. The last thing I want is to lose him. "What will we do?"

"Anything you want. Want access to the Elite library again? Go for it. Want another chai? I've got you."

I smile. Honestly, both of those things sound wonderful, and I also want to spend time with him. And that's basically what we're doing now, right?

"Or if you want to start with something with a bit less pressure, Stassi has been badgering me about throwing a party. I could do that. You could bring Lola and Janet." His voice drops. "Even Thompson if you want."

My eyebrows rise. Now, that's an idea. I can't tell if it's a great one or a terrible one, but it's interesting.

He's right though; the pressure would be lower.

People wouldn't make a big deal out of it. Just a demon prince throwing a party and inviting his ex and her friends. Maybe it would be a good way to ease back into a public friendship.

"Okay." I nod. "A party is—well, possibly a really bad idea, but let's do it."

31
FRIENDSHIP THERAPY

I sit with Janet and Lola in the common room. We have the entire room to ourselves tonight. A silly witch movie plays in the background while Lola does her homework and Janet whispers stories about her time in Major Hall with Marcus.

I try my best to focus, but my mind keeps wandering in and out, contemplating the party coming up this weekend.

From what I do gather, Janet has had really positive experiences. Everyone has been extremely welcoming and accepting in Major Hall, which she's surprised about. Often, upperclassmen still in Minor Hall are ostracized by the rest of the school, so dating outside of the hall is difficult. But so far, Janet has been treated well. I couldn't be happier to hear that.

Lola's book is smaller than average but still requires her to physically move her whole body in order to read it. She pauses suddenly, hovering over the pages. "Did you see Anita? How is she?"

"She avoids me." Janet shrugs. "Most of the pixies do, actually."

"Who's Anita?" I ask.

"My sister," Lola says casually, looking back down at her book.

Sister? I want to exclaim. I'm honestly embarrassed that I didn't already know this. There's a lot about my friends that I don't know, but I've never been good at asking the right questions to get close to people.

"We don't talk. At all." She shrugs, answering my unvoiced question. "So, I don't mention her much."

"And they know we're friends, so the pixies avoid me too."

"Hmm." I'm unsure what else to say. I had noticed that most of the pixies run in big herds, but Lola is always alone. "You don't get along with your family?" I try for a casual tone.

She shakes her head. "Most pixies are in Major Hall. A few exceptional ones make it into Superior. I'm the only one in the last decade to remain in Minor Hall past sophomore year. It was pretty rough the summer after I found out I didn't pass the exams to be moved up, but I'm over it now."

I suppose I should have realized. "I hate the way weaker supernaturals are treated," I say. "Magic isn't the only important thing about a person."

"Right!" Lola's wings wiggle.

"Lola has enough magic to pass," Janet says. "But she always gets super nervous for exams."

"What do you have to do to pass?" I haven't been at this school long enough to experience those kinds of exams. Not that it matters. The only way a human gets into a higher hall is by someone stronger claiming them. Jarron could get me into Elite Hall officially if we were still together, but I wouldn't have any desire to go.

"You have to win a fight against a full-grown troll," Lola says.

I lean in. "What? How is that even possible?"

"Pixie dust puts them to sleep. It's not actually that hard to do, but I always psych myself out and don't produce enough dust."

"Ooh," I say. "That sucks. To know you've got the power to do it, but somehow it just doesn't work."

She shrugs. "It's no big deal. I'm mad at my family for being jerks and acting like there is something wrong with me. But I just intend to prove that even Minor Hall pixies can do great things."

I nod sharply. "Love that plan."

When the movie ends, I begin to rise. "I'm gonna head to bed."

"Candice," Janet complains, "it's five thirty."

I shrug. "I have to be up early to check my potions."

Her eyebrows rise. "You've been hiding in your room every night this week. What's going on?"

I puff out a breath. "Nothing."

Lola stops reading to look up at me. "That's obviously a lie."

"There's something bothering you," Janet says. "I know you're a private person and don't like to express the things you're feeling, but I'm starting to worry about you."

"I'm fine."

"Lies!" Lola stands up and puts her hands on her hips. "Janet is right. Sit down and tell us all your problems."

I chuckle and flop back onto the couch.

"Much better," Lola purrs. "Now, lie back."

Both of them seem to be into this therapy idea all of the sudden, but I humor them and lie on the lumpy, stained suede couch like I'm in a shrink's office. Except, with a shrink, you don't have to talk if you don't want to. My friends don't seem to be as gracious.

"You've got to start talking to people, Candice." Janet sits beside me, arms crossed.

I huff. "Is this an intervention?" I'm one part amused by the tactic and one-part terrified they'll push me out of this really comfortable hiding spot I've found in the dark recesses of my mind, where no one judges me for falling in love with my dead sister's mate.

Over the last two days since I spoke with Jarron in Elite Hall, I've been more quiet than usual. Which is saying something because I'm not exactly a chatterbox.

"Yeah, you hold everything in. It's not healthy," Lola says, fluttering above me. I sneeze at the pixie dust that falls onto my nose.

"You're almost as dark and broody as Jarron these days. Did something happen when you went to see him?" Janet says.

"Or are you just worried about the party on Saturday?"

I grimace. "No." Yes. Sort of. "It's more like a piling up of a lot of things," I admit.

"Do you have any idea how much damage miscommunication can do to relationships?" Lola asks.

I want to tell her Jarron and I don't have a relationship to damage, but then again, I think that's her point.

"Just talk already!" Lola's yell is shockingly loud. It rattles my already unsettled nerves.

"I can't," I spit. "You don't understand." Pain clenches over my chest, and light floods the dark hiding spot in my mind, forcing all the unpleasant thoughts to the surface.

"Then tell us, stupid!" Lola lands on my stomach and puts her hands on her hips. "Explain!"

"It's something I'm not supposed to talk about. No one is. Even I'm not supposed to know it."

"What?" Lola tilts her head.

I groan and press my palms to my eyes.

My friends are quiet for a moment while I panic about my explosion of truth. I wasn't even thinking about the whole mate thing; it just kind of bubbled up.

"So, you know a secret you're not supposed to," Janet says slowly after a long moment of silence, working through the riddle I've dropped on them. "And it's eating you alive, but you can't tell anyone about it because you're not supposed to know. So, you're just pushing everyone away instead?"

I release a breath. "Yes." Yes, that's exactly it. Never mind that I could talk about it with Jarron, sort of, but I don't because I'm an absolute coward. But talking about it won't change anything. And he can't admit anything anyway because that's some demon-y sacred secret. "I think Jarron knows that I know anyway."

"Are you sure?"

"No?" I sit up, and Lola flies up to my shoulder. "But he was there when—" He was there, stabbed and drugged. "He was possibly unconscious when I found out."

"Oh hell, this is a big one, isn't it?" Lola whispers. She hovers, spins around, and then resettles on my leg. "Tell us how you know this secret. You learned it somehow at the Akrasia Games thing?"

I swallow and nod. "In the arena, when... Mr. Vandozer..." I trail off again, suddenly uncertain. Obviously, Mr. Vandozer is not a great source of information.

"Mr. Vandozer told you some incriminating information about Jarron, and you're sitting here like a dummy, believing him? Even now?" Janet's voice remains hushed even as her tension grows.

"But—" My brow furrows as I consider. "It wasn't just him. Bea implied it as well, several times. I just didn't understand it at the time."

"Bea isn't any better!" Lola squeaks.

"I talked to Trevor too! And I believe it, okay?"

They quiet. I readjust on the couch, arms crossed. "It's complicated," I whisper. "I can't ever know if it's entirely true, but that's part of the problem. And I know Mr. Vandozer believed it wholeheartedly. He built his entire plan around it."

Silence stretches for a few minutes. "It would be really helpful if we knew what the secret was," Lola mutters.

I bite my lip. Would it be breaking some sacred trust if I told them the full truth? I want to. Embarrassment swirls in my chest. What if I tell them the secret burning a hole in my heart—that Jarron was destined to be mated to my sister—and then, I change my mind and want to be with him again?

They'll know. I'll know that they know, and it'll eat me up in a new way.

But they could also help me understand it. Maybe they'd keep me from him, and maybe that's what I'm afraid of. Maybe they'll judge me for wanting my sister's fated mate.

And maybe that fear is actually really telling.

I suck in a long breath. I trust Lola and Janet. They won't

judge me; they'll just give me an honest perspective and tell me if I'm being an absolute idiot or if my hesitancy is justified.

"Swear you'll never repeat it to anyone ever. No one."

Their eyes widen.

"I mean it." I bite my lip. "Trevor said it's sacred. Like I'm pretty sure talking about it at all is a betrayal of some kind."

"We can do a swearing spell," Lola suggests. "We'll swear never to reveal the secret to anyone ever, no matter what."

Janet's jaw drops. "You really want to do that?"

"If the secret is really that big of a deal, then yeah, I think we should," Lola says. "It'll help us make sure we never break our friend's trust or overstep another world's culture."

"Isn't it dangerous?" Janet asks.

"Only if we have loose lips." Lola winks. "No one has to know we know either. We'll stay safest that way too."

I take in a long breath. This might be a bad idea, but they're right, the information has been suffocating me for weeks now. I need a little perspective.

I don't know much about swearing spells, but I have heard they can be deadly. It depends on the type and how strong they are. "I'll do it, but only if you guys want to."

"I do." Lola puffs out her chest.

Janet sighs. "Okay, fine. But if we're doing illegal magic, we're going to my room."

32
Mr. Vandozer Wins

Janet's room is very similar to mine, cramped and dark, except her window is a tad larger and there is a couch where the second twin-sized bed would be.

"You don't have a roommate?"

"Not since last year. They usually let seniors room alone if they want. There aren't many of us as it is."

I didn't get that option, but I can't really complain since I'm now technically alone too, ever since Corrine changed rooms.

She also has some more personalization than my room. Her bedspread is lavender with white flowers, and she has a vase of fresh daisies on the table. There's a floating shelf of books and a couple pictures of her family.

Janet hops around to light several candles and then grabs a big leather-bound book from the shelf, drops it in the middle of the floor, and sits cross-legged in front of it.

Janet flips carefully through the worn, yellowed pages of her book and then places her palm in the middle of it once she's apparently satisfied with her find. "So, if we're going to do this, I've got a few requirements."

"Okay," I say. All of this is new to me, so I'm just trusting them to make sound choices.

"We're going to blood bond first."

"Janet!" Lola exclaims.

My eyes widen, even though I have no idea what a blood bond means.

"Not like a full bond, where our lives are connected or anything. Just a link. It's like a permanent friendship bond. I'll be able to find you if I need to, and vice versa. Given everything going on, I kinda feel like this is a good idea anyway."

I sit next to Janet and read the spell she's chosen. There are words in Latin and symbols I can't tell the meaning of. I'm really useless here.

I've never dealt with this kind of magic before because it's not something I'm even capable of. "How does it work?"

"This one is a secret link. The secret is the thing that bonds us. If any one of us even gets close to spilling the secret, we'll know it. No one will die if the words come out of our mouth, but there will be pain, and if you want to add a tongue lock, we can."

"I don't think that's necessary," I say. This is already overkill as it is. Ensuring the secret can't go beyond us three does make me feel better about sharing it, though.

Lola drops to the floor by my knee, looking up at the ragged pages of the old spell book.

"So, we perform the spell, and then what? Do we do that creepy swapping blood thing from the movies?" I ask.

Lola snickers. "Sort of, but not exactly. We each need to

add a drop of blood for the spell, but we don't, like, cut our palms open and shove them together or whatever."

"Okay, good."

"I'll do the spell," Janet says. "We drop our blood into the bowl, and then you tell us the secret. It's best if you do it as succinctly as possible, even if there isn't context. Just the heart of what the secret is so the spell doesn't get confused and snitch on us for saying some arbitrary information that's only kinda relevant to the secret."

"Got it." That makes sense.

"After the spell is over, you'll explain it all and we'll talk it through."

"We're allowed to talk about it even after the spell is complete?"

"As long as we're in this room, yes. The moment one of us leaves, the pact is complete and the secret is sealed."

"You should know you'll be part of this too, Candice," Lola says. "You'll be bound not to tell this secret to anyone else either. Even Jarron."

"Right!" Janet says. "But that's what makes the blood bond great. Me and Lola will both be able to approve your sharing. So, if someone begins to share the secret, we'll feel the pull of the bond, but we can choose to accept the remission of the secret so that no harm comes to the sharer. If we were to do just a secret vow, no matter what, we couldn't share the secret without another ritual. But this way, we can make exceptions if all three of us agree. If one person doesn't—well, that's when the pain will come."

"So, basically, if I want to share this secret with anyone, even Jarron, I need your permission?"

Janet nods. "But we will give it."

"If we think it's in your best interest." Lola crosses her arms and squints at me.

Oh boy. I'm second-guessing the complexity of this. I could just tell them and trust them with it.

But also... "Through this bond, we'll be able to find each other?" That's extremely intriguing to me. "How does that work?"

"We'll have a tiny magic link that you can tug on to find us. It might be tricky for you since you have no magic, but it's possible. May just take some practice."

I press my lips together, considering the implications of this. Quickly, my mind is made up. This is a fantastic idea. "Let's do it."

Lola sighs but takes her place in our circle around the book. Janet lights a set of incense and begins a short chant in Latin. Then, she pulls out a pin and pokes her thumb. A tiny bead of dark blood pools.

She holds it over a wooden bowl and waits until it drips.

"Lola," she whispers.

Lola hops forward, and hovers close over the bowl. I realize that the needle Janet used could carve little Lola's body up, so it's unsurprising that she uses her own nail instead. Her drop of blood is smaller than Janet's but still probably large for her body. She hops back to her seat and seems entirely fine, though, so I accept a new pin from Janet and follow suit.

There's a tiny sting as the point pokes through my skin with a pop. Bright-red blood pools and then drips into the bowl with the other two.

Janet chants again, and the bowl begins rattling.

"Tell us your secret now, Candice."

My stomach twists uncomfortably, but I know this is

important. My words matter now, so I just spit it out quickly. "Jarron imprinted on my sister. She was his chosen."

Lola gasps. Janet looks slightly pale. But then, she places a wooden lid over the now smoking bowl and closes the book.

I look down at my hands and wait for their reaction. I'm distracted by a tiny red dot on my inner wrist. It doesn't move when I wipe at it. A mark of the spell?

"You can tell us more now," Janet says softly.

I close my eyes. I don't want to force the cursed words from my lips.

"Do you know what it means? To be a demon's chosen?" I ask them. I don't know how much context they need. It's not exactly common knowledge.

Janet shakes her head. "I only know they mate for life. It's more intense for them than many other supernaturals. Except Fae, I think?"

"Is it like fae's fated mates?" Lola asks.

"No," I whisper. "It's not predestined or anything, and it's one-sided. As I understand it, males choose a mate before adulthood. Only they know who their chosen is until the bond is accepted. Trevor said it's forbidden for anyone to talk about it."

"So, Trevor and Bea?" Lola asks.

I nod. "Yes, she is his chosen, and that's common knowledge, at least to the demons, because she's accepted the connection. In their culture, it's a sacred rite of passage for the young demon to pursue his chosen. 'To earn your chosen is to earn your right to rule,' that's what Bea said. Until you've earned them, the secret is sacred."

"And Jarron's chosen—"

"Was Liz."

"Wow," Janet breathes.

"Is that why Mr. Vandozer..."

"Maybe," I say. "I don't know exactly how all of that happened, but he did imply he was going to use it against Jarron. He had proof Jarron's chosen rejected him and chose another."

"Why? What happens if your chosen rejects you? Or dies..."

"Um, I guess it can be used to weaken his right to the throne? He could be usurped."

Janet fidgets with her silver chain. "But Mr. Vandozer couldn't gain the throne, could he? It would go to Trevor or someone close to the queen?"

"I think he wants Trevor on the throne. Or maybe that's what Bea wants. They were working together in some capacity."

"This is so crazy," Lola says.

"I know."

"And now, your relationship makes so much more sense," Janet says.

I huff.

"Does it?" Lola whispers.

Janet and I both frown down at her. She hasn't left her spot sitting on the ground, which is unusual for her.

"I get that you have some bad feelings about Jarron and your sister, but..." She looks at her hands. "Were they ever even together?"

"No. Not really."

"Then, what does it actually change?" Lola asks. Her wings perk up and begin vibrating.

"Everything," I say quickly.

"It doesn't change how Jarron feels. He's in love with you."

I bite my lip.

"But he didn't *choose* her. That matters," Janet says. "Don't get me wrong, I agree that he's in love with Candice and maybe it shouldn't matter in the long term, but I get how this could feel... not good."

Lola's frown deepens. She doesn't seem to agree.

"Okay, wait, though," Janet says quickly. "The source of this information is still Mr. Vandozer."

I nod.

"First of all, do you really trust what Mr. Vandozer says?"

"I trust that he believed it." That wasn't manipulation; he believed what he was saying.

"Hmm, so you believe the information is accurate?" Janet asks.

I nod. "Bea strongly implied it as well. I asked Trevor outright after everything happened, and he's the one who told me Jarron would never admit to it. I can't ask Jarron because he won't tell me. Or can't, I'm not sure. But no matter what happens, I'll always wonder. It's irrelevant if it's true or not, it affects me the same."

"So, Mr. Vandozer wins, then," Lola says in a quiet voice. Her wings are still again.

Janet nods absently, staring at the spell book, like she understands exactly what Lola means. It's only me who's confused. "Wins?"

"Did you ever think there's a good reason outsiders aren't supposed to know who a demon's chosen is?" Lola hops up from the floor and flutters in front of my nose.

I press my lips together, and I wait for her to go on.

"Do you believe Jarron wants you? Maybe even loves you?" she asks.

"Yes," I whisper.

"And what if you had never learned this fun fact? If Mr. Vandozer had never told you about Liz being Jarron's chosen, what would have happened?"

My lips part. I don't know.

"It would've never even been a question in your mind. You'd still be with him. You'd be happy. He'd be happy. And you'd never have even known the difference."

I bite my lip.

Janet nods as Lola continues giving me the slap in the face I didn't know I needed and still don't know what to do with.

"Even if it's true information, you're letting him win. He told you to hurt you. To hurt Jarron. And it's working."

Janet taps her finger against her lips as she considers. My heart throbs. This conversation hasn't gone how I'd expected, but then again, I wasn't sure what to expect.

#

We sit there in silence for a while, the pain of this terrible truth settling in for all three of us.

"Lola has a point," Janet says eventually.

My next breath trembles. Are they both telling me I should try to forget it? Date the boy who should have been my sister's epic love and pretend I never learned this ugly truth?

"Don't get me wrong, I completely understand how

painful it is, and I don't blame you at all for pushing him away. You're coping the only way you know how."

Hiding. That thought is sharp and painful. That's how I cope with things I can't handle—I hide from them. Is that why I haven't said it outright? Why I haven't screamed and cried to Jarron, "*Why didn't you pick me?*"

Tears threaten to stream down my cheeks at the overwhelming sense of rejection I feel even thinking those words.

Janet gently squeezes my hand. "I think—I think I would have done the same thing. But have you thought about this from Jarron's perspective?"

"Of course I have," I whisper. I hate it. I hate that it's hurting him.

"All the way through? Just think about this: let's say all of what we know is true—though, I have a feeling there's missing information. We can't fully understand the details of another world's culture, especially since this is such a unique and important element of it. But let's work through what we do know. Jarron imprinted on a human at a young age, and they were separated for various reasons."

"Me," I blurt out. "I'm the reason they were separated."

I stare at the off-white, worn carpet. If Liz had known back then that the handsome prince wanted her as his mate, she would have fallen into his arms in a nanosecond, even after he'd hurt her. I'm the one who pulled them apart.

"I have to imagine that's fairly normal for demons," she says softly. "From what I understand, demons rarely mate within their own species, and you said it's one-sided. The chosen mate has no idea, right? No feelings, no draw, nothing?"

"So far as I know."

"I've never heard of demons regularly mating before adulthood. It's always been implied that Trevor and Bea are exceptions. I think either Jarron imprinted earlier than usual or it's entirely common for there to be a gap while the demon waits for their mate to be ready."

I blink. "That would be rather polite of them."

Her smile is amused but still so gentle. "I'm just speculating, obviously, but if earning your chosen is a sacred rite of passage, then demons don't want to just force a claim or manipulate their chosen into commitment. They lure them in slowly, become everything they need, before they reveal their intentions. Demons are all about the chase, like other supernaturals, but their mates are precious. The bonds are intense and emotional. You don't get that by a quick claiming. Especially since you also say they can't speak about their chosen until they've been accepted. The idea is to *earn* them."

"Get to the part where you agree with me." Lola places her hands on her hips.

"Right. Well, Jarron imprinted and had to wait a few years for his chance to woo his chosen. But before he could, Liz was killed. His chosen is gone, no chance for him to ever experience that sacred cultural rite. He's devastated, even though he likely never had any real feelings for her beyond the instincts pushing him to her." She sucks in a long breath to keep going.

"But then, Candice shows up, seeking justice for Liz. Jarron obviously jumps right on board, and they become allies and friends. He falls in love with her naturally, organically. But then, the evil villain of the story exposes the truth about his chosen, and Candice pushes him away because of it. So, now, he's lost his ability to ever earn a chosen and because of that loss, he loses the woman he loves. He loses all of it."

My stomach aches. Sadness and guilt are not a good combination. I lie back on the ground and stare up at the dusty tiles. "So, should I take him back out of pity, then?" I grumble bitterly.

"No, of course not. I'm just saying, this whole situation is unfair, and you have one person to blame for it. It's not you. It's not Jarron. It's not Liz."

I blink. The pain is still swirling around, but my mind turns sharp. Yes, anger is a much better emotion to focus on. "It's Mr. Vandozer."

33
HOT AS HELL

"Are you all right?" Thompson asks, his hand lingering on the shiny silver door handle.

"Nope." I wring my hands awkwardly. I breathe in deeply through my nose, unsure what to expect.

Lola nuzzles into my neck. "You got this, babe."

"And you look hot as hell." Janet grins.

My lips lift, despite myself. I'm wearing black shorts, a simple red tank with black boots, and dark eye makeup that Janet helped me with. They even convinced me to ditch the bandage today, meaning I'm sporting the wolf bite out in the open. Though, I did add on a choker necklace with a star charm that partially veils the embarrassing mark.

I'm not quite as overt as some of these other girls in tiny skirts, corset tops, and cat ears, but I do feel kind of hot, and that's all that really matters.

Lola is in a pretty purple dress that shows off her legs beneath a handkerchief skirt, and Janet is in jeans and a cute floral top. She didn't want to get too dressed up since she's planning to make an appearance at the Major Hall party after, and as much as it's fun that she's been to an Elite party, she doesn't want too much attention for it. Major Hall is much more casual, apparently.

Janet twists her arm in mine and squeezes tightly. I take in their comfort then pull armor over my heart and nod to Thompson. He pushes the door open, and the heavy music and bright lights pour into the hall.

We all step into Jarron's bedroom together, which has apparently become a rave. Heavy bass music, with a slow rhythm, pulses and pounds through the room. It's dark, but there are slow flashes of red, green, and purple lights matching the rhythm of the music.

It's so strange being in here again, and even stranger how different it feels.

The layout is all the same as the last time I was here. The four-poster bed with black sheets to the right, several armchairs and a couch surrounding a flickering fireplace. A table with four chairs in the other corner. A whole wall of glass, showcasing the large patio with a flickering fire table.

I half expect the pile of random books and papers to be sitting in the middle of the floor like before, but it seems Jarron finally cleaned that up. Or at least hid it elsewhere.

The difference now is the bass-heavy music, pulsing red lights, and bodies everywhere.

And, of course, the prince himself, sitting on his throne.

I swallow as my attention pins to Jarron slumped causally in an armchair like he's the damn king and we all bow down to him. His eyes are lidded as he considers me. He's wearing a black button-up with the top several undone and the sleeves rolled.

Again, this is not the Jarron I know, and it has me unnerved. Although, not exactly in a bad way.

Dangerous, maybe, but certainly not bad.

My mouth dries, but I am hyper-aware of all the attention on me, so I do my best to hide the blush creeping up from my neck.

"Wow, he's hot."

"Janet!" I exclaim. Her mouth falls open in shock.

I slap my hand over my mouth as a laugh bubbles up in my chest. Amusement shatters my anxiety, and soon my shoulders are shaking along with my uncontrollable laughter.

The absurdity, irony, and shock on Janet's face all compiled to hysterical laughter, but damn, it feels good. Everyone is watching now, and I could seriously not care less.

Lola zips off my shoulder and hovers in front of us. "What? She's just saying what we're all thinking."

I snort, and then I pull them forward into the crowd that parts for us. Jarron watches as we stroll out onto the patio, where snowflakes flutter around and several people gather around the fire table.

The music fades behind us, and I breathe in deeply to calm myself.

"Oh, it's kinda chilly out here," Janet says, shivering.

"But it's *hot* in there," Lola jokes.

I let out one final chuckle, and then my laughter finally subsides. I am beyond grateful my friends are here for this. I literally don't think I could survive it without them.

"Candice!" a smooth voice exclaims.

I blink and find Manuela and her girlfriend standing by the iron railing. Her skin is a shade darker than Janet's, her hair tied back into a braid. Unlike most of the girls here, she's in regular—though, expensive—black slacks and a button-up top. To be honest, she may be wearing the exact same thing as Jarron.

Her girlfriend, Lucille, is in a tight pink dress and heels, her shoulders covered by a leather jacket. They make a cute pair, though I still remember what Bea told me about Lucille —she's got a thing for Jarron.

Maybe that was more lies, fed to me by a girl trying to manipulate me into the Akrasia Games. Or maybe it was real.

And even if it was real, I probably shouldn't care, right?

"Hey," I say casually.

"Having a good time already?" Lucille asks. I examine her for evidence of criticism, but her smile is sweet.

"The best."

"What? Do my eyes deceive me?" a lighthearted male voice says from behind us. "Or have the three most beautiful ladies in school made it to the party?"

I spin to find a handsome wolf shifter approaching with a big grin. I smile at Stassi, but also notice Thompson's shoulders stiffen.

"Wait, I thought I was the prettiest." A blond girl sitting in front of the fire croons with a smile.

Stassi winks at her and then turns back to us. "So glad you brought your friends this time. I've been dying to meet them."

Lola settles back on my shoulder and wiggles her wings. "Hello," she says in her attempt at a sultry tone.

"Stassi, this is Janet and Lola. And you know Thompson, right?"

Stassi ignores Thompson entirely, but possibly only because he's focused so intently on my female friends. "Lovely to finally meet you." His voice is exceptionally low. That's new.

Stassi is hard to read because he flirts and compliments everyone, but there's something a tad different about him right now. Could he actually be into one of my friends?

"How about a round of drinks?" Stassi offers, waving his hand like a butler.

"Oh, yes! We'll come," Lola says sweetly as she flutters up and around, making her skirt flow in the chilly breeze.

Janet slips her arm from mine. "You'll be okay, right?"

I nod. The moment those three are out of reach, Thompson shifts closer.

"Are you protecting me, or am I supposed to be protecting you?" I lean in to ask.

"Both."

I smile. "Deal."

"Candice!" Manuela calls again. "Take a seat. Hang out with us. Your wolf friend is welcome too."

"Hello, Manuela," Thompson says smoothly as we take their offer and sit on the couch facing the fire next to a bulky male I assume is fae. He looks exceedingly uncomfortable with my presence.

"You know Lucille?" she asks.

"I don't," Thompson answers. "It's nice to meet you. Silverback pack, yes?"

Lucille nods.

An awkward silence settles. I cross my arms and lean into the warmth of the flickering fire.

"So," the blond witch across from us says, leaning in. "You have so many secrets, Candice. I don't even know what to ask first."

A vampire boy with red eyes plops down next to the blond. "How about this? You and Thompson screwing, or what?"

I cough. "What?"

Manuela and Lucille snicker. The blond smirks, like I'm a present she's eager to open. Or a treat she's eager to devour.

"If we were, I'd already be dead," Thompson says casually. He leans back, expression calm.

"Oh please," the blonde girl says. "Just because he protects her from harm, doesn't mean he'll get all pissy about a hookup. It's not like he's in love with her. He didn't even bite her when they were together."

"But he did nearly demolish the school when someone else bit her."

I bite the inside of my cheek to hide any reaction.

I thought for certain Jarron's actions this week would make it very clear where he stood with me, but maybe I was wrong. Maybe the Elite are stubborn enough to deny I belong here at all.

"They dated for like four weeks."

I resist the urge to roll my eyes. We dated longer than that. "It takes less than that to fall in love," Manuela says quietly.

"Plus, they've known each other for several years," Thompson says. "They were childhood friends."

I've never talked about my previous relationship with Jarron to Thompson. How does he know all of that? Maybe he talks to Lola and Janet more than I realized.

"It's complicated, okay? That's my answer to all of your questions." I hold up my hands, just wanting them to stop discussing me like I'm not even here. "Well, except for Thompson. We're literally just friends."

The blond grunts and then stands. "This is boring." She

saunters off, back into the main room of the party. The wolf shifter follows her in.

"We're going in to get refills as well," Lucille says, holding up an empty glass. "Do you two want anything?"

My eyebrows rise. I'm impressed with the offer and decide, finally, to like her. She's kind and talented and beautiful, and I shouldn't let my own stupid—admittedly, irrational—jealousy get the best of me. "No. I—sorry, I'd rather drink something I pour myself."

"Smart girl," Manuela says. "Not that either of us would even consider messing with your drink. It's just a good rule to keep."

"We could go get drinks too if you want?" Thompson offers, nudging me with his elbow.

I twist my lips, looking through the large glass pane at the party within. Jarron is still in the same position, with casual ease, like he couldn't care less what was going on around him.

A girl in a red dress leans against the armrest and whispers something to him. Jarron flicks a hand, and the girl jerks away. Jarron doesn't so much as blink.

"Something about that posture is sexy, isn't it?"

My eyebrows pull down, and I look at Manuela. I was under the impression she had no interest in men, but maybe I was wrong. But then, I see her expression. She's examining me like a mad scientist watching an experiment. She's measuring every reaction.

I do my best to give her none.

"I know, right? I just want to sit on him."

The breath rushes from my lungs, and I don't breathe for several seconds. The girl who spoke is a short brunette with all the right curves.

"Shut up, Samantha," Manuela says, though her gaze is still pinned on me.

The girl giggles and then winks.

"Go give it a shot. See what happens," Thompson says smoothly. "We'll rate your attempt."

Samantha curls a lip in annoyance but then sashays into the room. She pauses in front of Jarron... and then continues walking past.

Thompson laughs. "Coward."

"Or wise, depending on your perspective," Lucille says.

"If she were wise, she'd have kept her mouth shut to start with," I say.

Manuela rolls her eyes. "All right, we going in for drinks or what?"

I nod, and we all four head into the dark room that vibrates with lazy pulsing tones. The lyrics of the song are about choking and other not-safe-for-work activities. I zone it out. I really don't need more sexual suggestion. My body is already tense, my mind barely controlled from thinking about things I very much shouldn't be.

As much as I wanted to rip the girl's head off for saying that about Jarron, she did kinda have a point.

Nope, not thinking about that. Or him. Definitely not thinking about him.

"You okay?" Thompson side-eyes me as he pours a glass of red liquid and hands it to me.

I take the mollifying potion, wondering if I should just grab two while I'm at it. I'm not much of a drinker—potions or alcohol—but tonight could be an exception.

Unwise? Maybe. Needed? Remains to be seen.

This potion is common at parties because it has much the

same reaction as alcohol—decreases inhibitions and relaxes you—but without the negative side effects. There are also blue and green potions, which I know have a bit of a more intense effect. I wouldn't touch those with a ten-foot pole. And then, there's laced blood and a tar-like substance I've never had the courage to inquire about.

I gulp down the mollifying potion, finishing the whole thing in a few seconds.

"I'll take that as a no," he says then pours another.

"I'm fine," I say and turn to find Lola, Janet, and Stassi chatting in the corner near the bed. "Kinda."

We separate from Manuela and Lucille and spend a while chatting with Lola, Janet, and Stassi. I'm quiet, just sipping on my potion. Warmth slowly spreads through my chest, and my muscles relax.

Lola spins in a circle and lands on Janet's shoulder.

"So, this is an Elite party," Janet says, looking around.

There are three nymph girls wrestling on the bed while six boys of various species watch and laugh. Another six gather around the potions bar, including Manuela and her girlfriend.

"It's smaller than I expected."

"This is the *Elite*, Elite party," Thompson tells her. "It's exclusive to only those really *in*."

Jarron is still in his armchair, with four other males sitting in the chairs around him. Laithe, whose expression is equally as surly, even though a blond boy sits on his lap, playing with his hair. Across from them are mages, who look remarkably similar, down to their matching suit vests and messy black hair. Twins, I'd guess.

My eyes continually drift back to Jarron, like a magnet. He holds a glass of that same tar-like substance I remember from the last time we were at a party like this—Trevor's, that time. His silver rings gleam in the red light.

"Elite-Elite? Then, why the hell are we here?"

"Because we're besties with the hottest girl in school." Lola tinkles and flies around my head.

I cough.

"What? She's right." A massive shifter slides up next to me, followed by a tiny redheaded girl with glowing amber eyes and pointy ears.

"Well, maybe not the hottest." The shifter grins. "But certainly the most interesting."

I grimace.

"Careful," Thompson says casually then glances over his shoulder at Jarron, who's watching us all closely.

The shifter frowns but his expression smooths into arrogance. "You really think he'll kill for her? Over a wink?"

"Dude, he almost killed me for agreeing that she's beautiful." Stassi shivers. "And I'm his friend."

I was not aware of this situation, but I wonder if it's what motivated his "adequate" comment the other day. Stassi does make some interesting comments, but Jarron has to know he's not a threat.

To be honest, I enjoy the compliments that don't come with any expectations. It's nice to be built up without the pressure to react the right way.

The mollifying potion is definitely attempting to calm me down. I can feel the warm comfort swirling through my veins, even while my mind flashes through so many dangerous thoughts.

Thoughts I'd love to indulge, but the repercussions are too heavy to consider.

Like running my hands through Jarron's hair, the way that fae is running his through Laithe's. Like sitting on the Crown Prince of the Under World's lap and allowing his hands to run over my skin the way they slide over the leather of that chair.

I shake my head and force it back to reality.

"Honestly," Thompson says, "I think we'll be walking on eggshells until his mark covers the one Jimmy forced on her."

The large shifter sends a nervous glance to Jarron but then shrugs. "I'm not afraid of him. Jarron's powerful as hell, but he doesn't do anything."

Thompson smiles. "Well, in that case..." Thompson grins. "Elliot, right? Perhaps you'd be up for a game of truth or dare?"

"Are you gonna try to get me killed?"

"No. Just want something to pass the time. I was worried everyone would be too afraid to play. You at least talk like you're brave. Care to prove it?"

"Fine. But don't think I won't bail to save my tail. There's a clear difference between bravery and stupidity."

My eyebrows rise. The large shifter, Elliot, is wiser than I gave him credit for.

"I'm in too!" the redheaded fae chirps.

Truth or dare at an Elite party. This sounds like a terrible idea. "What if I'm not in?" I ask.

The two new-to-me Elite glare at me. Thompson nudges my arm. "She's in."

I sigh. I'm equal parts curious and dubious. But much like the shifter, I'm not going to be too afraid to bail if I feel uncomfortable.

"It'll be good for you. Promise."

Janet inches in closer and tugs my arm. “Hey, um... is it okay—”

I hold up my hands and smile. “Yes. Go. Tell Marcus I said hi.”

She throws her arms around me. “Thank you so much. This was—well, insane but an experience I’m glad I was special enough to earn.”

I pull back to look her in the eye. “This—” I wave around, “—does not make you special. You are incredible. This is all just luck.”

She blushes and shrugs. “Still. Not many people get invited to these. It’s exciting to be one of the few for at least one night.”

I kiss her on the cheek. “I’m glad you came.”

“Me too.” She looks over her shoulder to find Lola blushing and chatting with Stassi. “You coming, Lo?”

Lola freezes. “Uh, is it okay if it—”

“Yep. I’m totally okay with going alone.”

“A Janet-and-Marcus date.” I grin.

She smiles bashfully. “Keep an eye out for her, okay?”

I nod. “Of course.” One of the reasons Minor Hall students don’t generally go to upper-level parties isn’t entirely because of access. Sometimes, it’s literally just not safe. It would be easy for a powerful dickhead to invite a weak student just to prey on them. Most wouldn’t accept an invite even if it came their way. Janet and Lola had Jarron’s assurance of their protection, so it was a little different, but there’s still some risk.

Lola flutters into Janet’s chest. “Stassi and I will walk you out of Elite Hall.”

“Protector Stassi on duty!” He stands up straight, his face

serious for only an instant before the grin spreads wide over his face.

"I'll be back in a few," Lola chirps to me, and those three make their way out of the room.

"Come on," Thompson prompts me. My heart hammers, despite the relaxing potion swirling around in my mind, lightening every muscle. Well, almost every muscle.

The walk across the room feels like it takes a million years with the powerful prince's eyes on me. His gaze is not quite as oppressive as his dark magic that fills the halls these days, but it lingers like a whisper over my shoulder, haunting each step.

It's bitter and sweet. It's terrible and beautiful.

It's everything I want and everything I'm trying so damn hard to avoid.

Wanting Jarron is one thing, but knowing he wants me back and still resisting is something else entirely. Knowing that any female in this room could come on to him and he'd cast her away with the flick of his wrist and barely a glance in her direction, yet if I were to saunter over and sit on his lap...

I swallow. I don't know what he'd do, and it's a very, very bad idea to imagine it.

Is there a potion for forcing your mind not to wander? There are focusing potions, of course, but you can't control what you focus on, and with my luck, I'd focus on him.

What I need is to stop picturing it. Stop imagining—*an imagination restrictor.* That sounds good. Maybe I'll invent that potion for moments like this.

A flicker of silver light catches my attention in the corner next to Jarron's bed. On the nightstand is something new. A silver knickknack I've never seen before. Jarron isn't one for décor, so his tabletops are generally bare.

This bit of abstract art is uncharacteristic. I'm pulled toward it, my curiosity again getting the best of me. I stop a foot before the bedstand and blink as I realize what it is.

It's not a statue. Not abstract art. Not décor.

My mouth dries, and the breath rushes from my lungs.

It's a set of silver handcuffs, crushed into a heap, as if—well, as if a massively powerful being crushed them between his hands.

Why—

"Something wrong?"

I suck in my lost breath and turn to Thompson with a smile I'm certain is more manic than happy. "Nope. I'm wonderful. Let's get the hell out of this room." I rush past him.

Jarron has nothing personal in his room for show. Except that.

Except the handcuffs he used to show me how much power I have over him, crushed into a ball.

34
DANGEROUS PARTY GAMES

I don't remember sitting down on the couch beside the flickering fire table outside or the others settling in around me. I don't pay attention to what they're saying; the chatter just floats around me like dust to be ignored.

I stare at the red and orange flames, my mind entirely elsewhere.

What does it mean? Jarron left those handcuffs, which he used to lock himself, hands up, to his bedpost and told me I had complete control over him.

Nothing happened that night, not really. I touched him in PG-13 places and then stopped it. It was more of an idea. He'd willingly submit to me. Be and do anything I wanted.

Even if it's nothing.

I think the stopping was part of me proving I really did have control. Because I could see how much he wanted more. And my body was not far behind his. But there was so much between us I didn't understand, and I didn't want to rush anything physical.

Jarron is a million times more powerful than I am, yet he insisted I have power over him. I tasted that power that night, and it was delicious. I wanted more.

I still do.

So, what, exactly, do those crumpled handcuffs mean?

Does he want to remind me of that moment? Or is the fact that they're crushed mean I don't have a right to that control anymore?

I don't know what to think, honestly.

"She just needs a minute."

I blink rapidly, my mind finally coming down from the avalanche of thoughts. "What?"

The blond from earlier is back and smirking at me with a decidedly unkind expression.

"She was talking to you," Manuela says. "But you were—"

"Right, yeah sorry. What were you asking?" I force a smile.

"I was just telling her all the potions you used in the fight against those wolves," Thompson says casually. "Stunning spells and poison, that's all I know for sure."

Poison. Right.

"Yes, I asked," the blond drawls, "how you killed that shifter. I've never heard of a human killing an Elite with potions."

"You've never heard of poisons?" Manuela rolls her eyes.

"Not used during a fight," the girl claps back defensively.

I shrug one shoulder. "Well, now you have."

She grunts. "We getting this game started or what?"

I take in a long breath to prepare myself for truth or dare among enemies.

There's a fine line between friend and enemy.

It's a good distraction, so even though it's dangerous, I'm not going to be the coward tonight.

A large group settles in close to the fire. Lucille sits on Manuela's lap on one of the smaller chairs. The large arrogant shifter Elliot, the blond girl, and a massive male I'm not familiar with are all on the couch across from us. There's also the girl in the tiny red dress leaning into a vampire against the railing.

"How does this work exactly?" I ask, taking a small sip of my red liquid. My glass is becoming empty faster than I'd planned.

"You've never played truth or dare?" Manuela accuses, quirking one brow.

"I have. With humans. If there is one thing I know about supernaturals, it's that they won't share their secrets. Certainly not for some drinking game."

Manuela smirks, her eyes gleaming in that predator way.

"Ask your questions, knowing we will lie," the large shifter says. "But that's part of the fun."

I pick at the nail on my thumb. The hell does that mean?

"Even the lies can reveal truths," Manuela says ominously. "Pay attention, little ones."

"Or as I like to play—" Thompson leans forward, toward the flickering flames, "—use dares to reveal truths."

I swallow. This may be a very, very bad idea.

"Let's start simple, with the lady of the evening." Manuela grins at me. I have to resist a shiver. "Candice, truth or dare?"

I bite the inside of my cheek not to react. "Truth."

"Do you have feelings for Jarron?"

My stomach twists. My first instinct is to lie. *No.* It's on the tip of my tongue.

But they'll know it's a lie. I know they will. That's what they mean when they say lies reveal. If I say no, it'll be clear I have feelings I'm hiding.

"She's pale," someone snickers.

"Yes," I say definitively, keeping my head high and gaze set on Manuela.

It's true. I do have feelings for Jarron. And it would remain true even if I wasn't trying to force my mind not to imagine his hands on my thighs, sitting on his lap inside that dark and music-filled room.

Feelings could mean a million different things.

"He is my friend, and I care about him. Those are feelings."

They don't need to know that the thoughts swirling through my mind are anything but innocent. Although, with this game and these potions, I wonder how long I'll be able to keep that secret to myself.

Manuela nods sharply, almost as if she approves of my answer. "Your turn."

Well, this part could be just as difficult, but at least this time, I'm in control. I consider asking Thompson some of the things I've been wondering about his motives, but this isn't the setting I'd even want those answers.

If I uncover his secrets, I want them to be mine. I don't want to share them with already powerful schmucks.

Instead, I turn to the girl in the little red dress leaning into the vamp against the railing. "What's your name again?"

She faces me with a grimace. "Samantha."

"Samantha, truth or dare."

She tilts her head curiously. "Truth." She sighs.

"You implied you were going to come on to Jarron earlier. Why didn't you?"

Her nose flares. She's definitely imagining my death right now. "Because I knew he'd turn me away."

My brows rise. Was that an honest answer?

"Jarron has never responded to shallow or sexual interactions. He wants something deeper. That takes time."

My mind stutters to a stop.

A gust of wind sends a scattering of snow into the gathering then disappears over the heat of the flames.

Does that mean this girl is trying to get close to Jarron? I mean, logically, I know girls have been trying for years, so it's not exactly news, but for some reason it gets to me.

What if it worked?

Damn, I'm messed up.

"Thompson," the girl in the red dress says seductively. "Truth or dare."

"Truth. I'm not buzzed enough for dares yet."

I snort. Isn't that the truth?

"Why did you gravitate straight to Candice on the very first day at this school?"

The group goes quiet. Everyone stills. This is the question everyone has been asking, isn't it? Even me. I have no idea what his agenda is, but it's something.

"Her winning personality." He grins, exposing sharp canines.

"Bullshit," Samantha spits.

"You didn't even know my personality until after you sat with me," I say.

He grunts. "Fine. You want a real answer? Why does anyone powerful go to this school? We don't need to learn to use our magic, not really. We come here to be around others of influence. We come here to network. I decided she was an ally I wanted."

The girl scoffs, still not buying it. Manuela looks especially interested, though. Those predator eyes narrow in on someone other than me. Manuela was once on Jarron's inner circle list. She's close to him.

Is she acting as a spy for him tonight?

"Your first choice in ally is the magicless human?" Samantha puts her hand on her hip like she doesn't believe it for a second.

"A human who was recently in a romantic relationship with the most powerful student to attend here in a hundred years," Manuela says smoothly, swirling her drink with one hand and gripping Lucille's thigh with the other.

"A human who is kickass at potion-making and is the daughter of the most influential potion masters in the world," he adds.

"That's a lot of truths for one round," I mutter.

Thompson chuckles. "I quite agree."

They were all things I'd considered or that Thompson tried to pass off as truth. It doesn't reveal anything new.

Thompson scoots forward to the edge of his seat. "My turn." He rubs his hands together. "Elliot. Truth or dare?"

Elliot flinches but then puffs out his chest. "All right, I'll bite." He points at Thompson. "But you better not be a dick about it. Dare."

"Now we're getting started," someone says. All attention narrows in on Elliot and Thompson.

Thompson rubs his hands together. "Let's test my theory on dares that reveal truths."

"Oh boy."

"Elliot, I dare you to pin Candice's hands above her head for ninety seconds."

"Screw you," Elliot spits.

My eyes widen.

"She'd have to consent, of course. Totally innocent. You'd only be touching her wrists, nothing more."

"What the hell, Thompson?" I ask.

Thompson meets my gaze, his expression soft. "Trust me."

I groan. "Fine. Come on, big guy. If I'm in, you are." I finish off the rest of my potion and then cross behind the chairs to the stone wall a few feet behind us.

Elliot grimaces but rises to his feet. "First sign of Jarron, I'm out."

"I thought you said you didn't think Jarron would kill for her?"

"Over an insult. This is... different." He swallows.

I won't admit it, but I kind of like that he's scared. But then again, I'm a bit nervous too. I lean my back against the stone and lift my hands up over my head. Elliot stands as far as he physically can from me while still reaching my wrists with his one hand. It's almost comical.

Thompson starts counting.

My heart pounds, adrenaline rushing. I don't know what truth Thompson is trying to prove, but I'm guessing he's anticipating a reaction from Jarron. He wouldn't purposefully get Elliot hurt, right?

"Twenty-nine. Thirty."

A form stands in the now open doorway to the patio. "The hell is this?" Jarron's low voice rumbles.

There's a slight pause, where even Thompson's counting stops.

"Thirty-three. Thirty-four," he continues, but his voice is quieter. Even he is nervous.

Elliot throws his hands up, releasing me. "It was a dare, dude," he stutters. Then, he literally leaps over the railing into the darkness below.

I gasp. "Oh my God. Did he really just jump?"

"What dare?" Jarron asks, his voice eerily low.

"He had to pin my hands for ninety seconds. Not a big deal." I peer over the railing, but I can't see anything except pitch-black darkness. How high up are we?

"Who made the dare?"

"Doesn't matter. I'm fine," I say, turning back to him. "Though, is Elliot okay?"

"He's a shifter. He's fine," Thompson says.

"Who?" Jarron demands again.

I don't know what Jarron would do if he found out Thompson made the dare, and I don't want them at odds. Thompson has few allies as it is.

"Trust me," Thompson says, not for the first time. Except now, it's to Jarron, not me.

My brows pinch. *The hell?* I recall Jarron's offer after the shifter attack. Are Thompson and Jarron more allies now than I'd realized? I shake my head. A question for another time.

"I need another drink." I march forward and stop in front of Jarron, still blocking the doorway. "Come with me?" I ask as casually as possible.

He blinks and then shifts aside to allow me to pass, then he follows me through the streaming red lights without a word.

"Interesting vibe you got going," I say as he catches up.

His lips twitch. "You don't like it?"

Oh, I like it. Even if it's a bit much. "I didn't say that."

"Mmhmm. You really are okay? No one pushed—"

"Nope, I'm good. It was a dare for Elliot, not me. I agreed to it."

"All right. Are you... having a good time? You're drinking more than usual."

I look down at my newly poured mollifying potion. Cool red liquid swirls in the glass. He's noticed that, has he? "I'm still a bit out of my element here. But I'm good."

The flutter of something purple grabs my attention. "Lola!"

She nuzzles against my chest and then whirls around my head.

"Are you having a good time?" I ask her. She soars around Stassi's head.

"We are wonderful," he says.

Lola lands on my shoulder and whispers in my ear all about how cute Stassi is and how she thinks he likes her. He showed her all around Elite Hall before coming back to the party. I'm grinning wide and lost in her story, so much so that I don't notice when Jarron slips away.

I turn to find him back on his throne. His posture is straighter now. Stassi and Lola follow me back out to the patio and are greeted by the group.

By now, my mind is fuzzy and my body light. Definitely my last potion of the night.

The game has continued in my absence, and I find the male fae in only his underwear and a wolf shifter nursing a cup of what appears to be blood, a look of disgust on his face.

Ick, I'd fail that dare immediately.

The next several rounds are truths that I barely follow. I

guess I'm not in enough on the Elite gossip to care very much about who cheated on who. My mind slips off again until I hear my name. I refocus on the conversation instantly.

"Oh please. You act like he's in love with her, but I call bullshit," Samantha says. "He's protective, yes. He cares, yes. But to my eye? He sees her like a sister."

My stomach sinks. What in hell are they talking about?

Several people talk over each other after that.

"Didn't you see them together last year?" the fae practically yells. "He barely touched her. Certainly never bit her."

"That was because of her, not him," Lucille says.

"So, you think the Crown Prince of Oriziah is smitten, desperately in love with a human girl, who won't give him the time of day? That's way twisted, bro."

"Let's test it," Manuela says, and the group pauses. "She picked truth last time, so she's obligated to a dare." Her smile is wicked and suddenly my heart is pattering faster than a bat's wings. I didn't realize that's how that worked. I feel like I did do a dare, but I guess it wasn't mine.

"Yeah, dare her to seduce him. See how he reacts," the fae in his underwear says.

"That's certainly a way to uncover truths with a dare," Thompson agrees.

"Thompson!" I bark, annoyed he's leaning into this so much.

"But it's not your turn," Thompson says. He crosses his arms and leans back. "It's mine. Candice, truth or dare."

I lift my chin, gritting my teeth hard. "Am I not allowed to pick truth?"

"No."

"Then, why ask?"

"You can choose truth," Manuela says, her expression dimmed now that the power behind her plan is stolen away. "But you'd technically lose. Do you know the penalty for losing a game of truth or dare here?"

I shake my head.

"You wear your shirt backward throughout the day on Monday."

I frown. That doesn't sound so bad.

"No, not the worst punishment, except that everyone who's in enough to know what it means will know you failed and why. Your revealed truths here only remain between us if you successfully finish the game. Lose and we spill it all. The rumors will be fierce but the pranks even worse. The backward shirt gives the other Elites that were playing a pass to mess with you. Ever hear of the girl spelled to act like a dog for a full hour during combat class?"

Uh, yes. Yes, I have heard of that.

"That's what that was about?" Lola chips.

"Yep. She was a Major student at an ascended party and lost a game of truth or dare. That was her punishment. Of course, no one would do anything too ruthless with you, not with the way Jarron is acting, but..."

Right. Got it. Failing is a possibility but not a desirable thing.

"Trust me," Thompson says under his breath. "We'll do this on your terms."

But truthfully, I don't think I do trust him. With my life? Yes. But to push me farther than I'm ready or willing to go? Nope. He'd totally do that.

"You better not give her something stupid, Thompson," the redhead says. "Or I'm declaring you the loser."

"You can't do that."

"Sure as hell can."

I sigh. Thompson is still the better option. "Fine, dare." I spit it out before I change my mind.

Again, the group quiets, everyone zoning in on me and Thompson.

"You've been looking into that room every few minutes for the last two hours."

Has it been two hours?

"I want you to do it."

My stomach sinks. "Do what?"

"That thing you've been thinking about but are too afraid to do."

My cheeks heat. Again, my attention drifts straight to Jarron. I can barely see him through the glare in the glass. A few people in the group begin whispering. Someone mutters, "That's lame."

But the majority of the group watches curiously.

"Th-that's my dare?"

"Yep."

I guess I see what he means about it being on my terms. I don't have to do something ridiculous, like give Jarron a lap dance or a strip tease or bite his neck. I can do whatever I choose—as long as it's something believable.

Realizing that my gaze has already given me away, I blink back to the group. *Shit.* Okay, it's not that bad, but also, it's really bad. I now have to get up, walk into the party while everyone watches, and... do something to Jarron.

There are several somethings I've thought about during the last few hours. But this dare is part truth. No one will know for sure if my action is what I've been thinking about.

I could serve him a drink. Sit at his feet and begin a conversation. Run my hands through his hair and then walk away. Will any of those things appease my audience? I'm not sure.

I stand, and several of the Elite around me chuckle. I meet Samantha's stare. Her glare tells me she's waiting for me to fail. Waiting for me to do something to prove her right when Jarron pushes me to the side the way he has every other girl that's come on to him tonight.

That's the moment I decide.

I'm not near bold enough to do something extreme, but I sure as hell have a point to prove, so I'm not going to take the easy way out.

My head pulses, vision moving in and out of focus as I approach the demon prince. He meets my stare with a confused frown and a flexed jaw I'm not supposed to find sexy. My chest rises dramatically with each step toward him.

Part of me wants to straddle him, press my whole body against him. Part of me wants to kiss him and taste the forbidden fruit. But I'm not bold enough for that, or perhaps not drunk enough. But still, determination swells in my chest, eager to prove my worth.

I know Jarron wants me. And I want him.

Right now, I'm determined to prove it while everyone watches.

He doesn't move. Once his eyes meet mine, they do not budge, not for one second. He doesn't examine the crowd piling into the room behind me, eager to watch the show. He doesn't move to anticipate me.

Jarron remains utterly still as I walk right up to him and then slide onto his lap.

35

I DARE YOU

Maybe it's the release of inhibitions from the mollifying potion, the determination to prove myself, or fear of what might happen if I lose the game, but somehow, I find myself settling down on Jarron Blackthorn's lap in the middle of a party.

Jarron is frozen in place for exactly three seconds, which doesn't sound that long but feels like an eternity. Finally, his muscles relax ever so slightly, and his hands slip over my thighs, tucking me in tighter against him.

It's not an overly sexy position, my legs are simply hanging over his thighs, my back partially against the armrest, partially against his side.

He leans in slightly, his nose grazing the hair at my neck. "What are you doing, Candice?"

I shiver at the gravel in his tone.

My throat sticks for a moment, and despite the mollifying potion, anxiety begins pooling in my chest. I try my best to swallow it down. I've technically completed my dare. I could hop up and run away like a coward now.

But my blood heats, overcoming the anxiety. I find I don't want to move.

Jarron leans back and brushes my hair over my shoulder to examine me. I still give no answer, mostly because I'm not sure I could make my lips work currently. Apparently, he finds no answer on my face or body language because he then turns to the audience crowding the open door from the balcony.

"What was the dare?" Jarron asks, his voice low.

Now, everyone in the room is watching. *Great. Perfect, exactly what I was hoping for.*

Thompson grins. "I dared her to do the thing she kept thinking about but was too afraid to do."

Jarron's fingers tighten over my thigh, and I swear I can feel his heart racing.

Dammit, I really like that.

His attention turns back to me. "Interesting," he murmurs against my shoulder. But then, he relaxes against the chair, expression back to that lazy arrogance that I don't dare admit does things to me.

"As you were," he says to the group still watching. When they remain still after another moment, he flicks one brow and they all scatter.

I barely hold back a laugh at how quickly they move. The truth or dare group is back outside, chatting wildly, presumably about me and Jarron. The other pockets of supernaturals inside go back to what they were doing before. A group of fae girls dance by the bed. Two wolf shifters wrestle in the corner.

"Welcome," a smooth voice says. I turn to Laithe, still with that same blond boy on his lap.

"Yeah," the boy purrs. "It's about time, Candy."

My face morphs into an expression of disgust, and I slowly turn my attention to the boy. Terror drops over his face, like he's facing a rabid bear. Good, that's what I want. "Call me that again, and I'll gut you."

There's a pause, and then Laithe and Jarron both start howling with laughter at the same time. The blond boy hops up and flees into the darkness around us.

I cross my arms.

"Next time, make your threat about potions or poisoning," Laithe says as his laughter dissipates. "You'll have the entire school shivering with just a look in no time."

I roll my eyes, but then I sigh. "Sorry for chasing away your boyfriend."

"Not my boyfriend." Laithe shrugs. "It is too bad though; I was getting hungry."

I tilt my head. "Hungry?"

Laithe smiles, showing off his elongated canines. The breath catches in my throat. Oh. That.

"But I thought—" I glance at Jarron, who looks entirely at ease, his eyes lidded as he watches me. "Jarron said that wasn't something demons had to do. Just something they... enjoyed?" I barely squeak out the last word. Warmth has crawled its way up my neck. Realistically, Jarron implied biting for a demon was erotic.

Bea compared the pleasure a bite brings to an orgasm.

Laithe sniffs. "Ahh the ease of being a royal," he drawls. "Not all species from our world have the luxury of being able to choose how and when we eat. Though I only feed every week or so, I will grow weak if I don't."

"Oh," I say stupidly. So, it's only an optional act for the royal line?

"Don't feel sorry for them," Jarron murmurs. "Though it's an act of sustenance, it's still enjoyable for both parties, and there is no lack of students that would gladly allow Laithe to feed on them."

Laithe reclines back. His expression smug.

Well, all right then. I suppose Laithe is vaguely attractive, despite the two-inch horns sticking up through his long dark hair. There are probably plenty of people attracted to that anyway. Plus, his relationship with Jarron puts him pretty high on the influence chain.

"So, Laithe is popular, got it."

Laithe smirks.

"Would you like me to call someone over for you?" Jarron asks with a cocky tone. He scans the room. "Lucinda would be here in a second."

Laithe scoffs. "Not my type."

I don't know who Lucinda is, so I have no idea why she wouldn't be his type. "Because she's female?" I ask uncertainly.

He shakes his head. "Gender is meaningless to me."

Jarron brushes a few strands of hair off my shoulder. "Technically, Laithe's species are genderless."

"Oh!" I say too loudly. If he's genderless... that would mean Laithe himself isn't male? Or female?

"So, should I not call you he?"

Laithe shrugs.

"They/them is more correct. Laithe just doesn't particularly care."

"I am simply Laithe. Our language does not have gendered

pronouns, but this is not my world nor my culture, and how I am perceived here means little. Call me whatever you wish."

Hmm. Does he truly not care, or is he just too passive to advocate for himself? I give him a short nod. "They/them it is."

His lips twitch.

"So, how is Lucinda not your type, then, if gender means nothing to you? Is it her species? Personality?"

"Because gender is not a norm in my culture, I find extreme femininity and masculinity to be off-putting."

Jarron points out a willowy girl with perfect black curls down her back, wearing a black mini dress, fishnet stockings, and super high stilettos. "That's Lucinda."

Okay, so super girly is not his type.

"What about him?" I point out a large shifter in a simple muscle tee and buzzed hair. I think I know the answer but am just curious at this point.

Laithe shakes his head. Wait, *their* head—the pronoun thing takes a little getting used to. "Wolf shifters in general are usually a no for me."

"Okay, so like, Manuela. She would be your type?"

Laithe nods quickly, not even needing to find her. "But she'd never desire me. She is solid in her attraction to females."

I look around, seeking another androgynous supernatural in the crowd. I find a girl with a pixie cut and dark-painted nails. She's wearing a skirt and a corset top. "Her?" I ask.

They tilts their head, examining the girl. "Perhaps."

There are few others I'd define as androgynous. Most people here push their sex appeal as hard as they can, which usually means punctuating things our culture likes about their particular gender. Girls with long hair, skirts, heels, and makeup. The men with tight tees, large, defined muscles, and short hair.

I've never considered myself overly girly, but maybe even I'm too feminine? Who knows? "What about me?" I blurt out.

There's a pause, and then a low rumble begins in Jarron's chest.

"Are you trying to get me in trouble, Candice?" Laithe asks lightly, but their gaze focuses past me.

"Oh, sorry. I didn't—never mind." My cheeks warm again. That was a stupid thing to say, wasn't it?

"It's all right," Laithe says. "It's those potions you've been drinking. They loosen lips and make you say things you wouldn't usually."

Jarron takes in a long breath. "You're right," he says to Laithe. "Maybe you should leave us alone so I can ask her a few questions."

Without missing a beat, Laithe slides from the seat and is lost to the crowd.

"Hey," I complain. "I was enjoying that conversation."

"I'm glad," he purrs. "You'll have many opportunities to continue it if you wish."

I grunt in annoyance. But then quickly I find my muscles tense, wondering if he's right. Maybe I'll pour out all of my true feelings here and now without being able to stop myself.

A sudden swell of emotions crashes into me, followed by a wave of panic.

What the hell am I doing? Sitting on Jarron's lap and flirting with him? It's already gone too far.

I move to stand, but Jarron's hands clench my waist and tug me back. "Please," he begs. "Please stay."

My heart clenches and then doubles its speed.

"You know I'd never pressure you to do anything you don't want."

My feet are on the ground, but my legs are still resting against his. His hands are spread over my waist, holding me firmly but gently.

"Even sit on your lap?" I whisper.

His breath shudders, and then he releases me, hands up in surrender. I step away but pause, and I watch as his expression turns into that devastation I remember from the day he saw my bite.

My heart clenches again. Dammit, why does this boy have to have such a chokehold on me? I swallow and then slowly retake my place on his lap.

He releases a breath, and the look he gives me now implies that I am giving him the greatest gift he could ever imagine, and dammit, I really like that too.

His chest rises and falls in quick succession. He stares at me, and I stare at him. The intensity is so strong that I don't dare move. Or at least, I thought I wasn't moving. Somehow, our faces have gone from at least a foot apart to mere inches.

We're going to kiss, I realize.

And I'm not sure how to feel about that. I want it. So badly, I want it. But there are reasons we shouldn't, right? For some reason, that's bad.

My brain can't quite grip those reasons, though.

"Why did you leave the handcuffs out?" I blurt. I'm not sure where that thought even came from.

Jarron's adorably confused as he leans back. "What?"

I turn to glance at the mangled handcuffs across the room

on the bedside table. "You destroyed them. Cleared out everything else from your room. But you left those. Why?"

He examines my face. "I didn't—I don't really know. I guess, I keep them there as a reminder."

"Of what?"

He swallows. "What I almost had."

A shiver washes over me.

His lips ghost over my shoulder. "What was in my grasp and somehow slipped away."

My breath catches.

"I still don't know why. What did I do, Candice?"

I close my eyes. Butterflies soar through my whole body.

"Nothing," I whisper. "Nothing you have control of. You're fucking perfect."

Then, I make a decision. Maybe it's the potions in my system; maybe it's my walls being slowly worn away by his disarming sincerity and Lola's insistence that pushing Jarron away is a win for Mr. Vandozer.

But my realization is as clear as day: there is nothing I want more than to be desired the way he desires me. To be looked at like *this.*

Before I can change my mind, I crash my lips into his.

Jarron is ready for me, pulling me tightly against him, and somehow, I find myself straddling him. His chest vibrates softly. I pull back just enough to smirk. "Purring again?"

"Only for you." His hand curls over the back of my neck and tugs me to him. His lips are gentle but firm, and his taste is intoxicating.

His hands slide up my thighs until his fingertips are just under the hem of my shorts. His nails dig into the skin as he drags them out.

My back arches, and the gasp that escapes my lips is barely just shy of a moan. I'm in big trouble here.

I lean away again and notice people herding from the room, a crowd forming at the open door, streaming into the hall.

I straighten. "What's happening?"

"Party's over." Jarron smirks. He palms my thigh, sending another jolt through me. Dammit, if he stops doing that, I might riot.

I bite my lip as I watch the traffic jam of supernaturals at the door. Jarron didn't say a word. How did everyone get the message all at once? Did I miss some announcement?

Thompson looks over his shoulder from the crowd and winks in our direction. I get the feeling it was not for me. "What the hell is his deal?"

"Thompson?"

"Yes."

Jarron leans in, running his nose along my collarbone. "You're only friends, right?"

I shiver. "Yes. But isn't it weird he's so forward about pushing us together?"

"Why would it be? Wouldn't your girl friends do the same if they thought two people should be together?"

I bite the inside of my lip. Maybe? I'm not positive Janet or Lola would be so manipulative, even if they thought it was in my best interest, but I could definitely imagine some girls doing that. So, is it actually weird? Or am I thinking too much into it?

"Wait," I say suddenly, jerking my head back. "What about Lola?"

"What about her?"

"Who is she with? She needs—"

"She's taken care of," Jarron assures me with another squeeze to my thigh. "Stassi," he calls, his voice low enough I doubt anyone could have heard it over the still-blaring music.

And yet, Stassi approaches within a second, Lola sitting daintily on his shoulder. "What's up, boss?"

"You wouldn't dare hurt that girl, would you?"

Stassi stands up straight. "Never."

"You are in charge of making sure she makes it back to Minor Hall safely. Understood?"

He nods.

I point straight at Stassi's face. Unlike Laithe's friend, Stassi is not intimidated. "If anything happens to her, I'll kill you."

Stassi smirks. "You mean your boyfriend will kill me."

I slip my fingers into my pocket and pull out a tiny vial full of glistening blue liquid. "No. I mean I will."

Stassi's eyes widen. Jarron's fingers clench over my thigh, fingers digging into my skin.

"That's what I'm talking about." Laithe lifts a fist in my direction just before tossing their arm back over the small blond boy and walking through the open door behind several other supernaturals.

Lola flutters up and around until she's buzzing beside my head. "We'll talk tomorrow. Janet will want a full report from both of us."

I grin and watch as they leave the room together. The door clicks shut behind them, and the room is empty, though still with the red flashing lights and heavy music.

"Is the music necessary?"

Jarron tilts his head, and the music halts, just like that. "Not if you don't like it."

"I didn't say I didn't like it."

"Would you like it to stay on?"

I breathe deep. If we leave it on, we'll keep kissing, and if we keep kissing... I don't know that I can be responsible for what else happens tonight. Though, even knowing that risk, I'm not ready to leave. "Not right now. I'm kind of surprised by your taste, though."

"I have eclectic tastes. That felt more appropriate for a demon prince's party than say Ella Fitzgerald or even Jimmy Hendrix."

"Hmm, I suppose you're right. 'Hot Demon Bitches,' after all..."

Jarron raises a brow then grins. "That's not exactly my type of woman."

"But certainly fits your brand."

He shakes his head in mock disapproval. The silence settles around us and somehow makes every touch stand out more. My heart pounds. There's fear somewhere in my chest, but it's buried beneath layers and layers of other, much more important feelings.

Jarron's lips graze gently over my collarbone. I allow my head to loll back, taking in the incredible sensation. Then, I gasp when two sharp points press into the lingering marks of my wolf bite.

I wait, expecting the pain to increase. Wanting it.

My muscles tense, anticipating his fangs carving into the mark and erasing the pain of that moment, replacing it with him. I hadn't considered wanting that before, but it's all I can think about now. I need it.

A moment later, Jarron lifts his head without so much as scraping my skin.

My heart hammers. "Do it."

Jarron flinches.

"I mean it," I say breathlessly, suddenly desperate. Certain beyond words that is what I want. What I need. I need that mark gone. Even with the wolf dead, it won't fade for weeks or months—unless a stronger being covers it. "I don't want that douchebag's mark on me. I want yours."

A rumble of a growl escapes Jarron's chest as he examines me, but he doesn't move, not an inch. He watches me for what feels like hours. When he responds, his voice rumbles with alien power.

"Do you wish for me to claim you, bright one?"

I jerk back. "What?" I squeak. "I—that's not the same thing, is it?"

His dark smile sends a thrill all the way to my spine. A bite and a claiming mark are very different. From the outside, they're similar. The marks will warn off other supernaturals from bothering me because it's a symbol that I'm of interest to someone powerful. But a bite will fade quickly. Laithe feeds from different people weekly, he told me. He does not claim them.

A bite is a casual hookup. A claiming mark is a commitment, the first step in a true bonding.

"He claimed you." The demon studies the puncture marks on my neck. "He had no right, and he did so without permission, so it holds little power, but that is what you ask me to cover. To replace."

I swallow. "You can't get rid of it without claiming me?"

"I can," he purrs and then leans in to nuzzle his nose against my neck.

I suck in a desperate breath.

His voice eases to his normal tone. "But you should be very clear what you're asking of me, sunshine."

"Do it, please. Bite me. Make it go away."

Jarron pulls away to look me in the eye, and he sighs. "No."

My heart plummets. My mind spins, unable to understand the rejection. I stand, and this time, he doesn't stop me. My heart aches as I face the empty room. "Why?"

Slowly, Jarron stands. I don't move as he maneuvers himself to face me, our chests inches apart. He gently places two fingers under my chin and lifts it until my gaze meets his. "I can tell you with absolute certainty there is nothing in the universe that I want more than to cover that mark with my own."

"Then, wh—"

"Because I want more than now. More than tonight. I am playing the long game, Candice."

Something flutters in my chest, but my tension has not alleviated.

"If you wake up in the morning, after all the potions have left your system, and you can look me in the eye and tell me you want this, I will not hesitate. But not now. I can't right now."

I close my eyes against a rush of emotion, then I lean my forehead against his chest. He curls his arms around me, and we stand like that for several minutes.

Eventually, the tension seeps away from my limbs, but he feels so good. Warm and comfortable.

My body begins to feel heavy. My eyelids flutter closed.

Soon, I'm weightless and wrapped inside arms so strong it's the safest I've ever felt. Then, I'm tucked inside silk sheets.

"I missed you," I murmur to the demon tucking me in.

"Mmm. You have no idea how much I missed you, sunshine."

36

BITE ME BETTER

Smooth silk slides against my calves, decadent and perfect.

I twist and look out into the darkness around me. The silhouette of the bed frame surrounding me and a set of chairs in the corner. I'm in Jarron's room.

My heart skips a beat, and then my mind jolts to awareness of everything that happened last night.

That was not the plan.

Not even a little bit.

And yet, I honestly feel nothing but contentment.

The potions are long gone from my system, but there is this sense of ease in my body that I can't explain.

I love it.

I don't want it to end.

I find the demon prince standing on the balcony outside, head dipped low as he peers toward the mountains in the distance. His clothes are the same as last night, wrinkled and twisted.

I look down at myself. Well, I suppose I didn't change my clothes either, but I was also borderline intoxicated. I fell asleep shortly after everyone left—embarrassing.

But perhaps for the best, given the circumstances.

I run my hand over the puncture wounds just above my collarbone.

Jarron must finally notice my movement because he turns to meet my stare through the glass. His expression is wary and almost sad when he approaches. He stops to lean against the doorway between the patio and his room.

"I didn't do it," he says without inflection. "Bite you."

"I know," I whisper. "That's the problem."

Jarron tenses. I find it a relief when shock replaces the sad look in his eyes.

"Come here," I say. His bed is so comfortable I'll be sorry to leave it. But then again, maybe I don't have to.

He swallows but obeys with careful steps. "Something wrong?"

"Well, not wrong, per se. But I do want something from you."

"Oh?" He quirks a brow.

Jarron approaches slowly, as if I'm an animal he's afraid to spook. I sit on the edge of the bed and peer up at him. He stops just before his legs hit my knees.

I feel powerful again at this moment. Even with those handcuffs mangled, I still have power over my demon prince. I can feel it.

"Bite me."

Every muscle in Jarron's body seems to clench at once. His eyes turn pitch-black.

Snow flutters in through the door behind him, but I don't

feel the chill. I feel only the heat of his gaze and the pounding of my own desperate heart. I want this more than I should, but I won't let fear stop me. Not this time.

This time, I'm taking back power from my assailant. Even from the grave, that asshole has a hold on me, and I'm determined to remove it. There is only one person I trust enough to do it for me.

I can't decide if it's a good thing or a bad thing that I desperately want this as well. I'm afraid of the pain, particularly because what I'm asking for is more than a pleasure bite. I want him to burn away the dead wolf's claim.

"You told me last night that if I were to look you in the eye and ask, you wouldn't hesitate."

He begins breathing again. His teeth stretch into long points.

"Please," I whisper.

A growl reverberates through his chest. He leans in but not close enough. He's still resisting. Annoyance, followed by determination, wells inside of me. I fist his shirt by the lapel. "Bite me now," I demand.

He leans into me, panting hard. Clearly the gentleman-human side is winning, but I don't want to be cherished and protected. I want to be devoured.

I lay back on the bed and touch the uncomfortable bite marks just above my collarbone. He places a knee between my legs and crouches over me.

"Candice," he whispers like a prayer, and he closes the gap between us. I gasp as his lips close over the skin of my neck. The sensation is one-part wonderful and one-part uncomfortable.

My belly flutters.

I want this.

I'm terrified of this.

"Are you sure?" he asks one more time, murmuring against my neck. It sends a shiver down my spine, but he still has not carved into that soft skin, and it's driving me crazy.

This time, I growl. "If you don't fucking bite me, Jarron, I'll get someone else—"

I don't even finish my words before he finally obeys. A monster's sharp teeth breaks open my flesh, digging deep.

Burning, fiery pain rages through my whole body. My muscles clench, but then, in an instant, the pain is gone, washed away like it never happened.

In the instant between, I can feel the pull of blood from my body into his. He grabs both of my wrists and pins them against the bed as he devours me, exactly as I wanted.

Another wave of sensation builds, one so overwhelming and shocking for a moment that I think it's a new form of pain, a bite so cold it hurts, but it soon reveals itself as impossibly intense pleasure. An inferno flaring to life inside my body.

My back arches into him as he takes and takes, and I internally beg him never to stop.

This is a dangerous, terrible *bliss.*

A moan escapes my lips as somehow, impossibly, the pleasure continues to build until my mind cannot handle any more.

My vision goes black, body soaring with a new indescribable high. My soul flares to life and meets the darkness of his.

I couldn't say which way was up or down. I couldn't tell you my own name.

It could have lasted moments, or it could have been hours, wrapped in only him. This darkness and I are one.

Then, all at once, he releases me and I fall to the bed, panting and dizzy.

"No," I whisper. "Keep going."

The predator crouches on top of me and drops his mouth back to my neck. Except, instead of the sharp bite of his fangs, he gently sucks at the sensitive skin.

I squirm as an achy discomfort spreads throughout my neck.

He slides his tongue over my skin, savoring every last drop. I tug him in tightly, fingers digging into his shoulders.

"Fuck, Candice."

I shiver at the desperation in his tone. "Don't stop." Those are words I didn't think I'd ever say about being bitten.

"I have to," he whispers.

I frown. That's not the answer I expected.

"If I take too much, I could hurt you." He nuzzles my neck gently.

"Oh," I squeak stupidly.

"I swear to never harm you. But until we are bound magically, I can't tell when I've taken too much. Let me claim you, sunshine, and this will never have to end."

I shiver, remembering our conversation from last night. I press my palm over the bite.

"It's just a bite," he assures me.

He pushes up, so that our chests are several inches apart. His eyes are hazy, his expression slack. There's bright-red blood on his lips.

He stares at me, at my neck, at my body laying helplessly below him in absolute awe. "You are everything, Candice," he whispers. "Everything I hope for. Everything I desire. Everything I fear."

I sit up on my elbows. "What do you fear?"

His expression falls. "Losing you. Never earning you, truly."

I grip the back of his neck and pull myself up to press my lips into his. My kiss is desperate and claiming. After a beat of surprise, he meets my passion with his own. His tongue slides between my lips, tasting.

His fingers dig into my thigh and pulls me to him as he sits up. I slide onto his lap, strapping my legs around his waist. I want more, so much more.

I want to never leave this room and face reality. I don't want to think about the past or the future. I want only now.

This moment.

This forever.

I don't know how long we stay like this, but I can't get enough of his skin on mine, of his lips, or his taste. All of it.

At some point, though, a deep growl grabs my attention, and we both pause.

Jarron smirks, his eyes shining with a light I haven't seen in weeks. "I think my sunshine is hungry."

I huff out a laugh. Heat rushes to my cheeks. Right, that was my stomach.

Jarron stands, pulling me with him, legs still wrapped around his waist. "Let's go find you something."

"Wait," I squeak. "I—I'd like to clean up first." Who the hell knows what I look like right now?

He reroutes toward the bathroom and slowly sets me on my feet. His eager stare lingers on my neck.

I bite the inside of my cheek to hide my anxiety. I don't feel any new pain right now. Maybe a small ache but nothing sharp or burning like last time. But I don't know if that's because of the blissful rush of our kissing. Will the pain begin when the adrenaline fades?

Once the door shuts behind me, I lean against the marble counter and take in a few deep breaths to calm myself before forcing my gaze into the mirror.

As expected, my hair is an absolute wreck and there are smears of red all over my neck and chest. Upon closer inspection, my new bite mark is bright-red but not any bigger than before.

My fingers shake as I steal a washcloth—which is like baby-butt soft, by the way—and run warm water over it. Carefully, I wipe the smeared blood from my upper body.

I let Jarron bite me.

Begged him to, actually.

While I refuse to feel anything negative about that decision, I do consider how bizarre it is. Less than a year ago, if someone had told me I'd be standing here now, I'd have taken myself to therapy, stat.

I finish wiping the fresh wound and find—it doesn't hurt at all.

No pain? How is that even possible?

The pads of my fingers drift over the bright-red puncture marks. I squirm at the sensation. It's not painful, or even uncomfortable, like that last one, but it is sensitive. Almost like I'm hitting a nerve that sends a jolt through my belly.

Weird.

I brush out my mess of hair into some semblance of tame, and when I open the door, I find Jarron patiently waiting on the arm of the nearest chair.

"How?"

He tilts his head. "How what?"

I run my fingers over the bite marks. The skin is warm to the touch. "The last time I was bitten, it tore me apart. I could barely move my arm for days. This doesn't hurt at all."

Jarron lowers his chin, looking at me through his lashes with dark, angry eyes. He stands and slowly approaches. He palms the side of my face tenderly, but his voice is harsh. "I want to kill him again."

I lean into his touch.

"This is how it always should have been," he whispers, eyes softening. He runs the pad of his thumb over the mark. "He was not careful. He did not care how it would harm you."

I guess I should have realized, given what I know about demon bites—they're supposed to be pleasurable for both parties. What happened with the wolf... wasn't. It was an attack.

"He was trying to mark you. Claim you. You did not accept the mark, and he had to battle through that resistance, creating even more damage. What I did was entirely different. The only magic I used was to clear out what lingered from him. I didn't claim you. And I only took what was given."

"Thank you."

Jarron's smile doesn't reach his eyes. "I'm sorry I didn't protect you."

"I wish you'd stop blaming yourself."

"Maybe one day," he says. "Maybe one day you'll understand why I blame myself and always will."

I run my hands up his chest, and his eyes flutter closed. He relaxes against my touch, and that power is intoxicating.

Without thought, my fingers grip the lapel of his button-up, and I tug him until he brings his lips to mine.

"Is this a dream?" he murmurs against me.

My smirk widens. "No."

He swallows and then rests his hands on my hips. "What changed?"

I don't know that anything did change, truthfully. I still have a lot of those conflicted feelings; it's just that I chose this desire over the pain and fear. I want him. He wants me. And that's all I even want to think about.

"Are we still *friends*?" he asks when I don't answer.

I twist my fingers into his. "I don't know what we are. Let's just take it a day at a time, okay?"

"Okay." He smiles, warm and hopeful. I don't know what this changes, but my own joy is undeniable.

37

DEAR CANDICE

It's funny how one small piece of information can change everything, isn't it? You have these scattered pieces, some that almost fit together, but they don't make sense.

Until you find that seemingly meaningless missing jigsaw piece and it all comes together.

What piece are you missing, Candice?

As for me? If I knew the truth back then, I never would have entered the games.

The Jinn

38
ONE LITTLE BITE AND NOW I'M A PRINCESS

"Hey, Candice," a beautiful voice singsongs. I whip my attention to a blond girl I don't recognize at all. Based on her glowing green eyes, she's powerful. An Elite student, randomly greeting me in the halls?

So strange.

"Hi?" I say awkwardly.

"New BFF?" Janet asks, curling her arm in mine once we pass her by.

"I honestly don't even know who she was."

"Bridget," Thompson says between bites of his chocolate muffin. "She was at the party." Crumbs fall from his lips.

A set of short fae girls smile at me.

"It's the bite," Thompson says. "Well, that, and the hot public make-out session with a certain powerful prince."

I sigh. "It wasn't technically *public.*"

"Well, a quarter of Elite Hall witnessed it, and the others want to pretend they saw it because they don't want to admit they weren't there."

The day after the party, Jarron and I spent a good portion of the morning together. He fed me a luxurious breakfast of peppered bacon steak and the most delicious waffles I've ever tasted. It was heaven.

Then, I worked on potions for a few hours and gossiped the rest of the night away with Lola and Janet. Overall, it may be my favorite Sunday ever.

Today is a whole different story. Not that it's terrible, but my bite-high is wearing off, leaving me with many questions and a whole lot of expectations.

Even my teachers treat me differently. My Orizian teacher is casual, but his gaze drifts to my neck with quiet interest. My next three teachers treat me like royalty, offering me prime seating, extensions on homework, and giving rapt attention anytime I speak.

They didn't act this way when I was officially dating Jarron before. Now, I get one little bite and I'm a pretty princess in their minds.

Again, the supernatural world is weird.

I guess it's a little different for me too, though. I haven't committed to the idea of being with Jarron long-term, but at least I know now that it's what he wants. So, it's within my grasp if I choose that route. I just don't spend a lot of time considering that option yet.

One day at a time.

As I walk toward the lunch hall, I receive smiles and waves, where last week, I'd been getting glares and scrutinizing stares.

A large shifter paces in the lobby outside the lunchroom. His white button-up is on backward and the word COWARD is painted in red on his back.

My lips twist as I stop beside him. "You guys can go ahead in," I tell my friends. Janet's eyes are wide, staring at the large shifter pacing around. Thompson pulls her forward, and Lola soars over their heads.

"Elliot?" I ask.

He blinks as if he's in a daze. "Candice?"

"Are you headed in?" I point to the doorway to the lunchroom.

"No, I don't think so."

"Something wrong?"

He nods rapidly. "Yep. Uh-huh. But uh, nothing I didn't see coming. Just don't wanna make it worse."

I tilt my head, watching him. He's fidgety, but he doesn't seem particularly fearful. Nervous and awkward, yes. But not afraid.

"Were you spelled?" The backward shirt, I remember, is the sign that he failed the game at the Elite party, so it's open season on messing with him.

"Confusion stun. Almost wearing off, though. Much better than the itching hex Manuela performed earlier this morning."

I wince. "Don't lose truth or dare in Elite Hall," I mutter as a reminder to myself. This does not look fun.

"Don't worry, no one would mess with you even if you lost. Jarron wouldn't allow it."

"Well, you don't deserve it either."

He nods rapidly again. "Damn Thompson put me in a lose-lose situation."

"Would you like to come sit with me and my friends? We won't do anything to you."

He swallows. "Can I walk in behind you?"

I nod. "Stay close."

I try not to laugh when Elliot crouches behind me as we walk between the tables. Elliot slips into one of the inner chairs, eyeing Thompson suspiciously, as soon as we reach my usual group.

I point to the chuckling Thompson. "You don't mess with him."

"Damn, I was hoping you'd have a fun curse potion for him."

I grimace. "He didn't do anything wrong. If anyone deserves the ridicule, it's you for making that stupid dare to start with."

I flop down in my chair.

"As I seem to remember, my dares did quite well by the end of the night." Thompson grins.

I try to pretend I'm not blushing. I resist the urge to touch my shiny new bite marks. I make no attempt to hide these ones today, and I will not dwell too long on why that is.

Several tables, including the Elite table, watch us, and I can't tell if their attention is on Elliot or me. Maybe both. I turn away quickly when I meet Jarron's hooded gaze, but my lips betray me with a bashful grin.

I introduce Elliot to Janet and Lola. He waves. "I don't know many pixies," he comments. "Or trolls, I suppose."

"You're missing out," I say with a smile.

"How did ya'll like the party?"

"Oh, I didn't stay long. I just wanted to check it out and then hang out with my boyfriend." Janet curls her fingers between Marcus's.

"She was too cool for us." I wink.

Lola's wings shimmer, shedding purple dust.

"Lola had a great time," I say for her.

"I'm glad someone d—" Elliot freezes as a shadow falls over the table.

Jarron's face is expressionless when he says, "Mind if I sit here?"

My stomach does a stupid flutter.

"Of course not!" Janet answers quickly with a near-panicked expression, looking around for an open chair. Jarron wordlessly finds his own, scooting in behind Janet, Marcus, and Thompson, across the table from me.

I smile at him, but it flickers out quickly. Not because I'm unhappy he's here, but because my mind is spinning through entirely too much, and most of the feelings welling up are not things I want to give much attention to.

Then, the ridiculousness of the situation hits me, and it seems the rest of the cafeteria as well. The chattering rises to a crescendo.

Jarron, the Crown Prince of the Under World is sitting at a Minor Hall table, next to a low-level human, a troll, and a pixie.

But then again, as I look around at the friend group we've established, there's also a Major Hall mage and two Elite wolves. Maybe this isn't the outcast table anymore.

Jarron fidgets with his silver rings. It's the only sign he feels anything more than ease and confidence. When I glance up, I meet his dark stare, and a jolt of emotions I won't dare name shoots through me.

I force logic to take hold. Jarron is my friend.

"I'm glad you're here," I tell him with a soft smile.

His throat bobs.

"It's about time you joined the cool table," Thompson says, elbowing Jarron's bicep.

Lola darts around the table like she can't control her happiness. She settles back down on her perch and then forces a chat about Janet's painting project. Janet explains that she's sketched the layout—she decided on a carnival theme.

"Ooh, that'll be so cool," I tell her.

"If I can get the music right, it will be."

"Oh, maybe I can help," Lola offers happily.

Elliot asks a few polite questions about the project. He seems genuinely interested by the end of the conversation. As a shifter, magic is not his strongest suit. But he seems to like understanding people different from himself, which I can respect.

For the first time in weeks, I've stopped noticing the reactions happening around me. All that matters are the people here with me.

Jarron's body language oozes ease. He does that powerful alpha male, casual slouch that I secretly like, but I also notice the tension in his shoulders that he tries to hide. And I think everyone notices the way his attention continuously darts to me then back to his hands, or whoever is talking at the moment.

Elliot is a bit distracted most of the time, but it's still kind of nice having him.

"So, Lola," Thompson drawls, "what's up with you and Stassi?"

Lola's wings tinkle, and she glows slightly. "Oh, nothing really. He's fun to flirt with, but I don't think anything will come of it."

Elliot snorts. "True. Hard to imagine a long-term relationship between a wolf and a pixie."

Lola rolls her eyes.

"Why don't you have a pixie mate?" Elliot asks. "Don't you usually have an arranged mate early in life?"

Lola doesn't respond to that, and I watch her reaction carefully. She doesn't giggle or correct him, but she also doesn't wiggle or sparkle like she would if she were being bashful.

"You're, like, not even around pixies ever. I always assumed you were a major dud or an outcast or something."

I glare at Elliot. "How is that something you say to someone?"

He blinks at me. A low sound reverberates from Jarron's chest, and that's when Elliot seems to realize how rude the comment was and blushes. "Oh, sorry. I don't usually hang with people who care about that sorta thing."

"Everyone cares about that sorta thing; you just get away with it because you're strong. If you wanna be here with us, you're nice to all of my friends or you're out. Or better yet, I'll use my truth-telling potion on you. You're still free pickings thanks to truth or dare, right? I'd be willing to bet you've got a secret or two you wouldn't like getting out."

Elliot swallows hard. "Yes, ma'am. I'll behave."

I huff and cross my arms, sincerely worried he struck a nerve with Lola. Janet begins a conversation about weird wolf traditions with Thompson, who plays along nicely. Before long the conversation is forgotten and the tension eases.

But the fact that Lola is quiet for the entire rest of the lunch period tells me she hasn't quite let the comments go.

Our group eventually disbands. Lola soars off on a search

for extra credit, Janet and Marcus slip away to make out probably, and Elliot rushes into a crowd to hide from his hecklers.

"You coming to hang in Elite Hall today?" Thompson asks casually. I resist the urge to glare because I know he's only asking for Jarron's benefit.

I sigh. I actually wanted to—that library is tempting now that it's an option again—but I'm concerned about Lola.

"No, not today," I answer without comment on his meddling. "I wanna spend time in Minor Hall with Janet and Lola."

He nods absently. "All right, I accept that excuse. Tomorrow, then?" He grins widely and then skips off down the hall without waiting for an answer.

"You don't have to feel pressured," Jarron says under his breath.

"Everyone thinks we're together again, ever since the bite."

Jarron tenses but doesn't comment. Right, that was probably a stupid comment. We are almost, kind of, sort of together again?

"It was good to have you sit with us today," I say quietly to cover my awkward comment.

"Was it?" he asks.

I nod. "I liked you being there." When I meet his eyes with a sincere smile, he returns it with one of his own. This boy is going to be the death of me. I sometimes have to actively remind myself of Janet's and Lola's assessment that I really can get past the idea of my sister being his mate. I'm still not convinced, even though I do accept the logic.

Other times, being around Jarron just feels so incredibly

right that I forget every doubt I've ever had. I live for those moments.

This is not one of them.

"Origins of magical objects, right?" he asks as we turn down a hall toward the eastern wing.

I nod. He knows my entire schedule now. Even though the black magic suffocating the entire student body is noticeably absent today, he still insists I'm never alone. He's recruited Stassi to walk with me from occult ethics to potions, and Thompson is with me in the mornings. Laithe tends to show up to and from combat class. There is at least one Elite student with me every moment between classes.

"Learning anything interesting in that class?"

"No, not really. It's more history and basic foundational information. We don't really get into anything cool until level two, which I won't reach before graduation."

"Well, if you want to learn it, I'm pretty confident you will."

I nod. "Potions take up most of my focus for now. Maybe one day, I'll be able to do something cool with objects."

"Mastering one thing before dabbling in another is a wise choice."

We reach my classroom, and I stop. "Hey, by the way, I just wanted to mention that I got another... message."

"From the jinn?" His brow pinches. "I'm half tempted to make you move into Elite Hall, whether you want to or not."

I laugh like it's a joke, even though I know it's not.

He twists his lips but shows no other emotions. "Bring it to classes tomorrow? I'll have Laithe do an investigation on it."

"Or maybe I can bring it to Elite Hall after classes tomorrow?"

"Really?"

"I could use a trip to that library." I force a smile and enter the classroom, pretending my heart isn't aching terribly at the sight of his eyes lighting up.

39

BEHIND ALIEN EYES

I don't know who I'm actually kidding. I'm in way too deep with Jarron to pretend this isn't real.

A swarm of butterflies performs an elaborate dance in my stomach when he smiles at me from the entrance to Elite Hall. His hand is in his pocket, and that half smile carves its way through my heart.

Is this my future? I ask myself for the first time.

It's too soon to think about that, though, and I force the question to the very back of my mind.

"Hey," I say shyly.

He greets me casually and guides me through the massive Elite entryway to find Laithe in the brightly lit main lobby beneath the array of windowpanes. They're leaning against one of the armchairs but stand up straight as we approach.

I rummage in my bag to pull out the new note and hand it to Jarron first. His jaw clenches as he reads. "I never would have entered the games," he reads the last line aloud. "What does that mean?"

I shrug. "I have no idea," I say. It's hard to wrap my mind around what it could mean. "Do you think it's a clue?"

He shrugs and hands it off to Laithe, who scans it quickly but gives away no reaction at all before they stand and walk down the hall, note in hand.

"Should we follow?" I ask when Jarron doesn't move.

Jarron shakes his head. "Laithe will inform me of any updates. You and I are headed to the library."

"Really?" My stomach swoops as I take his outstretched hand. "I suppose I don't mind, but why aren't we going with him?"

We pass by the speakeasy hall and continue toward the library.

"It's unlikely we'll gain any significant information," Jarron explains. "We now know the notes are from someone involved in the games. They will not make it easy to find them, so our goal now isn't tracking; it's information gathering. We'll check in on our leads then send the information to the authorities. Before, when we thought it might be a vindictive student, we had very different goals."

That's very wise. And also, a tad frustrating. If the authorities find Mr. Vandozer, will I miss my chance to carve his heart from his chest the way I've imagined?

"Where did the last one lead? I never heard."

Laithe went on to track the notes into Oriziah, and I'm assuming they found a dead end because they never said anything.

"The spell faded before Laithe could get much more information. It led toward a mountain range where the Vandozer family line has lived for centuries, but it's not much to go on."

We stop at the top of the large staircase set into the

massive multi-story library with thousands and thousands of books. I'm overwhelmed by the beauty and possibilities of this place again.

"I had my parents send several patrols to search those mountains. No luck."

I blink back my focus, registering his words. "Do we think this new note will lead to the same place?"

Jarron gently tugs me down the stairs into the library of my dreams. I'm trying to pay attention to his words, but my mind is also spinning through all of the things I want to search out here.

"My guess is he had been hiding in those mountains until we tracked the note there. I'm not sure how much he's involved in these notes, but he may be keeping a close eye on our movements here. The possibilities for spies in this school are boundless. So, I suspect he knows we'd track his general location and fled. So, no, I think it'll lead us somewhere new."

I reroute our descent into the second story of the library. Jarron follows obediently and releases my hand only when I begin brushing my fingers against the spines of the potions books, seeking out the exact right one.

Jarron finds a comfortable spot against the railing, watching my every move with interest.

I anticipated browsing this section for a long while, but a title catches my attention almost immediately. I slide the book from the shelf eagerly. It's thin and worn, with dark-blue leather casing and silver lettering.

Combat Potions: A guide to using potions for defensive and offensive means.

The breath catches in my lungs. I don't even need to flip through it to know it's perfect. I consider continuing to browse, but there are other sections that I'm burning to get to, so I promise myself I'll be back here soon to look some more.

I smile at Jarron and motion for him to follow me deeper into the library. He wordlessly pushes from the railing and catches up with only a few long strides. I find another set of stairs near the end of the row, and I skip down to the main level and then twist and turn to where I remember the small Orizian section.

"For class," I mutter. The amused look in Jarron's eye tells me he knows it's a lie, but he doesn't comment.

There's more than one subject I'd like to peruse here, but I'm not sure if I'm bold enough to select a book on Orizian mating rituals while Jarron is watching me. I still want to know more about how the mates thing works, but it seems like everyone is hiding the details from me. Then again, maybe the information I need is not written in any books, otherwise it wouldn't be such heavily guarded secrets.

First, I look for a title that's been stuck in my head for days now.

I have no idea if it would be in this section or not, but given the context of my sister's journal entry, there's a possibility. I drift my finger over each title, one at a time. There are only maybe two hundred books in this section, so if it's here, I won't miss it.

My heart shudders when I find it. *Behind Alien Eyes* by Margarette Showalter.

I don't know what to expect from this book. For some reason, I have this overwhelming sense that this book will connect me with Liz. For better or worse, it will give me insight into her emotions in her last days.

I need it, but I'm not sure I'm ready for it.

My fingers tremble as I grip the spine and slide it from the stack. This book is shiny laminate, much newer than my potions book. The spine crackles when I pry it open. The title page reads:

Behind Alien Eyes.

A compassionate study of High Orizian culture through the lens of an outsider

I turn the next page, and something slips out, fluttering to the floor. Ice crackles against the shelves before I'm able to even register what the object was.

"What the hell is that?" Jarron growls.

I swallow, finding the small card that dropped from between the pages. A tarot card, with the image of a jinn on it.

The Akrasia Games calling card.

40
PLAY ALONG

Jarron paces on the main floor of the library. Shadows cover the ceiling, and I'm shivering in the chill permeating the room. Though there weren't many people in here before, now we're entirely alone. Even the librarians scattered once it became clear Jarron was upset.

My heart races, but the volatile demon in front of me is the most direct concern, so I hold on to my other questions.

His first reaction was to make a phone call to someone in the Interdimensional Courts. He was not calm when he yelled in an order to send in everyone they have now.

I don't even know what that means, but I don't have the gall to ask for details at the moment.

"How?" he mutters more to himself than anything. "How, out of thousands of books, would you select the one with that card in it?" He continues pacing back and forth.

"It was in her journal entry," I whisper.

His black eyes flash up to mine.

"The missing entry that showed up on my door a week

ago? She mentioned this book." I hold up *Behind Alien Eyes.* "That's why I picked it up. I don't know how long the card has been in there, but once Laithe arrives, I'm sure we can get a better idea."

Jarron growls. "They cannot have you."

I don't respond to that because, as much as I enjoy the violent protector thing, I have a deep intrinsic need to find and kill Mr. Vandozer. I'm not letting this go. So, if I have to follow the trace myself to find him, I will.

Jarron growls every time I even take a few steps away from the table. I'm assuming he's remembering the last time the games reached out like this and I went running. Never mind that we were fighting at that time, but I'm not going to argue with him.

"Laithe is coming, right?" I ask. Because there's something I need from them if Jarron won't let me move.

He nods and continues his pacing.

I sit at the table and wait, leg bouncing restlessly. I try to distract my mind from what all of this could mean by flipping through the book. They must have delivered that journal entry just so I'd go looking for the book, right? And left the card, knowing I'd eventually find it.

The big question is, why? Are they expecting me to do something? There are no other instructions like there were last time. And why not just deliver the card to my door? Obviously, they have access to my dorm room because they've been sending me messages for weeks. Is this all an elaborate scheme to get into our heads?

It's clearly working on Jarron. His fingers have been replaced by massive claws, and curling black horns have appeared on his head.

To control my own nervous energy, I flip casually through the book while Jarron paces back and forth until Laithe finally arrives.

Laithe stomps in, their expression wary.

Jarron points to the calling card like it's a snake that will strike me at any moment, before Laithe even reaches us. There is sweat on Laithe's brow, but otherwise, they seem calm as they approach.

"It was in the book," I explain when Laithe peers over at the card. When they still don't move any closer, I give them a quick summary of how I found it and why.

Still, nothing. I want to shake them both. What are you doing? Laithe's gaze shoots to Jarron then back to the card, tension growing in the lines on their face.

"We need to find Corrine," I say finally. "I need to know if she's still here, in the school. If she's not—"

Laithe's expression is slack as they say the words that send a shiver down my spine. "The games have begun."

I swallow. My mind spins.

If only I'd known the truth, I never would have entered the games.

My blood runs cold.

What piece of information are you missing, Candice?

"He's not going to let you out of his sight. I'll..." Laithe looks over their shoulder. "I'll go and send a messenger to Minor Hall."

I sigh, realizing they're right. Laithe is too strong to go in, and Jarron isn't going to let me go. "Find Lola or Janet. Send them."

Laithe nods then strolls purposefully from the room. My

skin is crawling, a feeling inside telling me I need to move. Telling me I'm running out of time for something.

But what?

Is that my instinct telling me to follow the card? To go chasing after the games a second time?

My hands shake as I flip through the book some more, barely able to register the words until I reach a page with notes in the margin. I pick the book up with both hands and lean over it, bringing it close to my face.

Is this why he attacked? one of the notes reads.

He was mine all along? Why didn't I see that?

I flip to the next page; there are more random notes and a few highlights in a section about Orizian mates. My heart pounds even harder.

The actual content of the book seems to be fairly tame, with no mention of chosen mates or imprinting, but instead focuses on how a demon will cherish their mate above anything else, even above their own kingdom. It does tell the story of a young demon that destroyed a goblin consulate in defense of his mate, but it's painted in a romantic light.

Why didn't he tell me? This one is written in harsh dark letters, like the writer was angry.

I turn to the next page. The end of the chapter. The page is half empty of text, but the rest is filled in by scrawled hand-writing.

Dear Candice,

. . .

I PRAY this message finds you. He doesn't know I've sent it, and it has to stay that way. There's so much to tell you and not a lot of time for me to pen this before the plan is set. Vincent is baiting you, expecting to lure you and Jarron in. He has this elaborate plan that I don't agree with, but I don't have a choice but to go with it. The more I play along the easier it will be to save you both.

I need you to play along too, with a few exceptions.

Follow the tattoo, not the card. It will lead you to me.

I will do everything I can to protect you both.

With all of my love,

Liz

41
ANOTHER PART OF THE GAMES...?

I slam the book closed. My face is burning hot, head pulsing.

What. The. Fuck.

It's another joke, right? Another tactic to mess with us. All of it has been. This is part of the game. Another puzzle piece that's supposed to throw me off and distract me from the real answer.

Jarron stops pacing and turns slowly to face me. He examines me closely, and I try my best not to show my panic.

"What is it?" he says with a voice so low I'm not sure if it's him or his demon talking.

I tap my knee anxiously. "Nothing. Just... everything."

He narrows his eyes.

I stand, unable to hold in my own tension now.

I pretend I'm going to browse more books, but Jarron follows right on my heels.

Follow the tattoo, not the card.

Without thinking, I run my fingers over the faded mark on

my forearm. It's not generally noticeable, even when I'm in short sleeves, since it's nearly translucent and really only stands out when light reflects off of it. Particularly because I wear makeup to cover it.

Jarron moves so fast it's near a blur as he grabs my wrist and twists, just on the verge of hurting.

"Hey!" I complain.

He bares his teeth and pushes me up against the endcap shelf. "What did you do, Candice?"

"I didn't do anything," I say through gritted teeth. "Let me go."

His whole body is shaking now. He looks again at the tattoo. "When did it happen? What is it?" The expression on his face is a mix of terror and rage, making me think he already has an idea.

"It just showed up—after the last time I spoke with Mr. Vandozer."

The sound that rips from Jarron's chest sends terror cascading through my body.

Swirling black clouds twists out and around my wrist.

"What are you doing?" I squeak, squirming in his grip.

"Breaking this magic. No one can have a claim on you."

Anger wells up and replaces the fear. I rip my hand from Jarron's firm grip. I'm sure he could have kept his hold, but not without hurting me. "No."

"No?" His skin loses all of the golden pigment until it's just grey. Wings shimmer into existence behind him.

"No, you cannot break the magic. We—we need it." I wince as the words leave my lips. *Follow the tattoo.*

If I believe that, does that mean I have to believe the rest of the note? If it was just a means to mess with me, then following its directions wouldn't make sense. "It's not a full mark, it doesn't have a hold on me, but it does give me a connection to them. We can use it to find the games. To find Corrine and Mr. Vandozer."

"You will not be finding anyone," the demon hisses.

I put my hands on my hips. "If Corrine is gone, it's because she was called in to the Akrasia Games. She is our only link to those games, and therefore Mr. Vandozer. If we lose her, we'll never find them, and my sister's killer will remain free. Tell me, do you have a way to track her?"

He squints. "The interdimensional authorities are tracking her."

"You know the game runners have covered her tracks as well as they possibly can. They'll have prepared for them to follow her."

His nostrils flare, chest heaving, but he does not give a rebuttal.

"After we find her, you can break the magic. But we need to find her first." I didn't realize this was something Jarron was capable of, but that doesn't matter at this point.

He stares down at the tiny magic on my wrist like it's a breathing parasite that might leap onto him at any moment. When he doesn't answer, I take this opportunity to escape and begin marching from the library.

"No," Jarron finally growls and prowls after me. "You are not going. I don't care if it's our last chance to find him. I don't care if that girl dies. I am not putting you at risk to save her or get to him. It's not worth it."

I walk quickly, not bothering to acknowledge Jarron's objection. He doesn't stop me, but he follows right on my heel, huffing with every step.

Stassi stares wide-eyed over my shoulder at the full demon stalking me when I enter the sunroom.

"Candice?" Stassi whispers. "I don't think—"

"He's fine," I say, waving off the demon from behind me. I might be terrified of this form, but I'm damn good at compartmentalizing, and this is important. I turn to face Jarron.

Even though I just faced him in this monster form moments ago, it's still a shock when I turn toward him once more. His leathery wings fidget behind him, his teeth are bared. His legs have an oddly curved shape.

"You," I point at him, ignoring the patter of my own heart, "sit."

He blinks several times and tilts his head curiously.

Both Stassi and Manuela take that opportunity to scramble away, and I note that it's the first time I've seen Manuela ever show any fear of Jarron.

"Take a deep breath," I tell demon-Jarron. "Calm down. Shift back if you need to." I'm not sure how comfortable it would be for him to sit in a human armchair in that form. "Then, sit down."

"What is your plan?" he asks, voice rumbling in that alien way.

"We're going to have a conversation." My mind is made up, and I'm done running scared. My heart is aching and confused and—I don't know, but if Corrine is gone, I'm going after her.

Finally, his body shimmers slightly as he shifts back into his human form. His face is anything but calm, though. His eyes are sunken, his cheeks sallow. He's angry and ready to explode at any moment, but reluctantly, he obeys me and sits in the chair.

Without missing a beat, I slide into his lap, wrapping my arms around his neck.

After a beat of surprise, Jarron's face softens. He curls an arm around my waist, and another settles on my thigh. He pulls me in tight and nuzzles into my neck.

Jarron breathes in deeply, like he's trying to savor this.

He's not yours.

His arms feel so good around my body, and I try not to wonder if it'll be the last time I have him like this.

What piece are you missing, Candice?

"Last time," I begin softly, remembering several weeks ago when he tried to stop me from entering Minor Hall, where I knew the Akrasia Games would begin. "We were not on the same page. You did everything you could to stop me, and I did everything I could to do it anyway. We can play that game again if you want."

His nostrils flare again, but he doesn't respond.

"But I think, instead, we could be a team."

The last time, I basically drugged him to get through the barrier. And he followed me anyway, which almost resulted in his death.

"We could make decisions together, instead of always against each other. I know you don't want me to be in danger. You feel like it's your job to protect me. But you told me once that you value my will. You know I cannot sit by and let the same authorities that failed my sister's investigation face my enemy for me. I don't trust them to do it right. I have to do something."

Again with that heartbreaking look. His wide, terrified eyes search my expression. My big, powerful protector that's utterly desperate to keep me safe.

"You make that face a lot these days," I whisper.

"What face?"

"The one that looks like someone killed your favorite puppy."

His brows furrow. "What?"

"You look sad. Like—completely devastated."

He takes in a long breath. "I'm fucking terrified, Candice."

I curl into him and wrap my arms around his waist.

"I'm so scared I'm going to lose you. I can't—I won't survive it."

That sounds a little melodramatic, but I assume it's not a helpful comment, so I keep it to myself. He's afraid. He's allowed to be.

"I know," I whisper.

"You don't, but that's okay. I understand this is something you have to do," he says. "There is a sting operation being formed now, getting ready to move in on the location we pinpoint by tracking the card. You're right not to trust them entirely. I'm afraid they'll be too slow or that the game runners will not show up."

My heart clenches. They'll get away like they have so many times before.

"But they seem to want you as badly as we want them," he says with a resigned sigh.

I let a beat of silence pass before I respond. "So, there is a higher likelihood that they will be there if we... play along."

He holds up a finger. "Only long enough for the authorities to arrive. They do the bulk of the work. We are the bait, and you never leave my side. I will demolish anything and everything, kill anyone, to get you out alive if something goes against this plan. Do you understand?"

I swallow and nod, heart racing.

He leans into my neck and breaths me in one last time before he pushes his body up, taking me along with him. He holds me like a bride. Or a damsel in distress.

I cling to him, wondering what exactly he's doing now.

"What's going on?" a voice calls.

I twist in Jarron's arms to find Manuela in the hall, her eyes wide with curiosity. Any fear she had before is safely tucked away.

"Get ready," Jarron says dramatically. "We're going to war."

"What?" She puts her hand on her hips.

"And go get Thompson," Jarron calls over his shoulder. "If he wants to be my ally, now is the time to prove himself."

Jarron strolls away from the gawking Manuela with me still in his arms, out of Elite Hall.

42
THIS ISN'T LIKE BEFORE

"You can put me down, you know?"

Jarron's lips twitch. "I know."

"So, can you? I feel super weird being carried like a baby through the school." We're heading in the direction I want to go, so I'm not overly concerned it's just... odd.

He doesn't respond to my request. We pass a few students who gawk and whisper at our odd performance.

"Jarron?" I ask.

"Can you just let me hold you while I can?" he whispers. "It makes me feel better about this. For now."

I bite the inside of my lip. Then, I finally whisper, "Okay."

Jarron carries me all the way through the school. Past the main lobby and the spiraling stairs. Up the set of wonky narrow steps. Down the old hall with linoleum floors. And he finally stops in front of the shimmering gates of Minor Hall, where Laithe is waiting for us.

"What is it?" I ask, squirming in Jarron's arms.

"Corrine is gone. They found this in her room." Laithe holds up a card to match my own.

Jarron's next breath shakes.

I let him take his time before finally setting me on my feet. I remain cocooned in his arms, heart hammering. Then, I curl my arm up over his neck, hop up on my tippy toes, and press my lips to his. The kiss is quick, but Jarron looks dazed all the same.

"What—"

"This isn't like before," I tell him. "I'm going through there and coming right back. I won't leave without you, I promise."

He runs the pad of his thumb over my bottom lip. "Okay."

I gently twist from his arms and pass through the magical barrier of Minor Hall.

I DOUBLE-CHECK all of my vials and ensure I've got every spot memorized. I didn't have the chance to finish up the potions Thompson suggested, so I won't have any stunning bombs just yet.

Maybe I'll never need them.

I take in a long breath and force a few sips of water down my dry throat, and then I leave my room behind and head out toward my hopes and terrible fears.

Janet throws her arms around me the moment I make it into the game room. Lola wiggles between us to join in on the hug.

"You're going after her?" Janet asks.

I nod against her shoulder. "I have to. It might be our only chance to shut the games down for good. Backup is on the way, but we don't want to lose the trail before they can get here."

Janet sighs and glances to Lola, who puffs out her chest and wiggles her wings.

"We're coming," Lola says definitively. "Right?"

Janet flinches.

"You really don't have to come," I assure her, ignoring Lola's confidence. It's great that she wants to come, but if Janet isn't as sure... "I mean it. I will not think one iota less of you. I swear it."

Janet's shoulders slump. "I'd like to help. We all want those games that take advantage of lower-lever supernaturals to be shut down for good, but... can I even help? Will I just be in the way?"

I want to tell her no, but I can't be sure of that. "I don't know. I don't know what we're walking into, to be honest. But I know you're strong. Stronger than me. So, if you want to come, I want you there. But I can't promise you'll be safe, so if you don't—"

"I'll go," she whispers.

I swallow, uncertain if I said the right thing. Should I push her not to go so she'll stay safe? Should I support her and convince her to come along?

I honestly don't know, but I don't have the time or energy for an internal debate. She's going to have to make the decision for herself.

"If you're sure—"

She holds out her hand, palm up. "Let's do this. For all of Minor Hall."

I allow an honest smile and put my hand over hers. Lola does the same.

Lola spins in the air. "The Akrasia Games are going down."

43
PORTAL TO HELL

Janet, Lola, and I march out of Minor Hall together with our heads up.

Jarron is leaning against the wall casually, hand in his pocket and everything. Except, his body exposes his emotions are less than calm, considering his eyes are pitch-black and there are curling horns sprouting from his hair.

I leave Janet and Lola at the gate and approach the volatile half-demon. "Hey," I whisper. "I'm here."

"I'm not doing a very good job of staying calm," he tells me.

"I can see that."

He steps forward until he's towering over me. His fingers have sharp blade-like tips, but when he carefully touches my cheek with the base of his palm, it's smooth and gentle. "My bright one." The words rumble from his chest, low enough the others may not have even heard it. "I'm supposed to protect you. You aren't supposed to ever have to face danger like this again."

I meet his stare like a challenge. "I don't need a protector. I need a partner."

Finally, his horns and claws retreat. "I know. But that doesn't mean it's easy."

I wrap my arms around him, cheek against his chest. His resounding sigh holds a hurricane of emotions. We remain like this, hearts pounding in unison, arms clinging to each other, for several moments before I finally pull back.

Pretty sure he'd have stayed like that forever if it meant delaying this dangerous quest.

I hold out my wrist. "Can you help me?"

His now entirely human fingers, silver rings and all, grasp my forearm. He runs the pad of his thumb over my wrist. "There are two," he whispers.

I glance down to find the small red dot that appeared after the secret vow. "One is a secret with Janet and Lola."

"Secret?" he whispers.

"Mmhmm," I say, trying to pretend not to be utterly distracted by the sensation of his fingers running up my forearm.

He gives me a knowing look.

"They're—they're in the Forest of Nails," he tells me. How he knows that I haven't a single clue.

My stomach sinks. Of course they are. The Forest of Nails is where my sister died, or at least, where they found her body, and it's not far from campus.

"Where are we going?" I ask as we pass the front door of the school and head down the corridor labeled *Portals.*

The Forest of Nails is only three miles away. I can't imagine there is a portal that leads there from here.

"Trust me," he says.

The hair on my arms rises as we enter the large corridor lined with portals on each side. Their pulsing magic all at once feels like electricity. The magnitude of so many worlds colliding into one presses down on me.

I cross my arms and try my best not to let the oppressive magic get under my skin. This is not an enemy I can fight, but it feels like an enemy all the same. These worlds, full of people who'd see me as a meaningless bug.

It's not the danger that bothers me. It's the realization of how little I am in comparison.

I wonder if that's how Lola feels on a regular basis.

At the end of the dozens of portals, two figures lean over a stone basin. I expected Laithe, but I hadn't expected Manuela.

"Is it ready?" Jarron seems so much more at ease right now than even minutes ago in Minor Hall. Perhaps the shock has finally worn off.

"Not yet," Laithe answers. "A few minutes."

Jarron looks around the room. "No Thompson?"

Laithe shrugs. "He said he'd be here."

"What are they doing?" Janet asks, standing on her tippy toes to peer over at Manuela's spell without getting any closer.

"Creating a shortcut, and an escape plan," Jarron answers.

My lips part. Manuela is casting some elaborate spell over an empty, shallow basin on the ground. A circle, only a few feet in diameter. "Do you mean to tell me that Manuela is *making* a portal?"

"Of sorts."

"She can do that?" Janet exclaims. Portals take days to create and chart, even for skilled magic users. The idea that a student in this school has the ability to just make one on the spot is absolutely ludicrous. Even if it will only take us a few miles away.

He nods. "The mixture of dryad and witch magic allows her to create a portal through specific tree root systems. We'll portal in half a mile from where the tattoo has pinpointed. We've been able to establish that there are no major players in that area so it will give us some cushion."

"How in the hell did you plan all of this in the last thirty seconds?"

"Your sense of time seems to be a tad off." He smirks.

"Five minutes, thirty seconds—what difference does it make? You only figured out where the tattoo led a few minutes ago."

"Laithe gathered supplies and our portal-making ally and was here waiting when I sent them instructions."

"*Sent them instructions*?" I repeat stupidly.

He tilts his head, as if surprised I'm not aware of the answer. "We are bonded."

"And that means you can, what, send Laithe psychic messages?"

He shrugs. "Not exactly. But close enough."

Right. Okay, so they do have a psychic link. I bookmark this in my mind to come back to later. I have a lot of questions.

"So, once she's finished with the portal," Jarron continues, "Candice and I, and whomever else chooses to join, will enter the portal. We will need to be quiet, but please each do whatever you can to memorize the spot of the portal in case you need to retreat."

"Got it," Lola says, voice firm. Janet looks less sure.

"Done," Manuela announces. She straightens and brushes her hands on her slacks. Her skin is paler than usual.

"Good luck," Laithe says to me with a solemn nod.

I squint. "You're not coming?"

"No. Laithe will be entering a different portal."

Laithe grins, exposing sharp canines and then marches right through a portal with red glowing power.

"The portal to Oriziah is open?" I nearly squeak. I thought they were supposed to be closed until someone from administration approves them being opened.

Jarron nods. "Manuela opened that portal before she set to work creating the new one. Laithe is going to rally help from home. In case we need it."

Last time, we only survived because Trevor was able to get to us in time. I try not to let any of that information—or the fact that Laithe just *casually walked through a portal to the Under World three feet away*—dig too far into my mind. I need to focus.

"I wouldn't bring Laithe either way, though. That really just gives them a sense of purpose rather than sitting around waiting to find out if we need help."

"What do you mean?"

"Our link means they're able to know if I'm in danger and where I am. Keeping them behind, where they can act as a messenger to Ms. Bhatt or my family, is the best help to our mission."

"I see." My stomach clenches. "Are we ready, then?" I say, mostly to ignore the anxiety swirling in me.

"I was hoping Thompson would show," Jarron says, looking disappointed.

"What is going on with you two anyway?" I did not miss his comment about being his ally. Has he made him promises? And if so, in exchange for what?

Rustling from the end of the room catches our attention. "I'm here!" Thompson calls, clomping down the hall.

"We nearly left without you," Jarron says, like a teacher chiding a student.

"Sorry. I had something to put together before I came."

Thompson stops short, panting. Jarron stomps forward and points to Thompson's chest. "Your job is to keep her safe. Do that, and I'll give you anything you want. Understand?"

Thompson's eyes flare, then he nods eagerly.

Oh great, more questions for me to be anxious over. What the hell? I'm going to have stomach ulcers before this is over.

Based on their interactions, I have to assume that they've had conversations about me in private. Does Jarron know what Thompson is after? He's uncovered the secret and believes he can trust him?

Or did Thompson tell him?

Why would he tell Jarron and not me? Why hasn't Jarron told me?

And most of all, why do I care so much?

44
I DON'T WANT TO BE A PAWN

The zing of the portal magic sends an uncomfortable shiver through my whole body, but then it's gone, replaced by the much more pleasant sensation of Jarron's arms around me.

An icy breeze bites into the bit of exposed skin at my neck. We are in the middle of a small forest clearing. Jarron tugs me a few feet away from the tree behind us, and in the next moment, Thompson is barreling out of the bark. He stumbles but keeps his balance.

Whoa. That's not like any other portal I've ever seen. Portals are usually in a blank space with some kind of border —a doorway, stone arches, or even between two trees. But I've never seen one that allows someone to travel *through the tree.*

"What is that?"

Jarron raises his finger to my lips. "Dryad magic," he whispers. "Ask questions later."

Right. No noise. Memorize the area so I can find it again. I never mentioned that I'm directionally disadvantaged. I couldn't say which way is south for my life. And those mountains? All look the exact same. So...

Jarron leans into the tree and taps a strip of bark that's lighter than the others. I'm not sure I'd have noticed it without him pointing it out. I guess that's how I'm supposed to find the tree?

That's helpful... I suppose. We'll see if I'll be able to find it again when I'm looking at three hundred trees all at once. He leans into me, moving slow, almost sensually. My heart patters at the thought.

He taps my ear three times.

Listen? I focus on the sounds of the forest and find—there aren't any. No rustling leaves, despite the cool breeze. No birds or bugs. It's unnervingly still.

Another hint. That one is easier to notice. I'll just have to pay attention to when sounds return so I'll know the radius of the sound barrier.

Janet and Lola exit the portal next and look around with surprised stares. Jarron reminds them to remain quiet with a tap to his lips, then he grabs my hand, and together we walk toward our collective enemies.

#

We walk slowly for a few minutes until the noise of the forest suddenly appears. Birds chirp, and branches rustle in the wind. *Candice,* I hear someone whisper.

Jarron stops me and grips my forearm. My partial tattoo warms, and I suck in a breath. "Can you feel it?" he asks.

I nod but look over my shoulder to uncover the source of the whisper.

No one else comments on it. Is it in my imagination?

"If anything happens and we're separated, you run far away from that feeling. Do you understand?"

I swallow but agree.

"I've cast a silence spell, so we can talk for now. Keep it down, though." Jarron releases my arm and continues his march through the forest, stepping through bushes and over fallen branches.

My group of friends gather around me, with Jarron up front, leading us forward.

"So, we gonna talk about that tattoo?" Thompson asks.

I eye him without turning his direction, arms crossed.

"We gonna talk about that offer Jarron made? What did you ask him for?"

His eyebrows rise, but his expression remains casual. "That's been bothering you?"

I mean, only for the last few minutes, but yes.

There's certainly a part of me that's annoyed that he'd tell Jarron his secret but not me—the person he's been developing a relationship with. There's more to it, though.

"Maybe I'm not a fan of being blatantly used as a bargaining chip."

"Candice." He says it like I'm a child making an absurd claim.

I pinch my lips together. I watch the trees closely as we pass them, trying not to get too lost. I'm certain it's a hopeless cause, though.

He grabs my upper arm and pulls me to a stop. "That's not fair."

Lola and Janet stare for a moment but then continue, apparently deciding this is a conversation we need to have on our own.

I rip my arm from his grasp. "Isn't it? You obviously have some kind of agenda. I've known that for a long time, but it becomes something different when you're keeping things from me while making promises to someone I care about."

"I have not and will not do anything that is not in your best interest. I thought we trusted each other by now."

"How can I possibly trust you, Thompson, when I don't understand your motives?"

That's it. That's the core of what's been bothering me.

"You want something from Jarron, I guess? That's all I can figure. But I don't know what. And if I don't know *what*, then how do I know how far you'd go? Would you lie to me to make Jarron happy? Would you manipulate me? Him? If you're only my friend for what you can gain from my relationship with Jarron, then what if someone else comes around that can do whatever you want from Jarron? Will you betray me? Or does this relationship mean something to you? Until I know those things, then no, I cannot trust you and we are not truly friends."

He doesn't move. Doesn't blink for several moments.

"Candice, I—"

"Look!" a high-pitched voice calls from up ahead.

Thompson and I simultaneously whip our heads in the direction of the voice. I rush forward to catch up through the trees to find Lola and Janet staring at a worn path and a rocky hill. Between a few of the loose stones is a small opening.

The magic simmers, pulls taught as Jarron touches it.

"They're not far," he whispers, meeting my gaze.

I step onto the stone and look down into the small black hole. "We have to go down there?"

Jarron nods then once again taps his lips with his finger. Back to silence, and now we have to go caving. My guess is demons and wolves have fantastic vision in the dark.

Me? Not so much. "I'm not going to be able to see very well."

Jarron climbs in first, leaping down the several feet until he reaches flat ground. Then, he holds out his hands to me.

Something flutters into my chest. "Me neither," Lola whispers.

"Let's stick together, then." Especially her. It'd be so easy to lose her down there if she can't see where she's going.

I climb down carefully, keeping care of where Lola clings to my chest.

Jarron guides me, one hand on my waist, one at my elbow until my feet are firmly planted on some kind of solid ground. I can't see anything, though. So, for all I know, there's a steep cliff just inches away.

"The farther you go in, the easier it'll be for your vision to adjust. Don't look toward the light at all."

I follow his guidance, stumbling over uneven stone. My arm brushes up against something cold and wet. It's even chillier down here than above ground, although I wonder if the lack of breeze will make up the difference.

"Wait here," he whispers.

"Uh-huh," I say, voice too high-pitched. I most certainly won't be going anywhere else, that's for sure.

Lola is trembling against my chest, so I fold my arm up to tuck her in gently.

"You okay?" I whisper.

"Not a big fan of being underground." She shivers.

Pixies aren't exactly underground creatures. Some flying creatures are okay with caves, but only ones with some alternate way of maneuvering and telling where they are.

Janet being half-troll should mean she's completely at home underground.

When Lola's trembling seems to build as opposed to settle, I aim for some distraction. "So," I say, "I spent the afternoon with Jarron in Elite Hall."

She wiggles against me. "You didn't get to spend much time with him, did you? What's going on with you two, by the way? He's looking at you like he's ready to sweep you away and hide you from the world for eternity."

My cheeks redden.

"I—I don't know what to make of it all," I say honestly. "It's, well, you know what's holding me back."

A tiny tug on my wrist distracts me from the pain in my gut. That's the first time I've felt the secret bond at work. I wonder what it would feel like if I were to begin saying something that edges close to the secret?

Would my whole arm feel like it's on fire? Like I've sawed it off? Or will the pain move to other places in my body?

"Yeah," she murmurs.

"I just don't know for sure that there's a future for us, and if there isn't—"

"That boy is in love with you, Candice. At some point, you're going to have to realize that. You let him *bite* you; didn't you like that?"

My cheeks heat, and I comfort myself with the knowledge that it's much too dark to tell. I know she's teasing me now, but then again, maybe she's trying to distract me too. "Yes. A lot more than I expected." And now, I'm thinking about how I'd like him to do it again.

She wiggles against my chest and tinkles out a little laugh.

Finally, the group makes their way down to us and Janet curls her arm in mine. "You guys good?"

"Just peachy," I say. My vision is beginning to adjust, just like Jarron said, and I can see the faint shadows distinguishing some rocks from others. It's not enough to be able to walk without dying, but maybe enough not to trip when someone else leads me through.

Our small group piles in close to each other, but then everyone stills, and I have to wonder if there was some message for everyone to stop that I couldn't see or hear.

Being human among supernaturals sucks.

I can feel the others near me, though, so I don't feel alone, and I suppose that should be enough. Fingers dance along the nape of my neck.

Jarron's touch sends chills down my spine and terror into my bones.

I followed the note's instructions to follow my tattoo rather than tracking the card. That means I believe there is some validity to the note.

If so, my sister could be alive. Somehow, after almost a year—

I shake my head. They found her body. This is just another trick of the games. Mr. Vandozer trying to get under my skin and push me away from Jarron.

Jarron, who seems to have noticed my unease and is sliding his arms around me. His warm hand slips over my stomach, the pads of his fingers under the hem of my shirt.

Here in the darkness, I am cocooned by a demon.

And I am utterly terrified. Not that he'll hurt me, but that this will be the last time he touches me like this.

Because if Liz is alive, then the note was right all along.

He's not mine.

He was never mine.

45

WELCOME TO THE AKRASIA GAMES

Our small group inches through the tunnel, step by step. Lola huddles on my chest, and I hold a hand gently over her to ensure she's never crushed by an accidental collision with a wall.

Walls and I are not currently on friendly terms.

Janet grabs my arm and pulls me back from what I assume would have been another hard collision, but she doesn't release me. She stands still. So, I wait.

"There's a cavern on the other side," Janet whispers. Jarron's chest brushes up against my back to lean over me and press his palm against the stone.

"I don't feel anything," Jarron says. "Can you tell how big? How far it reaches?"

There's a pause while I assume Janet uses her senses to get an answer to those questions. "Very large. Hundreds of feet each way at least. I don't know how far or how to reach it."

"Let's keep moving then. Keep an eye on it, please. That might be where they are."

We continue moving again, slower this time. There's a slight scraping sound of fingers against the stone. I don't know much about troll abilities, but maybe Janet needs physical contact with the rock to sense where things are.

We walk for another couple minutes before Janet gasps and we all stop.

"Here," she whispers. "There's... magic coming through here."

Keep walking, a voice whispers.

I lift my chin. "Did someone say to keep walking?"

There's a pause. "No," Janet says uncertainly.

"I heard a voice," I say, realizing that may make me sound insane. Then again, the supernatural world isn't quite as sensitive to those kinds of things.

"What kind of voice?" Jarron asks, voice suddenly lower.

"A woman whispering?" I shrug.

"Let me know if you hear it again," he says. "But I'm not exactly inclined to listen to a disembodied voice right now."

The groaning of a stone shifting against stone alerts me to some kind of movement. My breaths huff, and Lola shivers against me. Another shift, and light floods the tunnel. I cover my eyes but then blink the shock away. Between the stones, a soft yellow glow brightens the immediate area.

"There's a ledge up here; we should be able to see what's happening below," Janet says.

Jarron moves first, shifting past Janet, but he keeps his hand clenched around mine. I meet Janet's gaze, sharing our quiet fear, before I lean forward enough to look down over the ledge.

A hundred feet below, there's a pit filled with stone walls twisting through it to create a sort of maze. There are also four platforms on each side of the pit with stone chairs. Viewing platforms? My stomach churns.

This is a source of entertainment, I remind myself. How many people come to watch young people fight to the death? My teeth begin chattering. Is this it?

Did we really find the Akrasia Games?

I press my lips together tightly, if only to hide the way they're trembling. Is this where my sister fought and died less than a year ago?

I've faced these people before—this vile, evil game. The people who hurt my sister, who took her from me. But that doesn't mean I'm ready for it again.

Janet and Thompson are standing beside us now, looking down at the massive cavern.

"What now?" Lola whispers, asking the question we are all wondering.

As if on cue, an eerie tune rings out from somewhere below. Everything I can see from here is entirely empty, no sign of life, so I can't tell where the music is coming from.

The tone dips and bounds into a melody. Simple. Child-like. And slightly off-key.

I shiver at the odd sound. In this context, it's nightmare inducing, especially when it bounces off the stone walls of the cavern. The echo makes it sound like a purposeful round.

An echoing voice booms. "Thompson, Lola, Janet, Jarron, and Candice. You are all invited."

My eyes widen. Well...

"What in the world," Janet whispers.

"Take the stairs," the magical voice croons.

Iridescent magic shimmers on the edge of our small stone ledge and then unfolds one step at a time until it reaches a platform a good fifteen feet above the pit. It's still nearly a hundred feet down. Janet looks to me. I look to Jarron.

His stare is blank, focused on the magical staircase.

"They expected us," I say. I suppose I knew that, but the question is, should we continue forward? Does that mean we are walking into a trap? Is it too late to retreat?

I need you to play along too, the note said.

We want to keep our villains here as long as possible. If we retreat now, will they flee before the authorities arrive?

One of my questions is answered when the stone behind us crackles and groans. I gasp and twist to watch in horror as the stones move entirely on their own, spinning and filling in the gap we'd created.

That can't be good.

Janet slams her hands against the now-solid wall trapping us on the stone ledge.

Thompson does the same, slamming his fists against the wall. "We can't break through it," he whispers then stands and faces us. "At least, not without magic."

Jarron's eyes are pitch-black. His fingers are solid black claws. "They have other traps waiting for us." His voice is full of gravel as he turns to me with a lingering, unspoken question.

He's leaving the choice up to me.

But my mind is already made up. I'd follow along with the group if everyone agreed to run, but if it's up to me? I want answers. And there is one, in particular, that's clawing at me.

One thing I have to know, or it will torment me forever.

Without even bothering to answer, I begin walking down the luminescent stairs. It's a bit unnerving being able to see through them all the way down the hundred-foot drop. And you know, the fact that the magical being that created the stairs could snap their fingers and remove them at any moment.

That seems unlikely, though. If they want us dead, that's not how they'll do it.

My friends follow closely behind. Janet loops her arm in mine and Lola glides down beside us. "Are we sure this is a good idea?" Lola asks.

"Nope," I tell her.

"Right." She looks over her shoulder at the closed stone tunnel.

I stop. I think about telling Lola and Janet they could retreat if they wanted, but they couldn't, could they? "Jarron, can you blast through that wall, so we have an exit plan? Lola and Janet, you're welcome to use it now if you want. I just have a few questions I need answers first."

Jarron wordlessly turns. A sparkling black void appears over his palm, growing each second.

"I don't want to leave you, though." Janet squeezes my arm a little tighter.

I jump when his magic smashes the stone apart, sending debris flying.

Janet stares back at the barely visible tunnel. That's our only known route to safety. "I know," I tell them both softly. "But this isn't your fight."

Lola flies up and lands on my shoulder. "Of course it is. If it's your fight, it's ours."

Janet smiles. "It's all of Minor Hall's fight."

"How did I get so lucky to find friends like you?" I ask. Is it always the least strong that have the biggest hearts? It feels that way sometimes.

Jarron peers down at me. I nod, and we turn together to keep walking down the stairs.

The haunted carnival tune continues its melody, getting louder and louder the closer we get to the bottom of the iridescent stairs.

Finally, we reach the stone platform with a metal railing that gives a great view of the pit maze below.

Is this where Mr. Vandozer, my sister's lover, watched while she died?

There's no one here to greet us. No sign of the jinn or the source of the voice or music.

"Hello?" I call.

The word *Welcome* pops into existence in front of my face.

"We're so glad you all could join us," an inhuman female voice purrs. "The games are about to begin. Would you like to watch?"

I clench my hands into fists.

"Take a seat."

My throbbing heart is ready to explode with anticipation and fear. Did we make the wrong choice in coming here? What the hell is happening? *Are they going to make us watch the Akrasia Games?*

We all share wordless, panicked looks and then take one of the folding metal chairs.

I can't just sit here and watch as Corrine and the others fight each other to the death. I don't care what I'd get out of it, even my own life. I can't do it.

I don't want to watch this.

I take the moment of peace to examine the pit below. The maze is not simple—I have to focus to follow it through. There are several open sections throughout. One has a glowing cauldron in the middle, pink steam billowing up. Another has a dark pulsing hole in the middle. Another, what looks like a big boulder, but on closer inspection—it's breathing. A tail whips out, sliding against the ground. I don't know what it is, but I wouldn't want to face it.

This has to be the games, doesn't it? Does that mean at any moment, Corrine and the others will come out and begin fighting each other? Fighting that lizard creature? Will there be more challenges thrown in?

Nausea rolls through me.

"Where is the jinn?" I say loudly. "I want to meet with the jinn!"

Because I can't just sit here any longer. Jarron grabs my hand and squeezes gently.

"All in good time, love," a feminine voice I assume to be the jinn floats through the air.

I press my eyes closed.

Then, the whole cavern darkens. Shadows fill the pit below. I squeeze Jarron's hand tightly. "I can't just sit here and watch them die," I whisper to him because I don't know what I'll do when it comes down to it. Will I jump in to help? How stupid would that be?

"I know," he whispers. I don't know if he has a plan, but I hope he does. Has he been communicating with Laithe? Is help already on the way? Closing in on the cave system to trap the culprits inside.

That thought sounds too good to be true, but I cling to it anyway because helpless is soul-sucking bitch.

Help might be coming. For me and for the kids they're going to force into fighting.

Grinding sounds begin, and I notice a small platform

rising from the shadowed hole. Ten forms stand on the platform with black masks over their faces.

Their posture is odd, though. They stand up straight, heads high. Those—those can't be scared contestants, can they?

"The Cosmic Council welcomes you," one of them calls.

The Cosmic Council? How lame is that.

"Welcome to the Akrasia Games."

In the next instant, the world turns pitch-black, and the floor drops out from beneath me.

46

WE'RE NOT SPECTATORS— WE ARE THE CONTESTANTS

Sharp talons grip my waist as I fall, and I cling to the demon I should probably fear. But right now, he is my only lifeline.

I can't see anything except darkness but his warm, strong body is wrapped around mine protectively. When I'm set firmly on my feet, my heart is racing so fast I'm worried it'll do permanent damage.

A spotlight shines on a platform to our right, twenty feet up. The masked men and women are now above us, sitting in their stone chairs looking down on us.

We're not watching the games, I realize.

We are in the games.

The light serves to brighten the pit we've fallen into, enough for me to get a sense of my surroundings. My heart hammers as I stare at the stone walls covered in streaks of mud and what I'm choosing to believe is red paint.

This isn't the Akrasia Games, I tell myself. We are not bound to any games; we haven't signed any contracts. Our goal is simply to survive until help arrives. Which means there is little they can do to control us, except the physical threats they throw at us.

I will certainly not be harming any of my friends. The only question is, what do they want from us? A cool chill drops over me, and I realize how vulnerable I am. It would be easy for them to kill me if that's what they wanted. They have magic; I don't. All they need to do is drop the temperature low enough, and I'd freeze pretty quickly. Even Jarron couldn't save me from that without getting us out of here, and at the moment, it seems he's unable to do that.

I take in every detail around me. The pit is maybe a football field in length but with walls all around to make a sort of maze with different sections. Each section likely has something to fight or solve.

"Oh, that's better," the booming male voice says. "Let's try this again. Welcome to the Akrasia Games."

Jarron tenses around me, a constant growl vibrating in his chest. He's waiting for the moment he can kill those who would threaten us. I can feel the tension in his limbs, his eagerness to destroy. The fact that he doesn't, tells me he's waiting for something.

"This is a special event," an echoey male voice calls from the platform above. "We cannot begin our official game without our final contestant. Your name seems to be incomplete, Candice."

I flinch.

"Anyone who comes for her will die," Jarron says, his tone promising violence.

"So," the voice continues, ignoring Jarron, "we are going to play a preliminary game. Just for fun."

"Who will win? Who will fight?" a female voice says delightfully. "Who will piss themselves with fright?"

"My money is on the wolf," a deeper female voice purrs.

Janet inches closer to us, watching the scaled demon holding me warily. Lola is on her shoulder, shivering into Janet's neck. Are they regretting their life choices yet?

"What is the point?" I spit at the evil fucks standing on that platform. "Why not just kill us and be done with it."

"You don't need to give them ideas," Lola singsongs quietly.

"Entertainment, dear," one of the female voices say. "Just pure entertainment. You can end it now, though, if you wish." A contract appears in front of my face, my incomplete name on the dotted line.

Jarron swipes at the parchment with his talons, and it flutters to the floor in jagged pieces. "I'm going to kill you all."

"Oh good, the Crown Prince of Oriziah has decided to show up." The male in the center is speaking now, I can tell because his canvas mask puffs out slightly with each word. "What better way to test a future ruler than make him fight for his life. Will he protect himself? Or his chosen? But wait, is she truly his chosen? Or will another sway his affections?" He speaks like this is a reality TV show. It might just be the most disgusting thing I've ever heard.

The others on the platform chuckle.

"The ultimate competition. We cannot wait to see how it all plays out."

Again, darkness drops over the arena, and an inhuman roar sounds from deeper in the pit.

That was not Jarron.

A screeching sound comes next, almost like a squealing

door. I have no idea what that could be. There's a hissing sound like... like steaming liquid. The cauldron?

"Can you just kill them?" Thompson whispers. I can't see him in the darkness, but he's nearby. All my friends are terrified out of their wits and in very real danger, all because of me and my thirst for vengeance.

"There's a force field," Jarron answers. "We'd have to break it first. I could do it, but—"

"I'll protect her," Thompson answers quickly. "I swear it."

Jarron pulls in a long breath and looks down. I can't make out much more than the silhouette of his face and the voids of those eyes so deep they never stop astounding me. I wish I could read those depths, but they are entirely foreign to me. Finally, he nods.

"I need to know who they are," Jarron whispers. "Their entire worlds will be wiped out by morning if I uncover their identities."

My eyebrows rise. That sounds a bit extreme, but I also don't think arguing with him right now is wise.

"Unmask the assholes, survive, get out of here. Got it," Thompson says.

Shadowy magic explodes from Jarron's hand and slams into an invisible force just feet from the masked beings. His power crackles and explodes in quick succession, but the beings behind the shield don't so much as wince. I shift back and find another hard chest. Out of the embrace of one monster and into another.

Thompson doesn't hold on to me though. He shifts to the side and then transforms into a massive black wolf and crouches in front of me.

Get to the center, that familiar voice whispers to only me. *I'll get you out of here.*

Before I can even think through the voice sending me messages about the trap I've walked into, light blasts into the clearing so hot it burns. I duck away from the attack.

A swarm of birds screeches above us. They soar up, away from a blast of Jarron's magic. Thompson leaps at them the moment they come close, but whatever these white squawking birds are, they have magic that can shoot at us from afar. He can't get them from down here.

Jarron can, though. He alternates shots of magic at the birds and the force field.

Janet curls an arm around mine, and we huddle together, Lola between us. The fluttering of her wings is a comfort and terror. Can we all survive this? I've brought them into this.

Their bodies tremble, and though their fear is absolutely founded, I don't want them to be swallowed up by the panic. That's the easiest way to die. So, even though I don't feel at all confident, I say, "Are we going to let the boys do all the fighting for us?"

A hysterical laugh builds up in Janet's throat. "I'm not much of a fighter."

"No, but we're smart and resourceful. We have some mysteries to solve here."

"You mean like the identities of those people?" Lola asks. "There might be some breaks in the force field I could get through, but with those birds swooping around—"

"No, no. Don't put yourself in danger like that. We're going to stay together and near our protectors as much as possible, but did you see the maze before we fell into it? There was a cauldron in the middle. I think there's a message there. I need to find it."

I don't exactly explain what makes me think there's a message, but they don't ask additional questions. "Okay," Lola whispers, and Janet nods.

They built a maze for a reason. They want us to either find a way out or there is something hidden in the middle of it. I remember the cauldron. If this is set up for me, they'll know my strength. If this is about entertainment, they'll want to give me a chance out, right?

They also want me to finish signing the contract, but I have to hope there's another way to survive this. Our goal is stalling anyway. How long will it take for the authorities to reach us? No idea.

And then, there's the whispers in my ear.

I don't want to think too deeply about what it all means because if I do, I might implode here and now. What I need is to not give up and work through this situation logically. One step at a time.

I cling tightly to Janet's arm as we step away from Jarron.

"Where are you going?' he growls immediately. The air above cracks and sizzles. White ash begins falling from nothing, which I assume means he's almost through the shield. Did they plan for it to be that easy for him to get through? The masked people still seem to be at such ease behind the near-failing magical shield.

They've planned for the shield to fail. They want him to shatter it, the voice tells me.

The voice is trying to help us, the only question is, is it part of the games? Should I trust it? I grab Jarron's forearm. "I don't think breaking the force field is the right move."

He turns to face me full on. "Explain."

"They're expecting it. Look." I nod up to the masked people watching us casually. "I think it's part of their plan. And I, for one, would rather not follow their plan."

"Kinda hard not to at this point," Thompson mutters, sweat beading on his brow, despite the cold. "What do you suggest?"

"We move through the maze. There's something hidden here. Something for us to find."

"Isn't that following their plan?" Lola asks.

"In a way, I guess. But I don't think they've set us up to fail. A game is only fun if there's a way to win." I wave my hand. "Look, I don't have a full strategy; it's just that my intuition tells me that fighting them outright isn't the correct response. We have to go in." I point to the stone walls making up the entrance to the maze.

"Together, right?" Jarron asks.

I nod. "All of us."

"Ahh shit," Thompson says. "Fine."

"Together," Lola and Janet agree simultaneously.

"All right, let's do this. Let's beat the Cosmic Council at their own stupid game."

47

I DO NOT WANT—TO BE A SECOND CHOICE

For the first few minutes we walk as a team between the stone walls, everything is quiet. Eerily still. Both Thompson and Jarron shift back into their human forms, feigning ease. Jarron keeps my hand tightly clasped in his, and after a lull of quiet, he pulls me in and whispers, "I can get us out of here if needed." He says it like it's a secret. "But I can't get us all out."

He nods to the other three.

I swallow. I don't know what this unspecified mode of transportation could be that is only good for me and him—it's not like he can fly us out, we're underground—but either way, that's not even an option for me. I will not be leaving my friends behind.

"So, my first goal will be to get them out of here," he says.

"They want us, not them. If it comes down to it, we can probably make a deal to let them go. Then, we stall long enough for—whatever it is you can do?"

He nods.

I take in a long breath. Good, we have a very tentative plan. That makes me feel slightly better. Survive the maze. Get Lola, Janet, and Thompson out of here. Stall long enough for Jarron's magic to set us free or backup to arrive, whichever comes first.

Cool. I do kind of wish I knew what he had in mind, but saying it out loud could take away our element of surprise, so maybe we should keep it quiet.

We walk up and down a few pathways, only to find dead ends, but finally, we reach the first opening of the maze. There's a ball of glowing darkness suspended midair. There is no noise or movement.

That's not ominous at all.

"Welcome," a bodiless voice says, almost sounding like a computer-generated voice, "to the orb of unwanted truths. To pass through, you must reveal an unwanted truth. If you attempt to pass without my offering, you will perish in a most gruesome fashion. Do you understand?"

Janet whimpers.

"Who will go first?"

"I will," Thompson says, before anyone else can answer. He steps up to the black ball of nothing and looks up.

"Complete the phrase: I do not want..."

"To fail," he says, his voice nearly breaking at the two words. I flinch. Fail at what?

"Very good. You may pass."

Thompson slowly walks the rest of the way across the opening and waits on the other side. "This is a pretty basic form of fae magic. It will pull the answer from your soul. There is no possible way to get it wrong. Just don't resist."

Lola and Janet go next, together. They are asked the same task. Complete the phrase, "I do not want."

"To be a no one," Lola says.

"To be forgotten," Janet says.

"Very good. You may pass."

Jarron leads me forward, and we stand together beneath the void. I look up to find bits of smoke swirling within.

"Complete the phrase: I do not want..."

"To be rejected," Jarron says just as I say, "To be a second choice."

I suck in a breath and slap my hand over my mouth. How—how did it know that?

Jarron looks down at me like he's never seen me before. I avoid his stare.

I pull him forward to meet with our friends, and we pass on to the next section of the maze.

"What's the point of all of this?" Thompson says. "What are they trying to achieve? The maze isn't even hard."

I jab him in the back. "Don't say that."

"Superstitious much?" he jokes.

"No, but they might send in more of those fire birds."

Thompson shivers.

"They want entertainment," Jarron says. "They're observing us. For what, I'm not sure yet. But there is something unpleasant coming, I'm certain of it."

The next section of the maze is long and more winding than the last. Eventually, Lola flutters up a few feet and darts back down.

"Don't do that, Lo!" I scold her. "It's not safe."

"I'm good. Now, I know the way," she says beaming. She instructs Thompson which turns to take, and we finally reach a long corridor. At the end, there is a scraping sound and the rumble of a predator.

"Is it that lizard thing we saw from above?" Lola whispers.

Though I don't say it, I'm pretty sure that's exactly what it is.

We pause, waiting to see if the monster will attack, but everything goes quiet again.

Jarron prompts us forward into the open space. There are white scrapes carved into the stone flooring. Hay is gathered in the corner, and—ew, yep that's a big dump over in that corner. Something really big lives here, but it's nowhere to be seen right now.

This way, Candice, the voice says. I swallow and look behind me. A cool breeze flips my hair back as I turn to find a break in the wall to the left, and at the end of the opening, the cauldron waits for me.

It's massive, taller than I am, and glowing with pink bubbling liquid.

It calls to me. As stupid as it sounds, I can feel this pull deep in my gut.

A roar shakes the ground, and massive claws and teeth fly from the dark hole straight ahead of me. The squeal that leaves my body as I duck from the lizard monster that smells like death is beyond embarrassing, but another monster slams into his body and sends him flying in the other direction. Jarron crouches in front of us, panting heavily.

The lizard shakes off the hit and gets to his feet. The thing is like a Komodo dragon but five times bigger. Slobber drips from its jaws, and its tail swipes back and forth, sizing up his opponent.

"Move as far out of the way as you can," Jarron instructs.

I glance over to the cauldron again. That's pretty far, right?

The moment the Komodo dragon charges again, I pull Janet and carry Lola to sprint to the opening between the stones. The dragon sees us running and shifts course toward us, but Thompson, in wolf form cuts him off.

Janet barely keeps up with my pace until there's a zing of magic as we pass the barrier. I stop, noticing the quiet that permeates this part of the maze.

I turn back to find I can still see Jarron and Thompson fighting the lizard, but I can't hear it.

I put my hand up to the opening we just walked through, and my palm, instead, presses against an invisible barrier that's warm to the touch.

I curse under my breath.

"What?" Lola asks.

"There's a force field between us," I answer.

Lola and Janet pause, watching the fight beyond. "That's a good thing, right?" Janet asks tentatively. "The lizard is on the other side."

"Yeah, I don't think they put that there as a favor to us," I mutter, unsure what horrors will face us on this side, but I don't for a second think it'll be fun.

The ground trembles. Once. Twice. A third time.

I breathe in deeply. Something new is coming, and this time, we don't have Jarron or Thompson to protect us.

48

WILL HE STILL FIGHT FOR YOU ONCE HE LEARNS I'M ALIVE?

This opening of the maze is massive. In the left corner is the huge cauldron with pink steam billowing out, but to the right, it stretches at least a hundred feet in length, and that is where a huge monster watches us from. His steps are slow, but I don't make the mistake of thinking we have any time at all.

The beast stands on two hind legs, and it's tall enough for his head to be higher than the stone barriers—at least fifteen feet. It has horns not unlike Jarron's and fur on its legs. Is this thing from their world?

"It's a minotaur," Janet whispers.

A minotaur. Wonderful. I don't know much about them, if I'm honest, but I know it's not something I want to fight.

I look back over my shoulder to find Jarron screaming, pounding and clawing at the force field. His rage rattles the very stone, but he can't break the shield. He begins throwing that shadow magic at it. It will take him several minutes to break it down—we don't have minutes. This thing is going to charge any second.

The cauldron is a clue or a puzzle piece I need to work out. Maybe the potion inside will take down the minotaur? It's unlikely it'll be that easy, but there's something here for me to do. I just have to figure it out.

"Lola," I whisper.

She sucks in a trembling breath.

"I need you to use your sleeping powder."

"What?" she squeaks.

"On the minotaur. I need you to fly up and use that pixie magic to put him to sleep."

"I—I can't."

"You can. You need to. I can do this." I point to the cauldron. "I can figure this out, but I can't fight that thing at the same time."

"You're stronger than your family thinks you are, Lo," Janet says through panicked breaths.

"You're smarter. And you're braver. You're better than all of them combined."

"Yeah, Lo," Janet says. "You got this."

Lola flutters up and hovers in front of my nose and puffs out her chest. "Okay, I'll do it."

"Yeah, you will!"

She soars up, and immediately my stomach sinks.

"Be careful, though!" If anything happens to that girl, I will riot. I send a pitying glance to the demon form of Jarron, who is still frantically slamming his magic into the wall and roaring desperately.

With no time to spare, I sprint over to the cauldron and up

the two concrete steps beside it so I can have a good look at the contents inside. The pink liquid is hot—so hot it's uncomfortable to even get too close. The streaming smoke is acrid and bitter.

A heavy helping of purple dust drops down over the monster behind me. That thing is huge, though. Will little Lola have enough power to take him down? She failed to put a troll to sleep during exams—twice. This thing has to be twice the size of the average troll.

The minotaur swipes at her, but she expertly darts away each time.

I breathe the potion in, trying to use my nose or intuition or anything to figure out the key to this puzzle. The smell makes my head spin, so putting down the monster is certainly a possibility, but even touching this potion with a ladle or vial could be dangerous.

I don't think that's the right answer.

"It's waiting for something," I say my thoughts aloud. The potion is incomplete. I can feel the tension in the air around it. I'm not sure how completing a raging potion like this could help us. Maybe it'll turn into acid and burn a hole through the ground we can use to escape? Okay, wishful thinking.

I rush over to the shelves filled with ingredients. Most of them look to be decoration rather than usable. There are books made of plastic or filled with gibberish. There is a vial filled with gummy worms—yes, literal gummy worms.

Maybe this is all pointless and was set up by an actual buffoon, and I'm over here trying to think logically. They want us to suffer. They want the entertainment.

The answer is beneath the potion, the voice says.

I blink and look back at the cauldron. There's a gentle

glow at the bottom of the copper base. Is it possible the potion isn't dangerous and we need to jump inside to get to the magic beneath it? Not a theory I want to test without solid evidence. In all likelihood, I'd be boiled alive for my efforts.

A massive boom shakes the ground, and I spin to find a puffy cloud of dust rising from the minotaur lying flat on the ground—and Lola dropping, her body limp.

My heart lifts and sinks at the same time. Janet rushes to the little pixie falling, and I'm a few steps behind. Her lifeless body flutters down, twisting and making it hard to calculate exactly where she'll hit, but Janet leaps to grab her carefully between both hands and then pulls her into her chest, cradling her like a baby.

"Good catch!" I say, panting. Just a few feet away is that massive monstrosity, snoozing peacefully. It groans but remains down. "Is she okay?"

Janet holds Lola out, lying on her open hands. Her body is limp, but her chest rises and falls slightly.

"Mm okay," a tiny voice mumbles. Both Janet and I release relieved sighs. "Did I—did it work?"

"Yes!" Janet says. "Screw those Major Hall dicks."

I stare. Did Janet just insult someone? "You did amazing, Lola!"

"I bet you could get in now if you wanted," Janet says more softly.

"No," Lola whispers. "I'm not leaving Minor Hall. I can prove myself outside of school. I'll be more successful than all of them."

"Yeah, you will!" My heart is full of hope for my wonderful friends, who I wish I was better to. They're incredible all on their own, and I'm so happy they're beginning to see it. But first, we have to make it the hell out of here.

"Excuse me, but I have a potion to figure out." Who knows how long we have until a new threat arrives?

I glance at Thompson and Jarron still desperately clawing at the force field. The demon looks like a panicked wild animal. His muscles flex as he throws his whole body at the magic keeping us apart.

Something tugs at my gut, and I turn back to look at the felled beast snoring behind me.

Clear goo pours from its nose. I tap my knee, considering.

Troll snot is an ingredient in some potions—including my nullifier. Could minotaur snot have similar properties? Or maybe the venom? I wrack my brain, trying to think this through. Minotaurs are very different than trolls. They're stronger in magic.

Finish the potion, the voice tells me what I already know.

I rush to grab an empty vial from the shelves. There's only one, so I'm assuming it's the correct measurements. Then, I run back to the minotaur and drop to my knees beside its massive head.

I grimace as I place the vial under the sticky clear liquid.

Smart girl, the voice purrs in praise. *You always were the smarter of us two.*

My heart aches for several reasons at once. Jarron's roar shakes me to my core, all of a sudden loud and clear.

I glance back to find he has partially broken through the barrier and is trying to force his way through a small opening. The skin on his back is ripping, blood caking the invisible magic surrounding him. He will tear himself apart to get to me.

Look how desperately he fights for you, the voice whispers in my ear. Except, it's different now. It's closer and softer and so utterly familiar. My stomach squeezes.

"*Will he still fight for you like this once he learns that I am alive*?" she asks from over my shoulder.

49
WE'LL FACE IT TOGETHER

The glowing silhouette of a beautiful girl appears behind me.

The same kind of glowing figure that taunted me to enter the Akrasia Games a few weeks ago. She's the same.

I close my eyes before I react. Has this been Liz the whole time? Every message, every word whispered. She's been trying to help me?

It would make sense for her to help me. The letters and the note in the book would all fit.

Is that the puzzle piece I'm missing? Liz is still alive.

Liz is the jinn?

Is that also why Jarron's demon soul has been splitting? Because his chosen is alive but with another man?

I shake my head. I have to keep my mind straight. Finish the potion, help my friends, then freak out about the possibility of Liz being involved in all of this.

Tears sting the back of my throat as I ignore the glowing figure that appeared at my back and instead rush toward the force field.

Jarron's monster-void eyes stare at me frantically, but his body is still. "I need you to shift back," I tell him gently. "Your human body is smaller; you can get through that way."

He blinks twice. His muscles are tense.

I place my arm on the rough leathery skin of his forearm. "Trust me," I whisper.

He winces, and a soft whimper escapes his lips. Then, magic ripples over his body and he's back in his human form. He looks incredibly exhausted. His hair dips into his sunken eyes, and he looks up at me like I'm his last remaining hope.

"Gently," I tell him, "crawl through."

I place my hand on the top invisible barrier, feeling around where it begins and ends. It's jagged and sharp; no wonder it's ripped into him. I wince at the bloody mess he's made of himself already.

I carefully guide his arm through, and then I pull him the rest of the way in.

He slides onto the ground in a heap, panting. "Are you okay?"

I laugh bitterly. "Better than you."

"What's happening?" he asks.

"Well, you nearly killed yourself to get through a magical barrier instead of calmly thinking through—"

"I meant over here," he spits.

"I need to finish the potion," I say and pick up the vial of minotaur snot on the ground. "I'll be right back."

Jarron groans in frustration as I run to the cauldron,

leaving him on the ground. I won't be gone from him for long; he'll be okay. I absently notice Thompson crawling through the opening in the barrier in his wolf form.

The pink liquid gurgles angrily. Here goes nothing. I quickly pour the sticky liquid into the potion, and it only takes a second for steam to billow up and out in a massive hissing wave.

I stumble away as the acid roars its freedom and the smoke turns black and triples in size.

You need to go first.

I press my lips together, searching the spot I swore the jinn had been standing moments ago. Nothing is there.

Thompson, in wolf form, trots next to a hunched over Jarron at the same time as Janet and Lola arrive to see what's going on. We watch together as the entire potion pours from the cauldron up, up, up, in a streaming pillar to the stalactites high above.

"What now?" Janet asks.

"We wait for it to finish," I say. "There's something beneath it." I point to the gentle light that grows in intensity the more that the potion seeps into the air.

It's peaceful for the minute we stand there and wait. Or maybe, that's only me. I know I've done what I needed to do, and I know what I need to do next. That feeling of accomplishment, even in such a stressful situation, feels good.

The hissing potion finally settles, and I skip up the steps to peer inside.

At the bottom of the cauldron is gooey pink residue and a golden glowing ball.

Get inside. It'll bring you to me.

It's a portal?

I bite my lip and look back at Jarron. When I hold out my hand, my heart aches. "Together?" My voice comes out as barely a whisper.

He blinks, surprised, but takes my hand tightly. We step over the edge and fall in together.

50
HE WAS NEVER YOURS

The whole world spins, but his hands are around me, and when I land, my heart shatters into a thousand pieces.

But I wouldn't change that shattered heart for anything because what's in front of me is terrible and terrifying and everything I've prayed for the last several months.

We're in a new cave system with a low ceiling filled with glowing stalactites hanging down and a beautiful girl with radiant skin, her hands on her hips.

"I've been waiting for you," the jinn says smoothly.

I let the oddly familiar and yet so very foreign voice wash over me, and that's the moment I know for sure. Instead of shock or panic or happiness or hope, I feel *acceptance.* There's sadness too, but I push it to the back of my mind.

I don't understand how, but I can feel the truth now.

Liz is the jinn.

Which is more confusing than anything else, but it means my sister is *alive.*

Just when I thought I was finding my footing in my new normal, it's all flipped again. I want to be happy, but I'm terrified because Liz is Jarron's chosen.

He's not yours.

He was never yours.

Something bold and wild and desperate breaks free from my soul.

One moment. That's all I have left with him.

And screw it all, but I'm going to take it.

I turn around and revel in the pleased surprise in Jarron's eyes as I tug him down to me. I slam my lips into his. Without missing a beat, he deepens the kiss. That one taste of his tongue on mine sends my body soaring.

He's not mine.

But right now, for this one moment, he is.

A rumble escapes his chest when I pull away. His eyes are hooded but entirely black. "What was that?" he murmurs.

"A goodbye," I whisper.

His jaw clenches as confusion drops over his face, but I turn my back on him to face the jinn.

Her glowing skin makes it near impossible to make out her usual features, but her arms are crossed and her hip is popped in a posture that is so very Liz.

"Pleased with yourself, are you?" the jinn bites out.

"Not really," I say. "I know I won't win. I won't fight you. I just needed one more moment before I let him go for good."

Liz lets out a high-pitched chuckle. "When did you figure it out?"

"Figure what out?" Jarron asks, his voice lower now. I refuse to even glance back at him to gauge his reactions. I don't want to see the hope bloom in his eyes when he realizes his true chosen is alive. Or worse, I couldn't bear it if he were torn.

"Don't you recognize me, love?" she purrs. "My sister clearly does."

His attention whips to me, instead of staying on Liz. "What?"

I can feel his tension and the heat in his gaze, but I still refuse to give him my attention right now, or I might shatter for real, and I need to be strong. Far beneath the surface, covered in stone and surrounded by enemies, I am not safe.

Later. Later, when I'm back in my lumpy cot in Minor Hall where I belong, I'll allow myself to fall apart.

Right now, there's new hope I hadn't expected, and I'm only allowed to focus on that.

"I don't want to fight you, Liz. But I do need to know how the hell you're alive."

51

A Dream Come True and Nightmare All in One

The jinn flips her hair over her shoulder and tilts her head. "Aren't you happy?"

"Of course I am." I'm shocked, and sad to lose something amazing, but if given the choice, I'd always choose Liz.

"Where are my friends?" I whisper, for the first time realizing they haven't made it through the portal with us.

"You don't seem all that happy," Liz says, ignoring my question.

"Liz," I bark, annoyed with her teasing. "This is hard enough as it is."

"Oh, fine." She waves her hand. "Things have been interesting on my side of things this past year. I've missed you, you know? And your friends were not invited to this part of my game. They'll be fine though—for now."

My stomach sinks.

"You're sure?" I whisper.

"The Council will be scrambling to find you two. They won't care much about the three left behind."

I sigh and close my eyes. I have to believe she's right. It's not like I can just hop back to the maze. The portal has closed up. "Have you?" I whisper, allowing my mind to refocus on the situation in front of me. "Have you missed me? You've let me believe you were dead for almost a year."

She rolls her eyes, hand on her hip. "You think I didn't try to contact you? There are reasons I couldn't, okay? Meanwhile, you went on this bold quest for vengeance. It's sweet really."

"So, you couldn't contact me? You sent me veiled notes but couldn't share that you were alive?"

She purses her lips. "I had to let you believe I was dead. That was part of the deal. Part of the contract. I've only just now figured out a way to lure you in. They've kept me on a tight leash."

"I don't understand," Jarron's voice is low, but I try not to read too deeply into the emotion in his voice.

Liz smiles at him but turns her gaze, blazing with power, to me.

My sister steps forward, and for the first time, I really see her. Her beautiful blue eyes, delicate features, pouty lips, and a scattering of freckles over her nose that she usually used makeup to hide. My sister. My lifelong partner in crime. The one I trusted with everything. Every secret. Every fear. Every hope.

She didn't do the same for me.

She kept things from me.

My sister, who I constantly defended because she was soft and sweet is now a powerful supernatural, staring at me from supernatural eyes. My stomach sinks. There is so much to unpack here, but I decide there is one thing more important than all of it. Like a switch flipped, I release my fears and confusion, and I throw my arms around the jinn.

I breathe her in. There's a tingling zing that floats through my body as I do, but behind it is her. Her smell. Her warmth. Her soul.

My sister.

"I missed you," I whisper into her hair.

She returns the embrace and hugs me so tightly I worry she'll break something. Her face drops into the crook of my arm, and I feel her begin to tremble. "I missed you too."

I didn't know I started crying, but when I pull back, my cheeks are wet. I sniff, and Liz's smile is bright and sweet and everything I remember. "I can't believe it's really you."

"I know. It's been... it's been hard." Her voice cracks. She straightens her shoulders. "Look, he's much more relaxed now."

I follow her gaze to Jarron. She's right; his eyes are back to that near honey brown, his shoulders much less stiff. Though his chest is still rising and falling faster than usual, and his gaze is piercing. He's still working through a lot, which is fair. So am I.

"They found your body," he says stiffly.

"Oh, about that body... being a jinn has its benefits. I have magic not even supernatural experts are aware of. Magic even the most powerful in the universe would be envious of. There are signs that body was a fake, but none that are known to anyone who hasn't been magically forced to remain quiet."

She sounds so proud. But there's only one explanation as to how she got this power.

"And how did you become the jinn?" I ask, voice low.

"By winning the games, of course."

I breathe slowly through my nose. Well, that answers a few of our leftover questions about the games. "The losers die. The single winner becomes the jinn."

"You always were the smart one, Candice." She smiles sweetly, but then her eyes turn sharp and her head tilts. "Now, let's talk about you stealing my future lover—a literal prince—right out from under me."

52
THE JINN HAS A PLAN

Jarron's nostrils flare, but his face remains passive otherwise. He's working very hard to control his reactions. "What," he says through a clenched jaw, "are you talking about?"

Liz turns her softened look to him. Her beautiful blond hair falls from her shoulder, waving down at the ground. She's even more beautiful than before. She now has the luminescent skin of a supernatural. "Don't worry, love. I know. Vincent doesn't know how to keep his lips shut. He's got this ridiculous grand plan, you know? Steal the prince's chosen, make her powerful, bond to her, and then parade her around on his arm. Apparently, that's some big political move in your world."

Jarron stills, every muscle tense.

"But I've got a plan of my own," Liz purrs. She steps closer to Jarron and then runs her forefinger down his chest. Jarron doesn't so much as blink. "I don't like being a pawn in someone else's plots, you see. And I don't like being lied to. He pretended like he was giving me something incredible but left out the part where he was stealing a different life of power from me. The life as the queen of an entire world." She holds out her hands like she's reveling in that power here and now.

My heart races, watching my sister. She's the same in many ways, but there's something off. Something different. My sister was lovable and sweet and oh-so-beautiful, but something about the way she's acting is almost unhinged.

I swallow. She was manipulated by an older man, lied to and betrayed and forced to fight for her life. She's been through a lot, I rationalize. She's been controlled and "kept on a leash," as she put it. It makes sense for her to be a little... different.

It just scares me because it also means I don't know what she's capable of. I don't know what this new version of my sister will be willing to do to get what she wants.

Jarron clenches his hands in fists.

"So, I made some moves of my own," Liz says, relaxing her stance once more. "I made promises to Vincent, whispered sweet nothings into his ear, and told him I would forgive him for his lies and play along in his plans, but I wanted something in return. I wanted my sister to enter the games."

My blood turns cold.

"What?" Jarron growls before I could utter the same response.

She waves her hand. "Don't worry. I never had any intention of letting her come to harm. I told Vincent I wanted Candice to be my replacement and become the next jinn. She'd get power like me, and together we'd be the unstoppable Montgomery sisters."

I roll my shoulders. My mind spins through so many

different things. "But everyone would think we were dead." I'm not sure why, of all the things I could scream at her, that's the one that first comes to mind.

She waves her hand again. "Yes, yes. That's a snag for sure, but we could find a way out of it. Perhaps we'd take on new identities and become some other set of sisters, or we'd make up a tale about how we hunted down a jinn and took its power. Who cares? We'd have incalculable power. Me and you, together. Can't you see it?" She turns her frantic wide-eyed stare to me. "I know you didn't want anything to do with magic, Candice, but that was just fear. You knew you couldn't overcome your inadequacies, so you moved away from that world entirely. But this is it—the way we could both be powerful beyond reckoning."

"Liz," I warn. How do I tell her that's not what I want? Any of it.

"And besides, I didn't necessarily plan for you to actually get into the games. That was all a ruse just to get you here. My vulnerable sister, and her big protector—soon to be mine." She winks.

"You're going to have to explain this more." Jarron's voice is small and gravelly.

I nod in agreement. "This is a lot of new information," I tell her gently. "What happened? You won the games and became the jinn? What does that mean? I have so many questions."

Liz heaves a big sigh. "Yes, well, apparently Vincent had no intention of allowing me to die in the games. He cheated, as powerful people tend to do." She rolls her eyes. "I didn't know it at the time. He implied I'd be fine, but once the games started and—" She closes her eyes. "I thought he'd really, truly manipulated me and I was going to die for it. And, I mean, I certainly could have died, but things were set up to my advantage. And, well, long story short, I won. He confessed his undying love and told me his whole plan. There were so many things he left out before the games, though. Like that a prince was my freaking soulmate and that he was going to use me to start a civil war in his home world. And that once I won the games, I'd be trapped. A literal slave." She crosses her arms and pops a hip.

My mouth dries. "Slave?" I whisper.

"It's temporary, but yes. My power, though great, is limited, and I have to do what Vincent and the others tell me. I can't hurt him. Which is where Jarron comes in."

What exactly does she want from us?

"I need Jarron to kill Vincent for me. Why else do you think I brought you all here?"

I hold my breath.

She wants Jarron to kill Mr. Vandozer because she can't. Okay, that makes sense. We are now on the same side—sort of. At least we have that one big thing in common, but there's more to this. Liz is beholden to what Mr. Vandozer tells her, and she's very powerful, which means the moment he finds out what she's doing, we're dead. That's one *big* downside.

Still, it's better than the jinn being our enemy, so we'll work with it.

But there's another piece that's irking me.

I release my breath slowly.

"It's temporary," I repeat. "Temporary how?"

"I will be the jinn only until another is chosen. They will take my place, and I will be free, but I will keep my magic."

"Chosen." I'm beginning to feel like a parrot, but I need her to expand. I can't think straight.

"I'll only be free once another winner is crowned."

My eyes flutter closed.

"You need another set of games to take place," Jarron says, his voice low.

Her smile is sad. "Or I'll remain a slave forever. And if Vincent finds out I'm not intending to play along with his long-term plans, that's exactly what will happen."

53
NO GOODBYES

My breaths are shaky, panic pressing down on my vision.

"We want to help you," Jarron says slowly, "I want to kill him, but there is a lot more stacked against us than just one Orizian betrayer."

Liz pops a hip again and tsks at him. "I thought you were *so powerful.* So young but the most powerful demon prince in generations. I did not anticipate you being afraid of a few interdimensional beings."

She steps forward, her eyes pinned to Jarron like she's the predator and he's the prey. "Don't you want to impress me? Your mate?"

I wince and then rub my chest, where it feels like a dagger just sliced me open.

Jarron flexes his hands several times, every muscle tight and unmoving. Horns inch up from his hair, as if he's trying to hold back the transition.

Liz watches with interest as he fights to hold back his

demon. "No?" she finally says. "How disappointing. Well, I better get us back to our regularly scheduled broadcasting, then, before I'm found out."

She grins manically and lifts her hand to snap her fingers, but Jarron leaps before she completes whatever magic she'd been intending. A blinding white light flares just before claws swipe at me, and then darkness takes over my vision.

#

Rough hands grab me. I twist, my hair flying. I can't tell which way is up until my back slams against cold stone.

A monster's fangs flash in front of me. I wince but manage to keep still otherwise.

"Shhh," the monster tells me. He places a gentle clawed finger over my lips.

I blink, trying to get my bearings. Moments ago, I was with Liz, now I'm in a dark tunnel with Jarron's demon form. The body holding me tightly against the wall shakes. He's trembling.

What the hell is going on?

"Jarron?" I whisper.

He shakes his head. "We have to get out of here," he whispers so lightly it's hard for even me to hear.

"What do you mea—"

He presses his palm against my mouth. I squirm but otherwise accept his reprimand and keep quiet. I don't know what to think about everything, but if he's afraid... I should probably just shut the hell up and listen to him.

"Oh, *Candice*!" a sweet voice singsongs. "Where did you

and my future husband run off to?" A bite of anger enters her tone in the last words.

My heart pounds. Why is Jarron running from her? What did she try to do?

She said she was on our side—well, sort of. At least she wants Mr. Vandozer dead.

Of course, we have a few other issues to contend with also, like the fact that she's literally his slave. And the fact that the Akrasia Games need to take place to save her.

Liz's voice continues her gentle croon, but it fades into the distance. She's getting farther and farther away.

"I thought we were going to work together." Her voice is fading, but it's also getting increasingly tight. She's not pleased with our disappearance. "But I guess we'll have to be enemies once again. Just a little suggestion, you should move away from your boy toy before the spell takes hold. Wouldn't want to have to present Mom and Dad with another body to bury."

My eyes widen. What did she do? How could she joke about something like that? But still, I trust the demon holding me.

He remains still, other than the gentle tremble in his limbs.

Finally, he pulls back, removing the pressure on my chest and than leads me down the tunnel. I can't see where we're going. Can't see the dips and curves in the uneven ground.

I try my best to follow without making any noise, but every time my feet make scuffing sounds, his hand tightens around mine. When my shoulder hits a jutting stone and I gasp, Jarron whips his attention to me, his eyes nearly glowing red.

That's a new one.

Does that mean he's angry with me?

Apparently fed up with my human clumsiness, his arm snakes out, and the next thing I know, I'm off my feet and tight against his chest again. I release a breath and follow suit, wrapping my legs around him. He rests his chin on my shoulder and breathes in deeply then continues walking with me in his arms like a damn toddler.

His walk is seamless and soundless. I was just too clumsy. I want to ask so many questions, but I'm afraid of making too much noise again. Will he be angry with me? Will we be caught and killed?

Several minutes later, Jarron presses me up against a wall.

"Jarron?" I whisper. "Are you okay?"

Then, his body shivers and his skin smooths, but his eyes are still ruby red. Does that have something to do with the spell Liz cast? Either my sight has adjusted to the darkness or there is some small source of light nearby because while everything is shadowed, I can make out some of his features inches from my face.

His chest rises and falls dramatically. His face is wild and frantic, shadowed in the darkness, making it all that much more intense. What the hell is going on?

Then, his lips are on mine. He grips the back of my head, pulling me tightly into him. I gasp but part my lips, allowing him access. His body shudders, and he groans low when his tongue meets mine.

"Candice," he murmurs, pulling back to touch his forehead to mine, "no goodbyes."

Was that in reference to our last kiss when I said it was a goodbye?

"What's going on? Why did you grab me and run away from Liz?"

His grip on my waist eases, so I release my legs from around him. He remains close, his chest against mine, taking in sharp breaths.

I place my hands on his chest.

"Because we have to get out of here."

I shake my head. "Why? I mean, yes, we need to get out of here, but why away from Liz? Doesn't this change things?"

He grabs my chin and forces me to look up into his void-like eyes. They're full of pain and fear and determination. "It changes nothing."

"I thought it changed everything."

He clenches his jaw tightly. "It doesn't change how I feel about you. I swear it."

I release a sharp breath. Could that possibly be true? "Okay," I say.

"She—she tried to do something to me." He twists his neck and rolls his shoulders.

Tried to or did?

"Your eyes are red," I whisper.

He straightens and runs his hands through his hair. "I can't believe it. I cannot believe they'd target my chosen."

My stomach sinks again.

"It's—it's inconceivable. Disgusting. Vile. Unheard of. I never even thought—" He shakes his head. His chest continues rising and falling. "I'm sorry. I know this doesn't make much sense to you. But right now, I need you out of here. They went after Liz because of me. If I'd known that was true, I would have—" He shakes his head.

I hate the new reality we're facing, but I hate his reaction more. His stress carves its way through my heart. Everything is wrong.

"Liz is alive. She is on our side."

"No," he whispers. "So long as she's bound to the games, she's not. And she wants you in them. I don't trust anything here."

Jarron's back arches, and he winces as if he's in pain. His breaths come quicker.

Jarron is freaking out from learning that Liz was harmed because of him, and probably equally freaked out because I'm in danger now too. Was Liz telling the truth? That I'm being targeted now because she wants me to have power like her? Or is there another reason?

"Those fools believe they know what's in my soul." His voice is gravelly. "They've bet on it. How they don't see—"

He groans suddenly, holding his head between two palms. He curses under his breath.

"Laithe isn't coming. And I—Candice, I need you to get out of here. I need you to go."

"What's happening? What's wrong with you?"

I couldn't get out of here on my own even if I wanted to. Jarron's next sound is so inhuman it sends a shiver down my spine. I stumble away from him, tripping on the uneven stone and slamming into the rock wall.

Jarron's shift is so sudden I barely see it happen, but suddenly he's that inhuman monster I remember from my nightmares. And this time, he does not look at me like I matter. There is no recognition at all.

"There you two are," a sweet voice calls. "Better back away, Candice. He doesn't have any idea who you are anymore."

The monster's back is hunched like he's in pain; each breath comes with an audible wheeze.

I back away slowly from the beast, unsure what's happening and terrified I'll relive those moments from my past. The beastly Jarron that stalked Liz all those years ago... he didn't seem to notice or care who either of us were.

He didn't listen to my pleas. He didn't care that I was crying for him to stop.

I hated him for that moment of helplessness, and I can feel it welling in me now. That terror. The knowledge that I am nothing, and there is nothing I can do to stop him from whatever it is he intends to do.

The beast growls low in his chest. A warning.

A glowing being appears beside me, so bright I can no longer see Liz's face or features. This is the powerful jinn.

The beast roars with his whole chest, so powerful it blows my hair back but only makes the jinn chuckle.

"Cute, isn't he?"

"What did you do to him?"

Jarron's beastly form charges the two of us, and I cower against the cave wall, but the jinn just snaps her fingers. When I peek up, the monster is gone.

"Your friends were having too easy of a time in the maze, you see. It wasn't created for powerful beings, and Jarron defeated the most dangerous beasts. Well, and that pixie used her one shot on the minotaur." She shrugs casually. "They're cute, your new friends. Anyway, we needed a new obstacle to even things out a little bit."

"Excuse me?"

The jinn grins wide and horrifying. "Jarron is a monster. All we have to do is shut down his memory and increase his sense of danger. Now, he's a mindless beast that will destroy any being he comes across. He'll hunt them down mercilessly. We probably overcompensated because he will tear those little friends of yours apart in seconds. Oh well."

"Liz," I hiss.

"Shhh," she says quickly, "You're not supposed to know that part yet. We're playing along now." She winks at me.

My breath trembles. I grab her forearm. It's hot to the touch, but I force myself not to let go and make her meet my eyes. "Is there a way out of it? The maze?"

She blinks, her gaze finally softening. "Yes," she whispers. "Back the way you came. They'll have to climb. I'll clear the way, but—"

"Fine. Jinn, send me back. Send me back to the maze too." I say it loudly because I get the feeling she's concerned someone is listening to us now. I can't leave my friends alone to face this.

"You want to play the game?" The jinn tilts her head innocently. "Only if you insist. Terrible idea, though. Remember, you're nothing to him now." She snaps her fingers again, and the world disappears.

54

JARRON WOULDN'T HURT US. BUT THAT IS NOT JARRON

Alien shrieking shakes the very stone around me. I cover my head until my feet land on solid ground. My stomach clenches, ready to heave my lunch onto my boots.

"Candice?" a voice shrieks.

I'm once again in the massive cavern, the ceiling over a hundred feet high, with stone walls surrounding us. Two sets of arms circle me, and a tiny body drops to my shoulder.

"Where did you go?" Janet asks frantically.

"Jarron and I had a meeting with the jinn," I tell them.

"Where is he? Where is Jarron?"

I swallow. They let me go and look me over. Janet, Thompson, and Lola look no worse for wear than before. "He's... in the maze too, I think. What happened to you guys?"

"Not much," Thompson claims. "Just some more of those stupid light birds trying to eat Lola."

I wince. That sounds fun.

"But it sounds like something else is coming," Janet whispers.

"Yeah, I happen to know what's coming next, and it's not good news."

"That's ominous."

"But I do have some good news. I know the way out." I turn around, trying to get my bearings in the maze again. "Back the way we came," I say, not even sure how we get back there. "And climb." I point to the small opening where the luminescent stairs once stood.

"There was a force field before," Thompson says, squinting up.

I can't tell one way or another, but I'm praying that when my sister told me to climb, she meant she was going to remove the barriers to help us escape.

Together, we work our way back the way we came. Past the empty cauldron and the still-snoozing minotaur. To the corridor with the slaughtered remains of the giant Komodo dragon and into the winding maze.

The roar sounds again, closer this time.

"What the hell is that?" Janet whispers.

"That's a very angry demon prince," I tell her.

"What?" she shrieks.

The ground rumbles from some unseen destruction. Crashing and crunching and more roars. He's on a rampage, and with the way sound bounces through this place, I can't tell how far away he is.

"He's coming for us," Thompson says. "What the hell did they do to him?"

"I don't know. Took away his memories and made him

into this mindless beast, I guess? He won't know who we are. He'll kill without thought."

"Great," Janet says through panicked breaths. "Wonderful. Just what I was hoping to hear."

I pull her into my arms. "We're going to get out of here. I promise."

I don't like making promises I'm unsure I can keep, but sometimes it's for the best.

We continue running through the winding maze. Lola darts up and down, guiding our way so we don't have to double back and risk greeting this new version of Jarron face-to-face.

We make it to the beginning of the maze, and I look up at the wall of stone before me. It's straight up, over a hundred feet. There are a few boulders I can use to get started, but after that, there's nearly smooth stone. No foot holds and very few ledges.

But we have to get moving because Jarron's echoing shriek is getting closer.

Once we're in his sights, we won't be able to escape. He's too fast. Too strong. Even if I used the nullifier on him, I couldn't fight him off. I learned that the hard way with Mr. Vandozer.

I begin the climb anyway. I climb onto the first boulder, then the next, seeking out a reasonable path.

Lola flutters over my head. "Candice, can you even climb this?"

I press my lips together. Probably not. But I don't say it. Sweat drips down my temple.

"I can carry you," Thompson says. "But I have to be

honest, I don't think we're going to make it before he finds us."

I pause. My lips tremble, but I don't let emotions drown me. I keep climbing.

"Jarron wouldn't hurt us, would he?" Janet asks, voice shaking.

"Jarron wouldn't. But that's not Jarron," I say.

"Isn't it, though?" Lola squeaks.

"I know we have to get out, but..." Janet stops and looks down at the tunnel below us. "What if we wait for him? What if we can talk sense into him? Even as a demon he'd be intelligent. He'd be somewhat him."

"She did something to him," I say through my panting breath as I claw up onto the next bolder. "Made him go into full beast mode. There isn't any compassion in him right now."

"Yeah, but—"

"He won't hurt you." Thompson's voice is louder now, more determined. His words feel... definitive.

I stop. His words settle between us all for a moment. I face him, expression full of terror and sadness. My broken heart aches so badly it's almost worse than the fear.

Thompson stomps forward. He grabs my upper arm and pulls me to face him. His eyes are wild, intense. Desperate. "He will not hurt you."

My breath hitches. I don't know if I believe that.

"Listen to me very closely," he says.

Another roar shakes the ground. He's coming. He's almost here. I don't know what will happen when he gets here.

"He's coming after *you*, and anyone in his way will die. Do you agree with that?"

I swallow and force a nod. Problem is, he isn't coming to cuddle with me. I'm prey to him. Even if he doesn't want to hurt me, he will.

"I'm willing to carry you, and I will if that's what you decide. I swear. But I believe it will end with my death. And Janet's. Maybe Lola can outfly him; I don't know."

My stomach clenches.

"I can't climb that fast, and even on flat ground he's faster. So, if we run, we die."

I'm utterly terrified. So scared it's hard to think straight.

"We will die, but you won't. I honestly, truly believe that, Candice. He. Will. Not. Hurt. You."

"But he's—"

"He's in his demon form, with his brain scrambled. Yeah, I get it. But demons will not harm their mates."

Shock like ice pours through me. "What?"

How does he even... Most supernaturals don't know how the chosen thing works. It's not common knowledge.

"Candice." He swallows. "I have to explain this fast, but I came to Shadow Hills with one intention: make an alliance with Jarron. Make an alliance with him or my pack is wiped out for good. The packs surrounding us don't just want our territory. Not anymore. They want the witch-wolf hybrids gone forever. They will kill us all. And I didn't know what else to do, except find another supernatural to help us."

My heart clenches at this new information.

He's talking so fast; I'm trying to keep up with it. "It's the only way to stop it. At this point, it's just a matter of when they break through our defenses. So, I came here to befriend the young demon prince with so much power and influence he wouldn't know what to do with it. The demon prince who famously has no particular alliances and very few friends. When I learned he was gone, I thought I'd have to leave immediately and find a new target, but then I learned about you. I'd already done a lot of research on demons before coming here, before choosing who I'd seek out. I wanted to know their motives and what it would take to put me on their good side. I was willing to do anything. Preferably nothing that hurt anyone else, but I will be honest—I was desperate. Still am.

"But I learned about demons' mates. I learned they choose their mates young, and they are desperately and violently defensive of them. I learned they will stalk their mates for years before earning them. The information is scattered and little, but I put enough pieces together to decide that you were his mate. So, yes, that was why I sought you out. Because I knew he'd be back. I believed you were the key to getting to him. And I'm sorry if you think that means I manipulated you. Again, I was desperate. I never would have hurt you. I just wanted into his inner circle."

"I don't understand," I stutter. Lola and Janet's eyes are wide, shocked at this new information.

Thompson believes I'm Jarron's chosen. *Shit.*

"Thompson, I'm not his chosen mate."

He blinks, taking in my words. "What?"

"I'm not. He—" My wrist burns. "I'm not."

He glances to Lola and Janet, confusion on his face. "What do you mean? How could you know for sure?"

"Because I know who is." Pain shoots through my chest. "And it's not me." I wince as the burning travels up my arm into my heart.

He shakes his head. "I don't know what—you're wrong."

He says it definitively, certain he is right and I am wrong. "I've seen it, Candice. I've seen how he is with you. The soul splitting—it's because of you. His demon is desperate for you, not anyone else."

My stomach sinks. "What?"

"When a demon's chosen rejects them, it splits their souls in half. It's not complete yet with Jarron, but it's enough to cause that volatile magic as his demon fights for control."

I stumble back. No. That's—

Do you deny me?

I wince. I did reject him, sort of, but—wait, no. "There's another explanation. Janet, Lola, I need you to let me share the secret."

They both gasp.

"He already knows more about this than he's supposed to, so I don't feel bad." I point to Thompson's chest. "But you better not share this information with anyone else or I'll use that instant death potion on you."

He blinks. "I knew that wasn't just a poison."

"I am not Jarron's chosen." The burn comes hard and fast this time, but I give it a moment to see if Lola and Janet can release me from the vow. "I know because..." The pain eases, and I release a relieved breath. "It was my sister, not me. Liz was Jarron's chosen. And she died, or we thought she did. She's actually still alive, and I think that's the reason for his demon fighting him—she's alive, but he still wants me, and he's split between us."

He searches my face for a long moment.

"No," he mumbles. "No. Don't believe it."

Janet's arm curls around mine. "Liz is alive?" she whispers.

"Yes, but it's very complicated, and I don't have time to

explain it all. The point is, Jarron could very much still hurt me because I'm not his chosen. I wish I was, but—"

"Bullshit," Thompson says. "He hasn't told you this, right? He can't. And he hasn't bonded with her. So, no, I don't believe it. I've seen it, Candice. I thought maybe I was wrong when he came back and didn't pursue you but after the way he reacted to seeing the wolf bite, I've been one hundred percent convinced. All of the pieces fit. His demon magic comes out in those moments. With your theory, it would only be him who cares, but it's not. His demon is enamored with you."

"That's what you want to be true, Thompson. That doesn't make it—"

"He won't hurt you! And you're right, I need it to be true because if it's not we're all going to die."

I shake my head and curse under my breath.

"The Jarron I know will burn this world down for you. Especially right now, in this state. He will kill anyone in his way. I don't think you're in danger at all right now. But we are. The only way to save us is for us to keep climbing... and for you to run the other way."

55
WHAT IF YOU'RE WRONG?

My throat dries, but somehow my mind clears. Laser focus on what I have to do.

"What if you're wrong?" I whisper.

Jarron is in epic demon mode, stalking his prey. One wrong move and I'm dead. He could do it on accident even.

If I'm his chosen, as Thompson believes, he'll be focused on keeping me safe. If I'm not, I'll be expendable to a wild animal that's angry and scared.

"You might still survive," Thompson answers. "Or he might kill you. But what do you think our chances are if you run with us?"

I look up at the wall, knowing I can't climb it. Not without help. Again, I'm the weakling, pulling everyone else down with me. I let out a final shaky breath, and when I release it—

A roar blasts through the open cavern.

"The only way any of us survives this is if we can wake Jarron up from whatever this spell is. And you are the only one who can do that."

I nod, trying to pretend my lips aren't trembling. "Go without me. If you're wrong, at least you can survive and share what happened."

My horrified stare twists to find the monstrous demon slowly stepping out from the shadows of the tunnel. *Shit.*

He splays his wings out wide. His are talons long, sharp, and glistening.

"Go," I order Thompson without pulling my gaze from the monster.

This alien may be running on all instinct, but if there is anyone who can reach him right now, it's me.

So, I have to try. Because the alternative is allowing my friends to die helping me.

I can be the distraction while they flee. My chances of survival might be slim, but it's more than theirs would be. It's a worthy trade.

Thompson doesn't second-guess my decision; he just rushes past me and pulls Janet with him. "Candice?" Janet says.. Lola lands on her shoulder.

Thompson whispers something to them both, and then they begin scaling the stone wall.

The demon bares his teeth in our direction. An inhuman rumble rips from his chest, slow and menacing. He stalks forward, his piercing focus cast up to my friends.

I shift to the left.

The demon's eyes dart to me and narrow. I'm a few feet up on the stone boulders, so I have to look down to figure out where to head. It's not as simple as stepping away. I could fall if I'm not careful.

I can't spare a long enough glance to watch their climb,

but I can see Lola's purple wings fluttering up and up from the corner of my eyes.

"Jarron?" The demon hasn't charged yet, so I take that as a good sign. I at least need to stall long enough for my friends to escape. After that—after that, I'll live or die and be content with it.

The demon's taloned fingers flex, and he crouches. Usually, there is an endless eternity in those depths, but now it's barren. He's not him. He's not even the demon who calls me his bright one.

He is something else entirely.

The demon's gaze darts up to my friends, only a few feet above me, and releases a shrieking roar. Janet whimpers.

I press my hand over my mouth and try to hold back one of my own, then I act.

Quickly, I find a smaller stone below me, and I jump without thought, barely landing on my hands and feet.

The monster roars. I stumble awkwardly to my feet, hop to another stone, and then onto flat ground and sprint for my life. I nearly make it to the cavern wall when dark wings flash in front of me.

I jerk to a stop. My eyes are pressed closed, and I can't bring myself to open them.

I feel the hot breath on my neck. A rumbling clicking sound sends a jolt of fear through me.

This is Jarron, I remind myself. The Jarron who cares about me. The Jarron who maybe even loves me. My Jarron, who would never hurt me.

I've faced this monster hidden inside of him several times now. Once, he hurt my sister. Another, he saved my life.

I know which one I'm facing right now, but even so, that

fear is not helpful. This time, I know deep inside this being cares about me.

A rumble comes from his throat, closer to that purr I've heard from him a few times but more menacing. I'm not sure what to make of that sound.

I open my eyes to find his face inches from mine, slowly examining my face and body. My heart throbs.

My breathing is labored, but I manage to force air in and out of my lungs. "Jarron?" I whisper.

He responds with more of that clicking growl. His nose wrinkles. His gaze darts over his shoulder to where Thompson, Janet, and Lola are precariously hanging just a dozen feet below their escape tunnel.

Jarron growls again. This time, there is a stark difference between this one and the last. I wave my fingers, and his attention whips back to me. He snaps his jaw, sharp fangs inches from my face.

I whimper and take a slow step back.

Forget them, I secretly beg him. *Let them get out. Let them get out, and then...*

—what then? Even if this demon doesn't kill me on a whim, how do we get out of here? I need his mind back to normal.

As of right now, my sister is trapped in jinn form. Mr. Vandozer is here somewhere with another ten supernaturals, eager to force me into the games.

Jarron's long, taloned finger slowly lifts toward me. Running would be bad, but is this worse? I don't know.

He rumbles again, then he stalks forward, each step thudding on the stone ground. His head lowers, his knees bent. He's ready to chase if I flee.

My breaths become even more labored until my vision is peppered with black. This is bad. I need to calm down or I'll end up passing out.

The demon continues forward until my back slams against the stone at the edge of the open cavern. I whimper, and he clicks his tongue in response.

This time, his hands press against the stone on either side of my head, and he leans in. My chest rises and falls dramatically, but I remain still otherwise.

I don't know what to do, but I glance up and find the wall empty. My friends made it out. That's good. That's very good. At least they made it out alive. Now... now, it's my turn to roll the dice.

I've been awkwardly dancing with the beast form of Jarron for a good two minutes and I'm still alive, so that's a good sign, right? He hasn't shown any recognition, but he doesn't seem to see me as a threat.

His clicking rumbling begins again as he leans his face down toward my neck. I gasp but again don't dare move. I close my eyes.

He breathes in my hair, long and slow. *Well then.*

What in the world is he doing? He nuzzles into the crook of my neck, and an off-sensation drifts down into my stomach. I jerk slightly, and he reprimands me with a small growl.

My bite. He's examining his bite mark on me.

I release a breath.

So, he recognizes me as his because of the mark? I swallow and ignore the stupid hope that Thompson put in my heart. I didn't want to let it affect me, but obviously it has.

I wanted Jarron to protect me in this form because it

would mean—well, might mean—that we were wrong. All of us.

Liz, Mr. Vandozer, Bea, Trevor. Everyone believed Liz was his chosen. What are the chances they'd all be wrong? They know so much more about how it works. What demons are like during that time.

Thompson is still an outsider, with very limited information about a culture he doesn't understand. Why would I rely on his information, over those from his actual culture?

They could still be wrong.

There are many clues that he could be right.

I want you. Not her.

This doesn't change how I feel about you.

All the information I've learned about demons' chosen mates.

I bite the inside of my lip. It doesn't matter. What matters is that I'm pretty sure Jarron's demon is not going to kill me right now, and we have to get out of here before another demon shows up who will.

"Jarron?" I try again, this time with a tad more confidence.

He murmurs against me.

I learned his demon was capable of speech and deep thought the last two times I interacted with him, but right now, that doesn't seem to be the case.

"Jarron, we need to get out of here."

His murmur turns rumblier. When I try to move, he growls, low and menacing. He pushes his chest against mine.

"You," he breathes, forcing the words out. "Will not." He huffs. The words are clipped. "Escape me this time."

My heart begins to pound again. Okay, yeah not good.

"If you get me back to the school—"

He clenches his teeth over my neck. I suck in a breath. Heart pounding rapidly. Darkness presses in on my vision, but a new feeling settles in my stomach. A fear that is not entirely bad.

"There are people here who want to hurt me."

He releases me and stands up straight. He looks around the empty cavern, and then his gaze lands back on me. His lips purse, as if saying, *where are all the people?*

"They're back there," I say, pointing across the way to the tunnel we came from.

He wrinkles his nose. "No one will take you from me."

My stomach twists. "Please, Jarron. I want to get out of here. You can keep me, just not here."

"Can I?" he whispers. "Can I keep you?"

My heart flutters then aches. I don't answer that because I don't know how to.

He's speaking now when that seemed impossible a few minutes ago. Does that mean the spell is fading?

"Will you run from me again?"

"Jarron, please," I whisper again. "I'm scared."

He growls, determined. "No one will harm you with me here. I will destroy them all."

"They took away your mind for a little while. They could do that again. They—they're powerful. And I want to go home. With you."

He purrs against my neck again. "Okay, bright one. I will do as you please."

My heart lifts. "Really?"

"If you stay with me. Yes, I will take you away from the dark place to somewhere you will be comfortable."

Okay, he's definitely regaining his mind. Hope blooms in

my chest for many reasons at once. Jarron wants me. His demon wants me too. And he's willing to help us both escape. We're close, so very close to surviving this.

Suddenly, I'm swept off my feet, and I find myself hanging in the demon's arms.

"Are you ready?"

I nod, even as anxiety floods me. So does hope.

Jarron crouches, wings splayed, ready to take me up into the air when an eerie tune rings out. Jarron stands straight, wings tucked in. His talons tighten over my waist and legs. I squirm at the sharp bite, but it's not enough to break the skin.

"There you two are," Mr. Vandozer croons from the platform above. "Just in time for the crescendo."

56
ONE MASSIVE MISCALCULATION

Several forms appear on that platform above. Mr. Vandozer is unmasked, standing beside the woman covered in glowing white light.

Liz.

The nine forms behind him still wear their black masks. The rest of the Cosmic Council.

Jarron tenses. "These are the ones you fear?"

"Yes."

"Then, they will die."

"Wait," I say quickly. I lean in close and whisper, "The glowing one is my sister. She's—I don't know if I can trust her, but I love her."

That will be a moot point if she is his chosen, but just in case.

He tenses then nods sharply.

He drops me on my feet.

"Jarron," Mr. Vandozer purrs. "You're looking rather pale.

Though, you didn't break her into pieces, so that's a good sign you're not too far gone, eh?"

Jarron growls, low and slow. He steps forward. "You will die now," Jarron rumbles, his wings rising and falling.

"Will I?" Mr. Vandozer asks sweetly. "Do you even know who I am?"

"You are no one that matters."

"Incorrect," Mr. Vandozer smiles.

Jarron's back tenses.

"I am the future King of Oriziah, and I will not kill you today, Prince, only because I want you to watch while I take everything from you. Piece by piece. Starting with the human girl you've connected to. Your replacement mate when you thought yours was gone for good."

Jarron remains still, watching him. I can't see his face, but something about his posture suggests he's not angry. He's somewhat relaxed and curious. He is waiting.

"I'm going to carve her apart in front of you."

Someone clears their throat.

Mr. Vandozer sends a fleeting glance to the glowing form next to him. "Trust me."

Liz's eye roll tells me she has no intention of doing that, but she says nothing else.

"Then," Mr. Vandozer continues. "I'm going to fuck your true chosen in front of you. And then, lastly, I'm going to take your throne. I'm going to replace you. With your chosen by my side."

"So, that is your plan." Jarron stands up straight. "Foolish, foolish male. You will be remembered for your idiocy."

Mr. Vandozer smiles, but there's annoyance on his face. It's not the reaction he expected. He nods to Liz, who snaps.

Blazing light fills the cavern, and the rest is chaos.

Jarron leaps into the air and blasts magic at the half-destroyed force field. After only a couple hits, the entire wall crumbles like melting plastic, and Jarron darts right at Mr. Vandozer.

Something sharp carves into my shoulder and throws me back against the stone wall. The breath is sucked out of my lungs, and my body drops.

A raging, desperate roar pierces the air, shuddering through my bones. There are explosions of crackling magic and crumbling ancient stone.

Someone grabs me and forces me up. A sharp blade presses against my jugular.

I blink rapidly.

I squirm and push back against a firm chest behind me. It only presses harder. "You don't want to do that," a woman whispers.

I look over my shoulder to someone with a black mask holding me. All I can see are bright green eyes; the rest is covered with black cloth.

"What are you doing?" I whisper.

"Don't worry, love. We want you alive. So long as he cooperates." She winks. My stomach sours.

I curl a lip. "You're one of them? Part of the Akrasia Games council?" I have no idea who this person is, but the more information I have, the better.

"The Cosmic Council, yes. One of ten."

"Quit playing with your food," a male voice says from somewhere behind me.

"Think the prince will kill him?" the woman says. She seems entirely at ease, like this is just a job to her.

"No. We have his chosen," the man says. "He'll do anything to get her. Too bad he doesn't realize that we own her now."

I turn my attention to where the grey-skinned demon holds a man by his throat midair. His wings casually beat up and down, keeping him in the air. Jarron has Mr. Vandozer.

"What are you doing?" a familiar high-pitched voice cries out with a hint of panic. Two of the other masked figures are holding Liz by either arm. A third presses a black blade to her heart.

My blood runs cold. They wouldn't—they couldn't kill her, could they?

"Put me down," Mr. Vandozer barks. "We'll talk this out."

Slowly, the winged demon lowers onto the platform, but he doesn't release Mr. Vandozer.

"Bring Candice up here," he says.

Liz's face is filled with rage, but one of the masked beings releases her arm. She snaps, and suddenly, I am on the platform beside her, and the woman holding a knife to my throat right alongside me.

Liz is being held by those two men. On her forearm is a long scar. Even being a jinn has not healed it. That's the scar Jarron gave her as kids.

"What's happening?" I whisper to Liz.

She doesn't answer.

"Release me," Mr. Vandozer croaks. He gurgles suddenly, suggesting Jarron tightened his grip instead of doing as commanded.

The woman behind me tsks and presses the blade tighter against my skin. Warmth wells on my neck, and I squeeze my eyes closed. Liz's gasp suggests they're doing the same to her.

"There's nothing you can do," an unfamiliar man says. "You might be powerful, but we have something precious to you. Two somethings actually. You cannot save them both."

"Which will he choose?" the woman holding me says, then laughs like the answer is obvious.

My stomach sinks.

A man steps toward the winged demon slowly, his hands clasped behind his back. "Let me explain this to you simply," he says. "Since your mind still seems a bit scrambled." He chuckles.

Jarron's jaw clenches, but he watches the new threat closely.

"As a young, unbonded demon, you have a few vulnerabilities we intend to exploit. You cannot speak about your chosen, but we can. They already know, you know?" He points to Liz and me. "That was a fun game while it lasted, but there's another restriction I'd like to play with. You also cannot harm your chosen, nor can you *allow* harm to come to them."

I straighten. This is new information, and I work my mind over what I know, desperate for anything to help us out of this situation.

"I have both of them at my mercy. Your mate and the woman you love. How sad they're not the same." He mock-pouts at Jarron, who's still clenching his hand over Mr. Vandozer's windpipe. From what I know about demons, he cannot kill him this way, but his pain does give my heart a small bit of relief.

"You could set off a magical explosion to save your mate. It would be swift and violent enough. I can see you welling that power inside, ready to detonate." He nods to Jarron's chest, as if we can all somehow see the magic inside of him. How does one see something like that? What kind of being is this guy? "I certainly couldn't stop you. But you would kill Candice in the process. You do realize that, right? You cannot harm your chosen, but you can certainly harm her. Your magic would disintegrate her."

The man grins, and a new deep hatred forms in my chest. I don't know who he is, but I want him dead.

"So, you can choose. Save your mate but let the other one die. She'd still be our slave of course, but you'd probably kill a few of us in the process, and you yourself would escape to live another day."

My heart throbs.

"Or you could fight the old-fashioned way and hope you're fast enough. Note, Akira is quite swift, and it only takes a nudge with that blade to kill a human. Except, you see, I know your weakness. And the human is not the only one vulnerable. Killing the jinn would take more than a quick swipe, to be sure, but the moment you know she's in danger, your instinct will take over and you will not fight for Candice anymore. You will choose Liz. It's how your power works."

"You wouldn't harm her. She's your jinn," I spit.

"Ahh true!" the man says, holding up a finger. "Smart girl. But here's the kicker—that doesn't matter. The demon only has to feel that physical threat, and he will have no choice but to act. Logic plays no role."

This guy is really starting to piss me off. "Who are you?" I ask. "I'd like a face to picture killing before I die."

The man chuckles. "But allow me to present an alternative in which both girls survive."

I roll my eyes. Yeah, sure, this'll be a good option. Give me your soul, and I'll let you live.

"Candice will sign the contract into the games, and Jarron will sign this." A new parchment appears, suspended midair. "In which you admit that your chosen is Elizabeth Montgomery, who has rejected you. You forfeit all rights to the Orizian throne."

"Are you through talking yet?" Jarron's demon hisses, his eyes hooded and dark. His anger is quiet. He is too calm. Has he already made up his mind?

Jarron drops Mr. Vandozer, shoving him back onto the ground. Mr. Vandozer sucks in panicked breaths, and then scrambles on his hands and knees over to Liz— as if she'd protect him while he keeps her bound and threatened. He clings to her leg, even while others from the council hold a knife to her heart.

"You've put me in a difficult situation," Jarron says smoothly. "But you've made one miscalculation."

"Oh?" the man says. There's a stillness to his body, but his voice sounds confident. It's enough to make him recount his chickens and glance around the area to see if he's missed something. "What's that?"

Jarron smirks at the masked man.

Then, there's a flash as Jarron makes his decision and the entire world around me explodes into ash.

57

Never a Second Choice

Magic crackles around me as my vision flickers back. An orb of dark power surrounds me, and... someone is carrying me.

His arms are warm and gentle, cocooning me in safety.

Stone shatters and shoots around us, a swirl of dust. Then, all at once, the hurricane of rock ends and we're surrounded by a star-filled night sky. The dark magic falls away, and I am soaring through the sky in his arms.

His leathery wings beat smoothly in a rhythmic pattern, lulling my mind into a hypnotic ease.

This is a good dream, I think.

I'd like to stay in this dream forever.

"Where are you taking me?" I murmur through dry lips.

"Home."

Home. A word with so many different meanings. I like that word, though. It has such possibilities, but they all mean comfort and safety. I want those things.

My gaze drifts down to the treetops getting closer and closer. I blink, watching the green rolling hills. Dizziness sets in.

And recognition that I am very much flying through the air and moving toward the ground.

And the demon's claws are digging into my leg.

"Holy crap!" I holler, suddenly realizing this is not a dream, and I'm hundreds of feet up in a demon's arms. I twist to desperately wrap my arms around Jarron, pressing my face into his neck.

He chuckles softly. "You are safe, bright one. I will not let you fall."

The ease of moments before, when I believed I was dreaming, falls away and smashes on the rocks below, leaving a mess of panic. "What the hell is going on? What happened?"

"Stay calm. We're almost there. We'll talk then."

I squeeze him tighter. He seems comfortable cradling me through the air.

It's incredibly peaceful, despite my panic, as I watch the clouds pass over the moon beyond the mountains in the distance.

"The authorities have arrived," he murmurs. "Late as always."

Jarron dips down, and I squeal, squeezing him tighter, eyes pressed shut. Down, down, down.

My stomach twists, and then he drops onto solid ground with a thud.

"We're home," he says so casually, like my life didn't just flash before my eyes.

My eyelids flutter, and I find myself on Jarron's patio.

We're back at Shadow Hills, outside his bedroom. I'm not particularly ready to let him go, though.

"Can I set you down?" he murmurs.

"No." I shake my head against his shoulder.

He chuckles. "All right."

He carries me inside and shuts the glass door behind him, then he walks me over to his armchair and carefully takes a seat, with me still in his arms.

I curl up against him, head in the crook of his neck. I've never felt this willfully helpless, but he feels so comfortable and safe, and I know the moment I let go, reality is waiting for me.

Jarron doesn't ask me anything else for several minutes. He just holds me and lets me hide away from the whole world with him.

I always hide. I don't want to hide anymore.

But I'm so scared and overwhelmed.

"Jarron?" I whisper.

"Yes, sunshine?"

I look up quickly to find Jarron back in his human form. I'm not sure when that happened. Anxiety moves in quickly, and I wring my hands before leaping to my feet.

It all comes crashing down, like I knew it would. One moment, I was being held with a knife to my throat, and then there was an explosion and I'm totally fine, being flown out by Jarron.

"What the hell just happened?" I ask.

Jarron's calm stare digs into me.

"I told you I had a way to get us out of there."

He had said that. I'd almost forgotten about that. "But not

Thompson, Janet, and Lola," I recall. But they did make it out before us. "Are they back here and safe?"

He nods.

I begin pacing. That explosion... "Did everyone else in the cavern die?" I whip back around to face him. "Is Liz okay?"

"Some of them are likely dead. The jinn transported out, along with anyone who was near her. Mr. Vandozer being one of them."

I grimace. Mr. Vandozer got out? Anyone else around who wasn't able to snap their fingers and disappear in an instant would have died. Except me. Why? He had some secret way of protecting me?

A demon cannot harm his chosen.

I don't know that I'm ready to believe that just yet. Except, I really can't come up with another explanation.

I breathe in and out three times, then I blurt out the question plaguing me. "Did you imprint on Liz at Myre Island?"

Some tension returns to his body.

"Or did you imprint on me?"

After everything that happened underground, I can't imagine how any of this makes sense unless it was me all along, but even that doesn't make sense. How could they all have gotten it wrong?

But then, Jarron always seemed so sure. *You were never a second choice.*

His jaw clenches. "I wish more than anything I could just tell you the truth, Candice. I wish I could explain it all away, but it doesn't work that way. I can't."

"Why is your demon fighting you?" I blurt again.

He grimaces.

"Can't tell me that either, huh?" Why do these rules have to make everything so complicated?

I hold my hands over my mouth for a long moment while I compile my thoughts. "Before I say all this, I need you to give me one answer. I know there's a lot you're not allowed to explain—that's annoying, by the way, but I don't blame you—but this one, I need."

He waits, sitting at the edge of the chair, pleading with his intense stare, uncertain he can give me what I need but desperate to obey.

"Even knowing that Liz is alive, do you still want me?"

"Yes." His answer is so fast I almost miss it. "Yes. I want *you.*"

The hair on my arms stands up, and the breath rushes from my lungs as this realization settles in. He wants me. He stands and grips my neck with both hands.

I swallow as new fear wells up. Fear of being vulnerable, of exposing a very delicate part of my heart, but Jarron is worth this risk.

"Since you can't tell me the full truth," I say slowly, "I will give you my truth."

Irrational terror takes hold of my heart. I know I am safe with Jarron, and yet, admitting this truth is still so difficult.

"The *only* reason I've pushed you away, Jarron—the *only* reason—is because I thought you'd chosen her." My lips tremble. "And even then, I was ready to give myself to you. You're everything I could ever want. You're too good if I'm honest. I don't deserve you."

Jarron's hand tightens on the back of my neck, and then his lips crash against mine, desperate and needing. He pushes into me, and I stumble back until my back hits the wall. His hips pin me tightly, and I let out a low moan.

My cheeks warm, but Jarron only deepens the kiss, his hands roaming over me. I can feel his desire in every move, in every tension-filled gasp of air, in the way his hands cling to me as if he's terrified I'll run away.

He ends the kiss as quickly as he began it, panting hard. "You don't see yourself clearly, sunshine. You're perfect."

I shiver against the certainty in his voice. "I'm stubborn and foolish and a complete coward."

He growls. "You are not a coward."

"If I weren't a coward, I would have faced you after that night you hurt Liz on Myre Island and told you how pissed off I was. I would have started potions work years ago to prove my worth in the supernatural world instead of running away." Tears well in my eyes. "I would have told you how much it hurt to know you picked her. How much I wanted it to be me."

Tears stream down my cheeks. He wipes each one away, methodically, carefully.

"So much of this became more difficult because of my fear."

He brushes the tears from my cheeks with the pad of his thumb. "We all have flaws, sunshine. That doesn't make you imperfect."

I sob out a laugh. "That's literally what it means."

"I adore you for your stubborn will. You are strong and brave. And maybe you run from emotionally difficult things, but I am not afraid to fight for you, Candice. So long as I know you want it."

Butterflies soar through my belly. I close my eyes against the wave of hope that crashes into me.

I'm still scared, still utterly terrified, but I am willing to trust him with my heart.

"Tell me what you're thinking?" I say, tired of my own avalanche of honesty.

He presses his forehead to mine. "I'm—I'm a mess of emotions, to be honest. I'm filled with hope and relief. There's immense joy in my heart. But I'm also so incredibly pissed I must fight the urge to hunt down Bea and Trevor and tear them fucking apart."

I had no idea he was feeling all of those things. He seemed so calm when we arrived back here. Maybe that was just a front, hiding the fact that he was about ready to explode.

"I'm in awe. And sorry for the pain you've gone through and the fear you have now. I'm also terrified because something is wrong back home, and I might have to leave..." He looks over his shoulder toward the empty bedroom, as if someone were there waiting for him.

I fidget with the collar of my shirt. "That was a paragraph of more questions. Why are you angry? What did Bea and Trevor do now?"

He pulls at my chin, forcing me to look him in the eye. "How do you think Mr. Vandozer learned I'd imprinted on Myre Island?"

I swallow. Mr. Vandozer is not directly related to him. The only real connection he has is the school, but they didn't start going there until a year after that summer.

"A demon can choose their mate at any point before maturity. Though it often happens young, there are many cases of the mating urges not beginning until their mid-twenties. The only reason he could know it was one of you two is if someone told him. Someone close to us. My parents would never. The reason your sister was targeted is because either Trevor or Bea told him. That put you in danger. It put her in danger. And I want to destroy them—slowly—for that."

I swallow. "How did they know?" The whole concept is still foreign to me. Trevor said there were signs, but not what they were.

"A demon's first shift on another planet is significant and usually done in a controlled environment. It's a peaceful transition—unless something happens to upset the demon soul, then it can be a more intense experience. Violent, even. When I shifted, seemingly out of nowhere, there was little that could have triggered the change in that way."

So, that was unusual? My parents acted as if it wasn't a very big deal. We were okay, and that was what mattered. But then again, we also decided to avoid demon kind for good, so it's not like they had to make any parental decisions for us. They were visibly relieved we decided to leave the island and start attending human schools.

"I can't explain more without—" He closes his eyes. "It all feels so pointless now to keep the truth from you. It's all been ruined by a traitor to his own kind."

"You're not supposed to talk about your chosen."

He nods. "It's more than not supposed to. The demon cannot physically speak any words that would identify his chosen until the acceptance. It is important for our chosen to choose us back, without any assurances. Others could take guesses, read the clues, but it's highly, highly frowned upon."

"How does one... accept?"

His lips twitch. "They would have to allow a claiming. Two marks, in particular. One would connect the two enough to make it clear what the second mark would mean. The second mark is the big one."

I squint, wanting to ask more about this tradition, but I think it can wait. He's asked to mark me before, and I don't want to set myself up for more pressure when I'm still unsure about it. "Okay. What did you mean by immense joy?" That's an intense feeling for simply surviving.

He stares into my eyes, as if the answer to the entire universe has revealed itself. "I understand now."

My breath hitches.

"I thought you feared my demon side. I thought you didn't accept that part of me, and maybe wouldn't ever. Or maybe that you simply didn't have the feelings I had, but now I know that's not true. My demon told you he would uncover the secret and resolve it. We've achieved one of those things. Now, I can enact a plan. Now, I can resolve it."

My lips part. "Resolve it how?"

His lips curl into a vicious grin that makes my heart race like a jackrabbit facing a wolf.

"If you'd take my mark, Candice, you'd understand all of it. All of those questions plaguing you—it would all make sense. Isn't that tempting?" he drawls, an echo pulling into his voice. His demon is having a say here. He's trying to taunt me. Lure me into a trap. "Don't you want to understand all of it? Because I have all of the missing pieces now, and I can share them—if you'd take my mark."

My eyes fly open. Stupid, steely determination settles in my bones. "No."

Jarron releases me. My arms are suddenly cold where his skin is now noticeably absent.

"Sorry," I say. "I'm a stubborn bitch."

He releases a shuddering breath. "You've got to stop calling yourself that."

My lips curl up. "I'm just saying, if you want me—and I think that's what you're saying?" I pause, waiting for him to deny it. He doesn't, just stares at me with those deep, searching eyes. "You're going to have to do it the old-fashioned way."

Something flickers in his expression. Excitement? He's thrilled by the challenge.

My stomach twists pleasantly.

"Do you want to be chased, *bright one?*"

I suck in a breath at the otherworldly quality his voice has taken on.

I swallow, mouth dry.

He prowls forward. "You are fucking torture, Candice. In the best possible way."

He presses his hands on either side of my head, and I'm thrilled by the jolt of fear that flashes over me. The best kind of fear.

I run my fingertips up his chest and revel in the shudder that rocks through him. He is a powerful demon prince, stalking me, and yet, he's undone by my touch.

Maybe I should take him up on his offer. Maybe I should just let him mark me and get those answers I'm craving. Good or bad, I need to know. Right?

"You said something is going on back home?"

Jarron winces. His shoulders tense. "Laithe is with my family now. I—they've been asking me to come back. I should, but I really don't want to leave right now." He presses his forehead against mine and breathes deep.

"Why? What's wrong?"

“Mr. Vandozer has begun the second stage of his plan. I should have just killed him when I had the chance, but I wanted him to watch all of his plans burn away like ash and know what a fool he truly is.”

My head spins. “What’s his plan?”

He sighs and runs his fingers through his hair. “He’s brought Liz to our world and is presenting her as my chosen.”

My stomach sinks. “He’s—”

“Trying to start a civil war by claiming I am not fit to rule.”

NOTE FROM THE AUTHOR

Thank you so much for sticking with the Shadow Hills Academy series! These characters are challenging and fun and are very personal to me. And yes, I kinda enjoy putting them through all the emotional turmoil. I hope you don't hate me too much for that!

I swear I write happy endings, it's just the between time that's a little sketchy. In the next book, please expect more plot twists and emotional turmoil, but a whole lot of wish fulfillment too.

Until then, turn the page to learn more about my other (finished) series. Or find me on social media and vent all your feels about Candice, Jarron and all the others! I'd love to hear your thoughts.

If you want to be the first to hear news about my upcoming books, please join my newsletter. https://www.staceytrombley.com

Follow me on Instagram & Tiktok @StaceyTrombleyAuthor

Also by Stacey Trombley

If you'd love to read another tear-your-heart-out but leave-you-happy-at-the-end series by me, please check out my Wicked Fae series!

All that's standing between me and freedom are eleven bloodthirsty fae

As a convicted assassin, I've been banished from the fae realm for years but now I have the opportunity to compete in a ruthless competition to earn a full pardon.

Dragons and twisted mazes are the least of my worries now.

I can handle a few bullies and death-defying challenges. The thing that will keep me up at night is having to face those I betrayed. Especially Reveln, the prince whose brother I killed. Every time I see the hatred in his eyes it reopens old wounds, a reminder of the destiny that was stolen from me. And I only have myself to blame.

But I'll find a new destiny—by winning the Trial of Thorns.

The whole realm thinks I'm weak but I'm stronger than they could ever imagine. By the time this is through—I'll bring them all to their knees.

ABOUT THE AUTHOR

Stacey Trombley is a casino pit boss by night, urban fantasy author by day. She lives in Ohio with her husband, son, and German Shepherd, Riley. When she's not writing or reading her husband is probably dragging her along on one of his crazy adventures for this travel vlog or competing against him about who can pick the most Survivor winners in the first episode (hint: she's winning). But mostly, she's probably reading.

ACKNOWLEDGMENTS

Every book is a whole new adventure, even when it's smack in the middle of a whirlwind of life. I've written and published many books by now but they never take less work, or less help.

So, first thank you to my supportive family. I love you.

Also, my writing group The Queens of the Quill. I've learned so much from the group, but it's also such an honor call you my friends.

To every reader who took a chance on me, but especially those who went out of their way to encourage me and share their love for my stories.

Thank you to all of my early readers. Deissy, Andrea, Ines, Nicole, Talia, Karen and Lucy. Whether you screamed in delight and sorrow in my DMS, sent detailed notes or sent me lists of typos to fix before the final version went out, I'm so very thankful!

Thank you to my editor, Caitlin Haines. Even when life causes you to delay my edits ;) I enjoy working with you and I'm so very thankful for your help!

And of course, thank you to my God. Help me to always remember, you are the one thing I seek.

Printed in the USA
CPSIA information can be obtained
at www.ICGtesting.com
LVHW092037101024
793329LV00010B/166/J